Rise of the Ancients

Dragons of Vacari
T.A. McEvoy

Dragons of Vacari

T. McEvoy

Copyright © 2024 by T.A. McEvoy

All rights reserved.

No part of this publication may be reproduced, distributed, or transmitted in any form or by any means, including photocopying, recording, or other electronic or mechanical methods, without the publisher's prior written permission, except as permitted by U.S. copyright law. For permission requests, contact tmcevoy1121@yahoo.com

The story, all names, characters, and incidents portrayed in this production are fictitious. No identification with actual persons (living or deceased), places, buildings, and products is intended or should be inferred.

Book Cover by NovelStormDesigns.etsy.com

Map by Rob Donovan (Snikt5 on Fiverr.com)

Copyright Registration Number: TXu 2-456-196

Library of Congress Number: 2024923207

First paperback edition 2024.

DRAGONS OF ACARI

DRAGONS OF VACARI

A Word Before You Begin

A Note to Readers

Welcome to *The Dragons of Vacari* series. This saga is a tapestry of interconnected stories, where each book weaves its own unique arcs and resolutions into a larger, overarching narrative. While some mysteries will unfold within individual books, others will span multiple installments, slowly revealing their secrets over time.

This epic adventure is filled with dragon battles, complex alliances, and elements of dark fantasy. If you love high-stakes tales set in a richly crafted world, you're in the right place.

Planned as a nine-book journey, each installment of this series will take time to create and release. To stay current with updates and enjoy additional content between books, feel free to visit my YouTube channel, where I'll be sharing videos and insights about the series. (https://www.youtube.com/@theresamcevoy612)

Your patience and support mean the world to me as I bring every chapter of this story to life. Thank you for joining me on this adventure—I hope you enjoy the twists, turns, and surprises that lie ahead!

Dedication

Tom Vick

To my wonderful boyfriend, Tom—thank you for reading every draft of this book. Since we met, my life has improved in more ways than I can express. Your constant encouragement, always having my back, and reminding me that I can achieve anything means the world to me. A special thanks for handling all the marketers and promoters—though they seem too scared to contact you after they're told to! Guess you've got them figured out, huh?

Introduction

In the heart of the mystical land of Vacari, where the emerald forests whisper ancient secrets and the mountains cradle untold legends, a new saga stirs. It is a tale woven into the very fabric of this enigmatic realm—a story of bravery, friendship, and the indomitable spirit that resides within us all.

As you embark on this journey through the *Dragon of Vacari* series, you will travel from the Cerulean Expanse to the depths of the Hidden Isles. Every corner of Vacari holds a story waiting to be uncovered, a myth yearning to be unraveled.

At the heart of this epic lies a creature unlike any other—a dragon whose scales shimmer like molten gold and whose roar shakes the foundations of the earth. It is here, in the company of this majestic beast, that our heroes will face their greatest trials, their deepest fears, and their most profound revelations.

Yet, amidst the perils, there is also hope. For within the depths of Vacari, friendships will be forged, alliances tested, and the true meaning of courage revealed. As our heroes navigate the treacherous paths ahead, they will discover that the greatest power of all resides not in the strength of their swords, but in the purity of their hearts.

So, dear reader, as you turn these pages and embark on this epic quest, remember that you are not alone. Heroes and heroines stand beside you, their stories inspiring and their journeys captivating. Together, their destinies will shape the very fabric of Vacari itself.

Welcome to the *Dragon of Vacari* series—a tale of adventure, magic, and the unbreakable bond that connects us all. May your spirit soar on the wings of destiny as you journey through these realms of imagination and beyond.

Various Locations

Main Realm

Vacari

Vacari is an enchanting realm where nature's vibrant tapestry weaves together diverse landscapes, fostering a peaceful coexistence among elves, humans, dragons, and merfolk. Majestic cities like Goldmoor and Crystal Vale thrive in prosperity, their gleaming spires and flourishing trade routes nestled amidst lush forests, shimmering lakes, and serene oceans. Ancient magic flows through the very soil, influencing both the land and its people, while the skies above remain guarded by the vigilant wings of dragons. Vacari's rich cultural heritage reflects the harmonious balance between its peoples, sustained by an intricate connection to the natural and mystical forces that shape the land.

Main City inside Vacari

Goldmoor

Goldmoor, the shining jewel of Vacari, radiates a harmonious fusion of elven grace and human ingenuity. Majestic spires, adorned with intricate gold and silver filigree, reach toward the heavens, their gleaming surfaces catching and reflecting the sunlight like beacons of prosperity. The bustling streets form a living tapestry of elven elegance and human vitality, where vibrant marketplaces brim with goods from every corner of the realm. Artisan stalls display exquisitely crafted wares—delicate elven jewelry, sturdy human armor, and magical artifacts—while the aromas of exotic foods fill the air. At the heart of the city stands the grand castle, its walls a testament to the unity between elves and humans, built with precision and artistry that mirrors the strengths of both races. The city hums with life, laughter, and camaraderie, celebrating the enduring bond that has forged not only a shared kingdom but a shared destiny.

Notable City inside Vacari

Crystal Vale

Crystal Vale, a mesmerizing gem nestled in the heart of Vacari, stands as a testament to the perfect fusion of elven grace and human ingenuity. Its crystalline structures shimmer like diamonds, refracting sunlight into breathtaking cascades of light that dance across the city. Elven and human artisans work in harmony, crafting architectural wonders—delicate bridges that span glistening waterfalls and elegant towers that soar toward the heavens, their surfaces glinting with ethereal brilliance. The city's pulse resonates with the unity of its people, and nowhere is this more poignantly symbolized than in the union of Ong Swifthammer and Keisha. Their marriage, a celebration of love and alliance, echoes eternally through the crystal spires, binding the city's legacy to their story.

Celestial Realm

Lyra'el,

Lyra'el, the celestial realm, is a magnificent and ethereal domain where dragons and celestial beings converge in harmony. Floating high above the mortal world, this radiant realm is bathed in the soft glow of starlight and cosmic energies. The skies shimmer with hues of gold and silver, and vast, crystalline mountains rise from the celestial plains, their peaks touching the heavens. Here, dragons of divine origin soar alongside majestic celestial beings, their forms radiant with the essence of the stars.

In Lyra'el, the boundaries between time and space seem to blur, creating a timeless sanctuary where both beings of incredible power come together in unity. The realm pulses with an ancient magic, one that governs both the heavens and the mortal world below, and its inhabitants are entrusted with the balance of cosmic forces. It is a place of unparalleled beauty and serenity, where the celestial and draconic realms intertwine, their destinies forever linked by the will of the stars.

Dark Cities inside Vacari

Fel Thalor

Fel Thalor, once the forsaken city of the Druchii, now stirs with life once more, yet remains a haunting monument to its dark past. Its once-majestic spires, though still scarred by time, rise defiantly against a brooding sky, casting long shadows over the streets where whispers of ancient power still linger. The air is thick with the weight of forgotten rituals, as if the city itself remembers the blood sacrifices and dark magic that once permeated its core. At the heart of Fel Thalor, the sacrificial altar—a grim relic of the Druchii's ruthless practices—has stirred from its long dormancy, as though waiting for its masters to reclaim their sinister legacy. Though no longer abandoned, the city remains shrouded in an unsettling stillness, a place where the line between past and present blurs, and the presence of its dark history can be felt in every stone.

Old Flameford

Old Flameford, once the formidable stronghold of the warlock Phoenix Shadowwalker, was a city cloaked in darkness. Its ominous atmosphere, enhanced by the oppressive hues of black and red that covered every building, created an ever-present sense of dread. At its heart stood the Dark Tower, a foreboding structure that pierced the very heavens, once the source of Phoenix's malevolent power. This was the seat of his dark rule, where nefarious plans were forged and dark magic flowed freely—until the alliance rose against him, driving him into exile.

However, Old Flameford has since undergone a dramatic transformation. While the tower still looms over the city like a grim reminder of its past, the landscape has become even more treacherous. Evil dragon lairs now scatter the land, their dark inhabitants adding to the already sinister aura of the city. These draconic overlords have made their homes among the crumbling ruins, solidifying Old Flameford as a place of darkness where evil continues to fester, waiting for the moment to rise once again.

Shadowhaven

Shadowhaven lies on the edge of Twilight Glade, adjacent to the foreboding Cerulean Expanse. This dark and shadowy city is a place where the light barely penetrates, and an air of mystery and danger lingers over every corner. Once a thriving figure in Goldmoor, Maldrak now rules over Shadowhaven, having been exiled by King Alex for his treacherous actions. Under his iron grip, the city has become a haven for those who seek to escape the law, as well as those drawn to its darker energies.

The architecture of Shadowhaven is as oppressive as its atmosphere—blackened stone towers and gloomy streets blend into the ever-present twilight, illuminated only by the faint, eerie glow from hidden sources. Maldrak's influence casts a long shadow over the city, where whispers of rebellion and secrets seem to thrive in the gloom. Its residents, a mix of outcasts and dark-hearted souls, have adapted to this realm of constant dusk, living under the ever-watchful gaze of their exiled ruler.

Though menacing and dangerous, Shadowhaven also holds a certain allure for those seeking power or refuge from the light. It is a place where alliances are forged in the shadows, and where Maldrak's dark ambitions may one day extend far beyond the city's borders.

Forests inside Vacari

Purplefire Woods

Purplefire Woods, awash in a mesmerizing kaleidoscope of purples, stands as an enchanting testament to nature's vibrant palette. Every shade, from deep amethyst to soft lavender, blends harmoniously with the gentle rustle of leaves, creating a forest alive with color and serenity. This breathtaking realm, beloved by Keisha for its beauty and tranquility, became the perfect setting for her union with Ong in a magical wedding ceremony that will forever be etched in the hearts of those who attended. The regal shades of purple that drape the trees and blanket the ground serve as both a backdrop and witness to this sacred event. Beyond its beauty, Purplefire Woods is a vital passage, guiding travelers through its enchanted paths toward the majestic city of Goldmoor, making it a place of both natural wonder and symbolic importance.

Emeraldwoods

Emeraldwoods, a lush, verdant realm bathed in the soothing embrace of emerald green, serves as a breathtaking passage to Crystal Vale. The vibrant hues of the forest, coupled with its serene ambiance, create an enchanting landscape where nature feels alive and welcoming. This sacred forest witnessed the engagement ceremony of Ong and Keisha, marking the union of their souls in a celebration of love and harmony. Beneath the emerald canopy, they pledged their bond, setting the stage for the joyous festivities that awaited them in Crystal Vale. The forest stands as a symbol of new beginnings, a tranquil sanctuary where love and life intertwine before travelers continue their journey to the majestic city.

Emberwooods

Emberwoods, a captivating forest bathed in fiery hues of red and orange, stands near the volatile volcanic region, lending it an otherworldly glow. Despite the inherent dangers lurking within, the forest retains a haunting, untamed beauty that entices both awe and caution. Traveling through Emberwoods is a perilous journey, as it leads to the formidable Druchii stronghold of Fel Thalor. Now, a new layer of mystery and challenge awaits all who venture there. Copper dragons and pixies have woven their magic to create an intricate, twisting maze at the very gates of Fel Thalor, a cunning trap meant to confuse and thwart the evil Druchii. This enchanted maze, alive with illusions and deceptions, tests the wit and endurance of any who dare to enter, making the path to Fel Thalor even more treacherous than before.

Ivory Moonbeams

Ivory Moonbeam, the mystical home of the Sylvan Elves, is a realm bathed in hues of white and ivory, its landscape reflecting the pure, radiant beauty of its name. The trees, with bark that gleams like polished pearl, rise tall and graceful, their leaves and flowers shimmering with a soft, ethereal glow beneath the moon's gentle light. The entire forest comes alive at night, as the moonlight casts an otherworldly brilliance upon the landscape, enhancing its serene and enchanting atmosphere.

The Sylvan Elves, known for their deep connection to nature, dwell harmoniously within these enchanted depths, their lives intertwined with the magic of the forest. The pristine color palette, dominated by shades of ivory and white, reflects the purity and tranquility that permeates Ivory Moonbeam, making it a sanctuary of peace and wonder. Those who wander through its glistening paths feel the quiet magic of the place, as though they've stepped into a world untouched by time, where nature and mysticism reign supreme.

Twilight Glade

Twilight Glade lies in the delicate balance between the ethereal beauty of Ivory Moonbeam and the mysterious darkness of Shadowhaven. The color palette of this enchanted forest reflects its name, with soft hues of purple, blue, and gray blending seamlessly into the landscape. The interplay of light and shadow creates an ever-changing tapestry of colors, as the sunlight filters gently through the thick canopy by day, casting dappled shades across the forest floor. By night, moonbeams weave through the trees, their silvery glow dancing upon the ground, adding an air of quiet magic to the glade.

The forest itself seems alive with the subtle transitions of light, as if caught between two realms—one of purity and one of shadow. Twilight Glade serves as a mystical bridge, embodying both serenity and mystery, a place where travelers can experience the magic of both worlds. The shifting hues create a dreamlike atmosphere, inviting those who wander through to lose themselves in the tranquil beauty and the soft whispers of the wind

Sub-Areas inside of Vacari

Shimmering Coast

The Shimmering Coast stretches along the borders of the Cerulean Expanse, where the ocean's azure waves gently meet the land. This radiant coastline serves as a peaceful convergence point, where merfolk from Coraluna emerge from the depths to bask in the sun's warmth and converse with visitors from the surface world. The coast is named for the way the waters shimmer and sparkle as sunlight dances across them, creating a breathtaking spectacle of light and color.

More than just a place of beauty, the Shimmering Coast acts as a vital meeting point between the realms of land and sea, fostering friendships and alliances among different civilizations. Here, merfolk and surface dwellers exchange knowledge, form bonds, and strengthen ties between their worlds. The coast has become a symbol of harmony, a place where the boundaries between ocean and land blur, and the people of both realms come together in peace.

Hidden Sub-Realm inside Vacari

E'vahona

E'vahona, the hidden jewel of the Eladrin, was a sacred gift from Kadona, the benevolent goddess of light. Shielded by divine magic, it remains untouched and unseen by the evil Dominion, a sanctuary of peace and purity. Crystal pathways wind gracefully through the city, leading to homes seamlessly crafted from a delicate fusion of crystal and wood, blending the natural with the ethereal. Within the enchanting boundaries of E'vahona, the Eladrin share their lives with magnificent companions—majestic wolves and mythical creatures like Pumpkin the panther—who roam freely, adding to the city's mystical charm. The air carries the gentle, harmonious melody of nature, resonating with an otherworldly beauty that reflects the close bond between the Eladrin and their divine patron. E'vahona is not just a city; it is a living testament to the light and protection of Kadona, and a place where magic and nature dance in perfect harmony.

The Sacred Grove

Nestled within the heart of E'vahona, a breathtaking garden flourishes under the divine caress of Kadona, the goddess of light. Crystal-clear waterfalls cascade gently from moss-covered cliffs, their soothing symphony echoing throughout the lush, vibrant landscape. The air is perfumed with the delicate fragrance of exotic blossoms, their brilliant hues creating a mesmerizing tapestry of color and life. Elaborate pathways, adorned with luminescent flora, weave gracefully through the garden, guiding visitors on a journey through this enchanted paradise where ethereal creatures roam freely. Butterflies, shimmering in the soft glow of the flora, dance in a harmonious choreography, while the gentle hum of mystical energies pulses in perfect resonance with the natural world. In this sacred space, the beauty of nature and the divine touch of Kadona converge, creating a serene haven of peace and wonder.

Sub-Realm inside Vacari

The Hidden Isles

Tucked behind a mystical barrier, The Hidden Isles emerge as a sanctuary of breathtaking beauty. This ethereal realm, a collection of isles adorned with vibrant flora and encircled by cascading waterfalls, welcomes only those who can pass through its enchanted protections. At the heart of these mystical isles stands a majestic golden castle, a symbol of the noble dragons' grandeur and the sacred meeting place for allies from various races. The crystal-clear waters below reflect the brilliance of the azure sky, while the air hums with the harmonious melodies of unseen creatures that dwell among the isles. This hidden paradise, untouched by time or conflict, is a place where nature, magic, and dragonkind exist in perfect harmony, offering refuge and counsel to those deemed worthy.

Ardinia

Ardinia, a haven of enchantment shielded by a magical barrier, unfolds as a breathtaking realm where nature's beauty reigns supreme. Towering trees, their branches adorned with blossoms in every imaginable hue, stretch toward the heavens, creating a lush canopy that murmurs the ancient secrets of the forest. Crystal-clear streams weave gracefully through the verdant landscape, reflecting the vibrant colors of the surrounding flora and adding to the tranquility of the realm. In this mystical sanctuary, nymphs, fairies, and the elusive white unicorns roam freely, their presence adding an ethereal grace to the serene atmosphere. Occasionally, the skies above Ardinia are graced by the majestic flight of Pegasus, a rare and awe-inspiring sight reserved for those fortunate enough to glimpse the magic that thrives in this protected paradise.

Cerulean Expanse

Beyond the shores of Vacari lies the Cerulean Expanse, a vast and seemingly endless ocean teeming with life and untold mysteries. The azure depths of this boundless sea conceal countless wonders, from vibrant coral reefs brimming with marine life to the forgotten shipwrecks of ancient vessels long lost to time. The ocean's surface glistens under the sun's rays, reflecting a shimmering, almost magical light that stretches to the horizon.

Beneath the waves, the merfolk dwell in majestic underwater kingdoms, their cities crafted from coral and pearl—a breathtaking testament to the beauty and grandeur of the ocean realm. These hidden cities are sanctuaries of peace and wonder, where the ocean's currents carry stories of the deep and where nature and magic intertwine. The Cerulean Expanse holds many secrets, its waters whispering of adventures yet to be uncovered, making it a place where both beauty and danger coexist in the vastness of the sea.,

Underwater Kingdom inside Vacari

Coraluna:

Coraluna, a mesmerizing underwater kingdom, unfolds as a realm of vibrant beauty beneath the azure waves. Vast coral reefs, adorned with a kaleidoscope of colorful corals and teeming with exotic fish, create a breathtaking tapestry that stretches across the ocean floor. Lush underwater plants sway gracefully with the gentle currents, their movements in perfect harmony with the ebb and flow of the sea. The merfolk, diligent and wise, tend to the well-being of their aquatic home, ensuring that Coraluna remains a thriving and serene sanctuary. King Oceanous, a majestic and benevolent ruler, watches over the kingdom with compassionate eyes, guiding his people and maintaining the delicate balance of the underwater world. In Coraluna, the harmony between nature and its inhabitants creates a tranquil and magical realm, hidden beneath the waves yet brimming with life.

Luminaqua

Nestled in the heart of the ocean's embrace, Luminaqua stands as a stunning testament to the ingenuity and harmony of the Aquanar Elves. This underwater haven is a marvel of elven and aquatic architecture, where the boundaries between nature and artifice blur, creating a breathtaking spectacle. The city's structures are masterfully crafted from luminescent coral, casting a gentle, ethereal glow that bathes Luminaqua in perpetual light. Towers and buildings, adorned with pearlescent shells, shimmer like jewels beneath the caress of the ocean's currents, their surfaces reflecting the serene beauty of the underwater world. The city's layout flows seamlessly, mirroring the graceful movement of the tides, with elegant bridges and pathways connecting its various districts in fluid harmony.

Luminaqua is not merely a city; it is a living, breathing masterpiece, pulsing with the ocean's rhythm and the spirit of its elven inhabitants. The Aquanar Elves live in perfect balance with the sea, their culture deeply intertwined with the ebb and flow of the tides. Life in Luminaqua is a dance of elegance and resilience, as this sanctuary, hidden in the ocean's depths, has withstood the test of time. A glittering jewel in the vast underwater world, Luminaqua remains a beacon of beauty, unity, and strength, a place where magic and nature are forever intertwined.

Underwater Realm inside Coraluna

Abyssal Sovereign:

Nestled within the ocean's depths, Abyssal Sovereign is a magnificent underwater realm governed by the divine watch of Lysander, the God of the Sea. This ethereal kingdom is a breathtaking display of aquatic wonders, where vibrant corals sway gently with the currents and schools of iridescent fish dance in perfect harmony. The tranquil kingdom is adorned with stunning structures, masterfully crafted from seashells and precious gems, their surfaces reflecting the divine touch of Lysander. His protective aura envelops Abyssal Sovereign, ensuring that no darkness or malevolence can breach its serene depths.

The merfolk inhabitants, guided by their benevolent ruler, maintain the flourishing marine life, tending to the ocean's vibrant ecosystem with care and devotion. Under Lysander's divine leadership, Abyssal Sovereign has become a haven of peace and beauty, where the sea's mysteries and magic coexist in perfect balance. It is a realm untouched by conflict, its calm waters a reflection of the god's power and wisdom, a sanctuary beneath the waves where tranquility reigns supreme.

Neighbor Realm

Afor

The Neighboring Realm of Afor has undergone a dramatic transformation over time. Once a vast, treacherous swampland where Phoenix and the Druchii were exiled, Afor's landscape was forever altered when Vuarus, the god of the abyss, was released from his imprisonment. His chaotic power scorched the land, transforming the swamp into an unforgiving desert, a barren region of shifting sands and desolation.

Since the defeat of both Phoenix and Vuarus, Afor has begun to rebuild. Amidst the harsh desert, new cities have emerged, built by resilient inhabitants who have adapted to the unforgiving climate. Yet, due to the realm's dark history, the Noble dragons (Bronze) maintain a vigilant watch over the region, patrolling the skies and ensuring that no lingering threats arise from its troubled past. Though Afor still bears the scars of its dark legacy, life continues to flourish as its people and their noble dragon protectors carve out a new future in this once-forsaken land.

World Map

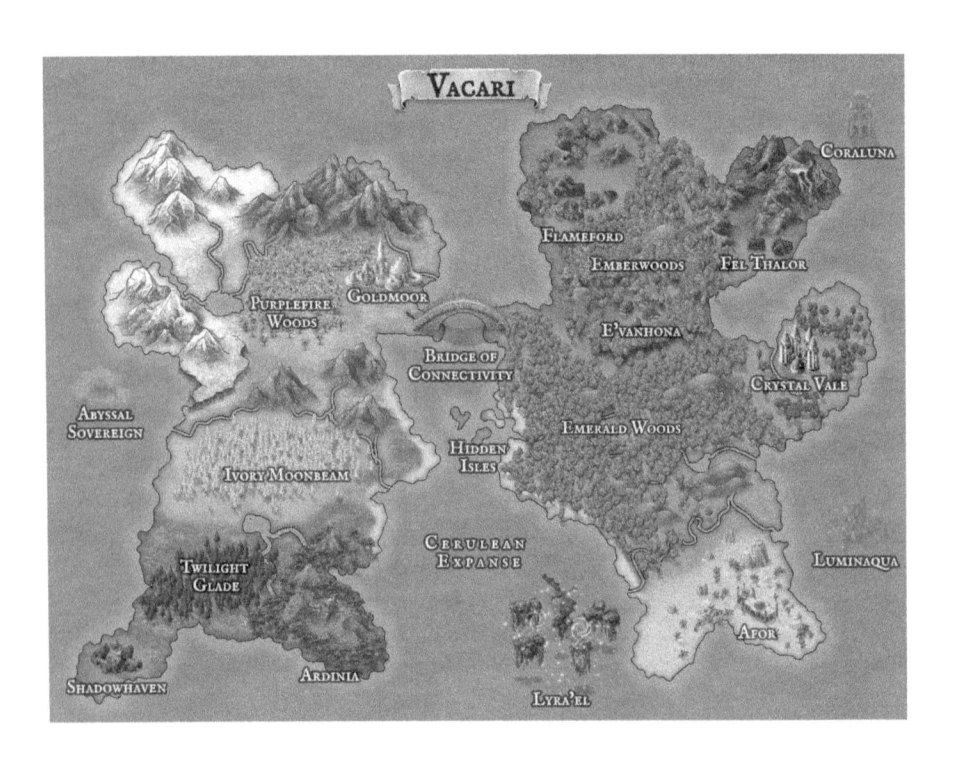

Dragons of Acari

List of Characters

Character List

Elves:

Eladrin:

- **Keisha** – A courageous Eladrin adventurer with elemental magic, skilled in archery, and driven by a strong sense of justice.

- **Lady Seraphina** – A wise and graceful figure on the Eladrin High Council.

- **Lord Karrenen** – Renowned for his mastery of magic and his unmatched command over the arcane arts.

- **Lord Thaldir** – A respected elder with deep knowledge of ancient lore.

- **Lady Elowen** – A skilled diplomat, adept at politics and negotiation.

- **Lady Lythia** – A talented healer and empathetic counselor, supporting the Eladrin community.

- **Lord Alaric** – A strategist and tactician, advising the council on defense matters.

Druchii:

- **Qellaun Deadcrusher** – A fearsome Druchii, formerly in service to Phoenix and Vuarus before their deaths.

- **Lyra Deadcrusher** – A cunning sorceress with a mysterious past, who once worked for Phoenix and Vuarus.

Humans:

- **Ong Swifthammer** – A loyal and skilled warrior, married to Keisha, and now an accepted member of Eladrin society.

- **King Manard** – The respected King of Crystal Vale.

- **Galien** – Son of King Manard and future dragon rider.

- **King Alex** – The noble King of Goldmoor.

- **Queen Jeanne** – Queen of Goldmoor, ruling alongside King Alex.

Dragons:

Noble Dragons (Good/Neutral Council Members):

- **Kimras (Gold Dragon)** – A regal leader, known for his wisdom and benevolence.

- **Silvara (Silver Dragon)** – Gentle and nurturing, embodying calm and serenity.

- **Talleoss (Silver Dragon)** – A battle-hardened dragon, known for resilience and freedom.

- **Dirona (Bronze Dragon)** – Ancient and wise, commanding great respect.

- **Aurelia (Crystal Dragon)** – Mysterious and ethereal, with vast ancient knowledge.

- **Verdantia (Emerald Dragon)** – Deeply connected to nature and the vitality of the natural world.

- **Amara (Amethyst Dragon)** – Spiritually insightful, with an aura of power.

- **Raelithar (Copper Dragon)** – Mischievous and witty, with a playful nature.

- **Azurina (Sapphire Dragon)** – A wise and serene dragon, connected to the sea and sky.

- **Aurix (Brass Dragon)** – Charismatic and commanding, with a strong presence.

- **Argentus (Mercury Dragon)** – Quick and elusive, Argentus's shimmering scales reflect his fluidity and unpredictability.

- **Aurelius (Celestial Dragon)** – Regal and wise, embodying cosmic balance with calm authority and power.

- **Radiantus (Platinum Dragon)** – The leader of the Noble Dragons, commanding respect with his radiant platinum scales and unifying strength.

- **Liora (Pearl Dragon)** – Elegant and serene, her pearl scales reflect her healing and nurturing magic.

- **Luminara (Opal Dragon)** – Adaptable and wise, with opalescent scales that shift and change in the light.

- **Aurora (Diamond Dragon)** – Unyielding and brilliant, her diamond scales symbolize clarity and unbreakable strength.

- **Ardentia (Ruby Dragon)** – Fiery and passionate, her ruby-red scales shimmer with the intensity of her spirit.

Young Brass Dragons:

- **Ciryth** – Spirited and inquisitive, eager to explore and learn.

- **Sylthar** – Swift and observant, always aware of his surroundings.

- **Lythor** – Curious and thoughtful, with a keen sight for details.

- **Valthor** – Patient and enduring, with a calm and steady nature.

Evil Dragons:

- **Zylron (Red Dragon)** – A treacherous dragon whose fiery scales mirror his fierce and unpredictable nature.

- **Glaciera (White Dragon)** – Ruthless and cold-hearted, Glaciera's icy presence mirrors the harshness of the coldest winter.

- **Zephyrion (Blue Dragon)** – Unstable and destructive, like a stormy sky, Zephyrion's electric blue scales crackle with malevolent energy.

- **Erebos (Specter Dragon)** – A shadowy and ethereal presence, Erebos is a dragon of the dead, moving between realms with chilling silence.

- **Pyrothos (Hellfire Dragon)** – Wreathed in flames and fury, Pyrothos embodies destruction, his hellfire burning everything in its path.

- **Noxus (Nightshade Dragon)** – A master of poison and darkness, Noxus's venomous breath is as deadly as the shadows he commands.

- **Voraxus (Dreadfang Dragon)** – Ferocious and bloodthirsty, Voraxus's presence instills dread, her fanged maw a symbol of merciless destruction.

- **Ixalis (Mirage Dragon)** – A master of illusion, Ixalis bends light and perception to her will, making her a cunning and deceptive opponent.

- **Vorathos (Abyssal Dragon)** – Rising from the depths of darkness, Vorathos's abyssal power is unmatched, her influence felt deep in the shadows.

- **Voraxia (Shadow Dragon)** – The ruler of all dark dragons, Voraxia's shadowy form and commanding presence make her a formidable leader of the forces of darkness.

- **Xalzorath (Black Dragon)** – Ruthless and cunning, Xalzorath's black scales hide a heart as cold and dark as the night.

- **Vorgrath (Green Dragon)** – Manipulative and calculating, Vorgrath uses his toxic breath and cunning mind to ensnare his enemies.

- **Zarathos (Topaz Dragon)** – Gleaming with malevolent brilliance, Zarathos's topaz scales shimmer with dangerous energy, reflecting his cruel and tempestuous nature.

- **Nocturna (Obsidian Dragon)** – Cold and unbreakable, Nocturna's obsidian scales give her a fearsome presence, her dark power mirroring volcanic stone.

- **Sanguis (Bloodstone Dragon)** – Pulsing with dark magic, Sanguis's blood-red scales are a reflection of her hunger for power and the blood she spills.

- **Nyxathor (Onyx Dragon)** – Silent and deadly, Nyxathor's onyx form allows her to blend into the darkness, striking with precision from the shadows.

Merfolk:

- **King Oceanous** – Ruler of Coraluna, a wise and just leader of the merfolk.

- **Adrianna** – Daughter of King Oceanous, a strong and noble figure.

- **Aqilus** – Adrianna's mate, and the right hand of King Oceanous.

Aquanar Elves:

- **Lord Caelumara** – The leader of the Aquanar elves, known for his wisdom and strength.

- **Lady Marinelle** – Mate of Lord Caelumara, respected within their society.

- **Thalas** – Guardian of the Aquanar's lore and history, keeper of their past.

- **Elenora** – Steward of arts and culture, ensuring the Aquanar traditions thrive.

- **Jorun** – Oversees the defense and security of Luminaqua, vigilant and dedicated.

Divine and Significant Beings:

- **Kadona** – Goddess of Light, protector of the Eladrin.

- **Lysander** – God of the Sea, ruling over the oceans.

- **Aeliana** – Guardian of the Mystic Realm of Ardinia.

- **Mysterious Person** – A powerful figure within the dark divine realm, their true nature and motives remain hidden.

Others:

- **Pumpkin** – A mischievous young panther with a mysterious connection to Keisha.

- **Malrik** – Chief Priest of Vuarus, devoted to dark forces.

- **Maldrak** – The exiled ruler of Shadowhaven, banished by King Alex.

- **Casper**-Queen Jeanne's cougar companion who protects her.

Note: Not all characters will appear in every book.

DRAGONS OF ACARI

Thank you

Thank you for reading Rise of the Ancients.

If you enjoyed the book, we would be immensely grateful if you could take a moment to leave a review at the location where you purchased the book. Your feedback is invaluable to us and helps other readers discover our work.

Thank you for your support.

This book contains some dragon battles and dark fantasy elements.

Also, by T.A. McEvoy

The Elves of Vacari Series:

The Wicked Published 11-01-2023

Shadows Unveiled- Published 12-05-2023.

Vacari's Resurgence: Healing Bonds 04-12-2024

Dragons of Vacari Series:

Rise of the Ancients

Coming Soon

Shadows of the Sylvan Series

Coming Soon

Depth of Destiny: A Merfolk Saga

Coming Soon

Passion's Quest

Coming Soon

Explore more about each book and series at: https://www.tamcevoy.com/

Contents

Prologue   1

1. Chapter 1   6
2. Chapter 2   16
3. Chapter 3   22
4. Chapter 4   36
5. Chapter 5   53
6. Chapter 6   61
7. Chapter 7   65
8. Chapter 8   71
9. Chapter 9   78
10. Chapter 10   85
11. Chapter 11   96
12. Chapter 12   106
13. Chapter 13   122
14. Chapter 14   128
15. Chapter 15   142
16. Chapter 16   165
17. Chapter 17   190

18. Chapter 18	206
19. Chapter 19	217
20. Chapter 20	241
21. Chapter 21	254
22. Chapter 22	266
23. Chapter 23	277
24. Chapter 24	288
25. Chapter 25	297
26. Chapter 26	306
27. Chapter 27	312
28. Chapter 28	318
29. Chapter 29	342
30. Chapter 30	368
31. Chapter 31	380
32. Chapter 32	390
33. Chapter 33	404
34. Chapter 34	411
Epilogue	420
Teaser	423
Acknowledgements	426

Dragons of Acari

Prologue
Shadows Stir

In the celestial realm, where the boundaries of the mortal world blurred into the divine, there stood a place untouched by mortal hands. Here, the gods convened, their presence illuminating the ethereal expanse with a brilliance mortals could only dream of beholding.

Lysander, God of the Sea, stood tall and resolute, his cerulean gaze fixed upon the gathering. Beside him, Kadona, Goddess of Light and Protector of the Eladrin Elves, cast a warm glow upon the assembly with her radiant presence. The other gods, their forms shimmering with divine energy, joined them in the celestial circle. Each deity brought their own domain of influence, their powers interweaving to shape the fabric of the mortal realm.

Amidst murmurs of agreement, Lysander's voice rang out, commanding attention. "We gather here today to discuss the events that have transpired in the mortal realm," he declared, his tone firm. "Certain... interferences have occurred, disrupting the delicate balance we've maintained."

Kadona nodded, her countenance radiant with warmth and wisdom. "Indeed," she spoke, her voice a soothing melody. "Some among us have stirred unrest among mortals, threatening the harmony we've worked tirelessly to preserve."

As the gods deliberated, Lysander's gaze narrowed, fixing upon a shadowy figure lingering at the edge of the gathering. "And what of you?" he addressed the mysterious presence. "Do you not see the consequences of your actions?"

The figure remained silent, shrouded in darkness that writhed and twisted with unseen malevolence. Though it said nothing, its presence loomed large, casting a pall over the assembly.

The celestial realm trembled with the weight of their discourse, as the fate of the mortal realm hung in the balance, waiting to be shaped by the gods.

During the divine assembly, the shadowy figure shifted, its form coalescing into solidity as it stepped forward into the circle. Its features remained obscured, but its presence exuded an aura of foreboding that sent shivers through the gathering.

"Lysander," the figure spoke, its voice a chilling whisper that echoed through the celestial realm. "Your actions have not gone unnoticed. By revealing the truth to the dragons, you've disrupted the balance we've labored to maintain."

Lysander's expression remained stoic. "The dragons had a right to know of the impending darkness," he retorted, his voice resonating with conviction. "Their role in preserving the mortal realm is paramount."

Kadona, her features etched with concern, interjected gently. "While it's true the dragons play a crucial role, we must exercise caution. Their intervention could have unforeseen consequences."

She paused, her gaze flickering with both wisdom and uncertainty. "When Radiantus, the Platinum Dragon, returns to Vacari, he will assume the mantle of leadership. His wisdom will guide them, and I trust his intentions are beyond reproach."

The shadowy figure inclined its head. "Indeed," it murmured, its voice dripping with an insidious undertone. "Powerful though they are, the dragons are but pawns in a larger game. Revealing too much to them courts disaster."

As the celestial assembly grappled with the implications, the shadowy figure's words lingered like a looming specter, a portent of darkness threatening to engulf them all.

Lysander's gaze hardened. "You accuse me of overstepping my bounds yet fail to acknowledge the true threat before us," he said, his tone measured, tinged with righteous indignation.

"Vuarus, in his twisted machinations, conspired with Phoenix Shadowwalker to sow chaos and destruction," Lysander continued, his voice heavy with revelation. "They sought to unravel everything we've fought for, even plotting to eliminate Kadona from our midst."

A ripple of murmurs spread through the assembly, Lysander's revelation sending shockwaves through their ranks. Kadona's expression darkened with remembered anguish, her gaze flicking to Lysander with a mixture of gratitude and apprehension.

"I acted not out of defiance, but necessity," Lysander declared, unwavering. "To thwart Vuarus and Phoenix, I could do no less. My actions protected Kadona and upheld the balance of Vacari, even in the face of treachery."

The shadowy figure regarded Lysander in silence before inclining its head. "Your actions may have spared us from greater calamity," it conceded, a grudging respect in its tone.

As the assembly absorbed Lysander's words, Kadona stepped forward, her gaze softening with understanding. "Lysander, your actions were guided by wisdom," she said. "You acted to defend Vacari and its people, sparing us from the darkness."

The other gods nodded in agreement, relief and appreciation evident in their expressions. Even the shadowy figure remained silent, its presence seemingly in accord with the consensus.

With the matter settled, the tension dissipated. The gods exchanged nods before dispersing, turning to their respective domains. As the meeting concluded, Lysander's gaze lingered on the shadowy figure—a silent acknowledgment passing between them before he, too, departed.

As the last echoes of the assembly faded, the shadowy figure remained, cloaked in obscurity. With a voice that reverberated from the depths of eternity, it delivered a chilling proclamation.

"If you think this is over, you are mistaken," it intoned. "Darkness will engulf Vacari. Time is of the essence if we are to bring about this darkness before Radiantus returns."

Its form seemed to smirk with malice. "Vuarus knew what he was doing, but he got careless. Lysander found out, and for that, there will be repercussions. I will ensure Vuarus's death is avenged."

With that declaration hanging in the air, the shadowy figure vanished, leaving behind a palpable unease. The divine realm fell silent again, but the ominous warning lingered—a harbinger of trials yet to come.

Chapter 1
The Stirring of Titans

At the heart of Goldmoor's glen, amidst a verdant oasis of tranquility, King Alex awaited the arrival of Kimras, the venerable gold dragon. The garden, a testament to the resilience of the kingdom, unfolded in breathtaking splendor. A magnificent sculpture of Kimras, wrought with exquisite detail, dominated the glen's center. The golden dragon soared in eternal flight, his wings a symphony of motion and grace. Atop his broad back, King Alex stood tall, a regal figure amidst the swirling currents of imagination and craftsmanship.

Surrounding the masterful sculpture, a reflective pool mirrored the azure sky, capturing the celestial dance of clouds and sun. In its rippling depths, Kimras appeared to glide effortlessly through an endless expanse of sky, a guardian spirit watching over the land below. The Garden of Resilience encircled this central marvel, its vibrant blooms are a testament to the kingdom's enduring spirit. Each petal and leaf whispered tales of rebirth and renewal, echoing the resilience of Goldmoor in the face of adversity.

Sunlight filtered through the canopy above, casting dappled shadows upon the garden's pathways. King Alex stood in quiet contemplation, and beside him, Queen Jeanne's gentle presence added warmth to the tranquil scene. Soon, the soft beat of wings heralded Kimras' approach. With a regal bearing befitting his station, the golden dragon descended gracefully into the glen, commanding respect and reverence.

"Kimras," King Alex greeted with a respectful nod, his voice carrying the weight of authority, tempered by camaraderie. "Thank you for joining me."

The gold dragon inclined his majestic head in acknowledgment. "It is an honor to convene with you, King Alex," Kimras replied, his voice resonating with age-old wisdom.

Together, they embarked on a discussion of great import—the training of the dragon riders, guardians of Goldmoor's skies and protectors of its people. In the tranquil embrace of the garden, amidst the whispers of flora and the watchful gaze of the sculpted dragon, their plans took flight, bound by a shared vision of peace and prosperity for their beloved kingdom.

"Kimras," King Alex began, his voice filled with anticipation, "as we delve into the training of our dragon riders, I believe it's crucial to ensure a deep connection between them and the dragons."

The golden dragon regarded the king with a thoughtful gaze, his eyes reflecting centuries of knowledge and understanding. "Indeed, Your Majesty," Kimras replied, his voice resonant. "The bond between rider and dragon is the cornerstone of our defense and the key to unlocking our true potential."

King Alex nodded, his expression grave yet determined. "I've reached out to Lord Karrenen, and the Eladrin elves are already crafting special saddles for the riders who prefer them. These saddles will provide comfort and stability and serve as a conduit for enhancing the connection between rider and dragon."

A spark of approval flickered in Kimras' eyes as he absorbed the king's words. "An astute decision, Your Majesty," the dragon acknowledged. "The Eladrin's craftsmanship is unparalleled, and their understanding of magic will undoubtedly imbue these saddles with powerful enchantments."

"But before a dragon accepts a rider," Kimras added, his voice carrying the weight of ancient wisdom, "there must first be a recognition—a mutual sensing of worthiness and intention. It is not simply the rider who chooses the dragon, but the dragon must also sense a quality in the person—a spark of courage, respect, or understanding—that resonates with them."

King Alex nodded thoughtfully. "So, it is a two-way bond, then? The dragon must feel this connection as well?"

"Indeed, Your Majesty," Kimras agreed. "The bond between rider and dragon is forged from mutual recognition. A dragon will never allow someone on its back without first feeling a sense of compatibility or trust. This is why the trial of acceptance is so important. It is a test not just of skill, but of the rider's spirit and the dragon's willingness to form that sacred bond."

King Alex considered this, appreciating the gravity of the ritual. "And if the rider is found lacking? If the dragon does not feel this connection?"

"Then the dragon will not allow the rider to remain," Kimras replied solemnly. "They have every right to reject a potential rider if the bond is not there. This ensures that both dragon and rider are united in purpose, bound by a connection that transcends mere practicality."

A sense of reverence filled the air as King Alex absorbed Kimras' words. "Thank you for sharing this, Kimras," King Alex said softly, his voice filled with appreciation. "It is clear now that the bond between dragon and rider is not merely a matter of utility, but of respect and mutual understanding."

Kimras nodded, a gentle smile gracing his lips. "Indeed, Your Majesty. The dragons of Vacari are not beasts of burden; they are partners in every sense. Their choices are as significant as those of the riders who seek to bond with them."

"Your Majesty," Kimras continued, "the process of bonding between dragon rider and dragon is sacred, requiring not only skill but also deep trust and mutual respect."

King Alex listened intently. "Please, continue," he urged, eager to learn more about the intricacies of the bonding ritual.

"The dragon rider must choose the dragon he wishes to ride and then embark on a trial of acceptance. He must climb onto the dragon's back, without the aid of a saddle or harness, and face the challenge of remaining there as the dragon attempts to dislodge him."

King Alex envisioned the gravity of the trial. "And if the dragon rider succeeds?" he inquired, his voice barely above a whisper.

"Should the rider prove himself worthy," Kimras replied, "the dragon will descend to the ground, signifying their acceptance of each other as partners."

As the implications of Kimras' words settled upon them, King Alex couldn't help but feel a sense of awe at the ancient ritual binding dragon and rider together.

A flicker of nostalgia danced in Kimras' eyes. "Years ago," he mused, "I first met Keisha, an Eladrin elf, and Ong, a human warrior. They sought the aid of the dragons in restoring Goldmoor to its rightful king." Kimras' smile widened. "I believe you are well aware of that battle."

King Alex's eyes lit up with recognition. "Yes, I remember it well. The courage and sacrifice of everyone involved were pivotal in securing our kingdom's future."

"They displayed great courage and determination," Kimras continued. "Through their efforts, the seeds of peace and prosperity were sown once more in Goldmoor."

With shared reverence for those who had come before them, King Alex and Kimras continued their discussion. Their shared memories wove a tapestry of hope for the future. In the hallowed garden, amidst the whispers of flora and the gentle rustle of leaves, the legacy of the dragon riders was poised to be reborn.

"Kimras," King Alex interjected, a thoughtful expression crossing his features, "I've always known Ong and Keisha to be unique individuals, steadfast in their dedication to Goldmoor in times of need. But I must admit, I never realized the extent of their connection to you and your kin."

The golden dragon regarded the king with a knowing gaze, silently acknowledging the bond that existed between him and the intrepid Eladrin elf. "Indeed," Kimras replied, his voice tinged with nostalgia, "Keisha possesses a very unique spirit."

A sense of wonder filled King Alex's heart as he contemplated the depth of the bond that had formed between Keisha and Kimras. "To think that she rides upon your back," the king mused, his voice filled with awe, "speaks volumes of the trust and friendship between you."

Kimras nodded in agreement, a faint smile playing at the corners of his mouth. "She possesses rare courage and wisdom," the dragon remarked, "qualities that endear her to all beings of Vacari, from dragons to humans, elves to fae, and merfolk alike."

As the echoes of their conversation lingered in the tranquil embrace of the garden, King Alex couldn't help but feel a newfound appreciation for the intricate alliances that shaped Goldmoor's destiny. In the shared memories of the past and the promise of the future, the legacy of friendship and unity burned bright, guiding them ever onward.

"Your Majesty," Kimras suggested, his voice carrying the weight of authority, "I propose you enlist your army's quartermaster to identify soldiers with the necessary skills and temperament for dragon riding. Once selected, the quartermaster can inform you when they are ready for training."

King Alex nodded in agreement. "An excellent idea. I shall task the quartermaster with this responsibility immediately."

With plans set in motion, King Alex and Kimras concluded their discussion. As they prepared to depart, the king and his wife bid farewell to the golden dragon, their hearts filled with hope for the future.

Returning to the castle, King Alex and Queen Jeanne resumed their duties, their thoughts consumed by the promise of a new alliance between humans and dragons. Meanwhile, Kimras took to the skies above Goldmoor, his majestic form a beacon of strength and reassurance to all who beheld him.

As the sun dipped below the horizon, casting a golden glow upon the land, Kimras soared into the endless expanse of sky, his wings carrying him toward a future filled with possibility and promise. Amidst the tranquil beauty of twilight, the legacy of Goldmoor's guardians remained poised to endure for generations.

In the heart of the realm, nestled amidst rolling hills and winding rivers, lay the Purple Fire Woods, a realm of unparalleled beauty and mystique. Beneath the verdant canopy of ancient trees, every leaf bore the regal hue of amethyst, casting the forest in a surreal tapestry of purple.

Tall spires of lavender blossoms reached skyward, their delicate petals unfurling in the breeze. Their fragrance, a heady perfume of sweet nectar and earthy musk, hung heavy in the air, enticing visitors to linger amidst the enchanted glades.

Amara, the Amethyst Dragon, guardian and protector of the Purple Fire Woods, stood at the heart of this ethereal realm. With scales aglow like molten amethyst, she watched over the forest and its inhabitants with a vigilant eye, her presence a beacon of strength and wisdom.

Beneath the shimmering canopy, nymphs frolicked among the purple-leafed trees, their laughter a tinkling melody that echoed through the woods. Meanwhile, young Amethyst Dragons soared through the skies, their iridescent wings catching the sunlight as they playfully honed their skills under Amara's watchful gaze.

As the sun dipped below the horizon, casting a warm glow upon the forest, Amara spread her wings and took flight, her form silhouetted against the fading light. With a mighty roar, she soared above the treetops, scanning the horizon for any sign of danger.

Amara's keen gaze soon fell upon a familiar figure. Kimras, the golden dragon, glided gracefully over Goldmoor, his majestic form cutting through the sky. With a joyful cry, Amara surged forward, her heart filled with excitement at the prospect of reuniting with her friend.

As she drew near, Kimras turned to greet her, his eyes alight with warmth and friendship. "Amara," he exclaimed, his voice carrying across the vast expanse between them, "how delightful to see you!"

"Kimras, my friend," Amara replied, her voice ringing with joy, "it has been far too long."

Drawing alongside her golden companion, Amara inquired about the situation in Goldmoor. "How fares the kingdom?" she asked, her gaze fixed on the distant horizon.

Kimras smiled warmly, his gaze drifting over the sprawling expanse of Goldmoor. "Goldmoor thrives," he assured her, "and soon, we shall begin the training of dragon riders to ensure the kingdom's continued prosperity."

Amara's eyes sparkled at the mention of dragon rider training. "Perhaps," she suggested, "we could include some of the Amethyst Dragons in the training exercises. After all, Purple Fire is the gateway to Goldmoor, and our presence could prove invaluable in safeguarding the kingdom."

Kimras nodded in agreement. "A wise suggestion, Amara. I shall bring your proposal before King Alex. I have no doubt he will see the merit in your words."

With a shared sense of purpose, Amara and Kimras continued their flight above the realm, their friendship and camaraderie a testament to the enduring bond between dragons. As they journeyed onwards, their hearts filled with hope for a future where dragons and humans could stand united in defense of their shared home.

Chapter 2
Forging Bonds and Blades

In the secluded haven of E'vahano, Lord Karrenen, patriarch of the Eladrin elves, walked along enchanting crystal walkways that led to the Grand Workshop, a marvel of Eladrin craftsmanship. The crystalline paths stretched before him like ribbons of light, connecting homes adorned with wood and crystals, each a testament to the Eladrin's unparalleled artistry. But today, his destination was not a home—it was the Grand Workshop, where the finest Eladrin artisans worked tirelessly.

The Grand Workshop, built into the heart of a colossal crystal tree, shimmered with enchantments. The air was alive with the sounds of diligent crafting and soft incantations. As Lord Karrenen entered, he was greeted by the sight of Eladrin craftsmen and women, their hands moving with practiced precision over various projects.

In a secluded section of the workshop, his daughter, Keisha, and her husband, Ong, were hard at work. Keisha's emerald-green eyes sparkled with concentration as she fine-tuned the intricate designs on a nearly completed dragon saddle, while Ong, his blue eyes and raven-black hair contrasting sharply, inspected a lance, ensuring its balance and strength.

Lord Karrenen approached them with a warm smile, his eyes bright with pride. "King Alex awaits the completion of the dragon saddles," he said, his tone serious but tinged with urgency. "He wishes for their swift delivery to Goldmoor."

Keisha and Ong exchanged a glance, already thinking ahead. "The dragon saddles are nearly finished," Ong replied confidently. "We've put our hearts into their creation, and they'll be ready for delivery soon."

Despite his outward calm, a knot of anxiety tightened in Ong's chest. The journey to Goldmoor was fraught with danger, and the weight of their task pressed heavily on him. Sensing his unease, Keisha placed a reassuring hand on his arm, grounding him.

Lord Karrenen nodded approvingly before Ong's gaze drifted to another section of the workshop, where several gleaming dragon lances rested on an ornately carved stand. Intrigued, he picked one up, marveling at its surprising lightness and the faint hum of magic coursing through it.

"These lances are extraordinary," Ong remarked, his voice filled with awe. "What are they for?"

Lord Karrenen's eyes twinkled with pride. "These are dragon lances, a gift from the Eladrin to the people of Goldmoor. Each one is imbued with our magic and the blessings of Kadona, our goddess of light. They symbolize the bond between our people and the noble dragons, and now they'll also strengthen the alliance between Eladrin and Goldmoor."

Ong traced the intricate runes etched into the lance's surface. "I can feel the power within," he murmured.

"These lances have a rich history," Lord Karrenen continued. "Long ago, when darkness threatened our world, Kadona saw the courage and purity of the Eladrin and allied us with the noble dragons. To seal this pact, she instructed our artisans to create these lances. Crafted from the rarest metals and imbued with dragon scale essence, their true power comes from the magic of our elders."

He paused, then added, "The elders, with their deep connection to the light, infused each lance with spells of protection, strength, and unity. The process, known as the Rite of Imbuement, is a closely guarded secret passed down through generations. It's said that when an elder imbues a lance, they impart a piece of their spirit, making each one a living testament to our legacy."

"These are more than weapons," Lord Karrenen emphasized. "They are symbols of hope and unity, meant to protect and inspire. Only those with pure hearts and noble intentions can activate their magic."

Keisha listened intently, pride and apprehension warring within her. The responsibility of transporting such powerful artifacts weighed on her, but she knew their mission's importance. "We'll make sure they reach Goldmoor safely," she vowed, her voice steady despite the unease gnawing at her.

The workshop buzzed with renewed purpose as Keisha and Ong, inspired by Lord Karrenen's words, redoubled their efforts. The grand hall echoed with the sounds of crafting and enchantment, each strike of the hammer and whispered spell a testament to their dedication and skill.

In the tranquil beauty of E'vahano, beneath the whispering leaves and shimmering crystals, Keisha and Ong resumed their work with renewed determination. The soft glow of the crystal walkways illuminated their workspace as they meticulously crafted each detail of the dragon saddles and lances, their focus unwavering.

Later, Keisha and Ong stood before Lord Karrenen, their mission clear. "My lord," Keisha began, her voice steady and determined, "the dragon saddles are ready. We've gathered a group of Eladrin to help transport them to Goldmoor."

Lord Karrenen nodded, pride shining in his eyes. "You've done well, both of you. May fortune smile upon your journey."

As Keisha prepared to leave, Lord Karrenen gestured for her to wait, a knowing smile on his lips. He motioned toward a nearby clearing where a young cougar roamed freely, its golden fur gleaming in the light.

"This cougar was orphaned when its mother was killed," Lord Karrenen explained solemnly. "We've cared for it, and now it seeks a new home."

Keisha's eyes widened with surprise and gratitude as she approached the cougar, extending her hand. "Thank you, Father," she said, her voice filled with appreciation. "This will be a wonderful gift for Queen Jeanne."

"Is there an Eladrin trainer who can help the queen bond with her new companion?" she asked, thoughtful.

Lord Karrenen nodded. "Any of our trainers would be honored. It's a noble endeavor that will strengthen the bond between our peoples."

Ong chuckled at the mention of the queen's companion, a mischievous glint in his eye. "At least Pumpkin will stop pouting now," he remarked with a grin.

With their plans set, Keisha and Ong bid farewell to Lord Karrenen and prepared for their journey. As they stepped into the shimmering light of E'vahano, the weight of their mission pressed upon them, but so did the promise of adventure and friendship.

Keisha turned to Ong as they walked. "The dragon lances are a surprise for Goldmoor. King Alex doesn't know about them yet. They'll be a crucial addition to the defense of the realm."

Ong nodded, though unease crept along his spine. "It's an honor to be part of this mission," he said, though the road ahead was uncertain.

Before they could continue, Lord Karrenen approached once more. "Keisha, Ong, remember this journey will be long and arduous. The saddles and lances must be handled with care."

He paused, his gaze serious. "Rest in the Purplefire Woods when you reach them. The enchanted forest will offer protection and a chance to recover. You must arrive in Goldmoor strong and with the lances unharmed."

"We will, Father," Keisha promised.

Ong nodded. "We won't let you down."

With a final nod from Lord Karrenen, they resumed their journey. The shimmering light of E'vahano gave way to the open path ahead, adventure and duty intertwined with every step. The Purplefire Woods awaited, a sanctuary where they would gather their strength for the trials to come.

As they walked, the weight of the lances and saddles mirrored the weight of their responsibility. But with each other's support and the wisdom of Lord Karrenen, they were ready to face whatever challenges lay ahead. Their journey to Goldmoor had begun, with the hope of safeguarding the realm shining brightly in their hearts.

DRAGONS OF ACARI

Chapter 3
The Guardian's Promise

Deep within the enchanted embrace of Purplefire Woods, where shadows danced in hues of violet and the air pulsed with ancient magic, Kimras, the golden dragon, and Amara, the amethyst dragon, stood together in silent communion.

"Amara," Kimras began, his voice resonating with the wisdom of ages past, "King Alex has accepted your proposal to integrate some of the Amethyst dragons with the gold dragons for the dragon riders."

Amara's eyes gleamed with satisfaction as she nodded. "I've already selected some of my finest young dragons for the task," she replied, her tone laced with pride. "They are eager to embark on this journey and forge bonds with their golden brethren."

Kimras chuckled at her confidence, a glint of amusement in his golden eyes. "You expected his answer to be favorable, didn't you?" he remarked, a knowing smile playing on his lips.

Amara grinned, her amethyst scales shimmering in the dappled forest light. "Of course," she replied with a touch of playful banter. "Who could resist the allure of the Amethyst dragons?"

With a shared understanding and a bond forged in the fires of friendship, Kimras and Amara gazed out over the vast expanse of Purplefire Woods. Their hearts swelled with anticipation for the adventures to come. In the heart of the enchanted forest, amidst the whispers of magic and the songs of the ancients, the destinies of dragons and riders awaited—bound by the unbreakable ties of kinship and courage.

In the heart of Goldmoor, within the grand royal palace where the air was thick with purpose, King Alex, Queen Jeanne, and the quartermaster gathered to discuss the selection of candidates for dragon rider training.

The quartermaster, standing with an air of deference before the royal couple, spoke with a steady cadence of authority, though a hint of concern tinged his voice. "Your Majesties," he began, "I've selected a handful of candidates from our ranks, men who have shown great interest in joining the esteemed dragon riders. However, the turnout has been... disappointingly sparse."

King Alex's laughter echoed through the chamber, his eyes sparkling with amusement as he exchanged a glance with Queen Jeanne, who stood regally by his side. "Ah, my dear," he teased, a playful glint in his eyes, "it seems our kingdom craves a touch of novelty."

Queen Jeanne's lips curved slightly as her expression turned contemplative yet firm. "Indeed," she replied, her voice a blend of quiet determination and resolve. "I've identified several capable women within the kingdom who aspire to master the art of dragon riding. Tradition should never stand in the way of progress."

The quartermaster's eyes widened in surprise at the queen's bold statement, though relief quickly washed over his features, transforming his expression into one of deep gratitude. "Your Majesties," he said, his voice full of appreciation, "such an enlightened decision is a beacon of hope in these uncertain times."

But amid the chorus of approval, one voice remained silent, his brow furrowed in discontent. Maldrak, one of the chosen men, could not conceal his displeasure at the queen's decree. "Women as dragon riders?" he questioned, his tone laced with disbelief. "Surely, Your Majesty, this is folly. They lack the strength and endurance required for such a demanding task."

King Alex and the quartermaster turned to Maldrak, their expressions stern yet composed. "Strength and endurance," King Alex replied firmly, "are not confined to one gender. If these women prove themselves during initiation, they will be granted the same opportunity as any man."

Maldrak's jaw tightened in frustration, but he dared not challenge the king further. With a curt nod, he yielded to the royal decree, though his heart simmered with quiet indignation.

As the meeting drew to a close and the candidates for dragon rider training were finalized, the echoes of change reverberated through the halls of Goldmoor—a testament to the kingdom's commitment to equality and the indomitable spirit of its people.

Trailing behind the group, Maldrak's discontent smoldered beneath the surface. Once they were out of earshot of the throne room, he could no longer contain his anger.

"Women as dragon riders? Preposterous!" Maldrak spat, his voice filled with disdain. "It's a mockery of tradition and the sacred bond between dragon and rider. They'll never have what it takes to command a dragon."

Unbeknownst to Maldrak, his words were not lost in the quiet halls. High above, a young gold dragon perched on a nearby balcony, its sharp ears catching every word of his rant. With a sense of duty to its kin, the dragon wasted no time in relaying the news to Kimras, the eldest of the gold dragons.

Moments later, Kimras emerged from the shadows, his golden scales shimmering in the soft light of the palace corridors. He nodded in acknowledgment to the young dragon before speaking in a voice that resonated with quiet authority.

"Thank you for bringing this to my attention," Kimras said, his gaze steady and unwavering. "But we must tread carefully. Dissent among the ranks can sow discord and weaken our unity—especially as the new dragon riders prepare for their initiation."

The young dragon nodded solemnly, understanding the gravity of the situation. Its eyes gleamed with determination, silently vowing to keep a watchful eye on Maldrak and anyone else who might challenge the queen's decree. Ensuring harmony between dragon and rider was paramount.

As Maldrak's discontented words lingered in the corridors, Kimras allowed himself a quiet chuckle. Memories of the Battle of Goldmoor flooded his mind—particularly of Keisha, the Eladrin elf who had once ridden him into battle with unmatched skill.

"Ah, young Maldrak," Kimras mused, amusement lacing his voice, "if only you knew the prowess of those who defy tradition. Keisha's mastery of riding and archery was unparalleled, a testament to her courage and skill."

The memory of that battle, one that had forever shaped their history, brought a smile to his face. Despite the doubts harbored by some, Kimras knew that those willing to challenge convention often held the greatest potential. In the trials ahead, he would watch closely, eager to see who would rise to the occasion and prove themselves worthy of becoming a dragon rider.

As the Eladrin approached the enchanting depths of Purplefire Woods, Amara, the amethyst dragon, emerged from the shadows to greet them with a playful glint in her eyes. Her sleek form glided gracefully through the air, landing before Keisha and Ong with a gentle thud.

"Welcome, dear friends!" Amara exclaimed, her voice warm and teasing. "It's been far too long since we last crossed paths. And Ong, my good fellow, have you finally learned to ride a dragon without falling off?"

Ong chuckled at her familiar teasing, his eyes sparkling with good humor. "Perhaps, Amara, perhaps," he replied, matching her tone. "But it seems there's always something around here that keeps me on my toes."

Keisha smiled at the banter between her husband and the amethyst dragon. "Shall we take a moment to rest and enjoy the beauty of Purplefire Woods?" she suggested, her voice filled with quiet anticipation.

Amara nodded, her gaze sweeping over the lush landscape with pride. "A splendid idea, Keisha," she agreed. "There's nothing like the tranquility of these woods to soothe the soul."

As the group settled in a comfortable spot amid the verdant foliage, Amara's keen eyes caught sight of a small cougar nestled among the trees. "And who might this little fellow be?" she asked, her curiosity piqued.

Keisha smiled fondly at the sight of the young cougar. "This is our newest companion," she explained, her voice soft with affection. "A gift for Queen Jeanne from Lord Karrenen. We believe he'll help protect her from any further trouble."

Their peaceful respite was soon interrupted by the sound of rustling leaves and the soft padding of paws. With a delighted gasp, Amara turned to see Pumpkin, Keisha's faithful black panther companion, emerging from the shadows, her green eyes gleaming.

"Well, well, it seems Pumpkin couldn't resist the call of the forest either," Amara remarked with a playful wink. "Shall we let these two new friends explore together?"

With a shared sense of excitement, the group watched as the young cougar and the sleek black panther greeted each other, their movements graceful and curious. In that moment, amid the beauty of Purplefire Woods, new bonds were formed, and the timeless magic of the realm embraced them all.

As the group relaxed in the serene surroundings, Amara leaned in closer to Keisha and Ong, her voice a soft murmur on the breeze. "Keisha, Ong," she began, "some of the young amethyst dragons will be joining the gold dragons. They hope to find riders to patrol this area and keep it safe."

Keisha's eyes lit up with excitement. "That would be wonderful to see," she exclaimed, her voice brimming with enthusiasm. "It's always heartening to witness the bond between dragons and their riders as they embark on their shared journey."

Ong nodded, his smile reflecting Keisha's joy. "Indeed," he said warmly. "But none will ever match the bond between you and Kimras, Keisha. That bond was forged in battle and strengthened by unwavering trust."

Keisha's cheeks flushed with a soft blush at Ong's words, her heart swelling with gratitude. "Thank you, Ong," she replied, her voice soft but sincere. "Kimras has been a true friend and ally, and I will always cherish the bond we share."

As the gentle rustle of leaves and the melodic chirping of birds filled the air, Keisha and Ong basked in the warmth of the forest and the camaraderie of their companions. In that fleeting moment of serenity, amidst the towering trees and shimmering light of Purplefire Woods, they found solace in the bonds of friendship and the promise of the adventures ahead.

But as the peaceful interlude came to an end, Ong's gaze met Keisha's with a mixture of reluctance and determination. With a heavy sigh, he knew it was time to bid farewell to the tranquil beauty of the forest and resume their journey to Goldmoor.

"Keisha," Ong began, his voice tinged with regret, "as much as I'd love to stay in Purplefire a while longer, duty calls. We must press on to inform the King that the dragon saddles are ready and deliver Queen Jeanne's surprise."

Keisha nodded in understanding, though a hint of disappointment flickered in her eyes. "I know, Ong," she replied softly but resolutely. "We can't delay any longer. Goldmoor awaits, and we must fulfill our promise to King Alex and Queen Jeanne."

As they prepared to leave Purplefire Woods behind, a sense of determination settled over them both. Their hearts were set on the task ahead and the adventures that awaited beyond the enchanted forest.

With renewed resolve, Keisha whistled for Pumpkin, her loyal black panther, and the small cougar followed closely. As Pumpkin bounded gracefully to her side, Keisha gently lifted the young cougar into her arms, cradling him with care.

Ong approached Thunder, his black stallion, who waited patiently. With practiced ease, Ong mounted Thunder's back, ensuring they were ready for the journey.

Before they departed, Ong turned to the assembled Eladrin. "Keisha and I will go ahead to Goldmoor to inform the King that the dragon saddles are ready and deliver Queen Jeanne's surprise," he announced. "You'll remain here with the saddles and lances. Await our signal for where the training will begin."

The Eladrin leader, Eldrin, nodded in agreement. "We understand, Ong. We will keep the equipment safe and be ready to move at your command."

Keisha added, "Stay sharp, and remain vigilant. We'll need you soon."

With a final nod of acknowledgment, Keisha and Ong signaled it was time to move. Keisha whistled for Pumpkin to follow, and together, they left the tranquil embrace of Purplefire Woods, their hearts focused on the path to Goldmoor.

The journey ahead was not without challenges. As they ventured forth, the lush greenery of the forest gradually gave way to the open expanse beyond. Rugged terrain and unforeseen obstacles tested their resolve, but each trial only deepened their bond and strengthened their determination.

"Do you think we'll make it in time?" Keisha asked, glancing at the setting sun.

Ong smiled reassuringly. "We will. Together, we can overcome anything."

As they approached the verdant glen of Goldmoor, the air shimmered with anticipation. The glen, bathed in the soft hues of twilight, offered a haven of tranquility amidst the chaos of the realm. Tall, ancient trees swayed gently, their branches whispering in the wind.

A sense of peace and hope filled the air, promising a brighter future for all who had journeyed to this sacred place. Keisha turned to Ong, her eyes filled with gratitude. "We made it," she said softly. "Now, let's fulfill our promise and ensure Goldmoor's safety."

Ong nodded, his heart swelling with pride and determination. "For King Alex and Queen Jeanne," he affirmed, and together, they stepped forward into the welcoming embrace of Goldmoor.

Amidst the serene beauty of the glen, Keisha approached Queen Jeanne with the baby cougar nestled gently in her arms. The Eladrin trainer stood nearby, a silent guardian ready to ensure the young cougar's well-being.

With a tender smile, Keisha presented the gift to Queen Jeanne, her eyes bright with anticipation.

"Your Majesty," she began, her voice soft as a melody in the tranquil air, "this little one is a token of our gratitude. We hope he will grow to be a loyal protector of Goldmoor and its people."

Queen Jeanne's gaze softened as she reached out to stroke the baby cougar's fur, her touch gentle and reverent. "What a precious gift," she murmured, her voice filled with emotion. As Keisha stepped back respectfully, Queen Jeanne's eyes shimmered with affection, and she cradled the young cougar in her arms. A single tear glistened on her cheek, reflecting the depth of her emotions.

King Alex, standing beside his queen, watched with a proud smile, his heart swelling with love for his wife and the new addition to their kingdom. Keisha motioned for the Eladrin trainer to step forward, indicating her readiness to assist in the bonding process between the queen and the cougar. With a gracious nod, Queen Jeanne accepted, her heart already embracing the young creature as her own.

As King Alex leaned in to whisper words of affection, Queen Jeanne's lips curved into a tender smile. "Casper," she murmured, the name a whispered promise of protection and devotion. And so, amidst the tranquil beauty of the glen, a bond was forged between the queen and the cougar—one that would stand as a testament to loyalty, courage, and the enduring power of love in the face of adversity.

As the evening shadows lengthened, King Alex turned to Keisha and Ong with a welcoming smile. "You've had a long journey. Let me show you to your rooms so you can rest," he said warmly.

Keisha nodded gratefully. "Thank you, Your Majesty. I'll see you and Casper in the morning with the Eladrin trainer," she informed Queen Jeanne, who responded with a gentle nod of appreciation.

King Alex led them through the grand corridors of the castle to their rooms, where they could finally unwind and prepare for the day ahead. The promise of a new dawn brought with it hope and anticipation.

As the first light of dawn painted the sky in hues of pink and gold, Goldmoor stirred to life. The morning air was crisp and invigorating, carrying the scent of blooming flowers and the soft rustle of leaves—promising new beginnings and endless possibilities. In the tranquil glen, Queen Jeanne emerged from her chambers, her heart filled with anticipation for the day ahead.

Accompanied by the gentle presence of Casper, Queen Jeanne made her way to the designated training grounds where the Eladrin trainer awaited. The trainer, with her ethereal grace and wisdom, stood poised and ready.

"Your Majesty, Casper," the trainer began, her voice a soft melody in the serene surroundings, "Today marks the beginning of your journey together as companions and protectors of Goldmoor."

Following the Eladrin trainer's guidance, Queen Jeanne allowed Casper to roam freely, trusting in the wisdom imparted. "Never use a leash or any restraints," the trainer advised. "Let him run free and explore. He will be trained to protect—loyal and fierce when needed—but he must also be free to learn and grow."

Queen Jeanne nodded, her gaze focused and determined. She had long awaited this moment, eager to forge a bond with her newfound companion, free from the constraints of harnesses or restrictions.

With each gentle touch and whispered word, Queen Jeanne sought to establish a deep connection with the young cougar, fostering trust and mutual respect. Sensing the queen's sincerity, Casper responded in kind, his movements graceful as he explored the surroundings with curiosity and wonder.

Together, the queen and her cougar embarked on a journey of discovery, each step bringing them closer to a bond that would transcend words. As the morning unfolded, Queen Jeanne and Casper reveled in the freedom of their companionship, their hearts united in a shared purpose—to safeguard their realm and protect those they held dear.

And so, amidst the tranquil beauty of the glen and the gentle embrace of the morning sun, the seeds of destiny were sown, heralding the dawn of a new era for Goldmoor and its people.

As Queen Jeanne and Casper continued their training under the watchful eye of the Eladrin trainer, King Alex stood nearby, his heart swelling with pride and admiration for his wife. Observing their interactions with a smile, he felt warmed by the bond forming between the queen and her loyal companion.

Chapter 4
Wings of Destiny

Ong broke the silence with a gentle suggestion as they stood together in the tranquil glen, having just arrived from the bustling city. The only sounds were the distant rustle of leaves and the soft murmur of a nearby stream, creating a peaceful backdrop. "Perhaps it's time we consider finding a suitable location for the initiation of the dragon riders," he proposed, his voice carrying a note of anticipation.

King Alex nodded in agreement, his mind already turning to the task. "Yes, we need a place that can accommodate the dragons' needs and the riders' training."

As they ventured beyond the city limits, the landscape unfolded before them in all its natural splendor. Rolling hills stretched as far as the eye could see, punctuated by clusters of ancient trees and winding rivers. The air was crisp and invigorating, carrying the scent of pine and the distant sound of rushing water—promising new beginnings and boundless possibilities.

They explored the outskirts of Goldmoor, seeking a location that would serve as the perfect setting for the dragon rider initiation and training. Immersed in the sights and sounds of their surroundings, the rustle of leaves and the distant call of birds added to the sense of tranquility and anticipation.

At last, they came upon a secluded clearing nestled amidst towering trees. Surrounded by nature's beauty, they found their answer—a place where dreams would take flight and destinies would be forged. The clearing was expansive, with ample space for both dragons and riders to maneuver and train. A nearby river provided fresh water, and the surrounding forest offered both shelter and resources.

"This is it," King Alex said, his voice filled with certainty. "This is where the dragon riders will begin their journey."

Keisha nodded, her eyes sweeping across the clearing. "It's perfect. The tranquility here will help the riders connect with their dragons."

Ong smiled, satisfaction clear in his expression. "We should start preparations immediately. There's much to do to ensure everything is ready."

With a sense of fulfillment, they stood in silent agreement, their gazes fixed on the clearing before them. In this peaceful sanctuary, amidst the whispers of the wind and the rustling leaves, they knew the initiation of the dragon riders would be nothing short of magical.

Reflecting on their shared purpose, they silently vowed to prepare for the momentous occasion ahead. The training of the dragon riders would not only strengthen their defenses but also forge unbreakable bonds between riders and dragons.

As they returned to Goldmoor, their hearts swelled with a renewed sense of purpose and anticipation. The journey ahead would be challenging, but with determination and unity, they were ready to face it head-on.

"Today marks the beginning of a new chapter in our history," King Alex declared, his voice carrying across the crisp morning air. "Follow me, and together, we shall embark on a journey that will test our courage, strength, and resolve."

With a determined stride, King Alex led the way, the hopeful riders falling into step behind him as they made their way toward the designated site for the initiation ceremony.

As the group approached the training grounds, a hush fell over the crowd. In the distance, a magnificent sight unfolded—Keisha, riding atop the majestic Kimras, the gold dragon, his scales gleaming in the sunlight. The sight of Keisha, fearless and composed, riding the ancient dragon, elicited gasps of awe from those gathered.

Kimras soared through the sky with grace and power, his massive wings casting shadows over the land below. As they descended toward the clearing, his presence commanded attention and respect. Keisha, seated confidently on his back, held the reins lightly, her posture calm and in control.

Shortly after, the majestic Amara, the amethyst dragon, appeared on the horizon, carrying Ong on her back. The Eladrin followed below, moving swiftly and efficiently, each carrying a dragon saddle or lance. The arrival of this impressive group heightened the sense of awe among the assembled crowd.

Amara landed gracefully beside Kimras, and Ong dismounted with practiced ease. The Eladrin arrived shortly after, marked by the quiet efficiency with which they set down the saddles and lances.

King Alex stepped forward, a smile of pride lighting up his face. "Keisha, Ong, your arrival is a testament to the bond we share with the dragons. You and your companions embody the courage and unity we strive to achieve."

Keisha nodded, her emerald-green eyes meeting the gazes of the gathered riders. "It is an honor to stand with you all today. The journey ahead will be challenging, but together, we will forge unbreakable bonds with our dragon companions."

Ong added, "These saddles and lances are more than just tools—they symbolize our dedication to this cause. With them, we will strengthen our connection to the dragons and protect our realm."

King Alex turned his attention to the dragon saddles laid out before him. He marveled at the craftsmanship, running his fingers over the intricate designs and sturdy construction. "The work of the Eladrin is truly exceptional," he remarked, admiration evident in his voice.

As his gaze shifted to the dragon lances, his brow furrowed in surprise. "I don't remember ordering these," he said, turning to Ong.

Keisha laughed, the sound light and joyful. "It's a gift from the Eladrin to the people of Goldmoor," she explained. "We wanted to contribute something special to your efforts."

For a moment, King Alex was at a loss for words, clearly touched by the gesture. "Thank you," he said, his voice filled with emotion. "This is a most generous gift."

One of the Eladrin stepped forward, bowing slightly. "Your Majesty, there are a limited number of lances as they are difficult to wield and require great skill. Only the most adept riders will be able to use them effectively."

King Alex nodded thoughtfully, examining each lance carefully and appreciating the fine balance and deadly precision of the weapons. "We will train diligently to master these. Your gift will be put to good use in defending Goldmoor."

With the arrival of Keisha, Ong, Kimras, Amara, and the Eladrin, the atmosphere buzzed with renewed energy and anticipation. The dragon saddles and lances were arranged with care, ready for the initiation ceremony to begin.

Kimras turned his wise gaze upon the gathered riders, his voice resonating with authority. "Today, you begin a journey that will test your limits and strengthen your spirit. Embrace this opportunity to bond with your dragons and become the protectors of Goldmoor."

King Alex addressed the group once more. "In this tranquil sanctuary, amidst the whispers of the wind and the rustle of leaves, we will train and grow stronger together. The initiation of the dragon riders will be nothing short of magical."

As the group settled into the clearing, Keisha turned to Kimras. "Kimras," she called out, her voice carrying across the assembly, "would you share with us the story of how the dragons came to Vacari originally?"

Kimras nodded, his eyes reflecting centuries of wisdom. "Very well," he began, his voice deep and resonant, captivating everyone present.

"Long ago, before the rise of kingdoms and the building of cities, the land of Vacari was wild and untamed. It was during this time that the first dragons arrived from the distant realm of Aurelia. They were drawn to the pure magic that flowed through Vacari, a magic that resonated with their very essence.

"The dragons were not mere beasts, but intelligent and noble beings, each possessing unique abilities and wisdom. They saw the potential in the land and sought to guide its inhabitants. Over time, they formed bonds with the early settlers of Vacari, teaching them to harness the land's magic and live in harmony with nature.

"As the bonds between dragons and humans grew stronger, so too did the power and prosperity of Vacari. The dragons became protectors, advisors, and friends. They helped shape the land, using their abilities to cultivate fertile valleys, forge mighty rivers, and carve majestic mountains.

"But as with all great powers, there were those who sought to exploit it. Dark forces arose, threatening the peace and balance that had been achieved. It was then that the first dragon riders were chosen—brave individuals who forged a sacred bond with the dragons, riding them into battle to defend their home.

"The legacy of these early dragon riders lives on in you," Kimras continued, his gaze sweeping over the gathered riders. "Today, you honor that ancient bond. You are the next generation of protectors, destined to carry forward the legacy of unity and strength."

As Kimras finished his tale, the assembly fell silent, each person deeply moved by the ancient history that connected them to their dragon companions.

As the crowd began to stir from Kimras's captivating story, Ong couldn't help but overhear Maldrak's incessant grumbling. Suppressing a chuckle, Ong stepped away, his lips twitching with amusement as he discreetly tried to stifle his laughter.

Maldrak, oblivious to Ong's reaction, continued airing his grievances, punctuating his complaints with dramatic sighs and exaggerated gestures. Though he said nothing directly, Maldrak's unease at Keisha's confident handling of the golden dragon was clear. His earlier complaints intensified, a sour expression etched across his face as he watched her with narrowed eyes.

Keisha, unaware of Maldrak's silent scrutiny, approached King Alex with unwavering determination, her focus solely on the task ahead. Meanwhile, Ong exchanged a knowing glance with her, a silent acknowledgment passing between them. They both understood the significance of Maldrak's reaction—a clear sign that Keisha posed a threat to his ambitions.

As the sun climbed higher in the sky, casting its warm glow over the gathering, the stage was set for the next chapter in Goldmoor's history, one filled with challenges and intrigue. The air buzzed with anticipation, and the scent of pine and fresh earth filled the clearing.

King Alex addressed the potential dragon riders with authority and encouragement. "My friends," he began, his voice strong and clear, "before you stand a selection of young dragons, each eager to forge a bond with a rider."

He gestured toward the waiting dragons, their scales shimmering in the sunlight. "I invite you to walk among them, to observe and connect with the dragon that speaks to your heart," he continued, his eyes gleaming with anticipation.

Excitement rippled through the group as the potential riders dispersed, their footsteps soft against the forest floor as they approached the young dragons. Men and women moved among the magnificent creatures, their eyes filled with wonder and determination. Some reached out tentatively, offering a hand to be sniffed, while others gently touched the dragons' scales, hoping to make a connection.

The dragons responded in kind, their movements fluid and graceful as they interacted with the potential riders. One young rider extended his hand, and a dragon sniffed it curiously before nuzzling him in approval, while another rider stroked the scales of a dragon, earning a pleased rumble in response.

Among the group, Maldrak stood apart, his gaze fixed on the golden dragons with a hunger that bordered on obsession. With a sense of entitlement, he approached one, his expression filled with arrogance as he reached out to make his choice. But the dragon stepped away, subtly rejecting him. Maldrak's face darkened with anger as he scoured the group, determined to find a dragon that would submit to his will.

Meanwhile, Keisha and Ong observed from a distance, their expressions thoughtful as they watched the potential dragon riders make their selections. Each choice spoke volumes about the rider's character and their potential bond with the dragons.

Amidst the quiet rustle of leaves and the gentle whispers of the wind, the stage was set for the initiation ceremony—a momentous occasion that would mark the beginning of a new chapter for Goldmoor and its people.

As excitement filled the air, Maldrak's bitter complaints cut through the anticipation like a blade. His voice rang with disdain, dripping with prejudice as he objected to the idea of women riding dragons.

King Alex and Ong attempted to reason with him, pointing to Keisha's strong bond with Kimras as proof that women were just as capable. But their words only fueled Maldrak's anger, his stubborn refusal clear in his every gesture.

Keisha, standing nearby, listened to the exchange with a mixture of frustration and resolve. The sounds of the forest—a gentle rustling of leaves, the distant call of birds—clashed with Maldrak's harsh words. As his tirade continued, Keisha felt indignation rise within her, a fierce determination to prove him wrong.

Her mind drifted briefly to the challenges she had faced, the doubts she had overcome, and the strength she had discovered within herself. These thoughts fueled her resolve, pushing her to show the world what she was capable of.

Turning to Kimras, Keisha exchanged a knowing glance with her loyal companion. Without a word, Kimras stepped forward, his golden scales gleaming in the sunlight as he approached her.

In a quiet moment of understanding, Keisha whispered to him, her voice barely audible. "Show them what we can do," she urged, her eyes alight with determination.

Kimras nodded, lowering himself to the ground, allowing Keisha to mount him. There were no saddles or harnesses—just the unbreakable bond between rider and dragon, forged through trust and companionship.

As Keisha settled into place, a sense of calm washed over her, her connection with Kimras strong and unwavering. With a gentle nudge, they moved together, their motions fluid and graceful as they navigated the clearing.

They performed a series of intricate maneuvers, each one executed with precision. Weaving between trees, soaring into the sky, and executing daring twists, they left the onlookers breathless. Kimras executed a stunning loop, followed by a dive that pulled up just in time, sending a rush of wind through the clearing.

At first, the crowd watched in stunned silence. Then, cheers and applause erupted as Keisha and Kimras displayed their skill and unity. Faces lit with awe, and murmurs of admiration spread like wildfire.

As they came to a stop before the crowd, Keisha glanced back at Maldrak, her gaze steady. "You see, Maldrak," she said, her voice firm and confident, "gender, race, or any other label holds no power over the bond between rider and dragon. I have shown you that a woman—elf or not—can ride a dragon with as much skill and bravery as any man."

With that, Keisha and Kimras stood as living proof of the strength and unity that could be found in the bond between dragon and rider—a bond that transcended barriers and defied expectations. As applause echoed through the clearing, a new sense of hope filled the air, heralding the beginning of a new era for Goldmoor.

As Keisha's display concluded, King Alex turned his attention to Maldrak, his expression stern yet resolute. The clearing fell quiet, the assembled riders watching the exchange expectantly.

Maldrak," King Alex began, his voice firm with authority, "enough. Your incessant complaints have no place here in Goldmoor."

Maldrak's glare hardened at the king's words, his defiance evident in his stance. "I will not be silenced," he retorted, his voice dripping with contempt. "I refuse to be a part of this farce."

King Alex sighed heavily, his patience wearing thin. He glanced at the other riders, their faces a mixture of concern and anticipation. "Then so be it," he declared, his tone resolute. "If you cannot abide by the values of unity and acceptance that govern Goldmoor, I have no choice but to ask you to leave."

Maldrak scoffed, wounded pride flashing in his eyes. "I'll make my own way," he spat, his words laced with bitterness.

Before Maldrak could take another step, Kimras exchanged a glance with Amara, a silent understanding passing between the two dragons. With a graceful movement, Amara swept forward, lifting Maldrak by his arms. Her powerful wings beat against the air as she prepared to carry him away.

King Alex watched with resignation as Amara flew off with Maldrak, his heart heavy with the knowledge that not everyone shared his vision for a united Goldmoor. The clearing fell into a tense silence, the weight of Maldrak's departure hanging in the air.

The riders stood quietly, their expressions a mixture of relief and uncertainty. The tension had been broken, but the reality that not all would follow the path of unity remained palpable.

Turning back to the assembled riders, King Alex forced a smile, his determination unshaken. "Let us not be deterred by one man's narrow-mindedness," he proclaimed, his voice ringing with conviction. "Each of you has chosen your dragon, and now it is time to begin the journey of bonding and camaraderie that will define you as dragon riders."

With renewed resolve, the riders turned to their selected dragons, hearts filled with anticipation for the trials and triumphs ahead. One rider gently stroked his dragon's snout, while another whispered softly to her dragon, their eyes reflecting mutual understanding. As they forged bonds of friendship and trust, the spirit of unity and acceptance that King Alex championed lived on, guiding them toward a future of hope and possibility.

As the initiation ceremony progressed, some potential riders encountered difficulties connecting with their chosen dragons. Despite setbacks, they persevered, determined to find the bond that felt right. One by one, they moved on, exploring their options until they found a dragon that resonated with them, their spirits aligning in perfect harmony.

Amidst the activity, Ong and Keisha shared a knowing smile, their confidence unwavering as they approached King Alex. "Your Majesty," Keisha began, her voice warm with encouragement, "there is one dragon left, and we believe it's meant for you."

King Alex's expression shifted from surprise to uncertainty as he glanced at the remaining golden dragon. "Me?" he asked, his voice tinged with disbelief.

Keisha chuckled softly, a playful twinkle in her eyes. "Yes, you," she affirmed, her tone light but certain. "Remember the exhilaration you felt when you rode Kimras? You were meant to soar among the clouds."

Ong nodded in agreement, his expression earnest. "Your people would be honored to have their king join them on this journey," he added, his voice carrying conviction.

With a hesitant smile, King Alex nodded, his resolve hardening. "Very well," he declared, his voice steady. "I will join my people as a dragon rider."

And so, with determination in his heart, King Alex embarked on the initiation process, his steps guided by the promise of adventure and the bonds of camaraderie that awaited him. As he mounted the golden dragon's back, a sense of anticipation filled the air, heralding the beginning of a new chapter in Goldmoor's history—a chapter written in the skies, where dragons and riders soared as one.

As King Alex soared through the skies atop the golden dragon, exhilaration surged through him, his spirit soaring alongside his newfound companion. With each passing moment, he felt the bond between them strengthen—a testament to the power of trust and friendship.

Ong, Keisha, and the citizens of Goldmoor watched with pride and anticipation as King Alex connected with his dragon. The air buzzed with excitement, and the sun cast a warm glow over the gathering. When King Alex landed back on the ground, a sense of accomplishment radiated from him, his expression one of determination and resolve.

As Kimras and Amara descended, Amara approached King Alex with a solemn expression. "Your Majesty," she began, her voice tinged with concern, "Maldrak has been deposited far from Goldmoor. You need not worry about his presence any longer."

King Alex felt relieved, nodding his gratitude to Amara. His heart was lightened by the news, while Ong and Keisha exchanged a knowing smile, their faith in King Alex unwavering.

Turning to address the newly initiated dragon riders, Kimras and Amara spoke with authority and wisdom. "The initiation ceremony marks only the beginning of your journey as dragon riders," they proclaimed, their voices carrying across the clearing. "From this day forth, you will begin training every morning to hone your skills and strengthen your bond with your dragons."

The Quartermaster and Ong brought forth the dragon lances, their presence a symbol of honor and responsibility. King Alex hesitated at first, but as he reached for a lance, a sense of familiarity washed over him. With a determined grip, he lifted the lance effortlessly, and the crowd erupted in cheers of approval.

One by one, the other dragon riders attempted to lift a lance—some succeeding, while others struggled. Those who could wield the lances with ease were encouraged to keep them, a mark of their potential as dragon riders.

Meanwhile, Keisha addressed the group, reminding them of the importance of magic users and archers. "Their skills will be essential in the battles ahead," she explained. "Precise archery and powerful spells will support your dragons in combat, ensuring our success."

With roles defined and spirits high, the dragon riders prepared for their training and the challenges that lay ahead.

Turning to Keisha and Ong, King Alex nodded gratefully. "Thank you for your guidance," he said, his voice filled with sincerity. "We will not forget your help."

Keisha and Ong exchanged a glance before preparing to depart. "If you ever need us, just call," Keisha assured him, her voice steady as it carried across the clearing.

With their mission accomplished and their hearts filled with hope, Keisha and Ong set off for E'vahano, leaving behind a realm united by the bonds of friendship, courage, and the promise of a brighter tomorrow.

As King Alex addressed the assembled dragon riders, his voice carried the weight of authority and determination. "Remember, be back here in the morning," he instructed, his gaze sweeping over the eager faces. "Training begins then. And don't forget to visit the armory to choose your dragon saddle."

With that, King Alex and the others began to depart, their footsteps echoing softly against the forest floor as they made their way back to the city.

As they left, Kimras and Amara exchanged a glance, their expressions reflecting a shared concern. "I hope Maldrak won't cause any trouble," Kimras remarked, his voice tinged with worry.

Amara nodded, her gaze thoughtful. "Only time will tell," she replied, her voice calm but edged with uncertainty.

With a final look at each other, Kimras and Amara parted ways, each returning to their respective areas to prepare for the challenges ahead.

As the sun dipped below the horizon and shadows lengthened, the day ended—but the future remained unwritten, filled with both promise and peril.

Chapter 5
Exile's Journey

Maldrak stood at the edge of Purplefire Woods, his gaze lingering on the serene beauty of the Sylvan Forest beyond. The scent of pine and earth filled the air, while the distant murmur of a stream added to the tranquil atmosphere. Memories of his recent expulsion from Goldmoor churned in his mind, mingling with the simmering resentment that fueled his every step. He knew returning to Purplefire Woods would be futile; the Amethyst Dragons guarded the forest with relentless vigilance, and any attempt to breach its borders would be met with swift retribution.

With a frustrated snarl, Maldrak turned away from the woods, his eyes scanning the horizon for a path forward. The bridge leading to the other side beckoned, but he hesitated, weighing his options. Crossing it would take him deeper into unfamiliar territory, away from the safety of the forest he knew. Yet something within him rebelled at the thought of retreat.

As he deliberated, his eyes fell upon the distant Sylvan Forest—a lush expanse of towering trees, shimmering streams, and vibrant foliage that seemed to beckon him with promises of hidden power and opportunity. Without further thought, he set off toward the forest, driven by a desire for revenge.

Venturing deeper into the Sylvan Forest, Maldrak marveled at the ethereal beauty around him. The trees, their leaves glowing softly in the moonlight, cast a shimmering light on the forest floor. It was a sight unlike anything he had ever witnessed, and for a brief moment, even his burning rage was tempered by the magnificence of his surroundings.

But his awe was fleeting. As he pressed on, his mind consumed by revenge, the sounds of rustling leaves and distant wildlife faded into the background. Unbeknownst to him, he was being watched—gleaming eyes followed his every move from the shadows. The Sylvan Elves had seen him enter their forest, and they knew his presence could only mean trouble.

With silent exchanges, the elves made their decision. They would follow this intruder, this harbinger of darkness, and ensure he posed no threat to their sacred home. Like woodland spirits, they moved through the trees, their footsteps as light as the whispering wind.

Oblivious to his pursuers, Maldrak forged ahead. Suddenly, the sharp crack of a branch breaking shattered the silence—one of the elves had slipped. Instantly, Maldrak whirled around, his eyes blazing as he caught sight of the elf.

With a snarl, Maldrak drew his sword, the blade gleaming in the moonlight as he pointed it menacingly at the intruder. But before he could act, a chorus of voices rang out from the trees, and a group of Sylvan Elves emerged from the shadows, their bows drawn and aimed at Maldrak's heart.

In the center of the group, a figure stepped forward—graceful and imposing, draped in robes of green and silver. Their emerald eyes bore into Maldrak with unflinching resolve.

"Leave Ivory Moonbeams and do not return," the elf commanded, their voice carrying the weight of centuries of wisdom and authority.

Maldrak's gaze flickered to the pointed bows and the unwavering faces of the elves surrounding him. Outnumbered and outmatched, he knew better than to fight them in their own domain—at least, for now.

With a scowl, he lowered his sword and stepped back, his anger simmering just beneath the surface as he turned to leave the forest. Yet as he vanished into the shadows, his parting words lingered like a curse.

Maldrak seethed with disdain, his hatred for the Eladrin and Sylvan Elves festering like an open wound. It began with Keisha's effortless bond with Kimras, her graceful ride through the forest that mocked his every struggle. And when the Sylvan Elves had the audacity to order him from their lands, he swore they'd regret it. "More elves," he muttered darkly, his voice dripping with venom. "They will pay for this."

The Sylvan Elves watched him go, remaining vigilant. They knew the darkness would always seek to encroach upon the light, but they would be ready to defend their home against any who dared to threaten it.

As Maldrak ventured deeper into the Sylvan Forest, his eyes fell upon a glade bathed in ethereal light. The landscape before him was a study in contrasts: sunlit clearings melting into shadowy groves, vibrant wildflowers blooming beside eerie, phosphorescent fungi. Drawn by an unseen force, Maldrak felt an irresistible pull toward the heart of the glade.

With cautious steps, he entered, his senses immediately overwhelmed by the surreal beauty. The air was thick with the sweet perfume of blossoms, mingling with the earthy scent of damp moss. It was intoxicating, clinging to the senses. Wisps of mist drifted between the trees, and strange luminescent creatures flitted through the shadows, casting eerie silhouettes on the forest floor.

As he ventured further, an otherworldly enchantment seemed to wash over him. The boundary between the mortal realm and the faerie realm blurred before his eyes. Shifting colors of purple, blue, and gray danced in the glade's soft light, casting mysterious shadows.

Settling beneath a gnarled tree, Maldrak let himself be swept away by the hypnotic rhythm of the forest. Thoughts of revenge and conquest swirled in his mind, growing more potent in the enchanted atmosphere. But even as he closed his eyes, surrendering to the allure of the glade, he couldn't shake the sensation of being watched—unseen eyes trailing his every move, waiting for the perfect moment to strike. As night deepened and shadows lengthened, Maldrak remained vigilant. He knew that in this enchanted place, danger lurked behind every corner, and the line between reality and illusion was perilously thin.

Resting under the gnarled tree, Maldrak's mind churned with thoughts of retribution. The forest seemed to echo his desires, feeding the flames of his ambition. He needed a city—a stronghold where his authority would reign absolute, where the chains of his past and the interference of others could no longer bind him.

Closing his eyes, Maldrak envisioned the perfect city. It would be a place where his word was law, where defiance was met with swift, merciless punishment. He imagined streets teeming with loyal subjects, each one devoted to his will. Towering citadels and impenetrable fortresses would stand as symbols of his dominance, a testament to his power over any who dared oppose him.

But above all, Maldrak knew this city would be the staging ground for his revenge against the elves of Ivory Moonbeam. The memory of their command to leave burned in his veins, driving his every thought. They would pay for their arrogance—for daring to defy him.

With grim resolve, Maldrak vowed to make them rue the day they crossed him. He would show them the true meaning of fear, the full extent of his wrath. It would take time, but he would build his empire, and when the time came, he would destroy the elves.

As Maldrak lay beneath the stars, the weight of his ambition pressed upon him like a heavy cloak. His path was clear: he would build his city, gather his forces, and when the time was right, unleash his fury upon Ivory Moonbeam and all who stood in his way.

In the deepening night, the forest around him grew silent, yet Maldrak's resolve burned brighter than ever—a beacon of darkness in a world of light. His destiny awaited, and nothing would stand in his way—not even the might of the Sylvan Elves.

At dawn, Maldrak stirred from his restless slumber, his mind still ablaze with thoughts of conquest. Rising to his feet, he felt renewed determination as the remnants of his dreams faded in the morning light. Leaving the tranquil grove behind, he pressed onward, driven by the unyielding desire to find a city of his own. The forest seemed to whisper to him, urging him forward with the rustle of leaves and the song of birds.

Emerging from the woods into an open expanse, Maldrak's eyes caught sight of a distant city, its towering structures rising against the horizon. The silhouette beckoned to him, promising a new beginning and the chance to forge his destiny.

With purpose in his stride, Maldrak set off across the open landscape, each step bringing him closer to his goal. The anticipation within him grew like a raging inferno. Approaching the city gates, he felt a surge of exhilaration course through his veins. Within these walls lay the power and authority he had long desired.

Passing through the gates, Maldrak commanded attention as he strode through the bustling streets. People stopped and stared, sensing the aura of power that surrounded him. He relished the control he felt, knowing that in this city, the people would serve him, bending to his will without question.

Surveying the streets, Maldrak saw the perfect place to begin his conquest and build his empire from the ashes of his past. With a triumphant smirk, he christened the city "Shadowhaven"—a name that reflected the darkness lurking within its walls and the haven it would become for those who pledged loyalty to him.

Standing at the threshold of Shadowhaven, Maldrak admired the city's imposing beauty. Towering spires reached toward the heavens, casting long shadows over the cobblestone streets. The air buzzed with the hum of city life—the voices of merchants haggling and the laughter of children echoing through the narrow alleyways.

But it wasn't just the architecture that captivated Maldrak—it was the city's strategic location beside the Cerulean Expanse, a vast and mysterious body of water stretching to the horizon. Rumors spoke of ancient secrets and untold treasures hidden within its depths, and its waters teemed with life, both wondrous and dangerous.

Gazing out at the shimmering waters, Maldrak knew the Cerulean Expanse held the key to his ambitions. With control over Shadowhaven and access to the Expanse, he would possess a formidable stronghold from which to launch his campaigns of conquest.

A satisfied smile spread across his face as he set foot into Shadowhaven, his mind already buzzing with dark schemes. With the city at his command and the Cerulean Expanse at his doorstep, the possibilities were endless. Maldrak's hatred burned like a wildfire as he envisioned a pact with the dark dragons—an alliance powerful enough to bring vengeance upon the Eladrin and Sylvan Elves. His journey into the heart of Shadowhaven was just the beginning.

Chapter 6
The Rise of Flameford

As the first rays of dawn pierced through the thick canopy of storm clouds, a silhouette appeared on the horizon, growing larger with each passing moment. Zylron, the crimson dragon, descended upon Flameford, his scales shimmering in the dim light. Memories of his servitude under Phoenix Shadowwalker, the dark warlock who once ruled these lands, flooded his mind. Phoenix's reign of terror and whispered promises of power still lingered in Zylron's consciousness. But now, Zylron had a new purpose: to unite the dark dragons, rally them, and reclaim the realm of shadows that had slipped from their grasp.

With a powerful flap of his wings, Zylron landed in the heart of Flameford. His eyes scanned the city with a mixture of nostalgia and determination. Every shadowed corner held reminders of a dark past and the promise of a new future.

High above, Glaciera, the alabaster dragon, soared through the sky. Her wings sliced the air with graceful precision, her mind buzzing with anticipation. She had pledged her unwavering loyalty to Zylron's cause—to unite the dark dragons and restore their realm to its former glory. As she approached Flameford, the tales of its twisted majesty and dark beauty played through her mind, now becoming a reality.

Unlike Zylron, Glaciera had never set foot in Flameford. The thought of exploring this unfamiliar territory thrilled her. As she descended, her keen eyes absorbed the darkened streets, the obsidian towers, and the potential for transformation. This would be the perfect place to carve out a sanctuary for her kind—the white dragons of the frozen north.

Glaciera landed gracefully, spotting Zylron immediately. With pride swelling in her heart, she approached. "Zylron," she greeted, her voice a melodic echo in the city's stillness. "I have come, as promised, to stand by your side and aid you in our quest to restore the darkness."

Zylron turned to face her, appreciation gleaming in his crimson eyes. "Glaciera," he rumbled, his voice carrying the weight of centuries. "Your loyalty and unwavering support are invaluable. Together, we will accomplish great things."

Glaciera's gaze held a calculated resolve. She had witnessed Zylron's raw power during Phoenix's reign and recognized that aligning with the red dragons was the only way to safeguard her own. It stung her pride to admit that the white dragons could never surpass the red, yet she knew Zylron's purpose could serve her own interests, ensuring both their futures.

Standing amidst Flameford's looming shadows, Zylron gestured to the sprawling cityscape. "But first," he continued, "we must carve out a sanctuary for our kindred—a realm where the white dragons and our dark brethren can thrive," he declared. "A place where any dark dragon will feel welcome, a stronghold where we can gather, united, to shape our plans and forge our future."

With a nod, Glaciera spread her wings and soared into the skies, envisioning icy courtyards and frost-covered towers, places where the cold would reign supreme. After surveying the city, she returned with important news.

"Zylron," she began, her voice grave with her findings, "I have spoken to the Black Dragons. Despite Drakthor's fall at the Battle of Vacari, they remain loyal to our cause."

Zylron nodded solemnly. "Their loyalty strengthens our alliance," he replied, pride lacing his words.

"But that's not all," Glaciera continued. "I have reached out to the Green Dragons, who have also pledged their support. They seek revenge for Venfyr's death and are eager to stand by us in the coming battles."

Zylron's eyes gleamed with anticipation. "Their aid will be invaluable in reclaiming what was lost."

He turned to Glaciera, his gaze sharp. "What of the Topaz Dragons? Do you think they'll remain loyal?"

Glaciera considered the question. "The Topaz Dragons are driven by power and dominance. They may seek revenge for Thundria's fall, but they also recognize the strength of our alliance. As long as they see an opportunity to advance their ambitions, they will stand with us."

Zylron nodded thoughtfully. "Their allegiance is crucial. We must secure their support—at any cost."

With a shared understanding of the challenges ahead, Zylron and Glaciera stood side by side, united in their determination to forge a future steeped in darkness and power. The shadowed landscape of Flameford stretched before them, a jagged tapestry of spires and alleys, whispering promises of their destined rule. Yet, a flicker of doubt crossed Zylron's mind—could he truly unite all the dark dragons as Phoenix once did? Reds were powerful, but would it be enough? He would never yield to the forces of good in Vacari; instead, he would fight tooth and nail to make the dark dragons supreme. Together, they would stop at nothing to claim their world.

DRAGONS OF VACARI

Chapter 7
Echoes of Disquiet: Return to Goldmoor

As the sun rose over the majestic peaks of Goldmoor, casting a golden glow on the landscape, the dragon riders and their noble steeds assembled on the training grounds. The crisp morning air was filled with the flapping of dragon wings and the murmur of determined voices. From a distance, Kimras and Amara watched, their keen eyes taking in the scene with pride and satisfaction.

Earlier, they had traveled to the outskirts of Purplefire Woods to confirm that Maldrak was nowhere to be found. As guardians of Vacari, the duty to protect their homeland weighed heavily on their hearts. With sharp senses, they had scanned the horizon for any signs of danger and were relieved to find none. Satisfied that Vacari was secure, they returned to Goldmoor to observe the progress of the dragon riders' training.

What they saw filled them with awe. The riders moved with grace and precision, their bond with their dragons evident in every synchronized maneuver. It was a testament to their dedication, and Kimras and Amara felt a swell of pride as they watched. King Alex stood among his people, his presence inspiring the riders and instilling a sense of purpose in all who trained.

"They've come a long way," Kimras remarked, admiration in his voice. "I never would have imagined they'd progress so quickly."

"Indeed," Amara agreed, her gaze fixed on the training grounds. "King Alex's leadership has brought out the best in them. His presence has made all the difference."

As the training session came to an end, the quartermaster approached Kimras with a sense of urgency. "Kimras," he began, his tone serious, "I believe it's time to organize the dragon riders into sections for the next phase of training."

"Go on," Kimras urged, his golden eyes gleaming with determination.

"The riders wielding dragon lances should focus on mastering their weapons from the backs of their dragons. Aerial jousting and precision strikes in flight would be ideal practice," the quartermaster explained.

Kimras nodded thoughtfully. "And what about the archers and magic users?"

"They need to maintain focus amidst the chaos of battle. We could set up moving targets and simulate battlefield conditions to test their skills."

"I agree," Kimras said. "Tell the riders that starting tomorrow, they'll be divided into groups based on their specialties."

The quartermaster bowed and hurried off to relay the instructions, knowing their preparation would be key to success in the battles to come.

As the session concluded, King Alex approached Kimras and Amara, his eyes reflecting pride. "Kimras, Amara," he greeted them warmly, his voice filled with appreciation. "I'm amazed by how far we've come in just six months. Your guidance has been invaluable."

Kimras inclined his head. "Your people's dedication has exceeded our expectations. It's a testament to their resilience."

Amara added, "It has been an honor to witness their growth under your leadership, King Alex."

King Alex smiled. "Thank you. But I know the hard part is yet to come. Learning to ride is one thing; mastering weapons and magic while doing so is another."

Kimras chuckled. "Your presence has certainly benefited them. Your commitment hasn't gone unnoticed."

As King Alex made his way toward the Glen, his heart swelled with anticipation. The tranquil beauty of the Glen greeted him, and as he approached, he overheard the Eladrin speaking with Queen Jeanne. "I've taught you all I can," the Eladrin said. "Now it's time for me to return home, and for you to continue your training with Casper."

King Alex watched as the Eladrin departed, leaving Jeanne and Casper standing together. "Jeanne," he greeted, his voice filled with affection. "It's good to see you both. Casper's certainly grown in the last few months."

Jeanne chuckled softly. "Yes, he has. And I've grown to love him even more."

King Alex grinned. "It looks like Casper has grown quite attached to you as well," he teased.

Jeanne laughed. "He does seem to follow me everywhere," she admitted, her fondness for Casper evident.

With shared smiles, they made their way back toward the palace, Casper trotting happily at their heels. King Alex felt a deep sense of gratitude for the love and companionship surrounding him.

As Kimras soared above Goldmoor, a lingering sense of unease gnawed at him. Despite the peaceful scene below, the memory of Maldrak's threats kept him on edge. Increasing the patrols, Kimras scanned the landscape, searching for any sign of danger. "Stay alert," he **mentally communicated with his patrol, reinforcing the need for unwavering vigilance. Though the fields were calm and the villages alive with activity, an unsettling tension lingered. Kimras, as guardian of Goldmoor, knew that his instincts were rarely wrong, and now, they urged him to stay alert—something dark was on the horizon.**

Meanwhile, Amara led a group of young dragons on a training flight above Purplefire Woods. Her laughter faded, replaced by a creeping sense of dread. As her gaze swept over the forest, the feeling gnawed deeper, hinting that the disturbance stretched beyond the woods to all of Vacari. The unease shadowed her thoughts, and she resolved to speak with Kimras soon, suspecting that whatever lurked might soon disrupt their world.

In the shadowed alleys of Flameford, a cloaked figure approached Zylron and Glaciera with urgency. "Zylron, Glaciera," the figure's voice carried a heavy weight. "I bring news of an ancient darkness stirring once more."

Zylron's gaze narrowed. "What do you know of this darkness?"

The ancient darkness seeks resurgence," the figure replied with a glint of satisfaction. "And there are certain boundaries that must be upheld. Allowing it to flourish will alter the harmony of our realm, setting forces in motion beyond comprehension. But this is precisely what we desire.

Zylron and Glaciera exchanged a knowing glance, understanding the gravity of those restrictions. "The dark dragons will unite under your leadership," the figure continued. "Their allegiance is inevitable."

As the figure melted back into the shadows, Zylron and Glaciera stood in silence, resolving to proceed with caution. They knew the road ahead would be fraught with uncertainty.

As the sun dipped below the horizon, Amara and Kimras perched atop a rocky outcrop overlooking Goldmoor. Despite their patrols revealing nothing unusual, both dragons remained uneasy.

Perhaps it's not confined to one area," Amara suggested thoughtfully. **"Maybe what we're sensing spans across Vacari itself."**

"You could be right," Kimras replied, his gaze steady. **"We'll need to remain vigilant and connect with our allies."**

As twilight deepened and stars began to scatter across the night sky, a quiet resolve settled between them. With a shared determination, they prepared for whatever lay ahead, their bond a steadfast source of strength amid the unknown.

Chapter 8
The Whispering Darkness

As the shadows danced along the walls of Flameford, Zylron and Glaciera convened in the dimly lit chamber. The air was thick with the scent of burning incense, and the flickering torchlight cast eerie patterns on the stone walls, creating an atmosphere of mystery and foreboding. Their conversation circled around the enigmatic figure that had visited them, leaving behind whispers of dark promises and unsettling prophecies.

"The figure's words still echo in my mind," Zylron rumbled, his voice heavy with uncertainty. "The thought of the other dark dragons uniting under my banner... it's both exhilarating and unsettling."

Glaciera's piercing gaze met his, her alabaster scales shimmering in the dim light. "Indeed," she murmured, her tone cold and calculating. "But what of the figure's cryptic allegiance to you? It spoke as if you were destined to guide us into the shadows."

Zylron frowned, the torchlight casting jagged shadows across his crimson scales. "A curious notion," he mused, his voice sharp. "But one we cannot ignore. If the dark dragons are to unite under my leadership, we must prepare for the challenges ahead." Yet a lingering question gnawed at him. The figure had spoken of his leadership but had never sworn allegiance. A hint of darkness had accompanied their words—a presence unsettling and unknown. Who was this figure, and what lay behind their intentions?

Glaciera nodded, her icy gaze reflecting a precise and emotionless resolve. "We must ensure Flameford stands as a bastion of darkness, a stronghold from which we can rally our forces and unleash the ancient shadows upon our enemies."

With a shared sense of purpose, Zylron and Glaciera turned their attention to the tasks at hand. In the depths of Flameford, amidst flickering shadows and whispered secrets, the seeds of darkness were sown, ready to bloom into a force that would shape the fate of the world. Yet, despite their ambition, a lingering unease hung in the air—a reminder that their mysterious benefactor's true nature remained shrouded in shadow.

As they plotted, they knew they walked a treacherous path—one fraught with peril, yet brimming with untold power. Even as they delved deeper into their schemes, they couldn't shake the feeling of being watched—eyes glimmering with malice, hungry for chaos and destruction. But for now, their focus remained on their preparations, their minds consumed with visions of conquest and glory. In the heart of darkness, anything was possible, and Zylron and Glaciera were determined to claim their rightful place among the shadows, no matter the cost.

Suddenly, a presence materialized beside them, sending a ripple of surprise through the air. A cloaked figure stood, obscured by shadows, yet exuding an undeniable aura of power. The flickering torchlight cast an eerie glow on their form, amplifying the sense of mystery.

Zylron and Glaciera exchanged a glance, astonishment flickering in their eyes before they quickly regained their composure. Zylron addressed the figure in his usual harsh tone. "Who are you?" he inquired, suspicion lacing his voice. "What brings you to Flameford?"

The figure smirked, a faint gleam of amusement flashing in their eyes. Soon enough, the dark dragons would understand the true purpose behind this alliance. For now, Zylron would be given the illusion of leadership—a useful tool in setting their plans in motion. Composing themselves, they met Zylron's gaze, their voice resonating with an otherworldly timbre. "I am but a humble servant of the shadows," they replied, their words layered with enigmatic charm. "I have come to assist you in preparing for the arrival of the others," the figure continued, a hint of satisfaction in their tone. "Not all who come are of Vacari. I have summoned dark dragons from distant realms to strengthen our cause."

Zylron's crimson eyes narrowed, his gaze sharp and unyielding. The mention of dark dragons from beyond Vacari stirred something in him, a mixture of intrigue and suspicion. And this figure's claim to have summoned them only deepened his unease. He kept his expression controlled, masking his thoughts, but his mind raced. Who exactly was this "servant of the shadows" to command such influence? "And what assistance do you offer?" he asked, curiosity seeping into his tone.

The figure inclined their head slightly, a ghost of a smile playing on their lips. "I possess knowledge and abilities that may prove useful," they said cryptically. "But I demand one thing in return: that the tower in the center of Flameford remains untouched."

Zylron and Glaciera exchanged a silent glance, understanding passing between them. The tower held great significance—its ancient spires a beacon of power within Flameford. To leave it untouched was no small request, yet the figure's words carried an authority that could not be ignored.

After a moment of consideration, Zylron nodded. "Very well," he agreed, his voice firm. "The tower will remain as you demand. But know this: if you betray us, there will be consequences."

The figure offered a nod of acknowledgment before vanishing into the shadows. As they disappeared, a lingering unease settled over Zylron and Glaciera—a reminder of the mysteries that lurked within Flameford. But for now, they turned their focus back to their preparations, their minds filled with visions of the dark future ahead.

As the shadowy figure dissipated into the darkness, Glaciera turned to Zylron, her brow furrowed. "Zylron, what is the significance of the tower?" she asked, her voice cold and precise.

Zylron's gaze drifted toward the imposing tower that loomed over Flameford's skyline, its silhouette a dark reminder of ancient power. Glaciera's words echoed in his mind—artifacts belonging to Phoenix's father were said to lie within. Zylron recalled the tower's long-standing presence, a monolith that had stood for centuries, housing remnants of a legacy that stretched back to a time of forgotten shadows. Its purpose lingered in mystery, yet its influence could still be felt, drawing him in with the weight of history. "The tower holds great importance in Flameford's history," he explained. "It was once Phoenix's domain, where he delved into the mysteries of magic and ancient lore."

Glaciera's eyes narrowed as she absorbed his words. "Then it likely contains relics and artifacts that belonged to Phoenix, or perhaps even his father," she surmised, her tone calculating.

Zylron's gaze drifted toward the imposing tower that loomed over Flameford's skyline. "That tower holds the key to many mysteries," he said. "It was Phoenix's sanctuary. There may be knowledge within its walls that could aid us in our endeavors."

Glaciera nodded, a newfound respect for the tower blossoming within her. "That is why the figure wished to preserve it," she concluded. "It holds secrets that may prove invaluable in the days to come."

With a shared sense of determination, Zylron and Glaciera resolved to uncover the tower's mysteries. Whatever it held could be the key to their success. As they prepared to delve into Flameford's ancient legacy, they steeled themselves for the challenges ahead, their resolve unshaken by the shadows that surrounded them.

Zylron turned his attention back to their plans, mapping out sections of Flameford where the dark dragons would find solace. For Zylron, the fiery heart of the volcano between Flameford and Fel Thalor would serve as his domain—a realm where the flames of ambition could burn bright.

For Glaciera and her white dragons, a different landscape was needed—a realm of ice and snow, where the bitter cold matched the frost in their hearts. Zylron designated the towering peaks of the Frostspire Mountains as her territory, where Glaciera's kin could thrive.

In the quiet solitude of the tower, the mysterious figure moved gracefully through the chamber. Shadows danced around them as they surveyed the ancient artifacts scattered across the room. The scent of old parchment and burning incense filled the air.

With a gentle touch, the figure began to arrange the items with reverence. Their gaze lingered on a particularly ornate scroll, its edges frayed with age, yet pulsing with arcane energy. "What secrets do you hold?" they murmured.

As they pondered the scroll, their thoughts turned to the intricate web of alliances that lay beyond Flameford. "The Druchii could be valuable allies," they mused. "Their knowledge of ancient magic may be key to our plans."

With a determined nod, the figure resolved to seek out these allies. In the looming darkness, every advantage would be crucial, every ally indispensable. The darkness was coming, and with it, untold power. A thought crossed the figure's mind—if they could locate Lyra and Qellaun in Fel Thalor, they might hold the upper hand. Both had once served Vuarus and Phoenix with unwavering loyalty, their skills invaluable. Reuniting with them would be a powerful asset in the battles to come.

Chapter 9
Pact with the Dark Ones

The dark city of Fel Thalor lay shrouded in perpetual twilight, its towering spires casting long shadows across narrow streets. The air was thick with the scent of brimstone, emanating from the altar built around a bubbling pool of lava at the city's center. The altar, a testament to the dark elves' devotion to forbidden magic, glowed with an eerie red light, casting an ominous hue on the faces of its inhabitants. The distant murmur of incantations and the clang of metal echoed through the city, adding to its unsettling atmosphere.

Lyra and Quellan, siblings bound by blood and ambition, stood near the altar. Lyra's sharp, calculating eyes glimmered with the promise of untapped power. A formidable sorceress, her dark robes flowed around her like shadows. Quellan, clad in dark armor, rested a hand on the hilt of his sword, his stance vigilant. The rough texture of his gauntlets served as a reminder of countless battles fought and won.

A figure approached, cloaked in darkness, their features hidden beneath a hood. Lyra and Quellan turned to face the newcomer, their expressions a mix of curiosity and suspicion. The air grew heavier as the stranger drew closer, the bubbling of the lava pulsing like a heartbeat.

"Who dares approach unbidden?" Lyra's voice was cold, and commanding, her eyes narrowing as she tried to discern the stranger's identity. The raw energy of the lava mirrored her rising anticipation.

The figure paused at the edge of the lava-lit altar, a faint smile on their lips. "An ally," they said, their voice smooth and unidentifiable, echoing in the cavernous space. "One who shares your desire to bring darkness to Vacari."

Quellan's grip tightened on his sword, his eyes never leaving the figure. "An ally, you say? And why should we trust you?" His mind raced through potential threats, always a step ahead, always prepared for the worst.

The cloaked figure chuckled softly, the sound mingling with the bubbling lava. "Trust is earned, not given. But consider this: our goals align. Together, we can achieve what neither of us could alone."

Lyra's eyes flickered with interest. "You speak of power and alliances, yet you remain hidden in shadows. Reveal yourself." The promise of new power tantalized her, drawing her in.

The figure shook their head. "In time, perhaps. For now, know that I have information and resources to aid you. Vacari is ripe for darkness; we merely need to seize the opportunity."

Quellan stepped forward, tense. "What information do you offer, and what do you seek in return?" His senses were sharp, ready for any sign of deception.

The figure's eyes glinted beneath the hood. "I offer you the key to destabilizing Vacari, to sowing chaos and fear. In return, I ask for your cooperation and... discretion."

Lyra stepped closer, her curiosity piqued. "And how do you propose we sow this chaos?"

"There are scrolls hidden in a cave in Afor," the figure said, their voice lowering. "These scrolls contain ancient knowledge and spells that can tear Vacari apart. Retrieve them, and the path to darkness will be clear."

Quellan frowned. "Afor? The gate from Fel Thalor to Afor has been sealed for decades. How do you expect us to reach it?"

The stranger smiled, unseen beneath their hood. "That is a challenge for you to overcome. However, I can guide you to the threshold of Afor. Use your skills and cunning to find the rest of the way."

Lyra exchanged a glance with Qellaun, excitement gleaming in her eyes. "Very well," she said firmly. "We will retrieve the scrolls. But know this, ally: if you deceive us, there will be no place you can hide from our wrath."

The figure bowed slightly. "I have no intention of deceiving you. Our goals are aligned. I will take you to Afor." With a raised hand, shadows swirled around them, pulling Lyra and Qellaun through a tunnel of darkness. The air grew cold and thin, spinning around them. When the shadows receded, they stood on the barren, sun-scorched sands of Afor.

The desert realm stretched before them, an expanse of golden dunes and jagged rocks. In the distance, the sealed Abyss loomed—its massive, ancient structure a testament to the power of the Noble Dragons who had closed it.

Lyra scanned the horizon. "There is no cave here," she said, frustration lacing her voice. "Only the Abyss, sealed by the Noble Dragons and the gods themselves."

The stranger nodded. Indeed. The cave we seek lies deeper within Afor, and we must search thoroughly to uncover it. It is a hidden sanctuary, concealed from those who lack the knowledge to find it."

They began their journey across the desert, the relentless sun beating down on them. The heat was suffocating, and the sand shifted treacherously beneath their feet. As they ventured further, the landscape became more rugged, the jagged rocks forming a natural maze.

Suddenly, the stranger grabbed Lyra and Quellan, pulling them into a narrow crevice. "Brass Dragons," the figure whispered, pointing skyward.

Lyra peered out, her eyes widening as she spotted the gleaming forms of Brass Dragons soaring above, their scales shimmering in the sunlight. "Brass Dragons are vigilant guardians," she murmured. "They are here to ensure no darkness invades Vacari again."

They waited in tense silence as the shadows of the Brass Dragons passed overhead. Time seemed to stretch as they remained hidden. Finally, the dragons flew out of sight, disappearing over the horizon.

The stranger nodded. "We must move cautiously. The Brass Dragons are formidable adversaries."

Lyra and Quellan emerged from the crevice, their determination renewed. Pressing deeper into the desert, they noticed a narrow, hidden path veering off from the main route.

"There," Lyra gestured. "A hidden path. We should see where it leads."

They moved stealthily along the path, rounding a bend to find a group of Moon Seraphidians—half-human, half-snake beings whose scales glinted in the dim light. A faint hissing filled the air.

"There," Lyra whispered, pointing to another path partially obscured by rocks. "We need to reach it without being seen."

Quellan spotted a group of warthogs grazing nearby and formulated a plan. "We can use the warthogs as a diversion. If we spook them, they'll cause a stampede."

The stranger nodded in agreement. "Do it."

Quellan carefully picked up a handful of rocks and hurled them at the warthogs. Startled, the animals scattered in all directions, stampeding toward the Moon Seraphidians. The Seraphidians hissed and scrambled to avoid the panicked animals, allowing Lyra, Quellan, and the stranger to slip past unnoticed.

As the commotion died down behind them, they pressed on, the entrance to the hidden cave drawing closer. The narrow, winding path led them into cooler, darker territory, the light dimming as they descended deeper.

Finally, they reached the cave, its entrance concealed by rocks and thick vines. The stranger approached, a sinister smile on their face. "This is the cave we've been searching for."

Lyra and Quellan nodded, anticipation flickering in their eyes as they neared the entrance. But the stranger held up a hand. "Perhaps we should rest before entering," they suggested. "We need to be at full strength for what lies ahead."

Reluctantly, Lyra and Qellaun agreed. They found a secluded spot nearby and settled down to rest, their thoughts consumed by the promise of the power waiting inside the cave. Lyra closed her eyes, feeling the cool ground beneath her as the desert winds howled in the distance. Qellaun kept his hand on his sword, his mind racing with plans. Their ambitions burned brightly, even as sleep began to overtake them, knowing that their next steps would define the future of Vacari.

From a distance, the figure glanced over at Lyra and Qellaun, a smirk creeping across their face. The pieces were falling into place. They had found Lyra and Qellaun, and the dark dragons were beginning to unite. Soon, vengeance for Vuarus's death would be theirs, and Vacari would be plunged into a darkness that would reshape it forever—just as Vuarus had envisioned.

DRAGONS OFACARI

Chapter 10
The Depths of Discovery

As the trio stirred from their slumber, the oppressive darkness of the cavern enveloped them like a suffocating shroud, creeping into every crevice. The air was thick with the scent of damp earth and ancient decay, while distant echoes of dripping water added to the eerie atmosphere. Lyra's eyes, gleaming with malice, scanned the chamber, her vision piercing the gloom with unsettling clarity.

A wicked grin curled on her lips as she noticed the torches mounted along the walls, their flames casting twisted shadows that danced in macabre delight. **"Did you arrange these torches?"** she asked, amusement dripping from her voice, a challenge lacing her words.

The mysterious figure standing beside them shook their head slowly. **"No,"** they murmured, their voice a low, ominous whisper that sent a shiver through the group. **"The darkness here has its own will. It guides those who dare to enter."**

Quellan, his expression twisted into a sneer, approached the torches with contempt. **"It seems someone has been here before,"** he remarked, disdain in his voice. **"Though they have long since abandoned this place."** The weight of unseen eyes pressed on them, a constant reminder of the dangers lurking in the shadows.

The cave exuded an aura of malevolence, its walls adorned with symbols of ancient power and dark sorcery. Shadows clung to the stone like writhing serpents, whispering secrets to those willing to listen. The distant howling of the wind through narrow passages added to the unsettling chorus of their descent.

As they ventured deeper into the bowels of the cavern, their footsteps echoed ominously against the rocky floor, and the air thickened with the promise of impending doom. Each flicker of torchlight cast grotesque shadows, mocking their very existence with twisted visions of horror. The stench of sulfur and decay grew stronger, heightening their sense of dread.

With every step, the trio felt the weight of their dark purpose pressing down on them, the cave itself pulsing with malevolent energy. Yet, amidst the darkness, there was also a twisted sense of satisfaction—a perverse joy that simmered beneath the surface like a festering wound. The cavern seemed alive, feeding off their darkest desires and magnifying them.

Lyra, her eyes sharp and calculating, scoured the surroundings for hidden treasures or ancient secrets. Her gaze fell upon a cluster of artifacts strewn haphazardly in the shadows. Moving closer, she reached out to inspect them, her fingers tracing the intricate patterns etched into the surfaces of ancient relics. Among them lay a collection of weathered scrolls, their parchment yellowed with age and heavy with the weight of centuries past.

"These scrolls," Lyra murmured, her voice filled with reverence and greed. **"They could hold the power we seek."** The thought of wielding such power thrilled her, and she struggled to contain her excitement.

Quellan stepped closer, his eyes narrowing. **"We must be cautious. Power often comes with a price."** A creeping sense of unease filled him, as if they were being led into a trap from which there would be no escape.

The mysterious figure nodded, their face unreadable beneath the hood. **"Indeed. We must tread carefully. These relics are imbued with potent magic—not all secrets are meant to be uncovered."** Their voice was smooth, almost hypnotic, as if weaving a spell of its own.

In the eerie glow of the torchlight, anticipation and dread hung heavy in the air. The trio knew that whatever knowledge these scrolls contained could change their fate forever. The tension crackled around them, a delicate balance of promised power and looming destruction.

Lyra's eyes scanned the faded text with a mix of fascination and trepidation. The parchment, rough and brittle beneath her fingers, exuded a musty odor that spoke of ages long past. As she read, her brow furrowed in concentration, her mind grappling with the implications of the words etched into the ancient scroll.

"This scroll... it speaks of someone being imprisoned within this cave for centuries," she murmured, her voice barely above a whisper, the weight of the revelation settling heavily on her.

Quellan stepped closer, his expression grave as he peered over her shoulder. His eyes flicked over the text, concern and curiosity warring within him. **"Is this individual still here?"** he asked, his voice tinged with apprehension.

Lyra hesitated, her gaze returning to the scroll. After a pause, she shook her head slowly. **"No,"** she said, her voice firm. **"According to this, the prisoner was released."**

A shiver ran down her spine as the words left her lips. The realization that someone—or something—had been freed from this dark place sent a ripple of unease through her. Who had been imprisoned here, and what kind of power had they wielded? The shadows seemed to deepen, and the air grew heavier with the weight of ancient secrets waiting to be unearthed.

With the knowledge of a long-forgotten prisoner now set free, Lyra, Quellan, and their enigmatic companion pressed deeper into the heart of the cave. Their quest for power led them through narrow, twisting passages, the walls seeming to close in, whispering warnings in a language long lost to time.

Lyra's thoughts churned as she pondered the identity of the mysterious prisoner, her mind drifting to the vast expanse of Afor beyond the cave's confines. "**I wonder who this prisoner was,**" she mused aloud, her voice carrying a hint of unease. "**And whether they still wander the lands of Afor.**"

The figure beside them, still shrouded in shadow, offered a cryptic smile, their eyes glinting with a sinister light. "**No,**" they interjected, their voice dripping with malice. "**The one that was imprisoned within these walls is no longer among the living.**"

Quellan, ever the skeptic, arched an eyebrow, his gaze narrowing as it bore into the stranger. "**And how do you know this?**" he demanded, suspicion lacing his tone.

The stranger's smile widened, a twisted grin concealed by the shadows that clung to them like a second skin. They paused, contemplating their answer, a glint of amusement flickering in their hidden gaze. *If you only knew how I came by this knowledge, you'd begin to question who I truly am,* they mused silently. Out loud, they murmured in a voice that echoed with dark promise, "Some secrets are best left buried. For now, you must trust me. The time for revelations will come soon enough."

Lyra's gaze hardened as she regarded the stranger, a flicker of distrust sparking in her eyes. Yet, she knew they had little choice but to accept the stranger's cryptic words—for now. With a resigned nod, she reluctantly acquiesced, though she silently vowed to keep a close watch on their companion.

With uncertainty weighing heavy upon their hearts, Lyra, Quellan, and the enigmatic stranger continued their journey deeper into the bowels of the cave. Their fates were now intertwined, bound by the threads of destiny and the promise of untold darkness lurking just beyond the shadows.

As they ventured further into the cave's dark recesses, the air thickened with the weight of ancient secrets. The musty scent of earth and stone filled their nostrils, and the faint drip of water echoed ominously through the cavern, adding to the oppressive atmosphere. Strange markings and symbols adorned the rough-hewn walls, their meaning lost to time.

Lyra's brow furrowed as she tried to decipher the enigmatic glyphs, her fingers tracing the intricate patterns with both fascination and frustration. Her fists clenched in mounting irritation. **"I can't make sense of these markings,"** she muttered, turning to the stranger for guidance.

The figure, their features obscured by shadow, regarded the markings with a knowing gaze. A secretive smile curled on their lips. **"Some secrets are best left undisturbed,"** they murmured, their voice carrying a faint warning.

"But we need to know," Quellan interjected, urgency in his voice as he stepped forward to examine the markings more closely. **"These symbols could be the key to unlocking the mysteries of this cave."**

The stranger's smile widened, but their eyes remained inscrutable behind the veil of shadow. **"Patience, young ones,"** they whispered, their voice echoing off the cavern walls. **"All will be revealed in time. For now, the secrets of this place shall remain hidden."**

Lyra simmered with frustration but knew pressing the matter would yield no answers. Reluctantly, she accepted the stranger's cryptic response. Though she longed to uncover the truth hidden within the ancient glyphs, she realized their path forward lay elsewhere.

With a lingering sense of curiosity and apprehension hanging in the air, the trio pressed on, driven ever deeper into the heart of darkness by their quest for knowledge and power. Yet, with each step, they couldn't shake the feeling of being watched. The cave seemed to hum with malevolent energy, its secrets still guarded by forces unseen.

Finally, they descended into the depths of the cave, arriving at the bottom where they found themselves surrounded by a treasure trove of scrolls and artifacts, each pulsating with the energy of ancient magic.

The mysterious figure, their voice reverberating with authority, suggested they gather the scrolls and artifacts and return to Fel Thalor, the seat of their power. There, Lyra could conduct further research and share her findings with the dark dragons.

Lyra's eyes gleamed with anticipation, her mind already racing with possibilities. **"Yes, we must bring these back,"** she declared, her voice resolute. **"These artifacts may hold the key to unlocking even greater power."**

With careful precision, they began gathering the scrolls and artifacts, ensuring not to disturb the delicate balance of magic that thrummed in the air. Each item seemed to pulse with life, whispering tantalizing secrets that beckoned them closer to the truth they sought.

As they made their way back through the winding tunnels of the cave, their minds buzzed with the weight of what they had uncovered. Lyra couldn't shake the feeling that they were on the brink of something monumental. With each step, the responsibility grew heavier upon her shoulders, but she knew that the knowledge they sought was worth any sacrifice.

Driven by the promise of untold secrets and newfound power, Lyra, Quellan, and their mysterious companion pushed forward on their journey back to Fel Thalor, where the true nature of their discoveries would soon be revealed.

Quellan's keen elven senses guided them through the winding tunnels, his steps confident as he led them down a path he had discovered earlier. As they followed, the air grew colder, the shadows deepened, and soon they reached a fork in the path.

"This way," Quellan said with quiet certainty, leading them down a narrow passage obscured by darkness. The walls seemed to close in around them, whispering secrets of ages long past as they descended.

After what felt like an eternity, the passage opened into a cavern bathed in soft, ethereal light. At its center, a narrow path beckoned, leading deeper into the cave.

Lyra's heart quickened. **"This must be another secret path,"** she exclaimed in awe. **"But where does it lead?"**

The mysterious figure, still shrouded in shadow, stepped forward with a knowing smile. **"This path,"** they intoned, their voice heavy with ancient wisdom, **"leads back to the depths of the cave. But that is a path we will not take for now. These are the scrolls we sought, and we must return them to Fel Thalor to decipher their secrets."**

A sense of relief washed over Lyra and Quellan as they realized the significance of their discovery. With this knowledge, they could return to the source of their dark power whenever needed.

With practiced efficiency, they gathered the scrolls and artifacts, careful not to disturb the delicate balance of magic in the air. Each item thrummed with a life of its own, whispering tantalizing secrets that beckoned them closer to the truth.

As they retraced their steps through the winding tunnels, their minds buzzed with thoughts of the discoveries awaiting them. Lyra felt the weight of responsibility growing, but the allure of knowledge and power pushed her forward.

Back at Fel Thalor, Lyra and Quellan settled into the dimly lit chamber of their stronghold. The mysterious stranger watched from the shadows, their eyes gleaming with a knowing smile as Lyra and Quellan carefully unrolled the ancient scrolls. Their fingers traced the faded text, excitement and trepidation dancing in their eyes.

The stranger's smile widened as they wondered if Lyra and Quellan would uncover the hidden information buried within the cryptic texts. The secrets of the noble dragons and their connection to the abyss lay concealed, waiting to be unlocked by those with the insight and determination to piece together the fragmented clues.

With a final glance at the engrossed pair, the mysterious stranger melted into the shadows, their presence fading into the darkness. A question lingered in their mind: would Lyra and Quellan unlock the secrets that could change the fate of Vacari, or would the mysteries remain hidden, waiting for another to uncover their dark truths?

Lyra scanned the dimly lit corridors, searching for any sign of their enigmatic ally, but found only darkness staring back. With a resigned sigh, she turned to Quellan, a silent acknowledgment passing between them.

"It seems our companion has vanished," Quellan remarked, his voice tinged with curiosity and frustration. **"But their guidance has proven invaluable."**

Lyra nodded in agreement, though unease gnawed at her. The stranger had aided them, but their motives remained shrouded in secrecy. She couldn't help but wonder what role they would play in the events yet to come.

With a heavy heart, Lyra turned back to the scrolls and artifacts they had gathered, knowing their journey was far from over. As she prepared to delve into the mysteries they contained, she couldn't shake the feeling that the shadows held more secrets than they dared imagine.

And so, with the promise of newfound knowledge and the lingering specter of their mysterious companion, Lyra and Quellan continued their journey into the depths of darkness, their fate intertwined with the fate of Vacari itself.

Chapter 11
Whispers of the Ancients

In the heart of Goldmoor, where the sun bathed the land in golden rays and the breeze whispered among the towering trees, the dragon riders under King Alex's command stood tall and vigilant. Their majestic beasts, scales gleaming like precious gems, soared above—aerial guardians of a realm healing from the scars of war.

Kimras, resplendent in his golden glory, and Amara, with her regal amethyst hues, watched as the dragon lancers honed their skills. King Alex, a figure of authority and strength, led the charge, his presence commanding respect from both riders and dragons alike.

As the training exercise unfolded under the azure sky, a shadow passed through Kimras' thoughts—a subtle whisper of unease stirring within him. Beside him, Amara, her eyes shimmering with ancient wisdom, sensed the same disturbance in the air.

"Kimras," she murmured, her voice melodic in the peaceful expanse of Goldmoor, "do you feel it too? A tremor in Vacari's essence?"

Kimras inclined his noble head, the golden crest of his helm catching the sunlight in a dazzling display. "Indeed, Amara," he replied, concern lacing his tone. "A disquiet stirs on the winds of destiny, yet I see nothing to explain its source."

Amara's gaze drifted toward the distant horizon, where the shadowy outline of Vacari lay shrouded in mystery. "We must remain vigilant," she said, her voice carrying the weight of centuries. "If darkness stirs in Vacari's depths, we must uncover its source."

A silent understanding passed between them. Kimras and Amara vowed to keep watch over the realm they had sworn to protect. Should the sense of foreboding persist, they would journey into Vacari itself, where secrets lay buried beneath the rubble of a fractured past.

Amidst the tranquil beauty of Goldmoor, two dragons stood as sentinels against the encroaching shadows, their bond unbreakable, their resolve unwavering. For in the delicate balance between light and darkness, it was their duty to ensure that hope endured—even in the darkest of times.

As the dragon riders maintained their watch over the cerulean expanse, their attention was drawn to two majestic figures gliding gracefully across the horizon. Zylron, his fiery red scales shimmering in the sunlight, and Glaciera, her ethereal form veiled in pristine white, cast an enchanting spectacle against the boundless azure sky.

Among the riders, awe mingled with apprehension as they beheld the unexpected sight. Murmurs of curiosity and concern rippled through their ranks like gentle waves lapping against the shores of uncertainty.

Talia, a valiant warrior bound to her dragon with unwavering loyalty, raised her gaze to the heavens. "Zylron and Glaciera," she whispered, her voice tinged with reverence and wonder.

Aric, a seasoned veteran with a sharp eye for strategy, furrowed his brow thoughtfully. "What brings them to the Cerulean Expanse?" he pondered aloud, unease creeping into his voice.

Talia turned to Aric, her expression mirroring his concern. "Should we pursue them?" she asked, uncertainty lacing her tone.

A sense of duty stirred within Aric before he could even respond "No," he declared firmly, his gaze shifting toward the distant horizon where Flameford lay shrouded in mystery. "We must report this sighting to King Alex and the guardians of Goldmoor. They will know how best to interpret this omen."

With a solemn nod, Talia and Aric turned their dragons toward the heart of their kingdom, their hearts heavy with the weight of their discovery. For the presence of Zylron and Glaciera teetered the delicate balance of power within Vacari, and their sightings needed to be brought to the attention of those entrusted with the protection of their world.

As the dragon riders and their loyal companions descended upon the familiar grounds of Goldmoor, the air buzzed with anticipation. With practiced ease, they guided their dragons to rest, where the majestic beasts basked in the warmth of the sun until called upon once more.

Talia and Aric dismounted, their hearts weighed by the news they carried. With determined strides, they moved through the bustling streets of Goldmoor, their eyes scanning the faces of their fellow citizens for any sign of King Alex.

At last, they found him in the grand hall of the castle, seated upon a throne of polished oak, his presence radiating strength and authority. Talia and Aric approached with measured steps, their expressions grave yet resolute.

"Your Majesty," Talia began, her voice steady despite the turmoil within her, "we have news to report."

King Alex regarded them with a keen gaze, his eyes reflecting the weight of his responsibilities. "Speak, my loyal subjects," he commanded, his voice resonating with the authority of a ruler born to lead.

Aric stepped forward, his gaze meeting the king's with unwavering resolve. "We sighted Zylron and Glaciera over the Cerulean Expanse," he revealed, his words echoing in the hushed silence of the hall.

King Alex's brow furrowed at the mention of the two legendary dragons. "This is troubling news indeed," he remarked, his voice laced with apprehension. "We must tread carefully in these uncertain times."

Turning to Talia and Aric, King Alex's gaze softened with gratitude. "Go, seek out Kimras and Amara," he instructed, his tone firm yet compassionate. "Inform them of what you have witnessed. Together, we shall decipher the meaning behind Zylron and Glaciera's presence in the Cerulean Expanse."

With a solemn nod, Talia and Aric bowed before their king, their resolve unwavering in the face of the challenges ahead. They swiftly sought out Kimras and Amara, the guardians of Goldmoor. Entering the glen where the two dragons resided, they bowed respectfully before the regal creatures.

Kimras, Amara," Talia began, her voice echoing with urgency, "we have troubling news. We sighted Zylron and Glaciera flying over the Cerulean Expanse."

Kimras, his golden scales shimmering with an ethereal glow, regarded them with a solemn gaze. "Thank you for bringing this to our attention, Talia, Aric," he rumbled, his voice resonating with ancient wisdom. "This is indeed concerning."

Amara, her amethyst eyes gleaming with intensity, nodded. "Zylron's allegiance to Phoenix was well-known," she stated, a hint of apprehension in her voice. "If Zylron has returned, we must investigate his intentions."

As Talia and Aric prepared to take their leave, Kimras turned to Amara, a flicker of concern crossing his noble features. "At least now we have some insight into the darkness that has been lingering over Vacari," he mused, his voice heavy with thought.

Amara's expression remained grave. "But we must not underestimate the threat posed by Zylron and Glaciera," she cautioned, determination sharpening her tone. "Their influence could tip the balance in these uncertain times."

With a shared understanding, Kimras and Amara focused on the task ahead, their resolve unwavering. In the delicate balance between light and darkness, it was their duty to protect Vacari, no matter the cost.

As Kimras and Amara soared over the vast Cerulean Expanse, their sharp eyes scanned the horizon for any sign of Zylron and Glaciera. Yet the skies remained empty—devoid of the fiery and icy presence of the legendary dragons.

With a shared sense of determination, Kimras and Amara continued their flight, their thoughts turning to the enigmatic city of Flameford. As they approached, they were not met by the familiar sights of bustling activity, but by a scene of desolation and decay.

Amara's keen eyes swept over the landscape, noting the ominous changes that had befallen the once vibrant city. "It appears they are constructing a new stronghold," she observed, concern coloring her voice.

Kimras's gaze hardened, his golden scales shimmering with restrained fury. "A stronghold for dark dragons," he growled, his voice like distant thunder. "This cannot be allowed."

As they circled above Flameford, Amara's sharp senses detected movement near the remnants of the old tower. "Look, Kimras," she exclaimed, nodding her head toward a figure emerging from the shadows

Kimras's heart quickened with anticipation as they descended, eager to uncover the truth behind Flameford's transformation. But before they could reach the figure, it vanished into thin air, leaving only a lingering sense of foreboding.

With a heavy heart, Kimras turned to Amara, his eyes reflecting his inner turmoil. "We must return to Goldmoor," he declared, his voice resolute. "There is much to discuss, and little time to spare."

Amara nodded, her expression mirroring his determination. Together, they veered away from Flameford, leaving behind the mysteries shrouding the city, and set their course for the sanctuary of Goldmoor, where their allies awaited.

Just as they prepared to depart the desolate ruins of Flameford, a sudden disturbance shattered the air's stillness. Zylron, his fiery gaze fixed on Amara, unleashed a torrent of flames, a brazen challenge to her presence in his domain.

Before the flames could reach her, Kimras, ever vigilant and protective, intercepted the attack with a swift motion. With a defiant roar, he summoned a fiery shield, enveloping Amara and shielding her from harm.

Amara's eyes widened in astonishment as she realized Kimras had saved her. "Kimras, you..." she began, her voice filled with gratitude.

Kimras turned to face Zylron, his golden form ablaze with righteous fury. "You dare threaten my friend?" he thundered, his voice echoing across the expanse.

Zylron hesitated, his gaze flickering with uncertainty at Kimras's unexpected show of strength. For a brief moment, he considered the challenge, but discretion won over confrontation. With a disdainful snort, he veered away, his fiery form fading into the distance.

Amara's heart swelled with admiration for her steadfast companion. "Thank you, Kimras," she said softly, her voice tinged with emotion.

Kimras gave her a gentle smile, his eyes reflecting the depth of their bond. "You think I would let Zylron harm my friend?" he replied, his voice calm but resolute.

With the danger behind them, Kimras and Amara resumed their journey to Goldmoor, their spirits buoyed by the strength of their friendship and the certainty that together, they could overcome any challenge ahead.

As the golden hues of dawn bathed the tranquil grove of Goldmoor, Kimras and Amara returned from their reconnaissance over Flameford. The weight of their discoveries hung heavy on their minds, and a sense of urgency filled the air as they summoned King Alex.

Emerging from the shadows of the trees, King Alex's regal presence commanded attention. Kimras wasted no time in relaying their findings. "We observed the construction of a new stronghold in Flameford," he began, his voice grave. "It appears to be intended for dark dragons, and we must keep a vigilant watch over the city."

Amara nodded, her amethyst eyes gleaming with determination. "We also saw a figure emerge from the tower," she added, her voice trailing off as she recalled the encounter. "But they vanished before we could identify them."

King Alex listened intently, his brow furrowing as the implications of their discoveries sank in. "It seems we must tread carefully," he remarked, apprehension creeping into his voice. "But should we not send the dragon riders to watch over Flameford and keep an eye on Zylron and Glaciera?"

Amara's expression darkened. "No," she stated firmly. "Zylron's power is formidable, and the dragon riders may be no match for him. If it weren't for Kimras's quick action, I could have been injured—or worse."

King Alex's eyes widened at the revelation of the near-miss, concern deepening as he considered the dangers his allies had faced. "I see," he replied somberly. "Perhaps it's best for the dragon riders to continue their regular patrols for now. We can't afford unnecessary risks."

With a shared understanding of the gravity of the situation, Kimras, Amara, and King Alex pledged to remain vigilant against the looming threat. In the delicate balance between light and darkness, their duty to protect the realm remained paramount.

As King Alex departed for the castle to attend to his duties, Kimras and Amara took to the skies once more. Their wings sliced through the air as they headed toward the lush expanse of Purplefire Woods. Soaring over the verdant canopy, a sense of tranquility enveloped them—a welcome respite from the tensions of the day.

Amara glanced toward Kimras, her eyes filled with gratitude. "Thank you again for saving me from Zylron," she said softly.

Kimras smiled warmly, his golden scales shimmering in the dappled sunlight. "You're my friend, Amara," he replied gently, with a hint of playfulness. "I'd do nothing less for you. Besides, who else would constantly tease Ong if something happened to you?"

Amara chuckled at his jest, her laughter echoing through the forest as they continued their flight. Their bond, forged through countless trials, grew stronger with each passing moment—a testament to their enduring friendship.

When they arrived at Purplefire Woods, they descended into a tranquil glade, their hearts lightened by the peaceful surroundings. Together, they surveyed the area, ensuring that all remained well within the sanctuary of the woods.

Satisfied that Purplefire remained untouched by the encroaching darkness, Kimras and Amara shared a nod of agreement before taking to the skies again. Their spirits were uplifted by the knowledge that they stood united against the threats looming beyond the horizon. With the bond of friendship as their guiding light, they faced whatever challenges awaited them with courage and determination—knowing that together, they were stronger than any foe.

Chapter 12
Encroaching Shadows

An unsettling tension filled the heart of Vacari, nestled among the ancient trees of Emberwoods. Raelithar, the wise and venerable copper dragon who watched over the sacred groves, had made the arduous journey to Goldmoor to deliver troubling news to Kimras.

Raelithar's voice carried the weight of his centuries of wisdom as he addressed Kimras and Amara in the great garden of Goldmoor. "The shadows deepen in Emberwoods, Kimras," he began, each word weighted with concern. "Our kin and the pixies fight valiantly, but this darkness is unlike any we've faced. Its source eludes us, and with each passing day, it grows stronger. We risk losing all of Emberwoods if we do not act swiftly."

Kimras listened intently, his golden eyes narrowing in determination. "The pixies and copper dragons hold the line, yet they're uncertain what fuels this darkness," he said, absorbing the situation's gravity. "Their struggle may prove futile unless we can uncover and extinguish its source."

Amara's brow furrowed in concern. Emberwoods, with its ancient magic and mystical inhabitants, had always been a sanctuary of light and beauty. The encroaching darkness filled her with a deep sense of foreboding.

"We must help," she declared, her voice enigmatic, as if speaking for the forest itself. "Emberwoods is a precious jewel in Vacari. We cannot allow its light to be consumed by this shadow. We must pierce the veil of darkness and find its heart."

Kimras nodded, his golden scales gleaming with resolve. "Indeed," he replied, his tone resolute. "The roots of this blight must be severed before they spread further. Emberwoods must not fall."

Raelithar's voice resonated with the wisdom of his long guardianship. "The Druchii are not behind this affliction," he said, his ancient eyes reflecting the burden of his duty. "But the true source of this darkness remains hidden from our sight. We must act swiftly, or the forest will be lost to us."

Kimras, Amara, and Raelithar waited, united by urgency, for further reports from the other dragons, knowing the fate of Emberwoods—and all of Vacari—rested on swift action and unwavering resolve.

As the sun cast its golden light over the sprawling city of Goldmoor, a pair of dragons descended from the heavens, their silver scales glinting in the morning rays. Talleoss and his mate Silvara, noble guardians of Vacari, had arrived to deliver a crucial report to Kimras.

Talleoss spoke first, his voice carrying the weight of his message. "Darkness seeks entry into every corner of Vacari," he reported, his silver scales gleaming in the sunlight. "Our kin, alongside the nymphs, merfolk, and Eladrin, have managed to hold it back so far. But even E'vahona, the sanctuary of the Eladrin, has felt its touch. This force is driven by something far beyond the natural."

Kimras's brow furrowed in concern. E'vahona had long stood as a bastion of light and purity, its magical defenses unmatched. The thought of darkness breaching its sacred borders filled him with dread.

Amara's eyes mirrored Kimras's worry. "If E'vahona falls, it could be our undoing," she mused, her tone both cryptic and urgent. "We must rally our forces and stand united. The darkness we face may be guided by a will as ancient as it is malevolent."

Silvara, her silver scales shimmering with quiet strength, added, "This is no mere shadow. It moves with purpose, as if directed by an unseen hand. We must gather all our strength to uncover this malevolent force and put an end to it."

Kimras nodded, absorbing the weight of the situation. "We'll need to gather all the guardians and plan our next moves. Raelithar, continue to monitor Emberwoods closely and report any changes immediately.

Talleoss, Silvara, see if you can gather more information from the other noble dragons and our allies."

With their tasks set, the dragons dispersed, leaving Kimras and Amara momentarily alone. Kimras turned to Amara, his expression resolute. "We must be prepared for anything. The safety of Vacari rests on our shoulders."

Amara angled her body slightly, her gaze steady as it met his. "Together, we'll find the source and put an end to this darkness," she said with conviction. "We've faced many challenges before, and we'll overcome this one too."

Raelithar, Talleoss, and Silvara rejoined Kimras and Amara, their presence a welcome reinforcement as they gathered their resolve. Silvara echoed Talleoss's urgency. "We must return to E'vahona to aid the Eladrin and Kadona in defending their homeland."

Kimras nodded in understanding. "We cannot ignore the threat to E'vahona. Talleoss, Silvara, please return and offer whatever assistance is needed. Amara and I will join you shortly."

Talleoss and Silvara exchanged a glance of gratitude before spreading their wings and soaring into the sky, their mission clear.

Turning to Raelithar, Kimras issued his next command. "Return to Emberwoods," he instructed, his voice carrying the weight of their shared responsibility. "Help keep the darkness at bay, and if you observe anything unusual, inform us immediately."

With their plans set, Kimras and Amara prepared to embark on their journey, knowing the fate of Vacari—and all of existence—hung in the balance. Taking flight toward E'vahona, their hearts brimmed with determination to confront the darkness threatening their world.

In the ethereal realm of E'vahona, a desperate battle raged against the advancing shadows. Lord Karrenen, his heart filled with resolve, stood alongside the Goddess Kadona, channeling divine power to hold back the shadowy miasma threatening their sanctuary.

Beside them, Keisha, a mage of formidable skill, wove intricate spells of protection, her hands ablaze with arcane energy as she bolstered their defenses. Meanwhile, Ong and the Eladrin warriors scoured every corner of E'vahona, their sharp eyes searching for any trace of the darkness's origin, finding only eerie silence and empty shadows.

As tension mounted and hope waned, a new arrival brought a glimmer of relief. Kimras and Amara, their majestic forms soaring through the sky, descended upon E'vahona with the grace of avenging angels. Talleoss and Silvara followed, their silver scales shimmering with an otherworldly light, ready to lend their strength to the battle.

Pooling their abilities, the dragons and their allies worked tirelessly to erect a barrier of pure energy—a shimmering wall of protection, glowing with the combined power of dragons and divinity alike. With each pulse, the barrier grew stronger, pushing back the encroaching darkness and holding it at bay.

At last, the barrier stood complete, a testament to the unity and strength of those who fought to defend E'vahona. For now, the darkness was thwarted, its advance halted by the guardians' unyielding resolve. Yet a sense of unease lingered—E'vahona had never faced such a threat.

As Kimras and Amara surveyed their handiwork, foreboding weighed on their hearts. The source of the darkness remained elusive, and until it was found and destroyed, the safety of E'vahona—and all of Vacari—would hang in jeopardy. With renewed determination, they vowed to uncover the truth and vanquish the darkness once and for all.

Lord Karrenen stepped forward, his noble countenance filled with gratitude. "Thank you for coming to our aid," he said sincerely. "Your presence has made all the difference in our battle against the darkness."

Kimras nodded, his golden gaze meeting Lord Karrenen's in a silent understanding of their shared responsibility. "We are honored to stand by your side," he replied, his voice steady with determination.

Kadona, the ethereal Goddess of E'vahano, approached Talleoss with a gentle smile, her eyes reflecting both gratitude and concern. "I am glad to see the silver dragons here to protect E'vahano," she said, her voice tinged with worry. "But this darkness is unlike anything we've faced. It even touches the heart of E'vahano itself."

Ong, standing nearby, couldn't contain his unease. "How can darkness reach us here, in a hidden city?" he asked, brow furrowed in confusion. "E'vahano has always been protected from the outside world."

Kimras exchanged a glance with Amara before addressing Ong. "E'vahano is indeed hidden from most beings," he began, his tone calm yet serious. "But dragons, especially those aligned with darkness, have ways of sensing magic, even in concealed places. They can feel the pulse of power that emanates from sacred sites."

Keisha, her face tense with thought, added, "So they can find us if they're actively searching for places of power? That makes them even more dangerous."

"Indeed," Kadona agreed, her expression grave. "However, while dragons possess this ability, it is not always used. Zylron and Glaceria, for example, never detected E'vahano while serving Vuarus or Phoenix."

Keisha looked puzzled. "But why didn't they reveal our location if they could sense it?"

Kadona nodded thoughtfully, reflecting on the complexity of the situation. "Vuarus was focused on using you, Keisha, as a sacrifice to maintain his godhead in the abyss. His interest in E'vahano was minimal; he knew the Eladrin and Ong would never willingly aid him. So, he never commanded the dragons to search for it."

Kimras added, "And the dragons themselves were preoccupied with the destruction Vuarus commanded—razing forests, attacking Goldmoor. Their task was to create chaos and weaken your spirit. In their minds, that was their sole mission."

Ong nodded slowly, understanding dawning on his face. "So, they weren't looking for us because they were focused on their mission of destruction."

"Exactly," Amara interjected. "The dragons wouldn't volunteer information that wasn't asked for, especially while consumed by their given tasks. To them, it might have seemed as if E'vahano was hidden from them, just as it was hidden from everyone else."

Keisha took a deep breath, letting the explanation settle. "I see. So, it's not just about their abilities but also about their directives. Thank you for clarifying."

Yes," Kadona replied softly, her gaze steady. "This is why we must remain vigilant. The darkness we face is multifaceted, and our enemies are cunning. We must be prepared for any possibility."

Kimras and Amara exchanged a solemn glance, their minds already turning toward the next steps. "We must investigate the source of this darkness," Kimras declared, his voice firm with resolve. "But first, we need to return to Goldmoor and inform King Alex of what we've learned. The other gold and amethyst dragons must also be alerted to guard Goldmoor and Purplefire in our absence."

Kadona nodded in understanding, her expression grave yet determined. "Should you uncover anything of significance, please do not hesitate to inform us," she said, her voice weighted with their shared responsibility.

With their plans in motion and allies united, Kimras and Amara prepared for their journey, knowing that the fate of Vacari—and all of existence—hung in the balance. As they took flight toward Goldmoor, their hearts brimmed with determination to confront the darkness threatening their world.

As they soared through the skies, wings slicing through the crisp air, a sense of unease lingered between them like a shadow. Amara, her voice tinged with concern, broke the silence.

"Should we have told Kadona and the Eladrin about Zylron and Glaciera's return?" she asked, her amethyst eyes reflecting the worry gnawing at her heart.

Kimras considered her question, his golden gaze fixed on the horizon. "No," he replied finally, his voice calm yet resolute. "I doubt those two dragons are responsible for the darkness spreading through Vacari. Their presence is troubling, but I don't believe they are the source."

Amara nodded, her thoughts drifting to the dark dragons and the ominous stronghold they were building in Flameford. Though the news unsettled her, she trusted Kimras's judgment and knew their focus must remain on uncovering the true source of the encroaching darkness.

With a shared sense of purpose, Kimras and Amara continued their journey toward Goldmoor, their hearts heavy with the weight of their mission. The fate of Vacari—and all who called it home—hung in the balance as darkness loomed on the horizon.

As they neared Goldmoor, a dramatic scene unfolded in the skies below. The dragon riders, diligently patrolling their territories, suddenly came face to face with the menacing form of Zylron, the red dragon. A wave of vigilance swept through the riders, each acutely aware of the danger he posed.

Without warning, Zylron materialized before them, his eyes gleaming with malevolent intent. Instinctual fear surged through the riders as they turned their mounts to flee from the threat.

Before they could escape, Zylron launched into pursuit, his powerful wings beating a relentless rhythm as he bore down on them with deadly intent.

Unbeknownst to Zylron, King Alex, ruler of Goldmoor, was training nearby with his dragon lance. Sensing the danger, he sprang into action without hesitation.

With swift, decisive precision, King Alex closed the distance between himself and Zylron, his lance held steady as he prepared to face the fiery menace head-on.

As Zylron neared the fleeing riders, King Alex struck with pinpoint accuracy, his lance piercing Zylron's side. Zylron roared in fury as the blow sent him reeling in shock and pain.

Displaying skill and courage, King Alex intercepted Zylron's advance, lance poised. Feeling the sting of the king's intervention, Zylron roared defiantly but, recognizing the strength of his opponent, retreated, pride wounded by the unexpected resistance.

As the dust settled and the immediate danger passed, King Alex and the dragon riders returned to Goldmoor, hearts filled with relief and gratitude for the king's timely intervention. Though they had narrowly escaped disaster, Zylron's looming threat and dark ambitions still cast a shadow over them. Vigilance remained their watchword.

Meanwhile, high above, Kimras and Amara continued their journey, unaware of the perilous encounter in Goldmoor. When they descended upon the city, their minds filled with the urgency of Vacari's crisis, they were met with unexpected news.

Before they could discuss the spreading darkness, King Alex approached them, his expression grave. "Kimras, Amara," he began, his voice somber but steady. "There has been an attack on the dragon riders by Zylron. Without my expertise with the lance, they might not be here with us today."

Kimras exchanged a glance with Amara, a flicker of concern passing between them. The news of Zylron's aggression only intensified the gravity of their mission, reinforcing the need for swift action.

After a moment, Kimras spoke, his voice firm. "We must bolster our defenses," he declared, his gaze sweeping over King Alex and the dragon riders nearby. "From now on, each patrol will have an additional dragon rider, and one rider must have expertise with the lance."

King Alex nodded in agreement, his eyes reflecting their shared determination. "Agreed," he replied, resolute. "We'll redouble our training and preparation to ensure we're ready for whatever challenges lie ahead."

With their plan set and resolve strengthened, Kimras, Amara, and King Alex turned their focus to the looming threat of the spreading darkness. United in purpose, they stood ready to defend Vacari with every ounce of their strength and courage.

As the gravity of the situation weighed on them, Kimras turned to King Alex, his expression serious. "My king, we've received troubling reports from E'vahona," he began, urgency lacing his voice. "While the immediate threat has been neutralized for now, it's clear we can no longer afford to remain idle."

Amara nodded, her amethyst eyes gleaming with determination. "We must leave Goldmoor and Purplefire Woods to search Vacari," she added. "We need to discover what—or who—is causing the darkness to seep back into our land."

King Alex listened intently, his brow furrowed as he absorbed their words. "I understand," he replied, his voice tinged with sadness at the thought of their departure. "Your mission is of the utmost importance, and I trust your judgment."

Turning to Kimras and Amara, King Alex offered his blessing. "May the winds guide you safely on your journey," he said warmly. "Be careful, my friends, and know that Goldmoor stands behind you."

Kimras and Amara exchanged a grateful glance, their hearts brimming with resolve. With a final nod to King Alex, they turned to prepare for their journey, knowing that the fate of Vacari—and all of existence—rested on their shoulders.

Kimras took a moment to gaze around Goldmoor, the stronghold that had been their home and sanctuary. A pang of sorrow tugged at him, but his resolve remained firm. Sensing his thoughts, Amara brushed her wing gently against his, a gesture of solidarity

"We'll be back," she said softly, her voice filled with determination. "And when we return, we'll bring an end to this darkness."

With renewed purpose, Kimras and Amara set off to make their preparations, gathering their equipment and bidding their farewells. Their fellow dragon riders, friends and comrades, wished them well, their faces a mix of concern and hope.

As Kimras and Amara took flight once more, their hearts were heavy but resolute, ready to face whatever dangers lay ahead in their quest to save Vacari.

In the dim light of Flameford's cavernous depths, Zylron limped forward, his fiery gaze meeting Glaceria's with a mixture of pain and frustration.

"What happened to you?" she asked, concern lacing her voice.

With a growl of resentment, Zylron recounted the encounter in the skies over Vacari. "King Alex," he spat, bitterness dripping from his words. "He struck me with a dragon lance."

Glaceria's eyes widened, thoughts of retaliation flashing through her mind. But before she could respond, a figure emerged from the shadows, their presence ominous and enigmatic.

"You put yourself in harm's way," the figure remarked coldly, their voice calculating.

Zylron bristled at the accusation, his pride stung. "This is new to the King and Goldmoor," he retorted defiantly. "They've never used dragons, much less dragon lances. Only the Eladrin rode dragons, and they had no lances."

The mysterious figure frowned, regarding Zylron with a mix of curiosity and disdain. "You underestimated them," they replied sharply. "We cannot afford such mistakes."

Without another word, the figure turned to leave, but just before vanishing into the shadows, they paused and looked back.

"Remember," they intoned with a chilling whisper, "our plans hinge on precision and secrecy. Do not let your pride jeopardize what we have worked so hard to achieve."

With that, the figure disappeared, leaving Zylron and Glaceria alone to ponder the gravity of their situation. The cavern grew colder, the weight of impending conflict settling heavily upon them.

Before silence could take hold, the figure's voice echoed once more from the shadows. "By the way," they added, their tone dripping with menace, "I've sent messages to the dark dragons—and even the neutral ones with dark tendencies. It's time for them to start making their way to Flameford."

The pronouncement lingered in the air, a grim reminder of the forces converging for battle. As the figure's presence faded completely, Zylron and Glaceria exchanged a tense glance, the enormity of their situation pressing down like a suffocating weight. The darkness was gathering, and with it, the fate of Vacari hung in the balance.

In a secluded part of the cavern, away from prying eyes, the mysterious figure paused once more, mumbling to themselves. "The little tests I conducted on the copper dragons in Emberwoods and the Eladrin's secret realm... they should provide valuable insights. I need to understand their strengths and weaknesses if we are to defeat them."

With a final, contemplative glance into the shadows, the figure vanished entirely, leaving the cavern in an even deeper, more foreboding silence.

Chapter 13
Dark Tidings

IN the heart of Goldmoor, Kimras gathered the gold dragons, his commanding presence drawing their full attention. The majestic creatures, their golden scales catching the sun's warmth, reflected both their strength and the weight of the message about to be delivered.

"My fellow gold dragons," Kimras began, his voice resonating with authority and determination, "I have grave news. Amara and I will be departing on a mission to investigate the spreading darkness that threatens our land."

A ripple of concern passed through the gathered dragons, their eyes reflecting the gravity of the situation. Kimras continued, his tone unwavering.

"During our absence, I entrust each of you with the task of safeguarding Goldmoor," he declared, his gaze sweeping over the assembled dragons.

"Those with riders, ensure their safety at all costs. Avoid confrontation with Zylron if possible but remain vigilant against any threats to our home."

The gold dragons nodded, their expressions resolute as they accepted the weight of their responsibility. Kimras's words ignited a sense of purpose within them.

With his message delivered, Kimras bid farewell to his kin, confident that the gold dragons would remain steadfast in his absence. As he and Amara prepared for their journey, the burden of their mission settled heavily upon them. Yet, they found solace in the knowledge that Goldmoor would be guarded by dragons whose loyalty and resolve mirrored their own.

In the serene depths of Purplefire Woods, Amara stood amidst the towering trees, her presence a beacon of strength to the amethyst dragons gathered around her. With solemn duty, she addressed her kin, her voice carrying with quiet authority through the forest.

"My dear amethyst dragons," Amara began, her words gentle yet resolute. "As Kimras and I embark on our mission, I entrust you with the protection of Purplefire Woods."

The amethyst dragons listened intently, their violet scales gleaming as they absorbed her words.

"Those with riders," she continued, her gaze steady, "always ensure their safety. Watch over them with unwavering vigilance."

A murmur of agreement rippled through the group, their resolve solidified by Amara's charge.

"Remain alert for any signs of darkness that may creep into our beloved forest," she added, her tone urgent. "Protect the nymphs who call this place home and remember that Purplefire holds special significance to Keisha. We must do everything we can to keep it safe."

With her message delivered, Amara bid farewell, her heart heavy with shared responsibility. As she departed to join Kimras, she felt comforted knowing Purplefire Woods would be safeguarded. Together, they would face the encroaching darkness, united in purpose.

The landscape below shifted as Kimras and Amara approached Emberwoods, the dense forest stretching out like a sea of green. A silent exchange passed between them, their mutual resolve unspoken but clear. They were prepared for whatever lay ahead, trusting their bond and mission to guide them.

As they descended, the sight of Raelithar, the copper dragon, standing with pixies near a damaged cave drew their attention. Typically jovial, Raelithar's expression was marked by sadness.

Drawing closer, Kimras and Amara exchanged glances before Raelithar hurried over, his voice tinged with desperation. "Please," he implored, "you must help us restore the cave. It's become a shadow of itself, and the pixies are distraught."

Without hesitation, Kimras and Amara joined Raelithar and the pixies, combining their efforts to undo the damage. With each sweep of magic and every carefully placed stone, they worked tirelessly. Their labor became a testament to the resilience of Vacari's inhabitants.

After what felt like an eternity, the cave shimmered with newfound beauty, whispers of gratitude filling the air.

Gathered around, the pixies voiced their heartfelt thanks, their chorus one of joy. In a gesture of appreciation, several pixies crafted small wreaths of flowers and, with delicate wings beating, flew up to place them gently along Kimras and Amara's heads. The dragons stilled, touched by the simple yet profound gesture. A glimmer of emotion shone in their eyes, and for a moment, both Kimras and Amara felt a tear threaten to fall.

Kimras and Amara exchanged smiles, their hearts warmed by the act. With their resolve strengthened, they prepared to continue their journey, bolstered by the bonds forged in adversity.

Departing from Emberwoods, Kimras suggested a detour over Fel Thalor. "Let's fly over but stay high enough to remain unseen," he said cautiously.

"Agreed," Amara replied, eyes fixed ahead. "We must tread carefully."

As they soared over Fel Thalor, eerie sights met their eyes—an altar perched over molten lava, casting a sinister glow. Kimras spotted Lyra engrossed in her work, surrounded by ancient artifacts. Amara noted another familiar silhouette approaching Lyra, but distance obscured details.

"We should leave," Kimras advised, urgency in his tone. "Lingering may draw attention. Let's head to the Hidden Isles and assess the situation there. I suspect the Druchii's involvement, but this darkness feels different—targeted."

Amara nodded, and they guided themselves away, questions buzzing in their minds as they set their course.

Arriving at the Hidden Isles, the lush terrain greeted them with comfort. A young dragon approached with a message of importance. Kimras read it, concern settling over him.

"Our brethren are returning," he informed Amara, "including noble and gem dragons aligned with us."

Amara's eyes widened, but before she could speak, the young dragon added, "Radiantus, the Platinum Dragon, warns of the dark dragons—and others called from beyond. Dragons who have never set foot in Vacari."

Kimras and Amara exchanged a tense glance. "This changes everything," Kimras said. "We must act swiftly."

"Agreed," Amara replied. "The threat is greater than we imagined."

With a renewed sense of urgency, they prepared for flight. "Let's head to Afor next," Kimras said. "We need to ensure the abyss's seal remains intact."

"Yes, let's go," Amara agreed.

Upon landing near Afor's sanctuary, Aurix, the Brass Dragon guardian, approached. "Amara! Kimras! What brings you here?"

Kimras shared the troubling reports, stirring concern among the dragons.

Aurix's expression turned solemn. "I've noticed nothing unusual except new settlements nearby."

"Thank you," Kimras said. "We'll inspect the area."

After a thorough search, Kimras confirmed, "The area is secure."

"Let's inform Aurix," Amara suggested.

Returning to the sanctuary, Aurix nodded after hearing their findings. "We'll stay vigilant."

With their task complete, they departed. "We must act quickly," Kimras said, eyes determined.

"Let's make haste," Amara replied, her gaze resolute.

Back at Goldmoor, they relayed their findings to King Alex. "We must bolster our defenses," he declared. United, they prepared to defend Vacari with unwavering strength and courage.

Chapter 14
A Growing Darkness

In the dimly lit chamber of their hideout in Fel Thalor, shadows flitted like restless spirits as Lyra hunched over a collection of ancient artifacts and scrolls, her brow furrowed in frustration. The cryptic symbols and inscriptions taunted her, shifting just out of comprehension. She sighed, the heavy burden of her limitations pressing down on her chest.

Beside her, Qellaun shifted uneasily, the tension etched across his face. "Can you make anything of it, Lyra?" His voice, tinged with concern, was barely above a whisper, as though afraid to disturb the silence. His eyes scanned the corners of the room, expecting danger to emerge at any moment.

Lyra's frustration boiled over. "No, Qellaun. It's written in some encryption I can't decipher. It's maddening." She clenched her fists, resisting the urge to fling a scroll across the room. The fragile paper crinkled under her grip.

A sudden chill slid down her spine as a familiar figure emerged from the darkness, their silhouette growing more distinct as the shadows receded. Lyra stiffened, but recognition tempered her tension with wary hope. The figure moved with a fluid grace, their presence shifting the air.

"You again," Lyra said, her voice a mix of surprise and skepticism. "What brings you here?"

The figure inclined their head slightly. "I've come to offer my assistance," they replied calmly. "It seems you could use help with these artifacts." Their voice was smooth, almost hypnotic, and for a moment, the tension in the room seemed to ease.

Lyra regarded the figure warily but couldn't deny the potential value of the offer. "And what do you want in return?" she asked, her voice cautious.

The figure shook their head. "Nothing, Lady Lyra. My motives are my own," they answered cryptically. Stepping closer, the shadows bent around them, their movements ghost-like.

Lyra exchanged a glance with Qellaun, uncertainty flickering in her eyes. Her desire for answers outweighed her mistrust. "Very well," she said, nodding to the figure. "We'll take whatever help we can get." She couldn't help but feel a chill as she spoke, as if she were making a deal with the darkness itself.

Sensing the tension in the air, the mysterious figure spoke again. "Perhaps it's time we relocated," they suggested, their voice echoing softly in the chamber.

Lyra looked up, surprise flickering across her features. "To where?" she asked, her curiosity piqued despite her lingering reservations.

The figure gestured toward the packed artifacts and scrolls. "To Flameford," they said decisively. "There may be resources in the tower that could aid us in deciphering these mysteries."

Lyra weighed their words carefully, considering the potential risks against the rewards. She glanced at Qellaun, silently seeking his opinion.

Qellaun nodded, his expression resolute. "It's worth a try," he said, knowing Flameford well and the dangers that lurked there. Yet something in the figure's confidence stirred a reluctant hope.

With a nod of acknowledgment, Lyra turned back to the figure. "Very well," she said, her voice steady. "We'll go to Flameford."

Together, they gathered their belongings and prepared to embark on the next leg of their journey, their destination shrouded in uncertainty but tinged with the promise of discovery. Lyra felt a mix of trepidation and anticipation as her mind raced with the possibilities of what they might uncover.

As they entered Flameford, Qellaun's steps faltered, and he shook his head in disbelief. Lyra, noticing his reaction, furrowed her brow in concern.

"What's wrong, Qellaun?" she asked, her voice tinged with apprehension.

Qellaun sighed heavily, his gaze sweeping across the transformed surroundings. "This was Phoenix's home," he explained, his voice thick with nostalgia. "But it was never like this." His memories of the place clashed with the stark reality before him, a painful reminder of what had been lost.

The mysterious figure, unperturbed by Qellaun's reaction, offered a knowing smile. "Indeed," they interjected cryptically. "It's being redesigned for the dark dragons on their way." Their words hung in the air, a subtle hint of impending change.

Lyra and Qellaun exchanged incredulous glances, struggling to comprehend the implications of the figure's statement.

"But how is that going to work?" Lyra asked, skepticism lacing her tone. "The dark dragons rarely come together, let alone work as a cohesive force. And the one person who could have united them is dead."

The mysterious figure merely shrugged, their expression unreadable. "Perhaps there are other forces at play," they suggested. "Or perhaps there are other ways to achieve their goals." They moved closer to the shadows, their form blending effortlessly into the darkness.

Lyra chuckled softly, irony in her voice. "Well, whatever their plans are, I doubt they'll succeed," she declared with unwavering confidence. "Not without Phoenix to lead them."

The mysterious figure smiled serenely at her skepticism. "They will unite under Zylron's leadership," they stated quietly, their tone carrying an unsettling certainty that made Lyra's skin crawl.

Lyra and Qellaun exchanged startled glances, taken aback by the figure's assertion. Qellaun nodded slowly, considering the possibility. "Perhaps," he conceded thoughtfully. "Zylron did follow Phoenix, and if anyone could unite them, it would be him. But they'll need a compelling reason to come together."

The mysterious figure nodded in acknowledgment. "Indeed," they agreed cryptically. "But time is of the essence. The noble dragons have already begun investigating the darkness. We must act swiftly."

With that, they gestured for Lyra and Qellaun to follow them to the tower, where they could resume their efforts to decipher the artifacts and scrolls they had brought from Fel Thalor. As they made their way forward, the weight of their mission pressed upon them, driving them onward in the face of the looming darkness. The path ahead was fraught with peril, but also promise.

As they settled into the tower's confines, Lyra couldn't shake her curiosity. She turned to the mysterious figure, her brow furrowed as she asked the question that had been gnawing at her mind.

"Why not just destroy the noble dragons directly?" Lyra inquired, confusion lacing her voice. "If we already have the means, wouldn't that expedite our plans?" She folded her arms, watching the figure closely, searching for any hint of deception.

The mysterious figure regarded her with a patient expression, their eyes reflecting a depth of knowledge that seemed beyond mortal comprehension. "It is not yet time," they replied cryptically. "We must ensure our plans unfold without interference from other forces. The gold dragons are not easily destroyed, and other noble and gem dragons could create problems if they learn of our actions."

Lyra's confusion deepened. "Are they not all here already?" she asked, her mind racing to piece together the fragments of a larger puzzle.

The figure shook their head slowly. "No," they said softly. "There are still more powerful dragons yet to return. We must proceed cautiously to ensure success."

Lyra nodded, absorbing the weight of the revelation. Her expression was thoughtful, she returned to her task, though her mind swirled with questions and uncertainty. The figure's cryptic words lingered in the air, casting a shadow over their mission. But for now, they had work to do. Unraveling the mysteries of the artifacts and scrolls would occupy them until the time was right.

Qellaun's thoughts drifted to the past, a time when Phoenix and Vuarus had nearly plunged their world into darkness. His hand instinctively moved to his side, where an old scar from that era throbbed with the memory. Despite knowing how Vuarus and Phoenix had been defeated, he couldn't help but wonder what might have happened if they had succeeded. With a furrowed brow, he turned to the mysterious figure, curiosity burning in his eyes.

"If Vuarus and Phoenix hadn't been stopped, do you think they would have succeeded?" Qellaun asked, his voice tinged with the weight of the unknown. "What do you think would have become of Vacari if they had prevailed?"

His gaze locked onto the figure, waiting expectantly for insights into the potential consequences of past events and the darkness that now loomed over the realm.

The wicked smile that spread across the mysterious figure's lips sent a thrill of excitement through Qellaun. He listened intently as the figure confirmed his suspicions: if Vuarus and Phoenix had succeeded, Vacari would have succumbed to eternal darkness. A vision of a world shrouded in perpetual night flashed in Qellaun's mind, and he shivered—partly in fear, partly in fascination.

Qellaun's mind raced with the implications of such a reality, the power and dominance that darkness could have held over their world. As a dark elf, he felt a strange exhilaration at the thought, a primal instinct urging him to embrace the chaos it would bring.

With a nod of understanding, Qellaun accepted the figure's words, his resolve strengthened by the prospect of serving the darkness in its quest for supremacy. He stepped outside, his determination fueled by the anticipation of what lay ahead and the role he would play in shaping Vacari's fate according to the shadows' will.

Outside, the air was thick with an eerie stillness, as though the world itself was holding its breath. Qellaun paused, letting the weight of the darkness settle over him like a cloak. He welcomed its embrace, his resolve hardening like steel.

As the mysterious figure watched Qellaun leave, they turned their attention back to Lyra, observing her as she worked on the scrolls. In a low voice, they muttered to themselves, "Let's see if she can find the information about the noble dragons. Once they are gone, we'll use our knowledge to conquer the rest of Vacari. This time, no one will be able to stop us."

With a calculated gleam in their eye, they whispered, "I will also send disturbances to Purplefire Woods to test the strength of the gold and amethyst dragons. This will help us gauge their power and alliances. Only by understanding our enemies can we ensure their ultimate defeat."

In Goldmoor, a tension hung in the air—the calm before an inevitable storm. The commanding presence of King Alex awaited their arrival. He approached them with purpose in his stride.

"Kimras, Amara, I'm glad to see you return," King Alex said, his tone conveying a sense of urgency. "There have been reports of disturbances in Purplefire Woods. We need your assistance there immediately."

Kimras and Amara exchanged a brief, meaningful glance, silently communicating their readiness to heed the king's call. They took to the skies once more, their powerful wings swiftly carrying them toward their destination. The familiar landscape of Goldmoor quickly gave way to the lush greenery of Purplefire Woods, the canopy of ancient trees beckoning them closer with a sense of urgency. Every beat of their wings felt like a countdown to an unseen confrontation.

As they soared above the forest, the air thick with anticipation, Kimras and Amara kept a vigilant watch, scanning the treetops for any signs of trouble. The whispers of the wind and the rustling leaves beneath them echoed faintly with unease, signaling that all was not well within the depths of Purplefire Woods.

With each beat of their wings, Kimras and Amara drew closer to the heart of the forest, their senses attuned to the slightest disturbance in the land's natural rhythm. A sense of determination gripped them, steeling their resolve to confront whatever challenges awaited them in the shadowy depths below.

As they descended, the familiar sight of Purplefire Woods greeted them—now transformed. The once-pristine crystal waterfall flowed with a murky hue, tainted by the encroaching shadow threatening to consume the forest. Darkened creatures prowled the underbrush, their forms twisted and corrupted by the malevolent influence that hung heavy in the air.

Without hesitation, Kimras and Amara joined the fray, their formidable presence bolstering the resolve of the amethyst dragons and nymphs valiantly fighting against the spreading darkness. Aeliana, the Guardian of the Mystic Realm of Ardinia and protector of the nymphs with their deep connection to nature, stood at the forefront of the battle, her steely gaze focused on the task at hand.

"We must stem this tide before it engulfs the entirety of Purplefire Woods," Aeliana declared, her voice resolute as she rallied her forces against the encroaching shadows.

Kimras nodded in agreement, his thoughts turning to Keisha and the vow he had made to protect these sacred woods from the darkness threatening to consume them once more. "Not on my watch," he vowed to Amara, his determination unwavering. "These woods hold a special place in Keisha's heart, and I will not allow them to fall to the darkness again."

The battle intensified, each dragon and nymph fighting with desperate determination. Kimras and Amara, their strength renewed, fought alongside their allies, claws and magic striking out against the shadowy forces seeking to claim Purplefire Woods. Despite the relentless onslaught, they refused to yield, their resolve pushing them forward to restore balance to the forest.

Finally, after what felt like an eternity, the darkness began to recede, its malevolent influence waning under the collective strength and determination of the defenders. As the last remnants of shadow dispersed into the ether, a collective sigh of relief echoed through the forest, signaling victory over the encroaching darkness.

With the immediate threat vanquished, Kimras and Amara exchanged weary yet triumphant glances, their hearts swelling with pride for their role in defending the sacred woods. Though the battle had been won, they knew their vigilance was needed now more than ever to ensure the darkness would never again gain a foothold in this hallowed realm.

Amara and Kimras shared a knowing look, understanding the gravity of the situation. Gathering their friends and allies would be crucial in formulating a plan to confront the growing darkness, even as its source remained elusive.

"We need to inform everyone of what's happening," Amara said, her voice firm with determination. "And let them know the rest of the noble and gem dragons are returning to Vacari."

Kimras nodded, his gaze sweeping over the battlefield, where remnants of the darkness still lingered. "We should ask Aeliana to head to Crystal Vale and request King Manard to send the Etherwings to spread the word. We'll convene a meeting in Purplefire."

With a decisive nod, Amara turned to Aeliana, who stood nearby, her expression a mix of weariness and resolve. "Aeliana, we need your help. Can you go to Crystal Vale and ask King Manard to send the Etherwings to gather everyone for a meeting in Purplefire?"

Aeliana's response was immediate. "Of course," she said, her voice steady despite the weight of the task. With determined strides, she set off toward Crystal Vale, her mission clear.

As Aeliana departed, Amara and Kimras returned to the task at hand. With their allies informed and united, they stood a better chance against the encroaching darkness threatening Vacari once more. The stakes had never been higher, and they knew they had to act quickly.

As Kimras and Amara returned to the clearing within Purplefire Woods, the familiar sight of the ancient trees and mystical surroundings greeted them. King Alex stood nearby, his presence commanding respect as he awaited their return. As the gathering settled into an attentive silence, Kimras stood tall, his wings held with regal grace. His words, measured and authoritative, carried weight as he addressed the assembly.

"Friends, allies, we have convened today because darkness threatens our beloved Vacari once more."

His gaze swept across the faces before him, lingering on each person to ensure he had their undivided attention. "Amara and I ventured into Vacari to assess the situation firsthand. While we managed to dispel the darkness in some areas, it still lingers, like a shadow waiting to consume our realm."

A murmur of concern rippled through the gathering, the gravity of the situation weighing heavily on their hearts.

Amara stepped forward, her voice steady but laced with worry. "Indeed, Purplefire has felt the brunt of this malevolent force. We fought valiantly to repel it, but its presence was more pronounced than elsewhere."

The mention of Purplefire stirred emotions among the assembly, especially in Keisha, whose troubled expression spoke volumes. Ong's comforting embrace provided some solace, but her concern remained palpable.

"Why Purplefire again?" Keisha's voice, tinged with frustration, cut through the somber atmosphere. "What could be causing this relentless assault?"

Kimras met Keisha's gaze with empathy. "That, my friend, is the question we seek to answer. The source of this darkness eludes us for now, but we will not rest until we uncover the truth."

As the assembly began to disperse, Keisha and Ong lingered, their expressions grave with concern. They approached Kimras and Amara, speaking in hushed tones.

Keisha's question hung heavy in the air. "What of the seal on the abyss? Is it still secure?"

Kimras met her gaze with reassurance. "Fear not, Keisha. The seal remains intact. We ensured its stability during our investigation." He paused, adding more context to ease her worry. "From what we've observed, it is not the abyss causing the darkness; something or someone else is at play—especially considering the disturbances in E'vahona, which has never been threatened before due to Kadona's protection."

Amara nodded in agreement. "Our journey also took us to Fel Thalor. There, we saw Lyra with ancient artifacts and scrolls, but we were unable to discern her intentions."

Ong's jaw tightened with determination. "Those Druchii never cease their schemes. But neither shall we."

Kimras inclined his head in acknowledgment, watching as Keisha and Ong prepared to leave for E'vahona. Their resolve in the face of uncertainty gave him hope. He silently prayed for their safety and success as they departed.

As Keisha and Ong disappeared into the distance, Kimras and Amara remained, standing silently. The weight of their duty pressed heavily upon them, but they stood resolute, ready to confront whatever trials lay ahead.

With the setting sun casting long shadows across Vacari, Kimras and Amara exchanged solemn glances. The battle against the darkness had only just begun, but they would face it together, unwavering in their commitment to protect their realm.

Chapter 15

Journey into the Unknown

As Amara and Kimras soared gracefully through the azure sky, the verdant landscape of Goldmoor and the dense canopy of Purplefire Woods stretched out beneath them like a vibrant tapestry. Despite the breathtaking beauty of their surroundings, a sense of unease lingered in the air. The recent attack of darkness on Purplefire Woods weighed heavily on their minds, casting a shadow over their otherwise peaceful flight. Amara's keen eyes scanned the horizon, her heartbeat quickening as she searched for any signs of trouble, while Kimras remained vigilant, his senses attuned to the slightest disturbance.

Beneath them, the emerald foliage of Purplefire Woods shimmered with an otherworldly glow, its once tranquil aura now tainted by the lingering presence of darkness. Kimras's heart clenched with concern as he beheld the once crystal-clear rivers below, now tinged with an ominous hue. A chill ran through him, the sight serving as a stark reminder of the growing threat.

"Something feels off," Amara murmured, her voice laced with worry as she surveyed the landscape. "The woods should be teeming with life, but it's like... the very essence of the forest has dimmed."

Kimras nodded, his gaze sweeping over the canopy of trees stretching into the distance. "It's as if the darkness has left its mark on these lands," he remarked, his voice tight with concern. "We must remain vigilant. There may be more to this threat than we realize."

Just as they prepared to continue their reconnaissance, a sudden flash of light caught their attention. An etherwing, one of the special messenger birds of Vacari, flew towards them, its wings shimmering with urgency. Amara extended her wing, allowing the bird to land gracefully and deliver its message.

"It's from King Alex," Amara said, her voice barely above a whisper as she read the scroll attached to the bird's leg. The weight of the words settled heavily on her. "There's trouble in Goldmoor. He requests our immediate assistance."

Kimras's eyes narrowed with determination. "We mustn't delay. Let's head to Goldmoor at once."

With a shared glance, Amara and Kimras altered their course, banking gracefully toward the heart of Goldmoor.

Landing amidst the bustling city, they were greeted by a scene of growing unrest. King Alex approached them with a furrowed brow, his expression tense with worry. "Something is amiss in the grove," he informed them, gesturing toward the city's center, where the majestic golden fountains stood. "The waters have turned dark, and the trees are wilting."

Without hesitation, Amara and Kimras made their way to the grove. They were met with a chilling sight. The once-golden waters of the fountains now churned with an inky blackness, the shimmering surface tainted by the encroaching darkness.

Kimras clenched his jaw, his golden scales shimmering in the dim light. He felt the pulse of his draconic power rise within him, a primal force demanding release. "We must act swiftly," he declared, his voice resolute as he summoned forth his draconic magic.

Amara nodded, her own powers intertwining with Kimras's as they unleashed a torrent of radiant energy upon the tainted waters. Around them, other gold and amethyst dragons joined in the effort, their combined strength fueling their cause.

For long moments, the air crackled with energy as dragonfire clashed with darkness, each side locked in a fierce struggle for dominance. Despite the formidable might of their adversaries, Kimras and Amara refused to yield.

Slowly but surely, the darkness began to recede, driven back by the unwavering resolve of the noble dragons. As the last vestiges of shadow dissolved into nothingness, a wave of relief washed over the grove.

Yet, even as the immediate threat was vanquished, Kimras and Amara shared a knowing look. The source of the darkness still eluded them, lurking in the shadows, waiting to strike again.

"We must find the source of this darkness," Amara murmured, her voice laced with determination. "Before it consumes us all."

Kimras nodded in agreement, his gaze hardening with resolve. "Agreed. We cannot rest until Vacari is safe once more."

With their mission clear, Amara and Kimras turned their eyes to the horizon, steeling themselves for the trials that lay ahead. The shadows stretched and deepened across Goldmoor as the golden rays of the sun began to wane, casting an ominous stillness over the city. Their greatest challenge awaited them, somewhere in the depths of the darkness threatening their world.

In a secluded corner of Goldmoor, away from the bustling city sounds, they huddled to confer in earnest, voices low yet intense.

"It seems we've scoured Vacari without finding any trace of the darkness," Kimras murmured, his brow furrowed with concern. "Yet it cannot simply vanish without a trace. There must be some clue we've overlooked." His words hung heavy in the air, weighted by the shared frustration and uncertainty.

Amara's gaze remained fixed on the distant horizon, where the last glimmers of daylight faded. A newfound resolve hardened in her expression. "Perhaps we should return to Afor," she suggested, her voice determined. "The darkness emerged from there before. We may have missed something crucial."

Kimras considered her words, the intensity of his gaze softening with acknowledgment. "Afor it is," he declared firmly. "We'll comb every inch of the desert realm, leaving no stone unturned."

With their decision made, Kimras and Amara made their way to King Alex to inform him of their plans. The human king listened gravely, his face mirroring the weight of their task. As they spoke, the gravity of their mission seemed to settle over him, deepening the lines of worry etched across his brow.

"May the winds guide your journey, and may fortune favor your quest," King Alex intoned, his voice heavy with concern. "The safety of our realm depends on your efforts."

With a solemn nod of gratitude, Kimras and Amara bid farewell to their king, their hearts resonating with the gravity of his words. Taking to the skies once more, their wings beat in unison as they soared toward the distant horizon, driven by a shared sense of duty.

As they journeyed onward, the desert sands of Afor stretched out before them—a vast expanse of shifting dunes under the relentless sun, shimmering with an almost otherworldly heat. The howling winds created an eerie symphony, the sound echoing in the emptiness, stirring something primal within them. Yet, despite the harsh conditions, Kimras and Amara pressed on, undeterred. They exchanged a glance, drawing strength from their shared determination; each powerful beat of their wings a testament to their unwavering resolve.

Upon touching down on the outskirts of Afor, they were met by Aurix, the guardian Brass Dragon of the sanctuary. His scales glistened in the sunlight, a radiant shield that seemed to repel even the desert's most punishing rays. As he approached, his expression was tinged with concern, his keen eyes taking in the tension etched in their faces.

"Welcome back, Kimras and Amara," Aurix greeted, his voice touched with curiosity. "Is something amiss?"

Kimras nodded gravely, meeting Aurix's gaze. "Indeed, there is," he began, recounting the events in Purplefire and Goldmoor. "We believe the darkness we encountered may have its origins here in Afor."

Aurix's expression darkened with concern, his scales seeming to dull in the shadows cast by his wings. "I see," he murmured, his gaze sweeping over the desert with a thoughtful intensity. "You have my full support. Should you need any assistance, do not hesitate to call upon us."

With a grateful nod, Kimras and Amara set off toward their intended destination—the sealed abyss, where they hoped to find clues to the source of the darkness. As they journeyed, they passed by the new civilization that had sprung up in the wake of Phoenix and Vuarus's old stronghold, their senses keenly attuned to any sign of disturbance. The air felt thick with anticipation, and a subtle, unsettling energy hung in the distance, hinting at the trials yet to come.

The weight of their mission pressed upon them, driving them forward. In the heart of Afor, amidst the shifting sands and ancient ruins, lay the key to unraveling the mystery of the encroaching darkness.

Kimras and Amara descended from the heavens, their powerful wings cutting through the air as they approached the sealed abyss at Afor's core. The landscape stretched below them—a bleak patchwork of rugged terrain and remnants of a once-vibrant world, now muted by desolation.

Aurix, gliding alongside them, spoke in a low rumble. "We must proceed with caution. The sealed abyss holds many secrets, and we cannot afford to underestimate its power."

Kimras and Amara nodded in agreement, their senses attuned to any disturbance. As they touched down on the outskirts of the abyss, an eerie silence enveloped them—a stark contrast to the howling winds of the desert. The air was thick, carrying a chill that seeped into their scales, making each heartbeat resonate with heightened awareness.

"This land was once a festering swamp," Aurix murmured, his gaze sweeping over the barren wasteland. "Before Vuarus tainted it with his wrath. Water and life have long since fled, leaving only this endless desert in their wake."

"The power of the abyss still lingers here," Aurix growled softly. "Vuarus didn't just change the land—he consumed it, leaving only dust. Even now, the air tastes of despair, a reminder of the abyss's hunger."

Kimras and Amara exchanged uneasy glances, feeling the weight of this haunting past pressing upon them. As they landed on the edge of the abyss, an unsettling quiet greeted them, thickening the tension in their bones.

Kimras felt a chill creep up his spine, his senses alert to the palpable danger. He recalled the stories of Afor's once-murky waters, once teeming with life. Now, the landscape lay barren—a desolate monument to Vuarus's wrath. When the god of the abyss was unleashed, he twisted the land, draining the swamps and leaving only scorching sands.

With a shared glance, Kimras and Amara approached the sealed entrance to the abyss, their steps slow and deliberate. Each footfall echoed, swallowed by the oppressive silence. The ancient wards guarding the threshold glowed faintly, casting a ghostly light over the rugged terrain. As Kimras traced the intricate runes, a chill surged through him; each symbol pulsed with a dormant power, vibrating beneath his touch.

"It appears to be intact," Kimras murmured, his voice tinged with relief. "But we must be certain. The darkness that once threatened our realm may still linger within these depths."

Amara nodded, her eyes scanning the surface of the seal. "Agreed," she replied, her voice steady despite the unease. "We must ensure the abyss remains sealed."

Together, they meticulously inspected each rune, probing for breaks in the ancient barrier. Tension hung heavy in the air, their duty pressing upon their shoulders. Each movement felt deliberate, every breath a testament to the gravity of their task.

A sense of relief washed over them as they found no visible signs of damage or disruption. Still, they were not ones to leave anything to chance, especially when Vacari's safety hung in the balance. They continued their inspection, scouring the ground around the abyss for any sign of malign influence.

After completing their search, Kimras and Amara wove additional protective wards around the seal, strengthening its defenses. Their magic flowed seamlessly, intertwining and merging as they chanted ancient incantations. The air crackled with energy as their combined efforts fortified the barrier, creating a shimmering shield around the ancient runes.

Yet even as they reinforced the seal, a nagging sense of unease tugged at their hearts. The lingering presence of darkness was palpable, like a shadow waiting just beyond the edge of sight.

"We have done all we can to strengthen the seal," Kimras said, his voice grave. "But the darkness persists."

Amara nodded, her eyes reflecting the flickering light of their magic. "Agreed. We must remain vigilant. The darkness may be contained for now, but it will not stay dormant forever."

With a renewed sense of purpose, they redoubled their efforts, pouring their strength into the wards. United in their bond and their mission, they stood firm against the forces that sought to unravel their world.

As the last traces of their magic faded, Kimras and Amara stepped back from the seal, their hearts heavy with the knowledge that the abyss was not the source of the darkness. Yet, ensuring it remained sealed would keep one threat at bay as they sought the true origin of the encroaching shadow.

In the heart of Afor, amidst the shifting sands and whispered secrets, Kimras and Amara hovered above the sprawling city below. From their vantage point in the skies, the city appeared calm, yet a faint, almost imperceptible energy pulsed beneath the surface—a subtle undercurrent that stirred a sense of unease within them.

"There's something about this place," Amara murmured, her sharp gaze sweeping over the city's maze of streets and towering structures. "I can't quite place it, but it feels... out of balance."

Kimras nodded, his eyes narrowing as he focused on the towering mage tower standing sentinel over the city. Its spires reached skyward, an imposing symbol of knowledge and power. "Agreed. There's a strange energy here, like a shadow lingering beneath the surface."

He considered their options, feeling the weight of their mission pressing upon him. "We should investigate," he decided. "But we must be careful. If there is darkness here, we don't want to risk harming the city or its people."

With a plan forming, Kimras looked to Amara. "I'll transform into my human form and explore the city alone. You can remain above, keeping watch."

Amara nodded in agreement, her amethyst scales catching the fading sunlight. "Be careful, Kimras," she urged, her voice tinged with concern. "If you need me, I'll be here."

With a final glance toward the city below, Kimras began his transformation, preparing himself for the unknown dangers that might lie ahead.

With a reassuring nod, Kimras closed his eyes, drawing his energy inward. His draconic form began to shift and morph, his powerful scales giving way to the shape of a mortal man. Though his outward appearance had changed, the strength and resolve that defined him as a dragon remained undiminished.

As the last traces of his transformation faded, Kimras turned to face the city, his heart weighed down by the gravity of his task. But he knew he could not falter; the fate of their realm depended on uncovering the truth hidden within the shadows.

With purposeful strides, Kimras set off toward the city, his thoughts clouded by the unknown dangers ahead. Yet, he drew comfort in knowing he did not walk alone, for Amara remained his vigilant guardian, watching from above. Together, they would face whatever trials awaited, their bond as guardians of Vacari a steadfast anchor.

As Kimras ventured deeper into the city, he marveled at the diversity of its inhabitants and the intricacies of its architecture. Every building told a story, each design a testament to the rich tapestry of cultures that had come to call this city home. The air buzzed with the sounds of bustling life, and the enticing aroma of exotic spices and foods wafted through the narrow streets, embracing him in a warm welcome.

Reaching the city's heart, his attention was drawn to a towering structure that loomed above the skyline, its spires stretching toward the heavens as though yearning to touch the stars. It was a mage tower, its grandeur and intricate carvings contrasting sharply with the humble dwellings surrounding it.

Kimras stood in quiet awe, his eyes tracing the glyphs and sigils etched into the walls. Each symbol seemed to pulse faintly with ancient knowledge, hinting at mysteries long forgotten. He felt a deep reverence for the tower's majesty, its presence a reminder of a world that still held wonders yet unexplored.

Lost in thought, Kimras was startled by a soft voice breaking the silence. He turned to see a city resident standing before him, their gaze warm with curiosity.

"Welcome to our city," the resident greeted with a smile. "I couldn't help but notice you admiring our mage tower. Do you like what you see?"

Kimras nodded, his gaze lingering on the tower. "It is truly remarkable," he replied, awe coloring his tone. "Are there any mages who dwell here?"

The resident's smile faded, a hint of sadness clouding their expression. "Sadly, no," he replied. "Many in our city fear the tower and the magic it represents. They believe our city was cursed long ago, and they distrust those who wield magic."

Kimras's brow furrowed as he absorbed the resident's words. The city's past cast a long shadow, stifling its people's spirit and suppressing the potential for growth and unity.

Looking back at the mage tower, a glimmer of hope sparked within him. He sensed the possibility of change—a chance to reclaim the city's legacy and foster a new era of enlightenment and trust.

With a respectful nod, Kimras thanked the resident for their insight before returning his gaze to the mage tower. As he pondered the city's future, he realized that true magic lay not merely in spells and incantations, but in the courage of those willing to believe in its transformative power.

After a thorough exploration of the mage tower and the surrounding streets, Kimras continued his stroll through the city, his senses keenly attuned to any signs of darkness or malign influence. To his relief, he found none; the city pulsed with vibrant energy, its people immersed in the rhythm of daily life.

Confident that the city was free from any immediate threats, Kimras made his way to the outskirts, where Amara awaited him. As he left the city's confines, he shifted back into his true form, his majestic wings stretching wide as he approached his companion.

Amara greeted Kimras with a playful smirk, her amethyst scales shimmering in the moonlight. "Well, well, look who's back," she teased, her voice filled with amusement. "Did you enjoy your stroll through the city, Kimras?"

Kimras chuckled, a hint of wryness in his tone. "It was certainly... enlightening," he replied, his gaze drifting to the horizon. "But being human has its drawbacks."

Amara laughed, the sound echoing through the night air like music. "Ah, but it's nice to blend in with mortals every once in a while," she teased, nudging Kimras playfully with her snout.

Kimras smiled, a twinkle of amusement in his eyes. "Perhaps," he conceded softly. "But there's something to be said for the freedom of flight and the majesty of our true forms."

With a shared glance, Kimras and Amara took to the skies once more, their wings beating in unison as they soared toward their next destination. In the vast expanse of Afor, amidst shifting sands and ancient ruins, they felt the weight of their journey ahead. Together, they would face whatever trials awaited, their bond as guardians of Vacari unbreakable.

As Kimras and Amara approached another city nestled in the heart of Afor, they noticed its imposing walls and sturdy gates—a stark contrast to the openness of other cities they had visited. The air around it seemed heavy, tinged with an unease that gnawed at their senses. Amara cast a cautious glance at Kimras, her amethyst scales shimmering in the sunlight.

"Are you sure you want to enter this city, Kimras?" Amara asked, her voice tinged with concern. "It feels... different from the others."

Kimras nodded, his gaze fixed on the city's looming gates. "Yes," he replied, his tone resolute. "But we must proceed with caution. There's something... off about this place."

With a shared understanding, they landed outside the city gates, and Kimras transformed once again into his human guise. As he approached the gates, a growing unease settled over him, a silent warning urging him to tread carefully.

Each step he took was deliberate, his senses heightened to any signs of danger. At the entrance, he was met by a pair of guards who regarded him with wary eyes.

"Halt! State your business," one of the guards demanded, his hand resting on the hilt of his sword.

Kimras met their gaze, his demeanor calm. "I seek entry to your city," he said, keeping his tone steady. "I mean no harm. I wish only to explore and learn more about this place."

The guards exchanged a skeptical glance before nodding reluctantly, allowing him entry. As Kimras stepped through, a chill ran down his spine—a silent reminder of the hidden dangers lurking within.

With a quiet resolve, Kimras ventured deeper into the city, his senses attuned to any signs of malice. Amidst towering walls and whispered secrets, he knew that the true test of his courage and conviction lay ahead.

As he moved through the crowded streets, Kimras's attention was drawn to a tranquil oasis nestled among the bustling market. The water glistened like a rare gem, its gentle ripples soothing his thoughts. Seeking a moment of calm, he settled onto a bench nearby, letting the lively sounds of the city wash over him. He observed merchants hawking their wares, children at play, and couples strolling arm in arm, their laughter mingling with the rustling of palm fronds in the breeze.

But his focus soon shifted to an unusual sight—a grand, enclosed carriage adorned with intricate designs, drawn by a team of magnificent horses. It moved slowly through the streets, drawing curious gazes, before stopping in front of a large, ornate building.

Intrigued, Kimras watched as guards surrounded the carriage, their expressions solemn and watchful. Sensing his curiosity, one of the guards approached him, respectful yet cautious.

"That building is for our sultan," the guard explained with reverence. "He resides there with his court, overseeing the affairs of our city and ensuring its prosperity."

Kimras nodded thoughtfully, his gaze lingering on the grand structure. He could sense the weight of history and tradition surrounding it, a legacy carved into every ornate detail.

As the guard returned to his duties, Kimras remained seated, lost in thought. The city, with its walls and whispers, held a vibrant spirit yet seemed weighed down by an invisible burden. For beneath its splendor, he sensed a faint shadow—a darkness different from the malevolent force threatening Vacari, yet unsettling all the same.

Kimras left the oasis and continued exploring, his senses sharp for any signs of darkness. He walked through the city, observing the pulse of life around him, yet all the while, he felt that lingering shadow lurking beneath the surface. As much as he yearned to uncover its origin, he knew it wasn't his place to intervene further.

With a heavy heart, he finally decided to leave the city, content that he had learned what he could. He returned to the outskirts, where Amara awaited. Transforming back into his dragon form, he spread his wings and approached her, ready to relay his discoveries.

"I sensed a darkness within the city," Kimras explained, his voice tinged with unease. "But it wasn't the same darkness that threatens Vacari. It felt... contained, as though it clung to the city and its rulers, bound somehow within their walls."

Amara nodded, her gaze somber as she absorbed his words. "It seems we have stumbled upon a city with its own secrets," she replied softly but resolutely. "But our path lies elsewhere for now. Let us continue to the city against the mountains."

With a shared sense of purpose, Kimras and Amara took to the skies once more, their wings carrying them over the endless desert toward their next destination. Below them, the landscape stretched vast and barren, yet they felt the pulse of their shared mission, a steady beat beneath the endless horizon. Together, they would face whatever challenges awaited them, their bond as guardians of Vacari unbreakable.

As they approached the city nestled against the mountains, they noticed a narrow path veering off from the main road, partially hidden by dense foliage and shadowy undergrowth. From this secluded trail emanated an aura of darkness, subtle yet potent, sending a shiver down their spines and heightening their vigilance.

Their eyes met, a silent understanding passing between them. This was no ordinary path; a shadow lurked within it, and they both felt its pull. Without exchanging words, they nodded to each other, veering off course and descending toward the concealed trail just outside the city's reach.

The closer they drew, the denser the air became, thick with foreboding. Every beat of their wings felt weighted as if the shadows themselves were pressing against them. Yet, their determination remained unyielding. Together, they pressed forward, their bond a shield against the unknown.

Whatever lay along this hidden path, they would face it side by side. As they ventured deeper into the darkness, their senses remained sharp, each instinct attuned to the dangers that might await.

Soon, they glimpsed figures emerging from the shadows—the Moon Seraphidians. These ethereal beings moved gracefully in the moonlight, their half-snake, half-human forms shimmering as though woven from the night itself. Their movements were both mesmerizing and unnerving, adding an eerie beauty to the darkened path.

As they continued, they spotted a herd of warthogs grazing nearby, their grunts and snuffles punctuating the silence. Respecting the creatures' space, Kimras and Amara moved with care, gliding past the herd with quiet precision, keen to avoid any unnecessary disturbance.

Eventually, they reached a narrow trail that led toward a cave, its entrance a dark, gaping mouth beckoning them into the depths of the earth. The air grew cooler as they approached, and faint whispers floated from within the darkness, curling around them like tendrils of smoke.

With a shared glance, Kimras and Amara steeled themselves, their hearts steady yet expectant. They could feel the weight of the unknown pressing against them, a challenge cloaked in shadows.

Together, they stepped forward, bracing themselves for what lay within the cave. Amidst the shifting shadows and whispered secrets, they knew their true test awaited, a trial of courage and conviction that would push them to their limits. But, as always, they would face it together, their bond as guardians of Vacari unbreakable.

As Kimras and Amara stepped into the cavernous depths of the cave, they were immediately greeted by the musty scent of earth and the chilling echoes of their footsteps reverberating off stone walls. The dim light filtering in from the entrance cast long shadows that danced across the uneven floor, flickering like restless spirits.

With each step, the air thickened, the weight of the darkness pressing down on them. Yet, their resolve remained unbroken; a shared purpose drove them forward, undeterred by the oppressive atmosphere. As they ventured deeper into the cave, the whispers grew louder, their presence weaving through the air like tendrils, filling their minds with a strange mixture of urgency and dread.

Kimras's keen eyes scanned the surroundings, alert for any hidden threats. Beside him, Amara moved with equal caution, her amethyst scales faintly glowing in the dimness, casting a soft, ethereal light around her as she advanced with feline grace.

Suddenly, the narrow passage opened into a chamber, its walls adorned with ancient carvings and glyphs that pulsed with a faint, otherworldly glow. In the chamber's center stood a pedestal upon which rested an ornate, gem-encrusted box, shimmering in the eerie light.

Kimras and Amara exchanged a look, their shared understanding clear in their eyes. This was it—the source of the whispers, the artifact that held the key to unraveling the darkness that had begun to creep through their world.

With a mixture of awe and caution, they approached the pedestal, each step measured and deliberate. As they neared the box, the whispers intensified, flooding the chamber with a cacophony of voices that seemed to emerge from every corner, filling their minds with fragmented echoes.

But Kimras and Amara stood firm, rooted by the strength of their bond as guardians of Vacari. Together, they would confront whatever secrets lay within this box and face the darkness that threatened to engulf their world.

Kimras's gaze drifted to an ancient section of the chamber wall, where intricate symbols and carvings adorned the stone in a complex weave. His eyes narrowed as he studied the glyphs, a deep frown creasing his brow.

"What's wrong?" Amara asked softly, joining him by the wall.

Kimras turned to her, his expression grave. "This cave..." he began, his voice heavy with the weight of history. "This is where Azeron—known to us as Vuarus—was imprisoned centuries ago. His chief priest, Malrik, freed him from this very spot."

Amara's eyes widened. "But Vuarus is dead," she said, her tone edged with uncertainty.

Kimras nodded solemnly. "Yes, but the echoes of his dark influence may still linger within these walls," he replied. "Whatever traces of his power remain, they could be as dangerous as he was in life. We must proceed with extreme caution and be wary of anything we uncover here."

The two guardians shared a tense silence, each recognizing the potential peril that lay ahead. They had journeyed here seeking answers, but now they faced the remnants of a darkness that defied time, its echoes lingering like shadows that refused to fade.

With renewed determination, Kimras and Amara steeled themselves. They would explore the mysteries within this chamber and uncover the truth—whatever it took to protect their realm from the encroaching darkness.

As they ventured deeper into the cave, Kimras and Amara moved with utmost caution, their footsteps echoing in the darkness. Each sound seemed to reverberate back, amplifying the weight of their journey. In the heart of the cave, surrounded by ancient writings and long-forgotten secrets, they knew the true test of their courage and conviction awaited them. Though the shadows threatened to engulf them, they pressed forward, their bond as guardians of Vacari unbreakable.

Their search led them to a hidden alcove strewn with scrolls and artifacts, seemingly discarded in haste. Kimras's heart quickened as he approached, the unmistakable aura of darkness pulsing from the objects, filling the air with a malevolent energy that was all too familiar.

Cautiously, Kimras knelt and picked up one of the scrolls, its brittle parchment crackling beneath his touch. His brow furrowed as he examined the ancient markings, recognizing the same dark energy that had plagued Vacari. This was no coincidence; these objects were tied to the force threatening their realm.

Amara joined him, her gaze sweeping over the artifacts with a mix of curiosity and trepidation. "We should take these with us," she suggested softly, her voice resolute despite the unease in her eyes. "If we can decipher their meaning, we might uncover the source of this darkness."

Kimras nodded, though a sense of foreboding gnawed at him. "It seems someone has been here before us," he observed quietly, glancing around the alcove as if expecting shadows to shift. "We must remain vigilant. We may not be the only ones seeking these answers."

With the scrolls and artifacts secured, Kimras and Amara made their way out of the cave, their minds heavy with the revelations they had uncovered. The mystery was far from solved, but they had gathered clues that might lead them closer to the truth.

As they took to the skies once more, setting their sights on The Hidden Isles, the vast horizon spread before them like an open book, each chapter promising new trials. The mysteries of the past and the unknown challenges of the future loomed large, yet their bond as guardians of Vacari was unyielding, a steadfast light in the encroaching darkness.

Together, they soared into the distance, determined to uncover the truth and face whatever awaited them, their courage unwavering and their resolve stronger than ever.

Chapter 16
Prophecies Unveiled

Kimras and Amara soared through the skies, the mystical barrier surrounding the Hidden Isles shimmering before them like a veil woven by ancient magic. As they passed through, its protective energy cascaded over them, tingling with the essence of powerful, ancient spells. Kimras felt the familiar ripple of magic across his scales, a reminder of the formidable protections guarding this sacred haven.

On the other side, an awe-inspiring vista unfolded—the Hidden Isles lay spread before them in breathtaking splendor. Islands adorned with vibrant, otherworldly flora dotted the crystal-clear waters, their shores bordered by cascading waterfalls that sparkled like liquid sunlight. The air was alive with the sweet fragrance of exotic flowers, the gentle rustle of palm fronds, and the harmonious songs of unseen creatures echoing from hidden groves. Kimras inhaled deeply, allowing the tranquility of the

Isles to soothe his battle-worn spirit. Beside him, Amara closed her eyes briefly, savoring the peace that stood in stark contrast to the chaos they had endured.

At the heart of the Isles, a majestic golden castle rose like a beacon of hope, its towers stretching toward the heavens, bathed in sunlight. The castle, a symbol of the noble dragons' grandeur, served as a sanctuary and meeting place for allies across the races—a bastion of harmony and unity. Kimras's heart swelled with pride as he gazed upon it, a reminder of all they fought to protect.

Kimras and Amara descended gracefully, landing on one of the verdant islands. Their wings folded with practiced ease as their feet touched the soft earth. Exchanging a silent glance, they acknowledged the sacredness of this place and the weight of their mission. For Kimras, the beauty of the Isles only strengthened his resolve; their task here could determine the fate of Vacari.

The warmth of the sun and the gentle lapping of waves welcomed them ashore. The Isles embraced them, offering a moment of solace amidst the turmoil of the outside world. Yet, beneath the surface calm, an urgency gnawed at Kimras. Time, he knew, was not their ally.

Dragons filled the Isles all around them, each exuding a quiet nobility. Some were young and full of energy, their scales bright with untarnished vigor, while others bore the wisdom of countless years, their presence a testament to the endurance of their kind. They practiced aerial maneuvers, tended to the flourishing gardens, or conversed in hushed tones. Kimras marveled at the diversity of his kin, each dragon's unique abilities contributing to the harmony of the Isles.

Kimras and Amara spotted familiar faces among the gathered dragons, nodding in silent acknowledgment. Their presence was met with camaraderie, a shared understanding transcending lineage and age. Surrounded by their kin, they felt a sense of belonging that fortified their spirits. This unity, Kimras reminded himself, was why they fought—to preserve this sanctuary and the peace it embodied.

With a shared purpose, they turned toward the golden tower at the heart of the Isles. Its gleaming spires beckoned to them, a promise of answers waiting within. Kimras felt an undeniable pull, a mixture of anticipation and trepidation churning within him.

As they neared the tower, their steps quickened. Inside, the scrolls and artifacts they had recovered would be studied in detail, and the ancient texts from the cave would be deciphered. This was the place where they would seek the wisdom of their ancestors and unravel the secrets buried in history. Kimras felt the weight of his heritage pressing upon him, the silent voices of his forebears urging him forward.

Every step they took deepened their resolve. Their journey was far from over, but together, Kimras and Amara would face whatever challenges lay ahead. Drawing strength from their bond as guardians of Vacari, they prepared to confront the truths that awaited within the hallowed halls of the golden tower, determined to shield their realm from the encroaching darkness.

Flameford, once a bustling city ruled with an iron fist by Phoenix and Vuarus, had undergone a dramatic transformation since their fall. The oppressive regime had given way to a dark refuge, its streets now inhabited by shadowy dragons who prowled through foreboding alleyways. Despite the passage of time, Quellan could still feel the city's lingering malice—a testament to the brutal battles fought here and the simmering power struggles that refused to fade.

Within the city, twisted spires and jagged rooftops clawed at the sky, their long shadows casting an oppressive gloom over the cobblestone streets. The air was thick with the acrid scent of smoke and sulfur, stinging the senses and standing as a stark reminder of the city's corruption. Lyra wrinkled her nose as she followed Quellan and the enigmatic figure through the streets, her expression tight with distaste. Flameford was a city steeped in darkness, its scars far from healed.

Their destination lay in the heart of the city—a dark, foreboding tower rising like a sentinel against the night sky. Its silhouette was a stark reminder of the ancient power that lingered within its crumbling walls. As they approached, Quellan felt a chill creep up his spine, the oppressive atmosphere settling heavily on his shoulders. Danger seemed to seep from the very stones of the city, an unspoken warning that their path would not be easy.

Inside the tower, an eerie silence enveloped them, broken only by the soft rustle of turning pages and the rhythmic scratching of quills on parchment. The room was lit by flickering candles, their golden glow casting dancing shadows on the ancient walls. Lyra, Quellan, and the mysterious figure gathered around a large table strewn with dusty scrolls and enigmatic artifacts. The shadows seemed alive, twisting and writhing as though mirroring the dark secrets they sought to unravel.

As they pored over the scrolls, the texts began to reveal fragments of their mysteries—hints of forgotten knowledge and the promise of power buried within the ancient words. But with every revelation came a tide of new questions, each more perplexing than the last. Lyra's frustration bubbled to the surface with every undecipherable passage, her sharp sighs and muttered curses filling the air. In contrast, the mysterious figure remained composed, their calm demeanor an unsettling counterpoint to Lyra's agitation.

The deeper they delved, the more the room seemed to shift around them, the whispers of ancient incantations and the echoes of dark power pressing in from every side. The scrolls radiated a malevolent energy that seemed almost alive, creeping through the chamber and clawing at their senses. Quellan shuddered as he felt the palpable darkness emanating from the artifacts. These were no mere relics of history; they were conduits for something far more sinister.

Their quest to resurrect the darkness was fraught with peril. Allies and adversaries emerged from the shadows, each driven by motives cloaked in secrecy. Betrayal and treachery lurked around every corner, forcing them to tread carefully. Lyra's eyes darted nervously to the door, half-expecting an ambush, her trust in their supposed allies wearing thin with every passing moment.

Amid the constant threat of danger, the trio faced choices that tested their moral convictions. Each step closer to their goal brought them closer to the realization that the darkness they sought to unlock might consume them entirely. Quellan's resolve faltered as doubt took root in his heart, the weight of their mission pressing heavily on his conscience.

Lyra furrowed her brow, her composed facade cracking under the strain. Quellan noticed her unease and leaned closer, his voice low and concerned. "What's wrong, Lyra? You seem troubled."

She sighed, her gaze fixed on the scrolls spread before them. "Pages are missing from these scrolls," she admitted, frustration lacing her voice. "Without them, our task becomes infinitely harder. If we can't find them, we may be chasing shadows."

Before Quellan could respond, the mysterious figure interjected, their voice calm and assured. "Do not despair," they said with a soothing confidence that set Quellan's teeth on edge. "We will return to Afor and the cave where these scrolls were found. There, we may yet uncover the missing pages and complete our quest."

Though their words were steady and reassuring, Quellan couldn't shake the unease they stirred in him. Something about the figure's tone, so smooth and hypnotic, rang hollow—a melody that hid dissonance beneath its surface. But with no better option before them, he chose to remain silent, his unease tucked away as they prepared to press onward.

Lyra's expression softened at the reassurance, a flicker of hope igniting in her eyes. "You're right," she said, a determined resolve settling over her features. "We cannot let a few missing pages deter us from our goal. Let's return to Afor and retrieve what we need." Her renewed determination filled the chamber, rekindling her sense of purpose.

With shared resolve, Lyra, Quellan, and the mysterious figure rose from the table, their thoughts already turning toward the next phase of their journey. Though obstacles awaited, their determination to succeed remained unshaken. For the moment, even Quellan's doubts receded, replaced by a fierce resolve to see their mission through.

Lyra's expression softened at the reassurance, a flicker of hope igniting in her eyes. "You're right," she said, a determined resolve settling over her features. "We cannot let a few missing pages deter us from our goal. Let's return to Afor and retrieve what we need." Her renewed determination filled the chamber, rekindling her sense of purpose.

With shared resolve, Lyra, Quellan, and the mysterious figure rose from the table, their thoughts already turning toward the next phase of their journey. Though obstacles awaited, their determination to succeed remained unshaken. For the moment, even Quellan's doubts receded, replaced by a fierce resolve to see their mission through.

The journey to Afor was swift but charged with tension, each of them consumed by thoughts of the missing pages and their significance. As they arrived at the familiar cave entrance, the weight of urgency drove them forward into the cavern's depths. Lyra's heart pounded as her mind raced with anticipation—and dread—of what they might find.

Navigating the winding passages with ease born of familiarity, they soon reached the chamber where the scrolls had been discovered. Lyra halted abruptly, her breath catching as she took in the sight before her. The space where the scrolls had once lain was empty, the absence glaring and undeniable.

"The pages... they're gone," Lyra exclaimed, her voice echoing against the cold stone walls. A wave of frustration and unease washed over her, the stark realization that someone had tampered with their discovery clawing at her composure. Her fists clenched tightly as anger and fear surged within her.

The mysterious figure frowned, their features betraying concern, though their glittering eyes hinted at something else—satisfaction, perhaps? "It appears we were not the only ones drawn to this place," they observed, their tone even but edged with apprehension.

Quellan's gaze darkened as he stepped forward, his voice grim. "Most likely the noble dragons," he said bitterly. "They'll stop at nothing to keep us from uncovering the truth." His words dripped with disdain, the old rivalry with the noble dragons flaring anew in his heart.

As the gravity of their situation settled over them, the trio exchanged knowing glances. Though the road ahead seemed steeper than ever, their resolve remained steadfast. Lyra squared her shoulders, forcing back her frustration as she prepared herself for the next step in their perilous journey.

The mysterious figure broke the silence, their voice calm but insistent. "We need to return and work with what we have," they urged, their tone carrying a quiet urgency. Their gaze darted toward the cave entrance, as though sensing unseen eyes observing their every move.

The words lingered in the air, a stark reminder of the urgency of their mission. With a solemn nod, Lyra steadied herself, her determination hardening. "You're right," she said, her voice steady despite the unease that gnawed at her. "We cannot allow the noble dragons to gain the upper hand. We must decipher what we have and use it to our advantage."

Quellan nodded in agreement, his expression fierce. "Even if they possess the missing pages, they don't have everything," he declared with conviction. "We still hold part of the puzzle, and that will be enough for now. We'll find a way."

With their course of action clear, the trio retraced their steps and set out for Flameford. The oppressive atmosphere of the city greeted them once more as they returned to the dark tower. The flickering candlelight cast elongated shadows across the walls, whispering reminders of the lurking darkness that surrounded them.

Gathered around the table once more, Lyra, Quellan, and the mysterious figure resumed their work, their focus razor-sharp. The ancient scrolls lay before them, their secrets tantalizingly close yet frustratingly out of reach. Lyra's fingers moved swiftly over the parchment, her mind racing with the possibilities hidden within the texts.

Each deciphered fragment felt like a step closer to their ultimate goal, yet the danger and uncertainty of their path loomed larger with every revelation. Despite the peril, they pressed on, knowing the fate of Vacari hung precariously in the balance. Only by unlocking the secrets of the past could they hope to secure the future—a future shrouded in darkness, yet one they were determined to claim.

As Quellan stepped outside the tower to assess Flameford's transformation, he found himself marveling at the city's stark evolution. Twisted spires reached ominously into the night sky, casting jagged shadows across the cobblestone streets. Foreboding alleyways carved through the city's heart, offering refuge to those who sought solace in its dark embrace. The very air seemed heavy with the essence of darkness, seeping from the shadows that clung to every corner.

Walking through the transformed streets, Quellan observed areas meticulously designated for the various factions of dark dragons. Each section reflected the unique needs and preferences of its inhabitants, a testament to the careful planning and coordination that had reshaped Flameford into a sanctuary for the forces of darkness. Yet, even amidst this order, he couldn't ignore the simmering tension beneath the surface—a fragile balance that could shift dangerously at any moment.

As he continued his exploration, his attention was drawn to a familiar figure among the throngs of dragons. Zylron, a towering red dragon, stood out with his vivid scales and commanding presence. Quellan approached him with a nod of greeting.

"Zylron," Quellan said, his voice edged with curiosity, "do you know anything about the mysterious person we're working with?"

Zylron's gaze grew pensive, his crimson eyes narrowing thoughtfully. "I'm afraid I know as much as you do," he admitted, a trace of frustration in his tone. "They're an enigma, that's for certain. But..." He hesitated, his voice dropping to a low rumble, "there's a dark power within them—something I've never encountered before. It's not like Phoenix's power. This... this feels darker, more dangerous."

The weight of Zylron's words hung in the air, stirring an unease that gnawed at Quellan. He nodded solemnly, his thoughts heavy with speculation. "Thank you, Zylron," he said, acknowledging the insight. As he turned back toward the tower, a sense of foreboding followed him. There was more to the mysterious figure than they had realized—of that, he was certain.

Retracing his steps through Flameford, Quellan couldn't shake the sense of unease that lingered in his mind. Though progress had been made in deciphering the ancient scrolls, the mysteries surrounding the enigmatic figure and their true intentions loomed large. His thoughts spiraled with possibilities, each one darker and more troubling than the last. Could their ally be a savior—or the harbinger of an even greater peril?

As Quellan approached the tower, the flickering torchlight cast wavering shadows across the walls, their movement mimicking the uncertainty that plagued his mind. Flameford had transformed into a haven for darkness, but at what cost? And would the alliances they were forging ultimately secure their goals—or unravel everything they had worked for?

Lyra painstakingly deciphered a particularly cryptic passage from the ancient scrolls, her brow furrowed in concentration as her finger traced the intricate symbols. Doubt began to creep into her thoughts, and she paused, her eyes narrowing as she wondered if her interpretation was correct. With a determined frown, she started rechecking her work, scrutinizing every line of text with meticulous care. The weight of the task before her was immense, and the mounting pressure felt like a storm gathering above her.

Finally, after a thorough review, a triumphant smirk tugged at the corners of Lyra's lips. "It would seem," she announced, her voice tinged with satisfaction, "that there was a plan to eliminate someone." Her gaze flicked toward the mysterious figure, her curiosity sharpening. "But that page is missing," she added, her tone shifting to one of frustration. "I wonder who it was meant for." The missing pieces taunted her, their absence both maddening and tantalizing.

The mysterious figure's response was as enigmatic as ever. "Keep searching," they said, their tone calm yet urging, as if they already knew the answer. Their eyes glinted, betraying an undercurrent of satisfaction—one that Lyra, too engrossed in the scrolls, failed to notice.

As Lyra bent back to her work, the mysterious figure allowed the faintest, most wicked smile to curve their lips, unnoticed by the others. It was the smile of someone holding a secret too powerful to share, a fragment of truth cloaked in layers of deception. With a subtle nod, they silently encouraged Lyra's efforts, their own mind racing with dark schemes. The scrolls, they knew, held more than just historical significance—they were the key to an unimaginable power that lay within reach.

Their eyes alighted on a passage buried within the ancient text, its cryptic symbols stirring something within them. Slowly, their lips curled into a knowing smile. Amid the faded ink and forgotten runes, they found it: a revelation of profound importance—the sacrifice Vuarus had sought to retain his godhead. The implications were staggering. It was the piece they had been searching for, a glimpse into the dark force that had once consumed their former ally.

But their excitement was short-lived, replaced by a sharp pang of caution. The knowledge was dangerous, its revelation potentially catastrophic. If Lyra or the others discovered the true origins of the scrolls, or that

Vuarus had intended to sacrifice Keisha for his power, it could destroy everything. The delicate balance of trust and deception would shatter, and their plans would unravel.

Now was not the time. The group was not yet under their control, and revealing too much could spark questions that would unravel the fragile trust they had cultivated. Control, they thought, was a slow and deliberate process—one that required patience. Until then, certain truths had to remain buried.

Quickly and deliberately, the mysterious figure moved to conceal the passage. With careful precision, they obscured the incriminating text, ensuring no trace of its existence remained. Their hands moved with practiced ease, their heart pounding with the thrill of secrecy. They couldn't afford even the slightest slip; the risk was too great, and their ambition too vast.

Glancing around the room to ensure no one was watching, the mysterious figure's gaze flicked over Lyra, who was engrossed in her work, and Quellan, who had stepped outside. Satisfied they were undetected, the figure deftly hid the passage, erasing any evidence of its revelation. The room's flickering candlelight danced across their face, momentarily illuminating an expression of cold resolve.

With the passage safely concealed, they turned back to the scrolls, their focus sharp and their movements deliberate. Each line of text held potential clues, fragments of power that could be pieced together to serve their ambitions. The thrill of discovery mingled with the ever-present danger of exposure, a precarious balance they navigated with precision. Their mind churned with schemes, each more cunning than the last, as they delved deeper into the scrolls' secrets.

Lyra, oblivious to the figure's duplicity, continued her painstaking work, unaware of the concealed truths just beyond her reach. The chamber seemed to pulse with the weight of hidden knowledge, the shadows stretching and twisting as if alive. And amidst it all, the mysterious figure remained vigilant, their true intentions shrouded in darkness, their resolve as unyielding as the secrets they guarded.

As Quellan reached for the tower door, Zylron's voice called out from behind, sharp and commanding. Pausing, Quellan turned to face the red dragon, who approached with purpose. Zylron's expression was resolute as he made his request. "I need to speak with them," he said firmly, the weight of his words leaving no room for negotiation.

Quellan nodded, sensing the tension in Zylron's tone. Relaying the message, he watched the mysterious person's reaction carefully. Their brow furrowed, and a shadow crossed their face. The interruption was unwelcome, and Quellan noted the subtle shift in the atmosphere as the mysterious figure's expression darkened.

Stepping outside to meet Zylron, the mysterious person carried an air of authority, their gaze sharp and unyielding. "What is it that you need?" they asked, their clipped tone betraying their thinning patience.

Zylron met their gaze without flinching, his own demeanor equally firm. "Glaceria and I are ready to begin the destruction," he declared, his voice steady but filled with anticipation. His eyes gleamed with a chaotic energy, the promise of destruction burning within them.

The mysterious person's expression hardened, their glare cutting through Zylron's resolve. "Absolutely not," they snapped, their voice sharp with authority. "It is too soon. That is why Vuarus and Phoenix failed." Each word landed with calculated weight, meant to quell Zylron's eagerness.

Their tone turned icy, laden with contempt for the failures of the past. "Phoenix was reckless, driven by his insatiable thirst for power. He acted without foresight, blinded by his ambitions. Vuarus, in his arrogance, gave Phoenix too much freedom, trusting him to act wisely. That trust was misplaced. Phoenix's impulsiveness led to Vuarus's downfall and the collapse of everything we worked toward."

The mysterious person's gaze bore into Zylron, their voice dropping to a chilling tone. "We will not repeat their mistakes. This time, we act with precision. Patience is not a weakness; it is our greatest weapon. The destruction will wait until the right time."

Turning fully toward Zylron, the mysterious person's words came with deliberate finality. "The destruction will wait until the right time," they repeated, their voice cold and unyielding, their eyes locked on Zylron's with a warning that was impossible to ignore.

Zylron hesitated, his gaze flickering between the mysterious person and the destructive chaos he had envisioned. His defiance was palpable, but the mysterious person's unwavering authority pressed down on him like a weight. The air between them crackled with tension, the fragile threads of their alliance stretched taut.

After a long moment, Zylron lowered his head slightly, his defiance yielding to reluctant obedience. "As you command," he muttered, his voice low but edged with simmering frustration. The mysterious person watched him carefully, their sharp gaze ensuring the message was understood.

The tension lingered as Zylron turned away, a silent reminder of the fragile balance of power within their alliance. The unspoken threat of discord loomed between them, its presence undeniable even as the immediate conflict subsided. The mysterious person remained still, their mind already calculating the next move, their control over Zylron and others a delicate dance that demanded constant vigilance.

For now, the destruction would be postponed. But in the shadows of Flameford, power shifted with every decision, and alliances hung by a thread. The subtle dance of authority and defiance continued, unspoken yet ever-present, as each player in this dangerous game waited for the right moment to strike.

Amidst the serene beauty of the Hidden Isles, Kimras and Amara sat in quiet contemplation, surrounded by the gentle rustle of leaves and the distant murmur of cascading waterfalls. Before them lay the ancient scrolls, their weathered pages bearing secrets that could hold the key to saving their realm. Yet the calm of their surroundings stood in stark contrast to the turmoil in their hearts, the weight of their mission pressing heavily on their shoulders.

"We don't have all the scrolls," Kimras observed, his voice tinged with concern as his eyes swept over the fragmented collection spread before them. His gaze lingered on the faded symbols, searching for patterns, his mind racing with the implications of the missing pieces.

Amara nodded, her expression thoughtful as she stared at the scrolls. "Most likely, someone dropped these," she suggested, her tone contemplative. Her mind worked through the possibilities, piecing together the scattered clues that hinted at the scrolls' origins.

Kimras furrowed his brow, unease gnawing at him. "I have a feeling," he began gravely, "that whoever is behind the darkness has the rest of the scrolls." His words were laden with foreboding, the shadow over their realm seeming to grow darker with every moment.

Amara's eyes widened at the implication. Her voice, when she spoke, was resolute. "Then we must do the best with what we have," she declared, her tone unwavering. "The light of Kadona may cast away the shadows that cloud our path. We cannot allow the darkness to spread unchecked."

Kimras met her determined gaze, his own resolve hardening. "Agreed," he said firmly. "Without the light of truth to guide us, we are but leaves adrift in the winds of darkness. We'll use whatever knowledge we can glean from these scrolls to uncover the truth and put an end to this threat." His voice carried the weight of his duty, a reflection of the unyielding determination in his heart.

With their course of action clear, they turned their attention back to the scrolls, their minds focused and their spirits united. Each fragment they deciphered brought them closer to understanding the ancient texts and the secrets they guarded. A sense of urgency propelled them forward, their quest gaining momentum with every discovery.

As Kimras and Amara worked, a nagging feeling tugged at Kimras's thoughts. He stared at the scrolls, a hint of recognition stirring within him. "These scrolls," he said slowly, his tone contemplative, "seem to contain knowledge Azeron would have been interested in." The thought settled uneasily in his mind, the implications both troubling and perplexing.

Amara looked up, confusion furrowing her brow. "But how could he have brought darkness to Vacari?" she wondered aloud, skepticism lacing her voice. The idea of such betrayal felt too enormous to accept.

Kimras sighed, his gaze returning to the cryptic symbols on the parchment. "I'm not entirely sure," he admitted, frustration creeping into his tone. "There are still parts of these scrolls I haven't deciphered. And we can't forget—we don't have them all." His words were heavy with the weight of their incomplete knowledge, the missing pieces of the puzzle taunting him as he searched for clarity.

Together, they delved deeper, driven by a shared determination to uncover the truth. The mysteries of the scrolls loomed large before them, but Kimras and Amara pressed on, their bond as guardians of Vacari unshakable. The road ahead would be fraught with challenges, but they knew that only by confronting the darkness with courage and resolve could they hope to protect their realm from the shadows closing in.

Amara nodded in understanding, a flicker of determination lighting her eyes. "Right," she said resolutely. "Let's focus on what we do have and see what we can uncover." Her resolve was unwavering, driven by her unyielding commitment to protect Vacari from the encroaching darkness.

With renewed purpose, Kimras and Amara returned to the scrolls. Their focus was sharp, their determination unshaken. Though the road ahead was fraught with uncertainty, they pressed on, guided by the light of Kadona and their shared mission to safeguard their realm. Together, they would uncover the truth and confront whatever forces threatened to unravel their world.

As Amara combed through the ancient texts with meticulous care, her sharp eyes caught something that made her pause. "Kimras," she called out, her voice tinged with intrigue. "Your name is mentioned in this section." Her heart quickened, the implications of her discovery sending a shiver down her spine.

Kimras leaned in, his curiosity instantly piqued. "Let me see," he said, moving closer to examine the scroll. His gaze followed Amara's finger as she pointed to the passage. His brow furrowed as he read the words, his name standing out starkly amid the faded symbols. He noted with growing unease the mention of other noble dragons alongside his own.

"This doesn't make sense," Kimras muttered, his voice heavy with disbelief. "Why would the noble dragons be mentioned here? There's no way they would have assisted in ushering in the darkness." His words hung in the air, laden with the weight of his confusion and the sheer impossibility of what the scroll seemed to suggest.

Amara nodded slowly, her mind racing with possibilities. "Do you think there could have been a plan to eliminate them?" she ventured, her voice hushed with uncertainty. Her thoughts spiraled, the implications of such a scheme sending a chill through her. "Perhaps the darkness sought to target the noble dragons, knowing they would be the greatest threat to its rise."

Kimras's jaw tightened, his thoughts swirling as he considered Amara's suggestion. The idea of betrayal—or a plot to destroy the noble dragons—was almost too much to bear. Yet, the evidence before them could not be ignored. The scrolls hinted at a deeper, more insidious plan, one that could have far-reaching consequences for all of Vacari.

"We need to find out more," Kimras said firmly, his voice steady despite the turmoil within him. "If there was a plan to target the noble dragons, we need to uncover it—and stop it before it can do any more harm."

Amara nodded, her resolve matching his. "Agreed," she said. "If this darkness is trying to manipulate history or turn us against each other, we need to bring it to light. We can't allow it to divide us—not when so much is at stake."

With a shared sense of urgency, they returned to the scrolls, their determination renewed. The mention of Kimras's name, and the implications of the noble dragons' involvement, hung over them like a shadow. Yet, they pressed on, driven by the belief that together, they could unravel the mysteries before them and uncover the truth hidden within the ancient texts.

Kimras considered Amara's words carefully, the weight of their implications pressing heavily on him. "It's a possibility," he conceded, his tone troubled. "But we need more information to understand the full extent of what transpired." His mind churned with questions, each one deepening the mystery surrounding the scrolls.

With a shared sense of determination, Kimras and Amara turned their attention back to the scrolls. Their thoughts were ablaze with questions, their resolve steeled by the urgency of their task. The cryptic texts held answers they desperately needed, and the weight of their mission drove them forward. Every revelation brought them closer to the truth, yet it felt like the shadows surrounding Vacari grew darker with each step.

As they painstakingly worked through the ancient texts, their brows furrowed with concentration and concern. They unearthed passages foretelling ominous portents and dark machinations—threads of a larger, insidious plan. The darkness that had consumed Purplefire Woods, devastating as it was, now appeared to be only a fragment of a far greater threat. The realization sent a chill down Kimras's spine, the scope of the danger surpassing anything they had imagined.

Among the faded ink and cryptic symbols, they uncovered unsettling hints of a sinister plot to unleash darkness across Vacari. The texts spoke of an unknown entity orchestrating the chaos with a precision and malice that set them both on edge. What troubled them most was the revelation that the noble dragons were not just incidental victims—they were deliberately targeted for elimination. The notion struck at their very core, a chilling confirmation of the darkness's calculated intent.

"This goes beyond anything we've encountered before," Kimras murmured, his voice edged with apprehension. "It's as if someone is orchestrating a plan to drown Vacari in darkness, and they're willing to go to unimaginable lengths to achieve it." His words hung in the air, heavy with the weight of his fears, the enormity of the threat pressing down on them both.

Amara nodded, her expression hardening with determination. "Then we have no choice," she said firmly. "We must unravel this plan and stop it before it's too late. Whatever this entity is, it's manipulating events to sow destruction—and it must be stopped."

Kimras met her resolute gaze, drawing strength from her unwavering resolve. Together, they would face whatever lay ahead. Though the road before them was shadowed by uncertainty and danger, they knew they had no choice but to press on. The fate of Vacari depended on their ability to uncover the truth and confront the darkness threatening their realm.

Amara nodded grimly, her eyes reflecting the gravity of their discovery. "But why target the noble dragons?" she wondered aloud, her voice tinged with unease. The motivations behind such a plan eluded her, and the implications of their findings sent a shiver down her spine.

Kimras shook his head, his thoughts racing with possibilities. "I'm not sure," he admitted, his tone grave. "But we must tread carefully. Whoever is behind this poses a grave threat to Vacari and everyone within its borders." His resolve hardened, the weight of his duty pressing heavily on him as he prepared for the battle that lay ahead.

As they continued to pore over the ancient texts, the sense of unease deepened. The scrolls hinted at a carefully orchestrated plot, but the true scope and intentions of their adversary remained shrouded in darkness. Despite the looming threat, Kimras and Amara clung to their determination to uncover the truth and thwart the sinister plans endangering their realm. For in the heart of darkness, hope still flickered—a beacon guiding them through the shadows toward the light.

"It feels like we're facing an enemy we can't see," Kimras mused, his voice heavy with concern. "I fear for the safety of Vacari if we can't uncover the truth behind this dark plot." The idea of an unseen enemy lurking in the shadows chilled him, the weight of the unknown pressing down like a storm cloud.

Amara nodded, her expression mirroring his apprehension. "The light of Kadona may cast away the shadows that cloud our path," she suggested, her voice holding a glimmer of hope. "As the goddess of light and protector of the Eladrin Elves, she may offer insights that could aid us in our quest." The thought of seeking guidance from Kadona provided a sliver of optimism, a ray of light piercing the darkness surrounding them.

Kimras considered her words for a moment, the gravity of their situation pulling at him. Finally, he nodded. "It's worth a try," he agreed. "Let's gather the scrolls and make our way to E'vahano to seek counsel from Kadona." His voice was firm, the decision to seek the goddess's guidance infusing him with a renewed sense of purpose.

With their course set, Kimras and Amara prepared to leave the Hidden Isles. Their minds were fixed on the journey ahead and the hope that Kadona might provide the answers they sought. Yet, as they readied themselves, an unspoken tension lingered between them, the awareness that their path would not be without peril.

Little did they know, their journey would lead them into the heart of a conflict far greater than they could have anticipated—a struggle that threatened to engulf Vacari in darkness once more. The path ahead was uncertain, but their resolve was unwavering. Together, they would face whatever trials lay before them, driven by the belief that the light of truth and unity could withstand even the deepest shadows.

Chapter 17
Seeking Guidance

Kimras and Amara prepared to depart from the Hidden Isles, scrolls securely in hand, their thoughts fixed on their next destination—E'vahano, the realm of Kadona, goddess of light and protector of the Eladrin Elves. Their mission weighed heavily on their minds, the urgency of their task spurring them onward.

Before they could embark, a young gold dragon burst into the tower, her shimmering scales betraying her agitation. The soft glow of the chamber seemed to dim in the face of her distress.

Kimras and Amara turned toward her, concern etching their features. "What's wrong, young one?" Kimras asked, his voice gentle yet firm, offering a steadiness that seemed to calm her slightly.

The young dragon took a shaky breath before speaking, urgency lacing her tone. "Kimras, Amara, the citizens of Goldmoor are uneasy," she began.

"Zylron and Glaceria have been flying on the outskirts of the city, and their presence is causing widespread fear."

Kimras and Amara exchanged a meaningful glance, their silent communication conveying a shared unease. Zylron and Glaceria were known for their calculating natures—they rarely acted without purpose. Their behavior suggested something more than mere intimidation.

"Have there been any signs of aggression or attacks?" Kimras inquired, his expression tightening as he considered the potential implications.

The young dragon shook her head, worry shining in her eyes. "No attacks, no damage," she replied quickly. "But the citizens fear it's only a matter of time. Zylron and Glaceria wouldn't be there without reason."

Kimras's jaw tightened as his thoughts raced. "Return to Goldmoor and keep watch," he instructed, his voice firm with authority. "Under no circumstances are you to engage with Zylron or Glaceria first. Your priority is to protect the city if they attack."

The young dragon hesitated only briefly before nodding, her resolve hardening under Kimras's steady gaze. "I understand," she said, determination replacing her fear. Without another word, she turned and leapt into the air, her golden wings slicing through the sky as she sped back to Goldmoor.

As her silhouette disappeared into the horizon, Kimras and Amara stood in silence for a moment, their unease palpable.

"It's unlike Zylron and Glaceria to hold back unless someone else is pulling the strings," Kimras murmured, his voice heavy with thought. His mind churned with possibilities, each more troubling than the last.

Amara nodded, her expression mirroring his concern. "It would have to be someone powerful enough to command their loyalty or restrain their impulses," she said quietly. "But who?"

Kimras's gaze darkened. "Whoever it is, they pose a significant threat—not just to Goldmoor, but to all of Vacari," he stated gravely. "But for now, our priority is to seek Kadona's counsel. Her guidance might help us understand what we're dealing with."

Amara agreed, her expression firm. "You're right. Let us not delay any longer. We must make haste to E'vahano."

With determination blazing in their eyes, Kimras and Amara spread their wings and took flight, soaring toward the realm of Kadona. The wind rushed around them, carrying them closer to their destination, but the unease clung to them like a shadow—a chilling reminder of the growing threat looming over Vacari.

As Kimras and Amara made their way toward E'vahano, their flight was intercepted by the graceful forms of Talleoss and Silvara, two noble silver dragons observing from afar. With fluid movements, the pair descended, their shimmering silver scales glinting in the sunlight as they transformed midair and soared to meet them.

"Kimras, Amara, what brings you to E'vahano?" Talleoss inquired, his voice rich with warmth and curiosity.

Kimras exchanged a glance with Amara before responding, his tone earnest. "We seek counsel from Kadona," he explained. "We hope she can offer insights into troubling matters that have arisen in Vacari."

Talleoss nodded, his expression turning serious as he processed their words. "Of course. You are welcome to accompany us to The Sacred Grove," he said, gesturing toward the heart of E'vahano, where Kadona was often found.

With Talleoss and Silvara leading the way, Kimras and Amara followed, their steps light as they moved through the verdant greenery of the grove. The air was alive with the soft hum of nature, the serenity of the grove enveloping them in its embrace. As they approached the grove's center, their eyes fell upon Kadona, her radiant figure bathed in the gentle glow of the surrounding foliage.

"Kadona," Talleoss called, his voice filled with reverence. "Kimras and Amara have come seeking your guidance."

Kadona turned to them, her presence exuding tranquility and wisdom, drawing the attention of all who stood before her. Kimras stepped forward, holding the scrolls with care, his expression earnest as he spoke.

"These scrolls were found in the cave where Azeron was imprisoned," he began, his voice steady despite the gravity of his words.

A flicker of concern crossed Talleoss's features at the mention of Azeron, a silent reminder of the darkness that had once threatened Vacari. Kadona accepted the scrolls with a gentle nod, her gaze sharp as she began to examine them.

"And are these all the scrolls?" she asked, her tone grave as her eyes lifted to meet Kimras and Amara.

Amara shook her head sadly, her disappointment evident. "We believe these were dropped," she explained, her voice tinged with regret.

Kimras added, his brow furrowing with concern. "There is mention in the scrolls of a threat against the noble dragons," he said. His words hung in the air, heavy with the weight of the implications.

Kadona's expression grew solemn as she absorbed their words. The light surrounding her seemed to pulse faintly as her thoughts turned inward. "Give me some time to go over these scrolls," she said, her voice calm but resolute.

As Kadona retreated to study the scrolls, Talleoss and Silvara stepped forward, their gestures comforting. "Come," Talleoss said gently, "let us take you to the garden prepared by the Eladrin. It's where we often rest in our dragon forms—it will provide you peace while you await Kadona's guidance."

Kimras and Amara exchanged grateful glances before following the silver dragons. The garden was a haven of tranquility, filled with vibrant blooms and soft moss-covered stones. Here, the Eladrin had created a space where the silver dragons could find solace. As Kimras and Amara settled amidst the serene surroundings, they allowed themselves a moment of quiet, their minds lingering on the looming threat and the hope that Kadona's wisdom would soon illuminate the path forward.

As Kimras and Amara rested in the tranquil garden, soaking in the serene atmosphere, their peaceful moment was interrupted by the approach of familiar figures. Keisha and Ong, their close friends from E'vahano, walked toward them with warm smiles, their presence a welcome comfort amidst the uncertainty.

"It's good to see you," Keisha greeted warmly, her eyes alight with genuine affection.

Kimras returned her smile, though it was tinged with a hint of worry. "Likewise," he replied, his voice carrying gratitude for their presence. In this moment, their friendship felt like an anchor in the storm.

Ong, ever perceptive, noticed the subdued atmosphere and furrowed his brow. "Is something wrong?" he asked, his gaze shifting between Kimras and Amara with concern.

Kimras sighed softly, his golden eyes clouded with thought. "We found some ancient scrolls," he began, uncertainty threading through his voice. "We're not sure if they belonged to Azeron, but they mention a threat against the noble dragons."

Keisha's eyes widened in surprise, her expression growing serious. "That sounds grave," she remarked, her voice reflecting the weight of the revelation.

Kimras nodded solemnly, his gaze steady as he met hers. "It is," he affirmed. "That's why we brought them to Kadona. We're hoping she can help us understand the implications."

Keisha and Ong exchanged a meaningful glance, the silent communication of trusted allies. Turning back to Kimras and Amara, Keisha's voice was soft but resolute. "We're here for you," she said, her words carrying a promise of unwavering support.

Amara's lips curved into a grateful smile, her heart warmed by their steadfast friendship. "Thank you," she said sincerely, her voice reflecting the depth of her appreciation. In moments like these, their bond was a light against the encroaching darkness.

Meanwhile, Kadona, seated within the heart of The Sacred Grove, examined the scrolls with a contemplative expression. Recognizing the need for additional insight, she decided to call upon Lysander. With a soft yet commanding tone, she spoke into the ethereal currents, "Lysander, I need your counsel on something important."

Moments later, Lysander appeared, his expression marked by curiosity and concern. He inclined his head respectfully toward Kadona as she gestured for him to come closer, motioning to the scrolls spread before her.

"There is something we need to revisit," Kadona began, her tone laced with unease. She pointed to a passage within the scrolls, and Lysander leaned in, his features darkening as he read the text. The tension between them was palpable, the weight of the discovery hanging heavily in the air.

Kadona's voice softened, her eyes meeting Lysander's with a solemn intensity. "Do you remember, after Vuarus's fall, the figure—shrouded in darkness—who was furious when the noble dragons intervened to save Keisha?"

Lysander's expression tightened as the memory resurfaced. "I remember," he replied gravely. "That shadowed figure... they were seething with rage, though they remained hidden. They blamed the noble dragons for ruining their plans and somehow connected that failure to Vuarus's death."

Kadona nodded, her brow furrowed with deep thought. "I've been considering that this same figure could be behind the current threats. Their grudge against the noble dragons was unmistakable. They may be fueling these attacks."

Lysander's gaze sharpened as he recalled the intensity of that moment. "Yes," he agreed. "Their presence was powerful. Even though they stayed in the shadows, their fury was palpable. It was clear they wanted to remain anonymous, but their hatred ran deep."

After a moment of heavy silence, Kadona decided. "We need to share this with Kimras and Amara," she said firmly. Rising, she gestured to

Lysander to accompany her. Together, they left The Sacred Grove, their strides purposeful as they headed toward the garden where the dragons awaited.

"Friends," Kadona began, her voice resonating with the weight of their shared purpose, "we have made a significant discovery regarding the threat against the noble dragons and Vacari itself."

Kimras raised his head attentively, his golden eyes fixed on Kadona as she spoke. Beside him, Amara's reassuring smile faded into an expression of solemn resolve, her violet scales shimmering in the sunlight filtering through the canopy.

Kadona's tone was grave but clear as she continued. "After closely reviewing the scrolls and reflecting on past events, we believe there may be a figure from Vuarus's time—someone who has harbored a deep grudge against the noble dragons ever since they intervened to rescue Keisha. This individual was shrouded in darkness, their identity unknown, but their fury was unmistakable."

Standing beside Kadona, Lysander added, "We recall this shadowed figure's presence after Vuarus's downfall. Their anger at the noble dragons, particularly after the failure of their plans, was palpable. We suspect they have been waiting, biding their time, and orchestrating attacks from the shadows. Their power appears to be tied to the Abyss, which only deepens the danger."

Kimras furrowed his brow, his expression thoughtful. "If this figure has been plotting for so long, then they are far more dangerous than we anticipated," he said, his voice heavy with concern.

Kadona nodded in agreement. "We have learned that someone is orchestrating this threat, and their grudge against the noble dragons is deeply personal," she explained, her tone resolute. "The noble dragons and their allies are already heeding the call to return to Vacari, but more must be done."

Kimras's expression brightened slightly as he confirmed her statement. "Radiantus has informed me that the noble dragons and our allies are on their way," he said, his voice steady with resolve. "But he advises caution. This information must remain confidential, as someone stronger is pulling the strings behind the scenes."

Amara's somber nod reflected the group's growing unease. "We have to be cautious," she said. "This adversary has had years to plan, and their hatred for the noble dragons is deeply personal. They will stop at nothing to achieve their goal."

Kadona's gaze swept across the group, her determination unshaken. "We must remain vigilant. This figure's connection to the Abyss makes them a formidable foe, and their endgame is tied to the darkness that threatens Vacari. We need to be ready for whatever comes next."

She turned her attention to Kimras, her voice deliberate. "Kimras, I suggest you send word to the other dragons in Vacari about the threat we face. While Radiantus has already informed the noble dragons of his return, the others must also be aware of what is at stake. The strength of Vacari lies in its unity."

Kimras straightened, the gravity of Kadona's words reflected in his glowing golden eyes. "You're right," he said firmly. "The more prepared we are, the better chance we have to stand against this darkness. I'll see to it immediately."

With their hearts and minds united, the group understood the severity of the situation. They had uncovered a critical piece of the puzzle, yet the shadow of the unknown still loomed large. Even so, their resolve was clear—they would face the challenges ahead together, bolstered by Kadona's wisdom and their shared determination to protect Vacari.

Ong, ever curious, turned to Keisha with a thoughtful question. "Keisha, what did Kadona and Kimras mean about more noble dragons? And who is Radiantus?"

Keisha smiled warmly, her appreciation for Ong's inquisitiveness shining through. "Radiantus is the Platinum Dragon," she explained. "He is the leader of all noble dragons, including the gem dragons who align with us. There are indeed more noble, and gem dragons scattered across the world, not all of whom remain in Vacari."

She glanced at Kimras, a silent cue for him to elaborate. Understanding the importance of providing context, Kimras nodded and began. "Centuries ago, after fierce battles against the dark forces, some of our kin withdrew to the Hidden Isles. It was a time for safety and reflection, a sanctuary where they could recover and prepare for future threats. Others chose a different path—they ventured out into the world to monitor the dark dragons who had scattered beyond Vacari."

Ong listened intently, his brows furrowing as he absorbed this latest information. "So, the noble dragons spread out to ensure the safety of the world and to keep an eye on the dark dragons," he summarized thoughtfully.

"Exactly," Kimras confirmed. "It was a strategic decision. By spreading out, we not only protected our realm but also ensured the dark dragons could not regroup and launch another major assault. Radiantus has always ensured that we remain vigilant, even while apart."

Keisha's smile widened, pride shining in her expression. "Under Radiantus's leadership, the noble dragons have always been ready to answer the call to return to Vacari when the need arises."

Ong fell silent for a moment, his gaze distant as he processed their words. Then, his expression shifted, his features hardening with determination. "Then we need to make sure we're ready to support them when they do," he declared, his voice resolute.

Kimras and Amara exchanged approving glances, their hearts buoyed by Ong's steadfast resolve. "We will face this threat together," Amara said, her voice filled with quiet strength.

The weight of the situation hung heavily over the gathering, a stark reminder of the challenges ahead. Yet, amidst the gravity of their task, a sense of unity and shared purpose prevailed. They would stand together, unwavering in their resolve to protect Vacari and thwart the forces of darkness threatening to engulf their realm.

Lysander's words lingered, heavy with the weight of history and betrayal. Keisha's eyes widened as the pieces of the puzzle began to align in her mind. Concern and determination etched themselves on her features as she glanced at her friends, then back to Kadona and Lysander.

Her thoughts turned to the cryptic scrolls and the ominous threat they foretold. A deep unease settled in her chest as she contemplated the connection between the mysterious adversary and herself. Was she an unwitting pawn in a larger game, manipulated by forces beyond her comprehension? The thought sent a shiver down her spine, and she tightened her grip on Ong's hand, seeking comfort in his steady presence.

"So, whoever is behind this threat has ties to the Abyss," Keisha surmised, her voice trembling with unease. "And they were connected to Vuarus—Azeron—and to me."

Lysander nodded gravely. "Indeed. Their connection to the Abyss points to a dark and sinister influence," he affirmed. "Their fury at the noble dragons for intervening in your rescue suggests a personal vendetta that spans years."

Keisha's grip on Ong's hand tightened further as the weight of Lysander's words sank in. The realization that she was entangled in the machinations of such a powerful adversary unsettled her deeply. Her thoughts raced, overwhelmed by what this could mean for her and those she cared about.

"But why target the noble dragons?" Ong asked, his voice filled with genuine concern. "What do they stand to gain from their downfall?"

Kadona's gaze softened, her radiant presence exuding reassurance as she regarded the young couple. "That is a question we are still working to answer," she admitted. "But rest assured, we will do everything in our power to uncover the truth and protect Vacari from this threat."

The group exchanged determined glances, their resolve solidifying as they turned their attention to the challenges ahead.

Keisha approached Kimras, her expression tinged with remorse as she looked up at him. "I'm sorry," she said softly, her voice carrying a hint of regret. "I never wanted my rescue to lead to such a threat."

Kimras's gaze softened, a reassuring smile touching his lips. "Keisha, you have nothing to apologize for," he said firmly. "Protecting you was the right thing to do, and we won't let this threat go unanswered."

Keisha's expression relaxed at his words, gratitude washing over her. She nodded, her trust in her dragon friend unwavering. "Thank you, Kimras," she murmured sincerely.

Ong stepped forward, his presence a steadfast support beside Keisha. "We're in this together," he declared, his voice resolute. "If you need our help, just say the word."

Kimras nodded appreciatively, a sense of camaraderie strengthening the bond between them. "Thank you, Ong," he said sincerely. "Your support means more than you know."

The group stood united, their shared understanding and resolve a bulwark against the looming darkness threatening their realm.

Kadona turned her attention to Kimras and Amara, her expression growing serious. "Have you checked the seal on the Abyss?" she asked, her voice heavy with concern.

Kimras and Amara exchanged a quick glance before Amara answered. "Yes, we checked the seal," she affirmed, her tone certain. "There's no sign of any breaks or disturbances."

Lysander furrowed his brow in thought, his expression darkening. "The individual orchestrating this threat must have a deep understanding of the noble dragons' significance and power," he said gravely. "Their connection to the Abyss and the dark forces makes them a formidable adversary."

The weight of his words settled over the group, casting a heavy silence. Each member grappled with the implications, their thoughts turning to the shadowy figure whose intentions remained shrouded in mystery.

Keisha broke the silence, her voice steady despite the unease in her gaze. "Do you think the reason the noble dragons are being targeted is because this figure knows that unless the noble dragons are removed, their plans will fail?"

Lysander nodded thoughtfully, his gaze intense. "That seems likely. The noble dragons have always been a shield against darkness, their unity and power acting as a counterbalance to rising threats. Without them, Vacari would be left exposed and vulnerable."

Kimras and Amara exchanged concerned glances, their unease growing. "Zylron and Glaceria have been spotted on the outskirts of Goldmoor," Kimras said, his voice edged with worry. "They haven't made any moves yet, but their presence alone is enough to cause fear. We need to return to Goldmoor and Purplefire Woods to ensure their safety."

Kadona's expression grew solemn, her radiant presence tempered by the gravity of the moment. "Remain vigilant," she urged, her tone steady yet heavy with concern. "I will focus on uncovering more about this figure and the dark powers they wield. We must understand their plans before they strike."

With a shared nod, Kimras and Amara bid farewell to Kadona and Lysander. With a powerful beat of their wings, they ascended into the skies, their forms cutting through the air with purpose as they soared toward their destinations. The path ahead was fraught with danger, but their resolve was unyielding. Protecting Vacari and the noble dragons was not just their duty—it was their purpose.

Chapter 18
Veiled Shadows

As the sun dipped below the horizon, casting long shadows across the city of Flameford, the transformation wrought upon its once-bustling streets was unmistakable. Where vibrant hues of life had once flourished, a pervasive aura of darkness now lingered—a testament to the dominion of the shadows.

The city had been reborn, redesigned to cater to the dark dragons who now called it home. Twisted spires and jagged rooftops loomed ominously against the night sky, casting eerie silhouettes that spoke of ancient power and hidden menace. Dark alleyways wound through the city's depths, shrouded in shadows and whispered secrets.

Amidst this somber landscape, only one vestige of the old city remained—the towering edifice of the central tower. Rising defiantly above the surrounding darkness, it stood as a silent sentinel, a beacon of the city's past in a world consumed by shadow.

Within the tower's walls, Lyra and her companions continued their work, their faces illuminated by flickering candlelight as they pored over ancient scrolls. Each line of text held the promise of long-forgotten knowledge, a glimpse into the mysteries of the past and the secrets of the darkness. The air in the chamber was heavy, not just with age but with the weight of their ambitions.

Their intentions were veiled in shadows as dark as their ultimate goal. With every word deciphered, they edged closer to extinguishing the light that had long been the bane of their kind—a task that had eluded the Druchii for centuries. This was more than a quest for power; it was a bid for dominance over a world they sought to remake in their image.

Guided by the enigmatic figure who had joined their cause, they sought to master the darkness in ways their ancestors had only dreamed of. The whispers of the shadows seemed to grow louder with each discovery, urging them onward and promising the sweet taste of victory. Despite the perils ahead, their resolve hardened, fueled by visions of a future where darkness reigned supreme.

Quellan's voice pierced the chamber, laden with uncertainty. His sharp gaze shifted toward the mysterious figure at the center of their gathering.

"Are you certain the dark dragons will unite under a common banner?" he asked, his brow furrowed, and his tone tinged with skepticism.

The mysterious figure smirked, a subtle curl of their lips betraying confidence born of authority. "Cease your worrying, young Quellan," they replied, their voice calm yet commanding. "The dark dragons will heed our call. They will do as they are commanded."

Quellan's eyes narrowed as he absorbed the cryptic words. "But who holds the reins of command?" he pressed, curiosity gnawing at him like a restless ember.

A low chuckle escaped the figure as they leaned forward, their presence imposing in the dim light. "While they may rally under Zylron's banner, it is I who truly hold sway over them," they declared, their voice carrying a chilling finality.

Quellan's expression darkened as he processed the revelation. Without another word, he turned and strode toward the exit, his mind weighed down by newfound knowledge. The mention of his sister's involvement only deepened his unease.

Lyra's gaze lingered on the doorway where her brother had disappeared, a flicker of concern passing through her eyes before she redirected her focus. Her voice broke the silence, questioning the bold claim.

"The only ones I ever saw controlling the dark dragons were Phoenix and Vuarus," she began, her tone edged with skepticism. "Are you truly more powerful than they were?"

The mysterious figure met her gaze with a knowing smirk, exuding an unsettling aura of confidence. "You will see," they replied cryptically. "But for now, let us focus on the task at hand."

The tension in the room thickened as the shadows seemed to draw closer, the faint whispers almost audible now. The promise of darkness loomed large, but so did the questions that remained unanswered.

With a subtle gesture, the mysterious figure motioned toward the scattered scrolls before them, their gaze glinting with a sinister light. Lyra swallowed her rising unease and stepped closer, her mind swirling with unspoken questions.

As her eyes scanned the scrolls, a passage caught her attention. It mentioned the noble dragons, but the writing abruptly stopped, the rest conspicuously absent. Frowning, she turned to the figure. "The mention of the noble dragons... it's here, but the rest is missing."

The figure's expression darkened. "These scrolls should hold the key to dealing with the noble dragons, ensuring they never interfere again," they replied, their voice edged with urgency. "But we must decipher what's missing before the noble dragons call upon forces beyond Vacari."

Lyra's brow furrowed, her curiosity piqued. "What do you mean? Are there more dragons?"

A sly smile crept across the figure's face. "More than you can imagine," they murmured, their words hanging in the air like a foreboding shadow.

Lyra's thoughts turned to the noble dragons who had intervened during Keisha's rescue. "I know about the dragons who helped Keisha. Are you saying there are others?"

The figure's smile widened, their demeanor unshaken. "Indeed, there are many more. The noble dragons have allies scattered across realms, making them a far greater force than you realize. Their presence complicates our plans."

Lyra pressed her lips together, skepticism mingling with curiosity. "You realize my brother and I are Druchii, right?"

"I know," came the enigmatic response, accompanied by a knowing smile that only deepened her unease.

She leaned over the scrolls again, her eyes scanning rapidly. "This suggests a strategy to target the noble dragons' strongholds," she mused aloud. "But they don't have special areas under their protection anymore, do they?"

The figure chuckled softly, the sound carrying an edge of condescension. "It seems you've missed a crucial development. The noble dragons have returned to Vacari, and they've established new sanctuaries—Goldmoor is overseen by the gold dragons."

Lyra's eyes widened in disbelief. "I had no idea."

The figure's laughter echoed in the chamber, low and mocking. "Perhaps you should pay more attention."

Lyra's mind raced as she processed the revelation. "So, the Copper Dragons protect Emberwoods?" she asked, surprise lacing her voice.

"Indeed. The maze still stands because of their protection," the figure confirmed with a slight nod.

Lyra's frown deepened, the pieces slowly falling into place. "Then targeting these locations makes sense after all," she said, a flare of determination lighting her eyes.

The figure's expression shifted to one of satisfaction. "Precisely. Goldmoor and Purplefire Woods are ideal starting points. Once the other dark dragons arrive, we can expand our reach."

Their shared resolve thickened the tension in the room as shadows seemed to shift around them, responding to the growing ambition in their hearts. The battle for dominance was no longer a distant vision; it was a storm gathering on the horizon, ready to engulf them all.

A smirk tugged at Lyra's lips. "Poor Keisha," she quipped.

At the mention of the name, an unmistakable flicker of anger darkened the mysterious figure's face. Their eyes narrowed, and for a moment, their calm demeanor slipped, revealing a sinister edge beneath. The shadow of fury passed as quickly as it appeared, replaced by their usual air of control.

The figure raised an eyebrow, their curiosity tempered by the remnants of that fleeting anger. "Keisha? What is her connection?" they asked, their tone deceptively smooth.

Lyra's smirk widened, her tone sharp with amusement. "She has ties to the forests."

A knowing smile crept across the figure's face, though their earlier flash of rage lingered faintly in their gaze. "Well, it seems you knew something I didn't," they said, their voice now laced with intrigue.

Leaning forward, a gleam of mischief in her eyes, Lyra spoke with growing excitement. "What if we stage the attacks in phases? Keep the noble dragons on edge, never knowing when or where the next strike will come."

The mysterious figure nodded slowly, their expression calculating. "A clever plan. It would leave them vulnerable."

Their smile darkened as they continued, their voice dropping to a menacing undertone. "And when they are weary, we strike—not at their fortifications, but at the dragons themselves."

Lyra's excitement mirrored the figure's as she nodded in agreement. "It's risky, but it could give us the advantage."

The figure's gaze hardened, their tone sharp and commanding. "Yes, but we must be cautious. Any misstep could expose us—and the consequences would be... dire."

The tension in the chamber deepened, their shared ambition thick with danger. Yet, in the flickering candlelight, the faint remnants of the figure's earlier anger at Keisha's name hinted at an unseen grudge, one that might yet shape their plans.

They paused, their voice low and deliberate as they added, Eliminating the gold dragons first is crucial, especially Kimras. While the amethyst dragons are the most powerful gem dragons, the gold dragons are the strongest in Vacari. Taking them out early will give us a significant edge," the figure said, their voice low and deliberate. "We must act swiftly, before the Platinum Dragons arrive and tip the scales further in the noble dragons' favor."

Lyra blinked, her curiosity overtaking her expression. "Platinum dragons?" she asked, her tone laced with both intrigue and uncertainty.

The mysterious figure sighed, their patience wearing thin. "Pay attention, Lyra. I have told you, there are more noble dragons than you know. The platinum dragons are among their ranks."

Their eyes narrowed dangerously, their tone sharp and cutting. "Do not act like that fool, Phoenix Shadowwalker."

Lyra swallowed hard, the mention of Phoenix sending an involuntary chill through her. The weight of the figure's disdain was palpable, and she quickly redirected the conversation. "Once the noble dragons are gone, we move forward with the plan?"

The figure's smile twisted into something wicked and sinister, their aura exuding an air of dark triumph. "Yes. Once they are eliminated, we will open the gates to the Abyss and usher in an era of darkness like Vacari has never seen."

Lyra turned back to the scrolls, her mind racing with possibilities, the weight of the figure's plan pressing heavily upon her. Behind her, the mysterious figure spun on their heel and stormed out, their footsteps echoing through the darkened corridors of the tower. The air seemed heavier in their absence, as if the shadows themselves carried their malice.

Stepping into the cool night air, the figure paused to gaze at the sprawling city below. The twisted spires of Flameford loomed like sentinels in the dark, a stark reminder of their ambition. Their thoughts churned with calculations and resolve, the first pieces of their grand design falling into place. In the silent stillness of the night, only one thing was certain—Vacari would soon bow to the shadow.

Outside, the figure paused, their eyes fixed on the distant horizon, where the last traces of twilight faded into night. "I will seek vengeance for Azeron," they whispered, their voice trembling with a potent mixture of anger and grief. "Why did Azeron ever trust Phoenix? It cost him everything. I was the one who served Azeron when he was sealed away for those years, but his leniency toward that reckless fool led to his downfall."

Their fists clenched at their sides, and their eyes gleamed with malice as they stared into the encroaching shadows. "The noble dragons disrupted the balance... intervened where they were not wanted. If they had stayed out of our affairs, Keisha would have been sacrificed as planned. She would not be causing us trouble now. And Azeron—" their voice wavered momentarily before hardening again, "Azeron would still be alive."

The weight of that loss burned like fire in their chest, fueling the simmering rage in their voice. "Their meddling has cost us dearly. But they will not escape retribution."

A sneer curled their lips as they turned their thoughts to the next phase of their plan. "Perhaps it's time to bring in forces from outside Vacari," they mused, their voice laced with chilling resolve. "Dark dragons far more powerful than those within this realm. Dragons who will follow my command, who understand the true meaning of power and vengeance."

The thought of summoning such creatures brought a twisted satisfaction to the figure. Their mind raced with possibilities, each more sinister than the last. These outsiders would be instrumental in achieving the vengeance they sought, tipping the scales irreversibly in their favor and crushing the noble dragons once and for all.

With a final, decisive nod, their resolve hardened. Turning sharply, the figure strode back toward the tower. The oppressive atmosphere seemed to thicken with their return, as if the very air bent under the weight of their renewed determination.

Lyra glanced up from the scrolls as the figure re-entered, sensing the shift immediately. The flickering candlelight cast stark shadows on the figure's face, their steely gaze colder and more foreboding than ever.

In that moment, Lyra felt it—an unspoken certainty that their mission had taken on a new, more dangerous dimension. This was no longer just a quest for dominance, but a campaign fueled by vengeance, a vendetta sharpened by the promise of summoning greater, more terrifying powers. The weight of it bore down on her, yet she could not suppress the flicker of anticipation that danced in her chest.

The figure's voice, low and commanding, broke the silence. "The time is near. Prepare yourself, Lyra. We have much to do, and no margin for failure."

DRAGONS OF VACARI

Chapter 19
Skybound Warrior: Ong's Journey

In the serene embrace of E'vahona, the Eladrin city nestled within the verdant forests of Vacari, Keisha and Ong found solace in the cozy confines of their home. Sunlight filtered through the canopy above, casting dappled patterns of light and shadow along the winding pathways and tranquil glades surrounding their dwelling. Despite the tranquility, Keisha's eyes shone with determination, her voice filled with both resolve and concern as she spoke.

"Ong, I believe we should go to Purplefire Woods and Goldmoor to assist Kimras and Amara. Considering the threat that arose from my rescue, it's the least we can do." Beneath her calm tone lay a sense of urgency, the weight of responsibility heavy on her heart.

Ong met her gaze, his expression was solemn yet resolved. He understood the worry beneath her composed exterior, reflecting the same concerns stirring within him. "I agree, Keisha. We cannot stand idly by while our friends face danger. We must help." His voice carried conviction, though deep inside, a pang of fear gripped him. He had almost lost her once—could he protect her this time?

With a shared sense of purpose, Keisha and Ong sought out Lord Karrenen, the patriarch of their household. As they explained their intentions, Lord Karrenen listened intently, his brow furrowed with concern.

"Keisha, Ong, I understand your desire to help, but I must caution you to be careful. The danger is real, and the thought of losing either of you is unbearable."

Ong stepped forward, his stance protective. "Lord Karrenen, I will keep Keisha safe. We can't let fear hold us back when our friends are in need."

His tone softened as he turned to Keisha. "I won't let anything happen to you again," he whispered, pulling her close, his arms tightening around her as if the mere act of holding her could shield her from the threats ahead. "We'll face whatever comes together."

Keisha's heart swelled with gratitude and reassurance as she leaned into Ong's embrace, drawing strength from his unwavering presence. Beneath her calm exterior, however, fear gnawed at her. The road ahead held dangers they could not foresee, but with Ong by her side, she was ready to face them head-on.

Lord Karrenen, the esteemed leader of the Eladrin Council and a powerful mage in his own right, nodded, his expression softening with paternal affection. "Very well, my children. If you are resolved, then go with my blessing. But I urge you to be cautious."

With his blessing, Keisha and Ong began their preparations. Ong saddled Thunder, their loyal black horse with a steady, unshakable demeanor, while Keisha called forth Pumpkin, her majestic panther companion whose golden eyes gleamed with intelligence. Together, they set off from E'vahona, determined to aid their friends.

As they journeyed along the winding trails toward Purplefire Woods and Goldmoor, the bond between husband and wife radiated a warmth that defied the chill of the evening air. The crisp scent of pine and earth filled Keisha's lungs, but despite the beauty surrounding them, her thoughts remained fixed on the task ahead. Worry for Kimras and Amara lingered in her mind, alongside a silent doubt—was she endangering Ong by asking him to join her?

Keisha, her ethereal beauty illuminated by twilight, cast a glance toward Ong. His steadfast gaze met hers, radiating unshakable resolve. In his eyes, she found solace and strength—a beacon of hope in dark times. Their love burned brightly, a flame that refused to waver, even as shadows threatened to close in.

"Pumpkin, do you sense anything?" Keisha whispered, her voice soft yet commanding.

The panther halted, her green eyes gleaming with silent determination. A low, rumbling purr escaped her throat, a quiet reassurance of her unwavering loyalty. She stood like a sentinel, her sharp senses scanning their surroundings for any sign of danger.

Ong tightened his grip on Keisha's hand, his touch a comforting anchor against the uncertainty pressing in around them. With a silent nod, he conveyed his resolve to stand by her, no matter the challenges they faced.

"We must stay vigilant," Ong murmured, his voice low but steady. "Our friends are counting on us, and together, we'll face whatever lies ahead."

Keisha smiled, her eyes reflecting a quiet confidence. In Ong's presence, she found the courage to confront the unknown. No matter what trials awaited them, she knew they would overcome them—together.

Their resolve firm, Keisha and Ong reached the outskirts of Purplefire Woods. The tranquil forest seemed to hold its breath in anticipation, its stillness broken only by the rustling of leaves in the cool breeze. Awaiting them was Amara, the noble Amethyst dragon, her majestic presence casting a formidable shadow over the forest floor. Her scales shimmered in hues of violet and indigo, each movement a reminder of her immense power and grace.

Ong's breath caught as he took in the sight of the dragon. Keisha chuckled softly, turning to him with a playful glint in her eye. "I think she wants you to learn to ride a dragon," she teased, her tone light yet filled with gentle encouragement.

Ong's expression shifted from surprise to incredulity as he shook his head adamantly. "No way," he protested, his voice carrying a hint of unease.

"I'm a warrior, not a rider." The very idea seemed ludicrous. How could he, a man trained for battle on the ground, command such a powerful creature?

But Keisha, ever persistent, was undeterred. Her determination was unwavering as she met Ong's gaze with a knowing smile. "Yes, and it will be on Amara," she insisted, her tone leaving no room for debate. "You've faced worse. It's time you learned, my love."

Amara tilted her massive head, her keen eyes gleaming with what could only be described as amusement. It was as if she shared Keisha's confidence, her imposing presence silently urging Ong to rise to the challenge.

Ong sighed, his warrior's instincts wrestling with the uncertainty of this new challenge. He had trained with swords and fought enemies face-to-face, but riding a dragon? It was a completely different battlefield. "Okay," he relented, his tone resigned. His gaze flickered toward Amara, wondering if he could truly master this new skill.

Keisha laughed softly. "That's the spirit," she quipped, her voice full of warmth. "Now let's get started before Amara loses her patience."

Amara nodded in agreement, sensing Ong's inner conflict but offering her silent support. With a graceful sweep of her wings, she motioned for him to approach. As Ong stepped forward to meet his next trial, he knew that even as a warrior, with Keisha and Pumpkin by his side, he would face this new challenge head-on.

His heart raced as Amara dipped into a sharp turn, the wind whipping against his face. His grip on the dragon's back tightened, his knuckles white from the strain. Every instinct as a warrior urged him to maintain control, to stand firm as he had been trained to do on the battlefield. But this was different—this was the sky, and the ground was a dizzying distance below.

"Focus on me," Amara's calm voice echoed in his mind. "Feel the rhythm of the air. Let go of your fear."

Ong clenched his jaw, forcing himself to take a deep breath, steadying the panic rising within him. The vastness of the sky felt alien, overwhelming. Yet, as his gaze flicked downward, he saw Keisha standing below, watching with unwavering trust in her eyes. That look of quiet belief sparked something in him, shifting his perspective. He realized this was not a battlefield to conquer with brute strength or sheer willpower. This was about trust—trust in Amara, trust in the wind, and trust in himself.

Amara banked into another smooth turn, and Ong relaxed his grip slightly, adjusting to the sensation of the wind and the movement of the dragon beneath him. Slowly, his fear began to ebb, replaced by a growing sense of awe.

"You're doing well," Amara encouraged, her voice carrying a note of approval.

Ong exhaled, releasing some of the tension from his body. "Maybe," he muttered, half to himself. "But don't go easy on me. I need to learn."

Amara chuckled, a deep rumble reverberating through her body. "Oh, I won't."

With that, she surged forward, her wings slicing through the air with newfound speed. The landscape blurred beneath them, and Ong's heart leaped again—this time, more from exhilaration than fear. The rhythm of the flight began to feel less foreign, the vastness of the sky transforming from a source of terror into an endless horizon of possibility.

"Focus on your breathing," Amara advised. "Feel the rhythm of my movements. We are one in the sky."

Ong struggled to steady his breath, synchronizing his body to Amara's movements. Each passing moment felt less like a battle and more like a partnership. He thought of Keisha, her unwavering belief in him, and let that strengthen his resolve. Drawing from her confidence, he adapted to the new sensations, his warrior instincts reshaping themselves to suit this new battlefield.

Amara leveled out, gliding smoothly through the sky. "Well done, Ong. The first step is always the hardest. Now, let's see how you handle a little more speed."

Before Ong could respond, Amara accelerated, the wind roaring past him with greater intensity. Ong leaned into the movement, feeling a rush of exhilaration as he let himself trust in the dragon beneath him. As they raced through the sky, a sense of unity began to form—a bond between rider and dragon.

For the first time, Ong felt a flicker of true confidence. He was not just a passenger anymore; he was part of something greater, something powerful. And with that realization, he knew this was only the beginning of his journey as a dragonrider.

Despite the moments of doubt that lingered, Ong gradually adapted to the sensation of riding Amara. The rush of wind and the sweeping vistas below were both thrilling and daunting. Yet, with Amara's steady presence beneath him and Keisha's trust grounding him, he felt ready to embrace this new chapter.

"You're doing well, Ong," Amara's voice echoed in his mind, steady and calm. "But there is much more to learn. Trust is the foundation of our bond, and you must trust me completely."

Ong nodded, determination etched on his face. "I trust you, Amara."

"Good," she replied. "Now, take it to the next level. Trust me with your life."

Before Ong could fully process her words, Amara executed a sharp roll. The world spun, and Ong felt himself slipping from her back. Panic flared in his chest as he desperately clung to her, his heart pounding in his ears.

"Let go, Ong," Amara's voice was calm, almost soothing. "Trust me."

Fear and instinct screamed at him to hold on, but Ong forced himself to listen. With a deep breath, he loosened his grip and allowed himself to fall.

The world blurred as he plummeted, wind roaring in his ears. A rush of fear surged through him, and for a moment, he felt utterly untethered, vulnerable. But amidst the terror, Amara's voice cut through, steady and unwavering. "I'm here, Ong. Trust."

Seconds stretched into what felt like an eternity. Just as panic threatened to overwhelm him, Amara swooped beneath him, catching him deftly on her back. The transition was seamless, her presence a steady anchor in the chaos.

"See? I will never let you fall," Amara said, pride evident in her voice. "You must trust that I will always be there for you."

Ong's breath came in ragged gasps, but he managed to nod. The fear had not entirely vanished, but a new understanding had taken root. Trust was not just a word; it was a bond forged through shared experiences and unwavering belief.

"Let's try it again," Amara suggested, a note of challenge in her voice.

Ong's heart still raced, but he steeled himself. "Alright."

This time, when Amara rolled, Ong released his grip more readily. The fall was still terrifying, but it carried a sense of expectation rather than sheer panic. Again, Amara caught him effortlessly, and Ong felt a flicker of triumph.

They repeated the exercise several times, each fall less frightening than the last. Ong's trust in Amara grew with every successful catch, and he began to relax into the process. What once felt like sheer terror now carried a strange exhilaration, the free fall and the subsequent rescue bonding them closer.

"You're learning fast," Amara praised, her voice warm with approval. "Now, let's take it a step further."

Ong's eyes widened slightly. "What do you mean?"

Amara ascended higher into the sky, the ground a distant blur below. "This time, fall and don't expect me to catch you immediately. Trust that I will be there, but also trust yourself to remain calm and focused."

Ong's mouth went dry, but he nodded. As Amara initiated the roll, Ong let go, his body plummeting once more through the vast expanse of sky. The instinct to panic surged again, clawing at his resolve, but he fought it down. He focused on his breathing, on the steady rhythm of the wind, and on his trust in Amara.

Seconds stretched endlessly. Just as doubt began to creep in, Amara was there, her strong back beneath him once more.

"Excellent," she said, pride unmistakable in her voice. "This is the foundation of our bond. With this trust, we can face any challenge."

Each exercise built Ong's confidence further. The fear that had once gripped him during their flights gradually gave way to exhilaration and determination. He began to see the importance of trust and calmness in the chaos of battle. This was more than just a flight lesson; it was a crucial part of becoming a true dragonrider.

Amara, sensing Ong's readiness, decided it was time to move to the next phase of training. Together, they would forge a bond that would withstand even the fiercest of storms.

"Ong," Amara began, her voice firm yet encouraging, "now that you've learned to trust me and yourself during flight, it's time to work on your balance. In battle, you may need to stand on my back to use a weapon against another dragon. You must be able to balance yourself with unwavering confidence."

Ong nodded, determination gleaming in his eyes. "I'm ready."

Amara hovered in midair, her wings beating steadily to keep them aloft. "Stand up, Ong," she instructed. "Find your center of gravity and balance yourself."

With a deep breath, Ong carefully shifted his weight, rising to his feet on Amara's back. The initial instability sent a jolt through him, his heart racing as the wind whipped around him. He focused on his breathing, planting his feet firmly and keeping his gaze steady. Slowly, he adjusted his stance to maintain balance, his muscles taut with effort.

"Good," Amara encouraged. "Feel the rhythm of my movements. We are one in the sky."

Ong spread his arms slightly, using them to help balance as Amara gently swayed beneath him. The sensation was unlike anything he had experienced—a delicate dance between stability and motion. Each subtle shift in Amara's flight required him to adjust his stance, attuning himself to her every move.

"Now, let's add some maneuvers," Amara said, her tone carrying a hint of challenge.

She began to bank and roll, starting slowly but increasing intensity with each pass. Ong's legs trembled as he fought to stay upright, his focus locked on maintaining his balance. Each movement of Amara's body tested his ability to adapt and remain steady, the challenges growing more complex with every turn.

"Remember, Ong," Amara instructed, her voice steady, "trust yourself and trust me. We are partners in this."

Ong gritted his teeth, his muscles strained as he adjusted to the rapid changes in motion. He nearly lost his footing several times, but each time he managed to recover, finding his center and regaining his balance. Determination burned within him, spurred on by Amara's guidance and his own drive to succeed.

After several intense minutes, Amara leveled out, allowing Ong to catch his breath. "Well done," she praised. "Now, let's try it with some added challenges."

Ong's brow furrowed in concentration as Amara flew higher, the wind resistance growing stronger. "This time," she said, "imagine you have a weapon in your hands. You must maintain your balance while preparing for combat."

Ong visualized holding a weapon, his hands gripping an imaginary hilt. He adjusted his stance, anticipating the added weight and the need for swift movements. As Amara performed more intricate maneuvers, he focused on maintaining his balance, his mind and body working in unison.

Amara increased the difficulty, performing sudden dives and sharp turns. Ong's heart pounded, but he stayed upright, his balance becoming more instinctive with each motion. Confidence grew within him as his body responded with greater agility and precision.

"Excellent, Ong," Amara commended. "You are learning quickly. Now, for the final test of balance before we introduce a real weapon."

She ascended even higher, the air thinning and the ground a distant memory. "Stand firm," she instructed, diving into a series of rapid spins and loops.

Ong's entire being was focused on staying upright. He bent his knees slightly, shifting his weight as needed, his balance becoming second nature. The world spun around him, the dizzying height pressing on his nerves, but he remained steady, trusting in his abilities and Amara's guidance.

As Amara leveled out, Ong stood tall, a triumphant smile breaking across his face. "I did it," he breathed, exhilarated by the challenge and his newfound skill.

Amara nodded, pride evident in her voice. "Yes, you did. You are ready to take the next step and practice with a real weapon. But remember, balance and trust are your greatest allies in the sky."

With his balance tested and proven, Ong felt a renewed sense of confidence coursing through him. Amara, sensing his readiness, descended gracefully toward the clearing where Keisha awaited. The sight of his wife brought a warm smile to Ong's face; her presence was a constant source of strength and encouragement, grounding him even as he soared through the skies.

Keisha approached as Amara landed, her eyes shining with pride. In her hands, she held a magnificent dragonlance. Its shaft was intricately engraved with Eladrin runes, each symbol glowing faintly with latent magic, and its gleaming, razor-sharp tip exuded an aura of power. The weapon was a masterpiece, a testament to Lord Karrenen's unparalleled craftsmanship.

"Ong, this is for you," Keisha said, her voice brimming with love and support. "Lord Karrenen crafted this dragonlance especially for you. It will help you in the battles ahead."

Ong dismounted from Amara, his gaze fixed on the weapon as he stepped forward. Taking the lance from Keisha's hands, he felt its perfect weight and balance, marveling at the artistry and care that had gone into its creation. The runes seemed to pulse faintly beneath his touch, their magic resonating with him.

"Thank you, Keisha," Ong said, his voice thick with emotion. "And remind me to thank your father when we return home. This is truly a work of art."

Keisha smiled warmly, her eyes soft as she placed a reassuring hand on his arm. "Remember, my love, we believe in you. You can do this."

Ong nodded, the surge of determination in his chest fueled by her faith in him. His fingers tightened around the dragonlance as he mounted

Amara once more. Keisha stepped back, her heart swelling with pride as she watched him prepare for the challenges ahead.

With a powerful beat of her wings, Amara ascended into the sky, carrying Ong back into the realm of clouds and wind. The dragonlance gleamed in his grip, a symbol of his readiness for the battles to come. For the first time, Ong felt truly prepared—not just as a warrior, but as a dragonrider.

high above the forest, Amara's voice resonated in Ong's mind, calm yet commanding. "The dragonlance is a powerful weapon, but it requires skill and precision to wield effectively in flight. We will start with basic maneuvers and strikes."

Ong adjusted his stance, the dragonlance held firmly in his hands. The energy coursing through the runes seemed to hum in rhythm with his pulse, filling him with both focus and determination. "I'm ready," he said, his voice steady and resolute.

"Good," Amara responded. "Let's begin."

Amara started with gentle movements, her flight smooth and deliberate to allow Ong to acclimate. He gripped the lance tightly as he practiced simple thrusts and sweeping motions, adjusting to the resistance of the air and the added weight of the weapon. The rush of wind pushed against him, a constant reminder of the challenges of aerial combat.

"Focus on your target," Amara instructed. "Visualize the dragon you are fighting. Each movement must be deliberate and controlled."

Ong narrowed his eyes, picturing a fierce opponent in his mind—a dark dragon, its wings cutting through the air with menace. With the image clear, he executed a series of thrusts and slashes, each movement becoming more fluid and precise. The dragonlance began to feel like an extension of his arm, its perfect weight and balance complementing his growing skill.

"Excellent," Amara praised, her pride evident in her tone. "Now, let's try some more advanced maneuvers."

Her wings beat with renewed force, and she increased her speed, weaving through the sky with agile precision. Ong adjusted his grip, leaning into her movements, his body aligning with hers as he struck with the lance. The wind roared around him, but he remained steady, his focus unwavering.

"Remember, balance and precision," Amara reminded. "Trust yourself and trust in our bond."

Ong gritted his teeth, his determination sharpening as he executed a complex series of strikes. Thrusts flowed seamlessly into defensive sweeps, each motion carrying the weight of purpose and intent. The dragonlance sang as it cut through the air, its sharp tip gleaming against the sunlight.

He could feel the rhythm of Amara's movements beneath him, their coordination growing more synchronized with each maneuver. The bond between dragon and rider deepened, their trust forging a partnership of strength and grace.

The world blurred around them as Amara dove and climbed, pushing Ong to adapt to the ever-changing flow of the sky. Yet, with each passing moment, the lance in his hands felt more natural, its energy resonating with his own. The fear and uncertainty he had once felt were replaced by confidence and exhilaration.

"Well done," Amara said, her voice carrying a note of satisfaction. "You're progressing quickly, but this is only the beginning. There is much more to learn."

Ong nodded, his grip firm on the dragonlance as they soared higher. He was ready to face whatever challenges lay ahead.

"Now, let's see how you handle a moving target," Amara said, her voice carrying a hint of challenge.

With a graceful flick of her wings, she conjured an illusion of a dragon, its form shimmering with faint, ethereal light as it took shape before them. Its translucent wings beat steadily, and its agile body twisted through the air, mimicking the movements of a true adversary. Ong's eyes locked onto the target, his grip tightening on the dragonlance.

The illusion darted and swerved, its movements unpredictable. Ong adjusted his strikes, thrusting and sweeping as he anticipated its trajectory. The lance hummed with energy, each strike carving through the air with precision. Ong's balance wavered at times, but he quickly recovered, driven by determination and focus.

"Stay sharp," Amara urged. "A true enemy won't give you time to recover. You must strike with purpose and precision."

The training intensified as Amara increased her speed, weaving through the air while the illusion grew more erratic. Ong felt the strain in his muscles, the challenge of maintaining his balance while executing precise attacks. Each pass tested his limits, forcing him to adapt and push through the fatigue. The wind roared in his ears, and sweat beaded on his brow, but with each strike, his confidence grew, and his skill with the dragonlance sharpened.

Finally, after several grueling sessions, Amara slowed her flight, allowing Ong a moment to catch his breath. His chest heaved as he steadied himself, the lance still gripped tightly in his hands.

"You have done well, Ong," Amara said, her tone warm with approval. "Your progress is remarkable."

Ong nodded, panting but exhilarated. His voice carried a mixture of pride and gratitude as he replied, "Thank you, Amara. I feel... I feel ready."

Amara's keen eyes glinted with approval as she gazed back at him. "You are ready, Ong. But remember, this is just the beginning. There will be many battles ahead, and you must always strive to improve. Together, we are a formidable team."

A deep sense of pride and determination settled in Ong's chest. With the dragonlance in his hand and Amara by his side, he felt prepared to face the challenges that awaited him. The bond they had forged through relentless training filled him with unshakable confidence.

Yet, even as the moment lingered, Amara's gaze grew thoughtful. She knew that Ong's training, while intense and rewarding, was not yet complete. There was one more test he needed to face. It would push him to his limits, demanding not just skill and balance, but unwavering trust and focus.

As they hovered high above the forest, Amara's voice resonated in Ong's mind, calm yet commanding. "You have done well, Ong. But there is one final challenge you must face. This will test your ability to stay focused and hold onto your dragonlance, even in the most dire circumstances."

Ong's grip tightened on the lance, his eyes narrowing with determination. "I'm ready, Amara. What do I need to do?"

Amara's eyes glinted with a mix of seriousness and encouragement. "You must trust me completely. If you ever find yourself knocked off my back during battle, you need to hold onto your dragonlance and be prepared to strike a dark dragon while I come to retrieve you. Stay focused and ready, despite the fall."

Ong swallowed hard, the weight of her words settling over him. He nodded, steeling himself for what was to come. "I trust you, Amara. Let's do this."

Amara began to ascend, her wings cutting through the air with powerful strokes. They climbed to an even greater height, the ground below becoming a distant blur of green and brown. She executed a series of sharp maneuvers, testing Ong's balance and focus. Then, without warning, she rolled suddenly, sending Ong tumbling from her back.

The sensation of falling was immediate and terrifying. The wind roared around him, and the world spun in a dizzying blur. But Ong held tightly to his dragonlance, forcing himself to remember Amara's words.

"Stay calm. Trust me," her voice echoed in his mind, steady and unshakable.

Ong's grip on the lance was ironclad as he fought against the instinct to panic. His eyes scanned the sky, sharp and alert, searching for any sign of a threat. Suddenly, an illusion of a dark dragon materialized, its menacing form diving toward him with predatory speed. Without hesitation, Ong readied his lance, his focus laser-sharp on the target.

The illusionary dragon loomed closer, its eyes glowing with malice. Ong timed his strike perfectly, driving the lance into its chest. The illusion dissipated in a burst of light, and Ong's heart pounded with the weight of his achievement. But he did not allow himself to relax; he knew the real test was not over.

Seconds stretched into what felt like an eternity, but true to her word, Amara was there. With a swift and graceful dive, she swooped beneath him, catching him on her back in a seamless motion.

"Well done, Ong," Amara's voice carried a note of pride. "But we must do it again. You must be ready to repeat this in the heat of battle."

They repeated the exercise several times. Each fall tested Ong's resolve, his skill, and his trust in Amara. The first few attempts were nerve-wracking, but with every success, Ong grew more confident. He adapted to the sensation of freefall, his strikes becoming more precise, his focus unwavering. The bond between dragon and rider deepened with every pass.

Finally, after multiple successful attempts, Amara leveled out and flew steadily, her voice resonating with satisfaction. "You have proven yourself, Ong. You have shown courage, focus, and trust. These are the qualities of a true dragonrider."

Ong exhaled deeply, the tension in his body giving way to a profound sense of accomplishment. He felt ready—truly ready—for whatever challenges lay ahead. "Thank you, Amara," he said, his voice thick with gratitude. "I feel ready for whatever comes next."

Amara's eyes glowed with approval, her tone filled with quiet certainty. "You are ready, Ong. Together, we will face any challenge and emerge victorious."

As they descended back toward the forest clearing, Ong felt a profound sense of unity with Amara. He was not just a warrior or a rider—he was something more. The bond they shared transcended the battlefield, a partnership forged through trust and trials. The dragonlance in his hand symbolized not just strength, but responsibility, and with Amara by his side, he knew he could rise to meet any danger.

Together, they were a force to be reckoned with, their connection making them greater than the sum of their parts. As they landed, Ong looked toward the horizon, ready to protect Vacari and face whatever darkness awaited.

In the serene embrace of Purplefire Woods, Keisha and Ong found solace once more. The gentle rustle of leaves and the soft murmur of a nearby waterfall created a peaceful ambiance, the kind that seemed to cradle their hearts after the trials they had faced. Keisha approached Ong with a warm smile, her heart swelling with pride for the man who had embraced every challenge life had brought their way.

"Life has a way of surprising us, doesn't it?" Keisha said, her voice tinged with fondness as she gazed into Ong's eyes. "I'm grateful for every moment we've shared and every new experience we've had together."

Ong nodded, his eyes reflecting the depth of his emotions. "Meeting you was the best thing that ever happened to me," he confessed sincerely. "I feel even more connected to this new chapter of our lives, with you by my side."

Keisha's smile widened, her heart brimming with pride and affection. "I'm so proud of you, Ong," she said softly, her voice a gentle caress. "You've come so far, and I know we can face anything together."

As they stood together, surrounded by the serene beauty of Purplefire Woods, they both knew their journey was far from over. But with their bond unbreakable and their hearts united, they felt ready to face whatever challenges lay ahead.

Ong returned her smile, his affection for Keisha evident in the way he looked at her. Before their conversation could continue, however, Keisha's attention was drawn to something by the waterfall. A white horse stood there, its coat gleaming in the sunlight—a vision of ethereal beauty amidst the natural splendor of the forest.

Curiosity piqued, Keisha approached the horse with reverence, her hand outstretched in a gesture of friendship. She spoke softly, her voice a gentle melody that seemed to soothe the creature's spirit. The horse nickered quietly, stepping closer, its large eyes filled with curiosity.

Ong watched with amusement as Keisha interacted with the horse, a playful grin tugging at the corners of his lips. "Trying to tame a wild horse now, are we?" he teased, his voice filled with warmth.

Keisha laughed, shaking her head as she stroked the horse's mane. "No, dear," she replied, her eyes sparkling with humor. "I'm simply making a new friend."

As she turned back to Ong and Amara, she did not notice the white horse following her, its steps light and purposeful. Ong chuckled, his eyes dancing with amusement. "It would seem, whether you wanted a horse or not, you've got one now."

Keisha turned and laughed, surprised when she saw the horse standing close behind her. "It appears so," she said, her voice laced with amusement. She attempted to coax the horse back toward the waterfall, but it seemed determined to remain by her side.

With a resigned sigh, Keisha approached the horse again, her hand resting gently on its muzzle. She stroked its mane and felt a sense of kinship with the creature—a quiet, unspoken bond. "I suppose we have a new addition to our group," she mused, her eyes soft with affection. "I'll call her Celestia."

Ong smiled at the name, his heart warmed at seeing his wife and her newfound companion. "It seems we now have two horses," he remarked, his voice light with fondness. "A white one for you and Thunder, my black stallion."

Keisha's laughter rang through the forest, a sound of pure joy that mingled with the gentle rhythm of nature. As they continued their journey, now with Celestia walking alongside them, they felt a renewed sense of purpose. Their bond was stronger than ever, their hearts united in love and determination. Together, they knew they could face any foe, conquer any challenge, and embrace every new adventure life had in store.

Chapter 20
Fortifying the Strongholds

Kadona's expression was grave as she addressed Kimras, her voice tinged with urgency. "Given the dire threat revealed in the scrolls you and Amara brought, we must reinforce the protections around these areas immediately. We can't afford to underestimate the danger, especially with the mastermind still unknown."

Kimras nodded, feeling the weight of Kadona's words. He had always valued her wisdom, but this situation felt different—there was an unsettling air that even her presence could not dispel. "Thank you, Kadona. Amara and I understand the gravity of the situation. We'll take swift action to bolster the defenses of both Goldmoor and Purplefire Woods."

With a shared understanding, Kimras and Kadona parted ways, each determined to protect Vacari from the looming threat.

"Amara," Kimras began, his tone serious as he approached his companion. "Kadona advised us to reinforce the protections around Goldmoor and Purplefire Woods based on the threats described in the scrolls."

Amara nodded, her expression a mixture of concern and determination. Her gaze lingered on the horizon, as though sensing the darkness creeping closer. "I agree. We must act quickly to ensure the safety of our people."

The two began deliberating strategies, pouring over a magically enhanced map that shimmered with faint runes. They considered the terrain, resources, and potential vulnerabilities. Reinforced barriers at key entry points, natural fortifications like cliffs and dense forests, and an array of magical wards and traps became the foundation of their plans.

"Using the natural terrain is key," Amara suggested, tracing her claw across the map. A soft pulse of magic followed her movement, the map responding with a glow. "We can place barriers here and here, where the cliffs form natural choke points."

Kimras nodded in agreement. "Exactly. And we should place wards around the perimeter to alert us to any breaches. Our dragon guardians can patrol these critical areas."

Amara studied the map, her mind racing. "The crystal caverns beneath Purplefire Woods are rich in protective energy. If we tap into that energy, we can enhance the magical barriers to create a force field strong enough to repel even the most powerful dark dragon attacks." She pointed to a location marked with ancient runes. "We'll need the nymphs' help to harness it, but once active, it will form an invisible shield—nearly impossible to penetrate."

Kimras's golden eyes gleamed with approval. "That will make Purplefire nearly impenetrable. In Goldmoor, we can use the volcanic terrain to our advantage." He motioned toward the southern end of the map. "There are natural geysers and lava flows here. We can create thermal traps—hidden trenches that can be triggered to unleash molten lava on any invaders who breach our outer defenses. It will slow their advances and force them to retreat or suffer heavy losses."

Amara's gaze sharpened as an idea struck her. "The flora in Purplefire is also an asset. Many of the plants are poisonous to dark creatures. We can cultivate the venomous vines near entry points—living traps that will lash out at anything foreign. Combined with the wards, they'll be deadly to any dark dragon that dares to pass."

Kimras smirked, a glint of satisfaction in his expression. "Nature itself will fight alongside us." He paused, considering the next step. "We'll need to ensure the river running through Goldmoor is closely monitored. We can enchant the waters to detect any intrusions. A ripple in the current will notify the dragon guardians and set off alarms in the towers. Any dark force attempting to cross will be exposed immediately."

As they finalized their plans, the hum of magic in the air grew stronger, the land itself seeming to respond to their ideas. The protective energy of Vacari pulsed faintly, as if the land stood ready to aid in their defense.

"We'll need all the help we can get," Kimras said quietly. "But with these measures in place, we can turn Goldmoor and Purplefire into fortresses."

"And we'll be ready when the darkness comes," Amara added, her voice firm with resolve.

High above the grand halls of Goldmoor, Kimras, the noble gold dragon, descended gracefully to meet with King Alex. Bathed in sunlight, his majestic form radiated wisdom and strength as he approached the king with urgency.

"King Alex," Kimras began, his voice resonating with authority, "I bring troubling news regarding our safety."

The king turned, his expression grave as he awaited the dragon's report. "Continue," he urged.

"We have received word of a gathering darkness threatening our realm," Kimras said, his golden eyes flashing with concern. "Dark dragons are making their way to Vacari, and their intentions remain shrouded in mystery. However," he paused, his tone deepening, "some of these dark dragons are not native to Vacari."

King Alex's brow furrowed, the weight of Kimras's words sinking in. "Not from Vacari?" he repeated, surprise lacing his voice. "How is that possible? Have we not been isolated from outside realms?"

Kimras nodded solemnly. "Yes, Your Majesty, we have. But it appears that the mastermind behind this threat has found a way to reach beyond our borders. These dark dragons come from lands unknown to us—powerful creatures whose capabilities and allegiances we do not fully understand. This makes the situation far more dangerous. Whoever commands them wields great influence and is not bound by the natural barriers that have protected us for so long."

The king's expression darkened as he absorbed the implications. "If they are not from Vacari, they will not fight like the dark dragons we have faced before. We cannot rely on what we know to defend against them."

"Precisely," Kimras agreed, his voice steady but urgent. "Their methods, their strengths, their weaknesses—these remain a mystery. It is clear that the one pulling the strings has tremendous power and influence. We must not only prepare for an external invasion but also guard against internal collapse. We cannot let fear or uncertainty weaken us."

King Alex's jaw tightened as he straightened. "Then we must act swiftly. We cannot afford to underestimate this threat."

Kimras's wings unfurled with purpose, his voice resolute. "We must bolster our defenses immediately. Increase the patrols of our dragon guardians and maintain constant surveillance over the skies. Strengthen the watchtowers and equip them with signal flares for rapid communication. Above all, we must remain vigilant—this mastermind has proven they can reach beyond our realm, and they may yet have more tricks in store."

A grim silence followed, the enormity of the situation settling heavily over both leaders. King Alex's gaze turned steely as he met Kimras's eyes. "We cannot allow Vacari to fall into darkness. Whatever power this enemy possesses, we will face it head-on. I will rally our forces, and we will be prepared for whatever comes."

Kimras nodded, his golden eyes gleaming with determination. "I will continue to monitor the situation from the skies and ensure our guardians are ready. Together, we will protect Vacari."

King Alex nodded, rallying his people to action with commanding authority. His voice echoed through the halls and streets of Goldmoor, spurring the city into motion. As orders were dispatched, Kimras took to the skies once more, his heart heavy with the weight of the approaching storm yet resolute in his duty to defend their world from the looming darkness.

In the grand courtyard of Goldmoor, Kimras addressed the assembled soldiers and dragon riders, his golden form towering over the crowd. His voice carried the weight of their shared responsibility, reverberating through the space with clarity and strength. The warriors stood at attention, their gazes fixed on the noble gold dragon who commanded their respect.

"Brave soldiers and dragon riders of Goldmoor," Kimras began, his tone resonating with authority. "We face a grave threat. Dark dragons are approaching, and their intentions remain unclear. But know this: not all of these dragons hail from Vacari. Some come from realms beyond our borders, and we do not fully understand their powers or their methods."

A murmur rippled through the gathered ranks, unease flickering across the faces of some. Kimras's gaze swept over them, steady and unwavering, as he let the gravity of the situation settle over the group.

"These dark dragons are unlike any we have faced before. They do not fight by our rules, and their strengths may be unfamiliar to us. We must fortify our defenses and remain even more vigilant. Prepare yourselves for battle against adversaries who will use tactics and abilities foreign to us."

He paused, his golden eyes scanning the faces before him, ensuring his words left no doubt. The murmurs faded, replaced by a tense silence thick with understanding. The soldiers and dragon riders straightened, the weight of the challenge ahead reflected in their determined gazes.

"Strengthen the perimeter defenses and ensure the watchtowers are manned at all times," Kimras continued, his voice firm and commanding. "Our dragon guardians will patrol the skies in rotating shifts. Communication and coordination are critical—we must be ready for anything. Establish barricades and traps at strategic points and keep a close watch for any unusual activity. Trust your instincts and trust each other."

The soldiers and riders nodded in unison, their resolve mirrored in their eyes. Though the threat was unfamiliar, their readiness to protect their home and people was unwavering.

"We stand together," Kimras said, his voice rising with conviction. "In unity, we find strength. Protect our realm, protect our people. Trust in one another and in the bond we share. Above all, stay sharp. These enemies are new to us, and we cannot afford to be caught off guard."

With a collective sense of purpose, the crowd began to disperse, moving with precision to carry out their orders. Kimras watched them go, a surge of pride swelling within him as he witnessed their unwavering commitment. The defenders of Vacari understood the gravity of the situation, and their determination to stand against the encroaching darkness was evident in every step they took.

As the courtyard emptied, Kimras turned his gaze to the horizon. The weight of leadership pressed on him, but so did the strength of hope. Even in the face of an unknown threat, Vacari's defenders stood ready, their unity a shield against whatever darkness awaited them.

In the heart of Purplefire Woods, beneath the canopy of ancient trees, Amara, the regal Amethyst dragon, addressed her kin. Her shimmering scales reflected the dappled light as her voice, rich with authority and wisdom, carried through the forest.

"Brothers and sisters," Amara began, her tone steady but grave, "a gathering darkness threatens our land. More dark dragons are coming, their intentions still unknown."

The assembled Amethyst dragons listened intently, their eyes reflecting the weight of her words. The wind stirred the leaves above, carrying whispers of an ancient warning through the depths of the forest. Unity had always been their greatest strength, and now, more than ever, they stood together as guardians of their sacred home.

Amara turned her gaze to the nymphs of Purplefire, their ethereal forms blending seamlessly with the forest around them. "Nymphs of Purplefire," she addressed them, her voice imbued with both care and urgency, "the looming threat may endanger you. If any of you wish to seek protection in Ardinia, now is the time."

A nymph stepped forward, her expression resolute despite the tension in the air. "We will remain here, alongside our Amethyst brethren. Our roots run deep, and we shall not abandon them."

Amara inclined her head in gratitude, her voice softening with emotion. "Thank you, sisters. Your courage honors us all."

Before she could continue, another nymph emerged from the group, her eyes glinting with a mixture of hope and uncertainty. "Amara," she began, her voice tentative, "I've heard whispers... rumors that the Opal Dragons are returning to Vacari. Could it be true?"

Amara's eyes widened slightly, a glimmer of hope flickering within them. The Opal Dragons—ancient allies with cosmic knowledge—were believed lost to time. If they were truly returning, it could shift the tide of this impending conflict. "If the Opal Dragons are indeed returning," she said, her voice tinged with cautious optimism, "it would be a beacon of strength in these troubled times." She paused, the weight of the possibility settling over her. "Thank you for this, sister. We will remain vigilant and welcome their return if the rumors prove true. Their wisdom would be invaluable in this dark hour."

Turning her focus back to the younger Amethyst dragons, Amara spoke with renewed resolve. "To protect Purplefire Woods, we must create a barrier of vigilance. Patrol the forest, especially around potential entry points for the dark dragons. Use the natural terrain to our advantage—set traps and wards to alert us to any intrusion. Coordinate with the nymphs; their magic will enhance our defenses. Together, we can weave an unbreakable shield of protection."

Amara's voice grew firmer as she continued. "Rotate the patrols frequently, ensuring our defenses remain strong and unpredictable. Place enchanted barriers at key locations and establish safe zones for retreat if necessary. Be vigilant and trust in one another. In unity, we are unbreakable."

A ripple of magic shimmered through the ancient trees as the young dragons and nymphs dispersed to carry out her orders. The forest seemed to hum with their combined energy, the efforts of its protectors a reflection of their unity and shared purpose. Dragons unfurled their wings and soared into the sky, their movements swift and determined, while the nymphs moved with grace, their magic weaving through the air like threads of light.

Amidst the tranquil beauty of Purplefire Woods, a silent vow echoed through the ancient trees—a promise to stand united against the shadows seeking to tear their world apart. In that unity, they found strength—a beacon of hope shining amidst the encroaching darkness threatening to engulf their land.

With a gentle smile, Amara reminded herself that even in dark times, it was important to celebrate the small joys. These moments of light would sustain them through the challenges ahead, guiding them with hope. The memory of Ong's training brought a flicker of warmth to her heart, a reminder that even amidst danger, there could be growth and triumph. She knew she had to share this news with Kimras.

With grace, Amara spread her wings and took to the skies, her heart filled with determination. The golden light of the setting sun illuminated her path to Goldmoor, where she would prepare for the trials to come.

Upon reaching Goldmoor, Amara descended gracefully, landing beside Kimras with practiced ease. Her presence radiated quiet resolve as she approached her fellow guardian.

"Kimras," Amara greeted warmly, her voice carrying the wisdom gleaned from her recent experiences. "Even in darkness, we must celebrate the small joys. We have a new dragonrider—Ong. And there's news from Purplefire Woods that you should hear."

Kimras's eyes widened slightly, curiosity and intrigue flickering across his golden gaze. A smile tugged at the corners of his mouth. "Tell me about his training," he said, though his tone also hinted at interest in the other news.

Amara recounted the training sessions, detailing Ong's challenges, and his impressive progress. Her voice carried pride, not just for Ong's achievements, but for the bond they had begun to forge. As Kimras listened, his smile deepened, a knowing look spreading across his face.

"Ah, so your teasing must have worked wonders, Amara," Kimras remarked, his tone light and teasing. "We have another dragonrider thanks to your 'encouragement.'"

Amara chuckled, shaking her head. "Perhaps a little push was all he needed," she admitted. "But he has proven himself capable."

Kimras laughed softly, his pride in both Amara and Ong evident. "You've done well, Amara. In times of adversity, it is these moments of light that sustain us."

Amara nodded, then her expression turned more serious as she relayed the information, she had gathered in Purplefire Woods. "There is more. One of the nymphs told me that rumors are circulating—the Opal Dragons may be returning to Vacari."

Kimras's expression shifted from pride to contemplation, his mind already racing with the implications. "The Opal Dragons? If they return, that would change the tide. Their knowledge and power could tip the balance in our favor."

"That's what I'm hoping," Amara replied, her voice steady but cautious. "But until we have confirmation, we must continue preparing."

Kimras inclined his head, his tone now more solemn. "Agreed. The dark dragons from Vacari are dangerous enough, but if there are forces from beyond Vacari, we must be ready for whatever comes."

The two guardians stood in silent solidarity for a moment, the weight of their responsibilities balanced by their shared determination. United in their commitment to protect Vacari, Amara and Kimras prepared themselves for the battles ahead. Together, they would face any challenge with courage and resilience, drawing strength from their friendship, the potential return of powerful allies, and their unwavering hope for the future.

Chapter 21

Casper's Valor

Queen Jeanne cherished the rare moments of tranquility she found beyond the city walls, seeking solace in the serene beauty of the surrounding wilderness. Accompanied by her loyal companion, Casper the cougar, she often ventured into the forest to clear her mind and reconnect with nature. Today was no different. As she wandered along a familiar path, the soft sound of Casper's paw steps beside her brought a comforting sense of peace.

Dappled sunlight filtered through the canopy, casting a warm, golden glow on the forest floor. Jeanne smiled as she watched Casper explore, his sleek form moving gracefully through the underbrush. These excursions were her cherished escape from the pressures of royal life, offering her a rare chance to breathe freely and find balance in the quiet rhythm of the natural world.

Pausing to admire a cluster of wildflowers swaying gently in the breeze, Jeanne closed her eyes, savoring the calm. But the serenity shattered in an instant as a sudden rustling in the bushes caught her attention. She turned, expecting to see Casper emerging from the foliage. Instead, her breath hitched as she came face-to-face with Quellan.

The sinister figure stepped from the shadows, his eyes gleaming with malice. His presence struck like a thunderclap, obliterating the fragile peace of the forest. Jeanne's pulse quickened, and a wave of dread surged through her chest, her heart pounding like a drum. Not again.

Memories of their last encounter crashed over her—terror, a narrow escape, and the chilling threats that still haunted her. Her body froze, but her mind screamed for action. A sharp cry escaped her lips, the sound slicing through the air, only to be swallowed by the vast emptiness of the wilderness. She was alone—far from the safety of the city walls, far from help.

Quellan's lips curled into a mocking smile, his voice dripping with cruelty. "Well, well, Queen Jeanne... we meet again," he sneered, his tone laced with dark amusement. "Didn't think I'd try for a second round, did you?"

Jeanne's pulse thundered in her ears as fear snaked through her veins. *He has done this before.* She forced herself to stand tall, though her voice trembled when she spoke. "Why are you doing this?"

Quellan's laugh was cold and sharp, slicing through the quiet of the forest. "You weren't easy to catch the first time," he hissed, his eyes gleaming with sadistic pleasure. "But you won't be so lucky again. No one can hear you out here, Queen Jeanne." He stepped closer, savoring her fear as he loomed over her. "This time, there's no escape."

Jeanne's throat tightened, her mind racing as fear clawed at her resolve. Her hand instinctively reached for Casper, her only hope now, as the cougar prowled somewhere nearby. She had to trust that he would hear her call—that he would come—because this time, Quellan's intentions were unmistakably sinister.

Summoning every ounce of courage, Jeanne called out for her faithful companion, her trembling voice echoing through the silent forest. "Casper!"

The sound of her plea carried through the stillness, finding the ears of her vigilant protector. Casper, ever watchful and fiercely loyal, moved with the precision of a predator through the underbrush. His sleek fur melted into the dappled shadows, rendering him an almost ghostly figure in the dense woodland. Jeanne's pulse quickened. Quellan, too arrogant and assured in his dominance, remained oblivious to the approaching storm.

Then, like a bolt of lightning, Casper leapt from the shadows, his powerful form landing between Jeanne and Quellan with a thunderous impact. His arrival was so sudden, so commanding, that Quellan froze mid-step. Casper's muscles rippled beneath his sleek coat, his entire body coiled with lethal intent. His eyes, bright and feral, locked onto Quellan's, burning with a predatory intensity that made the intruder's blood run cold.

Quellan instinctively stepped back, his earlier bravado cracking under the weight of the cougar's presence. Casper's growl rumbled low and deep, the sound reverberating through the forest—a primal warning, unyielding and fierce. It promised violence, an unrelenting wrath that would be unleashed at the slightest provocation. The cougar's ears flattened, his lips peeling back to reveal gleaming fangs that spoke of nature's untamed fury.

Casper crouched low, every fiber of his being ready to pounce. His tail twitched, the movements precise and calculated, his attention locked entirely on the man before him. The air between them seemed to crackle with tension, the forest itself holding its breath. Quellan, faced with this embodiment of primal rage, felt a shiver crawl down his spine as the weight of his mistake sank in. He could see his own demise reflected in the cougar's unblinking gaze.

Quellan's confidence wavered, his steps slow and deliberate as he began to retreat, careful not to provoke the beast. Casper's golden eyes followed his every movement, daring him to make a single misstep.

"I'll remember this, Queen Jeanne," Quellan spat, but the venom in his voice was diluted by trembling fear. "But for now, I'll take my leave."

Jeanne, no longer the terrified queen, straightened, a newfound defiance hardening her gaze. A faint smile tugged at her lips, her voice cool and unwavering as she replied. "I suggest you never bother me again, Quellan. Or next time, I'll let Casper finish what he started."

Quellan's eyes widened, a flicker of terror breaking through his mask of anger. Without another word, he disappeared into the shadows from which he had emerged, his earlier bravado in tatters.

The forest remained still, the silence almost deafening as Casper held his ground. His piercing gaze tracked Quellan's every retreating step until the dark elf was gone. Only then did the cougar's growl subside, his body relaxing just enough to glance back at Jeanne.

When she was certain they were alone, Jeanne finally let out a breath she had not realized she had been holding. Her hand reached out to gently stroke Casper's head, her fingers trembling but filled with gratitude. "Good boy," she whispered, her voice soft but steady as her heart swelled with pride. Without his fierce intervention, the outcome of this encounter would have been far different.

Casper, his duty fulfilled, nuzzled her gently, a quiet reassurance of the bond they shared—a bond that no intruder, no matter how dangerous, could ever break. His steady presence grounded her, helping to calm the adrenaline still coursing through her veins.

Jeanne gathered her composure, her trembling subsiding as she patted Casper with affection. Her heart still pounded from the encounter, but something within her had shifted. The fear that had gripped her moments before was giving way to a new sense of strength. Casper had not only saved her life, but he had awakened a fierceness within her—a reminder of her resilience and determination.

As they made their way back to the city, Jeanne reflected on how moments like these had shaped her. Casper had been her protector, but he had also been her catalyst for change. The bond they shared was not just about safety; it reflected her own inner courage. She was not the same queen she had been years ago—cautious, hesitant, and dependent on others. Now, she felt the resolve to stand firm against whatever dangers lurked in the shadows, fortified by the love and loyalty of her companions.

Upon returning to the castle, Jeanne hurried to find her husband, King Alex. She found him in the great hall, deep in discussion with his advisors. As soon as he saw her, his sharp eyes caught the tension in her gaze. Sensing the gravity of her presence, he dismissed the advisors with a wave of his hand.

Jeanne recounted the harrowing encounter with Quellan, her voice steady but edged with a steeliness that had not been there before. Though the reality of the confrontation had shaken her, she no longer spoke from a place of fear. Her words carried the weight of someone who had faced danger head-on and emerged stronger.

Alex listened intently, his expression darkening with concern at each detail. But as he took in her account, he noticed something else—a quiet transformation in his wife. When she finished, he rose and embraced her tightly, his relief palpable.

"Thank the stars you're safe," he murmured, his voice filled with gratitude. "And Casper... he truly is a remarkable guardian."

Jeanne smiled softly, glancing at the cougar who stood calmly by her side, his golden eyes watchful. "It's thanks to Keisha that he's with me," she said quietly. "She brought him to me when I needed him most, though I didn't realize how much I would come to rely on him. I'm so grateful for that." Her voice wavered slightly, not from fear, but from the enormity of the realization—Casper had not just been her protector; he had been her reminder of the strength she carried within.

Alex pulled back, studying her intently. His eyes softened with admiration, and a small smile played at his lips. "You've changed, Jeanne," he said gently. "You're not just the queen who oversees this kingdom—you're a fighter, just as much as anyone else. I see it in your eyes."

Jeanne met his gaze, the weight of his words settling over her. But instead of feeling burdened, she felt empowered. Her voice was calm yet resolute as she replied, "I've had to be. Casper has reminded me of the strength I already had. He gave me the courage to stand against Quellan. And next time," she added, her voice unwavering, "I won't be afraid."

Alex nodded, pride swelling in his chest. "You've come so far," he said warmly, his hand resting gently on her shoulder. "I'm proud of you, Jeanne. But remember, you don't have to face these dangers alone."

Turning to a nearby servant, Alex issued a firm but kind command. "Prepare a special meal for Casper. He deserves the finest we can offer for protecting the queen."

The servant nodded and quickly departed to fulfill the king's request. Alex turned back to Jeanne, his expression a mix of seriousness and affection. "I'm grateful you and Casper are unharmed, but from now on, you must take additional guards whenever you leave the castle grounds. We cannot risk your safety. Even a noble protector like Casper needs support."

Jeanne nodded, meeting his gaze with understanding. She knew he was right, but for the first time, she did not feel like she was yielding to fear by accepting extra protection. She was ready to face whatever lay ahead, but she also understood the importance of unity and support. "I will, Alex. I promise."

As they walked together toward the dining hall, where a special treat awaited Casper, Jeanne felt a renewed sense of security, love, and strength. The bond between her, Alex, and Casper was unbreakable—a foundation upon which she could stand firmly, no matter the challenges to come. She was not just a queen sheltered by castle walls; she was a leader forged by trials, a woman empowered by loyalty and love.

And with Casper by her side, his golden eyes filled with unwavering devotion, Jeanne knew there was nothing she could not face.

Qellaun ran through the woods, his heart pounding, and his mind racing. The predator had become the prey, and it gnawed at his pride. He needed to put distance between himself and the cougar. When he finally felt safe, he stopped, panting heavily, his thoughts consumed by the unexpected turn of events. Where did that cougar come from? Queen

Jeanne had never had a protector like that before. Humans rarely had such fierce companions, especially one that seemed so perfectly attuned to her needs.

As he stomped back toward Flameford, frustration simmered within him, the sting of defeat fueling his anger. This was not how things were supposed to go. Upon reaching the fortress, he was met by his sister, Lyra, who immediately noticed the fury radiating from him.

"What is wrong, brother?" she asked, her voice calm and composed, though her sharp eyes betrayed her curiosity.

Qellaun growled in frustration, his fists clenched. "It was Queen Jeanne," he muttered bitterly. "She had a cougar with her—an animal I've never seen before. It thwarted my attempt to capture her."

Lyra tilted her head, her brow furrowing slightly. "A cougar? That is not typical for a human. Where could she have possibly gotten such a companion?"

Qellaun paced angrily, his frustration mounting. "Exactly. Where would she get such a beast?" He sneered, the image of his failed attempt gnawing at him. His eyes flashed with malice as the pieces clicked together. "That Eladrin—Keisha. I bet she had something to do with it."

Lyra raised an eyebrow, realization dawning. "Ah, yes. Keisha and Jeanne have grown close in recent years, haven't they?" Her voice carried a note of amusement. "Do you not recall her friendship with Keisha? That Eladrin has been involved in more matters than you give her credit for."

Qellaun's frustration boiled over. He slammed his fist into the nearest wall, his voice rising with fury. "Of course, Keisha! That meddling Eladrin is always interfering. She is another reason I wish she were out of the way! Her constant meddling has been a thorn in my side for far too long!"

Lyra watched him, her expression measured, but she nodded slowly, her agreement clear. "You're not wrong, brother. Keisha has been involved in too many things. Perhaps it's time we find a way to remove her influence."

Qellaun's eyes gleamed with malice. "Indeed. With that elf out of the picture, Jeanne will be vulnerable, and Vacari's defenses will crumble. Keisha has always been too close to the noble dragons for my liking."

With their focus now fully on their dark plans, Qellaun, Lyra, Zylron, and Glaceria gathered in the towering fortress that served as their base. In the dimly lit war room, the air was thick with tension and anticipation. The mysterious figure, cloaked in shadow, joined them, commanding immediate attention. An aura of power clung to the figure, a presence so formidable it sent a shiver even down Lyra's spine.

"The time for half measures is over," the figure intoned, their voice echoing with sinister resolve. "Our next move must be decisive. We will exploit every weakness, target every ally, and ensure that the first two noble dragons fall. Only then will Vacari be ripe for conquest."

Nods of agreement and murmurs of approval filled the room as the group steeled themselves for the battles to come. They knew the road to victory would be fraught with challenges, but their resolve was unshakable.

With their dark plans now set in motion, the fate of Vacari and its defenders hung precariously in the balance.

Keisha is becoming far too much of a problem," he growled. "She's interfered at every turn. We need to remove her—permanently."

Lyra nodded in agreement, her expression thoughtful. "She's more than just an annoyance, brother. Her alliances with the noble dragons and her influence over Queen Jeanne are destabilizing our efforts. If we are to succeed, she must be dealt with."

Quellan sneered, the glint of malice in his eyes sharpening. "Perhaps it's time we try to sacrifice her again. Without her magic—"

The mysterious figure's glare cut through his words like a blade, freezing him in place. A tense silence fell over the room as the air grew heavy with the figure's displeasure. When they spoke, their voice was low but thunderous, filled with cold authority. "That would be a foolish mistake."

Quellan stiffened, his confidence wavering under the figure's piercing gaze. "Why?" he managed, though his voice lacked its usual bravado.

The figure's eyes burned with intensity, their presence towering despite the shadow that cloaked them. "Because," they said, their tone chillingly precise, "Kimras and her husband are bound to her. If you harm Keisha, they will sense it. And when they come for vengeance, they will not stop until they've destroyed everything we've built." They leaned forward slightly, the room seeming to darken with their fury. "Do not be so reckless again."

Lyra shifted uneasily, but her curiosity overrode her caution. "Phoenix tried that once," she ventured carefully.

The mention of Phoenix made the figure's anger flare visibly. Their voice rose, sharp and cutting. "And how did that turn out, Lyra?" they snapped, their tone carrying the weight of judgment. The question hung in the air, and both Lyra and Quellan fell silent, their defiance withering under the figure's cold stare.

After a beat, the figure exhaled slowly, regaining their composure. Their voice was calm but carried a dangerous edge. "Keisha is indeed a problem. But it is a problem that requires more thought. Hurting her is not the answer. If we are to eliminate her influence, we must find a solution that does not provoke the wrath of the noble dragons or her allies." Their gaze swept over the group, daring anyone to challenge them. "Am I understood?"

Chapter 22
Shadows Stir

As Ong and Keisha rode into Goldmoor, with their loyal companion Pumpkin trailing closely behind, they were greeted by the welcoming smiles of the city's citizens. Despite the underlying tension in the air, a sense of anticipation and determination flowed through the streets. Merchants bustled about, setting up their stalls, while children's laughter rang out as they played games, a bright contrast to the uncertainty looming ahead.

Keisha's presence did not go unnoticed, her elegant mount, Celestia, drawing curious glances from the gathered townspeople. The horse's gleaming white coat seemed almost ethereal, adding to Keisha's already formidable aura. From across the bustling square, King Alex spotted them and approached, a warm smile lighting his face.

"Greetings, Ong, Keisha," King Alex said, his voice imbued with regal warmth. "It is good to see you both. And who is this magnificent creature you have brought with you?" He gestured toward Celestia.

Ong chuckled, sharing a knowing look with Keisha before recounting the tale of how Celestia had joined their group. As he told the story, laughter rippled through the growing crowd, the humor of the situation not lost on anyone. Keisha, her eyes sparkling with amusement, added her own playful embellishments, drawing even more smiles from the onlookers.

King Alex raised an eyebrow as the story concluded, his gaze shifting mischievously to Keisha. "I see," he said with a grin. "So not only do you have the respect of dragons, but it seems even the wild horses of Vacari are determined to follow you home."

Keisha's cheeks flushed, and she let out a soft laugh, shaking her head. "Oh, come now, Your Majesty," she replied with a grin. "I hardly think taming a horse compares to riding a dragon."

"True," King Alex teased back, his tone playful. "But at this rate, we may need to call you the 'Mistress of Creatures.' First Pumpkin, now Celestia—what is next? Will the hawks of Goldmoor start following you around as well?"

Keisha blushed deeper, but her laughter was infectious. "If they do, I'll let you know," she quipped, her eyes dancing with amusement.

The crowd chuckled, their spirits lifted by the exchange. Even Ong joined in, his affectionate smile for Keisha filled with pride. Despite the gravity of the times, these moments of lightheartedness and camaraderie were a balm for weary hearts. They reminded the citizens of Goldmoor that even in the face of darkness, joy could still be found, binding them together.

With the sound of laughter lingering in the air, Ong and Keisha exchanged smiles, grateful for the warmth and acceptance of their fellow citizens. These fleeting moments of connection fortified them for the challenges ahead, a reminder that unity and resilience would carry them through.

As the day progressed, the majestic forms of Kimras and Amara descended upon Goldmoor, their arrival heralded by the shimmer of sunlight on their gleaming scales. The dragons' presence commanded instant attention, drawing awe from the townsfolk. Whispers of reverence rippled through the crowd as the bond between humans and dragons was once again on full display—a vital alliance in a world on the brink of turmoil.

"Greetings, Kimras, Amara," Ong said with a respectful nod, his voice carrying the weight of his gratitude for their arrival. "We're glad to see you both."

Kimras returned the greeting with a solemn nod, his golden scales catching the sunlight, a reminder of his majesty and the burden of leadership he bore. "And we are glad to see you as well, Ong, Keisha," he replied, his tone heavy with responsibility. "Your presence strengthens us."

Keisha stepped forward, her eyes bright with determination. "Is there anything we can do to help?" she asked earnestly, her voice steady despite the unease bubbling beneath the surface.

Kimras exchanged a glance with Amara, a silent understanding passing between them before he turned back to Keisha. "Goldmoor's defenses have been fortified. The dragonriders are on a rotating patrol schedule, constantly surveying the skies. Magical wards have been laid along the city's perimeter to detect any intrusion. So far, these measures have held."

Amara's amethyst scales shimmered as she spoke, her tone both reassuring and urgent. "Purplefire Woods has been similarly reinforced. The natural barriers—the cliffs, dense forests, and rivers—grant us an advantage. We have placed magical wards that harmonize with the terrain, ensuring no movement goes unnoticed. The nymphs of Purplefire are weaving their own enchantments to strengthen the defenses."

Kimras nodded in agreement, his gaze steady and thoughtful. "The nymphs' magic, combined with our patrols, creates a strong defense for now. But the enemy is cunning. We believe they are testing us, probing for weaknesses in our fortifications."

Ong and Keisha absorbed the gravity of their words, the weight of the situation pressing upon them. Each detail sharpened their awareness of the battles that lay ahead. Ong's voice was steady as he replied, "We will remain vigilant. You can count on us."

Keisha's heart swelled with a mixture of pride and worry. The alliance between their people and the dragons was powerful, a bond forged in trust and necessity. Yet, the ever-present threat of darkness loomed on the horizon, casting long shadows over their hopes. She met Kimras's gaze and nodded firmly. "We'll do everything we can to ensure Vacari remains strong."

Kimras and Amara took to the skies, their powerful wings cutting through the air with grace. As they soared above the city, their majestic forms filled Ong and Keisha with a renewed sense of purpose. The sight was a reminder of what they fought to protect—and what they stood to lose.

"I'll take care of the horses," Ong said, his tone resolute. "They'll be safe in the stables."

Keisha nodded, watching as he led Celestia and Thunder toward the stables. The steady sound of hoofbeats echoed through the cobbled corridors, a calming rhythm amidst the activity of the city. Ong took his time, ensuring both horses were settled comfortably, patting their sleek coats and murmuring reassuring words. The quiet sanctuary of the stables felt like a haven, a brief respite from the weight of the world outside.

As Ong finished, he stood for a moment, his hand resting on Thunder's neck, his mind turning to the battles ahead. A deep sense of responsibility settled over him, but alongside it, a quiet determination. Together, they would face whatever challenges awaited them, drawing strength from one another and their unbreakable bonds.

Keisha watched him from the stable door, her heart swelling with pride and affection. Ong's steadfastness was a constant anchor for her, a reminder that in unity, they could withstand even the darkest storms. With him, with their allies, and with the dragons soaring above, she felt ready to face the trials to come.

The tranquility of Goldmoor shattered as Zylron and his cohort of young red dragons approached, their fiery forms a stark contrast against the clear skies. A palpable sense of urgency swept through the city as dragonriders sprang into action, their resolve reflected in the fierce gazes of their noble dragon companions. The air buzzed with the sound of wings, shouted commands, and the clamor of weapons being readied.

Keisha wasted no time, leaping onto Kimras's back with fierce determination. "Let's go!" she commanded, her voice steady despite the adrenaline coursing through her veins. With a powerful beat of his wings, Kimras launched into the sky, his movements precise and rhythmic as he climbed higher, carrying Keisha toward the encroaching threat.

As they neared the battlefield, Keisha's sharp eyes scanned the skies, quickly assessing the positions of the enemy dragons. With a flick of her wrist, she unleashed a barrage of magical energy. Bolts of crackling lightning arced through the air, striking true against the red dragons. Each burst of magic was a symphony of controlled power, her flawless precision forcing the young red dragons to scatter as their fiery breath faltered.

Below, the dragonriders and their mounts moved with seamless coordination. Riders leaned low against their dragons, loosing arrows that flew in deadly arcs toward their foes. Each shot struck vulnerable points in the red dragons' defenses, forcing them into disarray. Riders wielding lances and spears dove into the fray, their weapons gleaming in the sunlight as they drove them into their enemies with devastating momentum. The synchronization between rider and dragon was breathtaking, their trust in one another forged through years of battle and training.

One rider, perched atop a gold dragon, unleashed a torrent of arrows, the shafts streaking through the air like shooting stars. Her dragon twisted and rolled, dodging incoming fire with remarkable agility. Another rider, wielding a gleaming lance, struck a decisive blow against a red dragon's flank as his mount roared, slamming into the enemy with thunderous force. The red dragon spiraled downward, its wings struggling to regain control before it crashed into the forest below.

Above the chaos, Kimras and Keisha pressed forward, their attention narrowing on Zylron, the towering red dragon leading the assault. Zylron's imposing form dominated the sky, his flames scorching everything in their path. Keisha's eyes burned with intensity as she summoned a concentrated burst of magical energy, her hands glowing with radiant light. With a swift motion, she conjured a massive barrier of shimmering arcane force, deflecting Zylron's devastating fire breath and shielding the advancing dragonriders.

Zylron snarled, his frustration evident as his flames dissipated harmlessly against Keisha's shield. His fiery eyes locked on her, calculating his next move. Realizing the tide was turning, his voice boomed through the chaos, commanding his young red dragons to retreat. Reluctantly, the red dragons obeyed, their furious roars echoing as they beat their wings and vanished into the horizon.

As the last of the red dragons disappeared, a wave of relief washed over Goldmoor. Though the skirmish had been brief, it was a stark reminder of the dangers that lurked beyond their borders. The peace they had fought so fiercely to protect was fragile, always threatened by the shadow of war.

Amidst the chaos and uncertainty, a glimmer of hope remained. The dragonriders, their weapons still gleaming in the sunlight, guided their dragons back toward the city. Their noble companions—gold and amethyst alike—descended with grace and power, their wings folding as they landed with a thundering presence. Each step, each beat of their wings, was a testament to the strength and resilience of those who stood united against the forces of darkness.

When the riders returned from the skirmish, King Alex stepped forward to greet them. His face radiated pride and gratitude for their bravery. The courtyard, still alive with the energy of battle, fell quiet as his voice echoed through the space.

"Excellent work, dragonriders," King Alex declared, his tone carrying both strength and appreciation. "You have defended Goldmoor with valor and skill. Your efforts remind us all of what it means to stand united against darkness."

The dragonriders acknowledged his praise with solemn nods, their expressions a reflection of the gravity of the ongoing conflict. Though their resolve was unshaken, their eyes carried the weight of the battles still to come. They knew this skirmish was but a taste of the storm looming on the horizon.

Before they could depart, Kimras descended gracefully beside King Alex, his majestic golden form towering over the courtyard. The quiet power of his presence drew every gaze, his steady breaths carrying the weight of both their victory and the deeper realization of what lay ahead.

"Your Majesty," Kimras began, his voice resonating with authority and wisdom, "I fear that this was not a true attack, but rather a test."

King Alex furrowed his brow, confusion flickering across his face as he turned toward the noble dragon. "A test?" he asked, his voice tinged with uncertainty.

Kimras nodded solemnly, his golden eyes gleaming with the gravity of the situation. "Zylron's retreat was uncharacteristic. He is an ancient dragon, Your Majesty—formidable and ruthless. It is not in his nature to back down from a fight, especially one he initiated. I believe this skirmish was meant to assess our strength, to probe our defenses."

Ong, who had been listening intently, stepped forward, his expression resolute. "I agree with Kimras, Your Majesty," he said, his voice steady. "Zylron is no ordinary foe. His power is legendary, and yet... he held back. This attack felt like a probing maneuver, an attempt to identify weaknesses in our defenses."

Kimras's gaze darkened as he continued. "Zylron could have unleashed his full might, but he chose not to. He is capable of far more destruction than what we witnessed today. This restraint concerns me. It means he was gathering information, testing not only our strength but our responses. He will not make the same move twice."

King Alex absorbed their words, his expression growing graver as the weight of their revelation settled over him. "If this was indeed a test," he murmured, his voice heavy with concern, "then we must remain vigilant. Zylron may have retreated for now, but we cannot afford to lower our defenses. He is planning something far worse, and next time, we may not be so fortunate."

Kimras nodded gravely, his form casting a long shadow in the fading sunlight. "Zylron is an ancient dragon, and his mind works like a battlefield strategist's. He will be studying us—our tactics, our alliances. We cannot underestimate him. The next time he strikes, it will be with the intent to overwhelm us, and he will not hold back. We must strengthen every weak point, fortify Goldmoor and Purplefire Woods, and be prepared for the full force of his wrath."

A heavy silence fell over the courtyard as the full weight of Kimras's words sunk in. The defenders of Vacari exchanged determined glances, their shared understanding forging an unspoken vow of unity.

King Alex lifted his gaze toward the horizon, his expression resolute. "We will not falter," he said firmly. "We will prepare for whatever comes, and we will meet it together. Vacari will not fall to the darkness."

Kimras inclined his head, his golden scales shimmering as if reflecting the hope beneath the solemnity. "Together, we are strong," he said. "And together, we will prevail."

As the defenders dispersed to fortify their defenses and prepare for the battles to come, the shadow of Zylron's power loomed over them like a gathering storm. Yet, amidst the uncertainty, a glimmer of hope shone—a testament to their unity, courage, and unwavering determination to protect Vacari.

With noble dragons and steadfast allies, they would stand unyielding against the darkness. For their realm, their people, and the bonds that held them together, they would fight. Strong, united, and unbroken, they would face the coming storm.

Chapter 23
Shadows of Suspicion

In the heart of the battlefield, strategically positioned between the fortified city of Goldmoor and the enchanted expanse of Purplefire Woods, the clash of claws and the roar of dragons reverberated through the air. The skirmish unfolded with ferocious intensity. Red dragons, their scales shimmering with fiery malevolence, surged forward relentlessly, their eyes burning with malice as they sought to overwhelm their golden adversaries. The ground beneath was a treacherous mix of dense forest and open field, littered with hidden roots and jagged rocks. Each step taken was fraught with peril as combatants fought to maintain their footing amidst the chaos.

Kimras, his golden scales gleaming like molten sunlight, stood resolute in the face of the onslaught. His sharp, calculating gaze locked onto Zylron, the formidable leader of the red dragons, whose fiery breath scorched the earth with every exhalation. With a bellowing roar, Kimras unleashed his own searing flames, the two torrents colliding midair in a cataclysm of heat and light. The air warped and shimmered under the intense heat, creating a distorted haze that veiled the battlefield. Blinded momentarily, the surrounding combatants faltered, but neither Kimras nor Zylron wavered as their elemental powers clashed with thunderous force.

Above the fray, Keisha, perched atop Kimras, radiated an aura of arcane energy. Her hands moved with practiced precision, tracing intricate patterns in the air to summon shimmering shields that deflected incoming attacks. Bolts of crackling magic erupted from her palms, striking red dragons with unerring accuracy. Each spell she cast was a beacon of light cutting through the dark chaos, her growing strength a defiant stand against the encroaching threat. The weight of Vacari's survival pressed on her shoulders, but Keisha fought not just to endure—she fought to protect everything and everyone she held dear.

The skies above were a storm of motion, dragonriders and their steeds weaving through the melee with deadly grace. Arrows rained down from above, finding the small, vulnerable gaps in the red dragons' armor, bringing down enemy after enemy. Ong, wielding his dragonlance with lethal precision, was a blur of motion. Each thrust of his weapon was deliberate, his strikes powered by unrelenting determination. His resolve burned as brightly as the flames around him, his heart set on safeguarding Goldmoor, Purplefire, and the lives that depended on him.

Yet even as the red dragons faltered under the relentless assault, a gnawing unease took root in Kimras. His battle-honed instincts whispered of something amiss. The red dragons fought fiercely, yet their attacks were erratic, disjointed—moments of ferocity followed by sudden retreats. Zylron's strikes, though devastating, felt calculated in a way that eluded understanding. It was as if the enemy sought not to conquer, but to observe, to probe their defenses.

Kimras's sharp gaze followed Zylron as the red dragon circled back, flames roaring anew. Something darker lay beneath these tactics, a puppeteer pulling unseen strings. The way the red dragons moved—hesitant, almost unnatural—sent a chill through him. It felt as though their actions were guided by a force beyond themselves, manipulated like pawns in a grander, unseen game.

Amara, her amethyst scales catching the sunlight as she fought, shared Kimras's unease. Her eyes, glowing with suspicion, tracked the enemy's movements with precision. She, too, had noticed the irregular rhythm of the red dragons' attacks. Moments of hesitation where there should have been none. Her power flared in a wave of magic, cutting through a swath of red dragons, but her mind remained focused on the underlying threat. She caught Kimras's glance, and in that shared look, an understanding passed between them—this was only the beginning.

Zylron, ever the strategist, seemed to be laying the groundwork for something more sinister. Kimras's thoughts raced as he deflected another barrage of flames. Could this skirmish be a diversion? A calculated ploy to draw their focus while a larger trap loomed unseen?

The battlefield roared with renewed fury as golden and red dragons clashed, each strike resounding like thunder. But beneath the visible chaos, an invisible game of strategy unfolded. Kimras could not shake the feeling that they were being watched, their defenses measured, their every move scrutinized by an unknown force.

With that realization, Kimras's resolve only solidified. He would not let Vacari fall to treachery or manipulation. Whatever trap lay ahead, he would face it head-on. The light of their alliance would not falter, no matter how deep the shadows sought to consume it.

As the skirmish intensified, Zylron, the formidable leader of the red dragons, launched a vicious assault on Amara, his movement swift and calculated. With a deafening roar, he unleashed a torrent of flames aimed directly at her vulnerable flank, the searing heat blazing through the battlefield like a wildfire.

Kimras, ever vigilant, sensed the danger. His golden eyes flared with fury as he turned his attention to Zylron, understanding in an instant the true intent of this assault. This was no random act of aggression—it was a deliberate, calculated strike. Zylron was not merely testing their defenses or sowing chaos. This was a targeted effort to harm or kill Amara, one of the most powerful and revered of the noble dragons.

A surge of unrelenting anger welled up within Kimras, fiercer than the flames that danced around him. The realization that Zylron sought to eliminate Amara filled him with a righteous wrath. With a thunderous roar, he intercepted the attack, his golden form radiating power. A ferocious blast of flames erupted from Kimras, meeting Zylron's assault head-on. The force of their clash sent shockwaves rippling across the battlefield, the air heavy with the raw power of their elemental fury.

Above the chaos, Keisha sprang into action, her form wreathed in shimmering arcane energy. Her protective instincts surged, and with a commanding sweep of her arm, she conjured a crystalline barrier of magic that enveloped Amara and Ong. The shield pulsed with radiant energy, reinforcing Kimras's defense and creating an impenetrable bulwark against Zylron's onslaught.

As the flames subsided, Kimras stepped forward, his gaze locked onto Zylron. His voice roared across the battlefield, each word laced with fury and resolve. "You dare attack my friend?!" he bellowed, the weight of his words trembling in the air. "This wasn't just a battle—you sought to kill her!"

Zylron sneered, his eyes smoldering with malice. "This is war, Kimras," he retorted, his voice dripping with venom. "There are no rules—only victory."

The tension crackled like lightning between the two dragons, their confrontation transcending mere combat. It had become a clash of will and purpose: Kimras's unyielding loyalty against Zylron's ruthless ambition. The weight of Zylron's treachery pressed heavily on Kimras, the realization of how close they had come to losing Amara fueling his rage.

With a roar that shook the battlefield, Kimras unleashed the full force of his power. Flames of searing light and scorching heat erupted from him in a torrent, engulfing Zylron in an inferno that burned with the weight of his fury. The red dragon, formidable and defiant, struggled to withstand the onslaught, but even his might faltered under the relentless barrage. Kimras's fire burned brighter, hotter, fueled by his resolve to protect and his unshakable sense of justice.

Zylron roared in pain, his form battered and scorched. His wings faltered, his once-mighty stance weakening. With a final, ragged snarl, he staggered backward, his body trembling from the force of the attack. His venomous gaze burned with hatred as he snarled, "This is not the end, Kimras. We will return, and when we do, you will rue this day."

Kimras met Zylron's gaze, his golden eyes ablaze with righteous fury. His voice, steady and resolute, carried across the battlefield. "You will never win, Zylron. Your darkness will always fall before true strength and righteousness."

With a bitter roar, Zylron turned, his forces retreating in disarray. The battlefield grew quiet, but the tension of his parting words lingered like a dark cloud over the defenders. The promise of future conflict hung heavy in the air.

As the flames of battle died away, Kimras and Amara descended to the ground, their powerful wings folding as they landed with a graceful but weary rhythm. The weight of the skirmish showed in their labored breaths, but their spirits remained unbroken. Keisha and Ong dismounted, giving their dragon companions space to recover. They exchanged glances, their bond strengthened by the trials they had faced, knowing that this victory, though hard-won, was but the beginning of a far greater struggle.

Kimras approached Amara, his expression softening but shadowed by concern. His sharp eyes scanned her for any sign of injury, but Amara met his gaze with a steady nod, her composure unshaken. Their bond, forged in countless battles, was stronger than any weapon, yet the tension between them was palpable.

Kimras's mind raced, replaying Zylron's calculated assault. He leaned closer, his voice low, anger barely restrained. "Zylron wasn't just testing us today. That attack—it was not random. He was targeting you, Amara. He wanted you dead."

Amara's amethyst eyes widened slightly, the weight of Kimras's words settling over her. "You're right," she said, her voice calm but resolute. "This wasn't just about the battle. He aimed to eliminate me."

Kimras's fury simmered beneath the surface as he cast his gaze toward the horizon where Zylron had retreated. "He will pay for this treachery," he growled. "No one threatens my friends and gets away with it."

Amara nodded, her heart swelling with gratitude for Kimras's fierce loyalty. "Thank you, Kimras," she said, her voice steady. "We will be ready for whatever comes next."

Satisfied that Amara was unharmed, Kimras allowed himself a moment of relief before turning to Keisha and Ong. His gaze softened, and he offered them a nod filled with gratitude. "Thank you, both of you. Your bravery and insight have saved us today."

Keisha, her form still shimmering faintly with residual magic, smiled warmly. Ong stood tall, his pride evident as he acknowledged their collective efforts. Yet, beneath the surface of relief, a heavy tension lingered in the air.

As the dust settled around them, Kimras and Amara exchanged reflective glances. An unspoken understanding passed between them, rooted in their shared leadership and instincts.

"They weren't attacking as they should," Amara remarked, her voice quiet but sure. "It felt... wrong, as though their strategy wasn't fully engaged."

Kimras's brow furrowed, his thoughts immediately returning to Zylron's attack. "Except when Zylron went after you," he said, his tone dark. "That was deliberate—focused."

Amara nodded, her expression thoughtful. "Yes. That part was intentional, but the rest? Disjointed, hesitant. They weren't fighting to win; they were testing us."

Kimras's expression darkened further. "Testing us..." he murmured, his voice heavy with the implications. "Or probing for weaknesses."

Nearby, Ong and Keisha had been quietly discussing their observations. Ong spoke first, his tone uneasy. "They weren't pushing as hard as they could. That wasn't a full assault."

Keisha's eyes narrowed in thought. "But Zylron's attack on Amara—that was personal. It was a calculated move to take her out."

Ong's gaze sharpened. "Kimras reacted fast, but it's clear Amara was the target. This isn't just about territory or chaos—they're targeting Vacari's leaders."

Keisha's breath caught as the pieces fell into place. "If their plan is to weaken us by targeting our leaders, it could work. Without leadership, our defenses—our unity—would crumble."

Ong's eyes widened as realization sank in. "Without leaders, we'd fall apart."

Keisha and Ong quickly relayed their insights to Kimras and Amara. As they spoke, Kimras's expression turned stormy, his righteous anger simmering just beneath the surface.

"Zylron dared to lay a claw on Amara?" Kimras roared, his voice shaking the air, fury radiating from him like heat. "He will pay dearly for this treachery!"

His roar echoed across the battlefield, and for a moment, silence fell. Slowly, Kimras's rage subsided, his voice calming but still carrying the weight of command. "Thank you for your insight," he said to Keisha and Ong, his gratitude evident. "We must inform the others immediately. This was no ordinary battle—it was a prelude. We have to be prepared for what's coming."

Kimras turned, his expression resolute as he reached deep within himself to summon the magic shared between the noble dragons and their allies. A soft hum filled the air, growing into a gentle breeze that carried the scent of wildflowers. Moments later, a radiant figure emerged from the surrounding trees—a nymph, her translucent wings shimmering like spun crystal, astride a magnificent white Pegasus.

Pegasus's hooves barely touched the ground as it approached, exuding an air of grace and power. The nymph's eyes, glowing faintly with ancient magic, met Kimras's with a quiet understanding. She bowed her head in respect, awaiting his instructions.

"Go swiftly," Kimras said, his voice imbued with authority and urgency. "Warn the dragons of Vacari. Tell them these attacks are not what they seem. They must guard one another and fortify their territories. Zylron and the dark forces are probing for weaknesses, and we cannot allow them to exploit what they find. Stress the importance of unity—we must be prepared for their next move."

The nymph nodded solemnly, her hands glowing as she conjured radiant scrolls, the message magically imprinted upon them. With a graceful motion, she tucked the scrolls into a satchel at her side. Pegasus spread its powerful wings, and with a mighty leap, they soared into the sky, disappearing over the horizon in a blur of white and silver.

Kimras watched her departure, a weight lifting slightly from his shoulders. Though the message had been sent, the responsibility of protecting Vacari rested heavily upon him. He turned back to his companions, his golden eyes filled with resolve. "The message is on its way. Now we must prepare ourselves for the challenges to come."

The group stood together, their determination solidified. The revelation of Zylron's treachery and the calculated nature of the attack left no doubt that darker days lay ahead. Yet, their bond of friendship, loyalty, and shared purpose burned brighter than any shadow.

As they turned their thoughts to the future, a silent vow echoed among them. They would not be caught unprepared. Vacari's defenders, united and unyielding, would stand against the growing darkness. Together, they would face whatever came next, their resolve unbreakable, their hearts steeled for the challenges ahead.

Chapter 24

Whispers of Fire: Tensions Unleashed

Zylron returned from the skirmish near Goldmoor, his wings scorched and tattered from the battle with Kimras and Amara. Each labored beat of his wings carried him closer to Flameford, the embers flickering in his eyes—an outward reflection of the fury burning inside him. The acrid scent of smoke and ash clung to the air, mingling with the remnants of destruction he had left behind. He landed heavily before the looming figure cloaked in shadow, his growl reverberating through the chamber like distant thunder.

"I came within a breath of annihilating Amara!" Zylron hissed, the memory of the battle still fresh and raw. His voice crackled with bitter frustration, the taste of his near-victory souring in his throat.

The figure turned slowly, their eyes gleaming with icy disdain, the rest of their face obscured by shadows that seemed to cling to them like a second skin. "Nearly?" they snapped, each word a shard of frozen contempt. "Do not come to me with 'nearly.' Explain yourself!"

Zylron's growl deepened, his pride bristling under the weight of the figure's scorn. Flames flickered dangerously in his throat, the heat of his frustration boiling to the surface. "Kimras intervened," he snarled, his voice rough with fury. "He shielded Amara, thwarting my attack. Her life was in my grasp—and then gone." His claws gouged deep into the stone floor, leaving scorched marks as the battle replayed in his mind.

The figure stepped forward, the oppressive weight of their presence pressing down like an unseen hand. "Failure is unacceptable," they said coldly, their voice cutting through the air like a dagger. "There are no excuses for failure—only consequences."

Zylron's tail lashed in defiance, his frustration turning to anger. He bared his fangs, his fiery gaze meeting the figure's. "You think you can speak to me this way?" he roared, his voice shaking the chamber. "I am Zylron, leader of the red dragons, a force that has scorched realms into submission! I—"

The air grew heavy, the shadows thickening as the figure's eyes flared with an unnatural light. A cold, oppressive force seized Zylron mid-sentence, silencing him. The heat of his flames wavered, dimming as an ancient and overwhelming power pressed against him. His defiance faltered, and he felt, for the first time in centuries, a primal fear clawing at his chest.

"You think your flames can touch me?" the figure intoned, their voice a quiet, chilling promise of destruction. They took another step closer, and Zylron instinctively recoiled, his wings folding tightly against his body. The suffocating power surrounding the figure left no doubt—they were more than a mere ally or manipulator. They were something far greater, far darker.

The red dragon bowed his head slightly, his earlier bravado extinguished. "Kimras and Amara were stronger than expected," he muttered, his voice subdued. "They had help... Keisha's magic continues to grow. It's becoming... problematic."

The figure's growl deepened, reverberating through the chamber like an earthquake. "Excuses do not absolve failure," they said, turning away with an air of finality. "Keisha and the noble dragons are a threat—but they are not insurmountable. See to it that your next move leaves no room for error. The cost of another failure... will not be so forgiving."

Zylron watched the figure disappear into the darkness, their presence lingering like a shadow over his pride. His anger simmered, but now it was laced with the weight of his own doubt. The noble dragons were proving to be more resilient than expected, and Keisha's magic loomed over them—a force he had underestimated. The crack in his confidence deepened, gnawing at him as he stood alone in the suffocating silence.

As the figure disappeared into the shadows, Glaceria approached, her icy gaze tracing the scorch marks on Zylron's scales. "Kimras's doing, I presume?" she asked, her voice soft yet sharp as frost, a layer of concern lingering beneath her composed exterior.

Zylron nodded slowly, his mind still replaying the battle. "Partially," he admitted, though his thoughts lingered on a far more imposing presence. "But Keisha... her magic was stronger than before. She's no longer just a nuisance."

Glaceria's eyes widened slightly at the mention of Keisha, her mind stirring with old memories. "The elf," she murmured, her voice like the chill wind that cuts through bone. "Her magic resurfaces—more powerful than ever." There was a grudging respect in her tone, though it was steeped in resentment. Keisha had always been a threat, but now that threat had grown into something far more dangerous.

Zylron's claws scraped against the stone as he spoke. "Stronger than when Phoenix and Vuarus tried to harness her power." The mention of their former allies brought a flicker of ambition to his gaze—a time when they had come so close to victory, only to be thwarted by noble dragons and Keisha's resilience.

Glaceria's lips curled into a smile that did not quite reach her eyes. "I find myself yearning to freeze her again," she said with an eerie hint of amusement. "To remind her of her place."

Zylron chuckled, the sound hollow and bitter. "As tempting as that would be," he said, his voice darkening, "our troubles with the elf are far from over." His mind flashed back to the battlefield, the crackling energy of Keisha's magic a warning of what lay ahead.

Glaceria tilted her head, her sharp gaze narrowing as she studied Zylron's subdued demeanor. "But there's something else," she observed, her voice carrying a note of intrigue. "You backed down. From them." Her words hung in the air like frost clinging to glass. "What happened?"

Zylron stiffened, his eyes flicking toward the shadows where the figure had vanished. For a moment, silence reigned as he grappled with his pride, but the lingering weight of his earlier fear was impossible to ignore. "There is... something about them," he said carefully, his voice low. "Something I cannot place, but it would be unwise to argue with or stand against them."

Glaceria's brow arched, a flicker of surprise flashing across her otherwise composed features. "Unwise? Coming from you, that is rare." She stepped closer, her voice taking on a softer, more contemplative tone. "Do they hold power over you, Zylron? Or is it something more... primal?"

Zylron's growl rumbled softly, his tail flicking with irritation. "It is not power over me," he said, though the fire in his voice had dimmed. "It is their presence—something ancient and suffocating. It grips you, and for a moment, you feel as though no flame, no strength, could stand against it."

Glaceria watched him closely, her icy exterior momentarily thawing with curiosity. The idea of something that could cow Zylron was both troubling and fascinating. "Interesting," she said at last, her voice quiet. "If even you hesitate to challenge them, we tread more dangerous ground than I thought."

As they stood together, the flickering firelight reflected off their scales, casting long shadows across the chamber. The weight of the past bore down heavily upon them, but it was the future that pressed most urgently. In the icy gaze they shared, there was an unspoken understanding—they had to act swiftly or risk losing control over the very fate they sought to bend.

Elsewhere in the dark tower, Lyra, the dark elf, glanced up from her ancient scrolls, her crimson eyes gleaming with the hunger for more power. The runes that illuminated the chamber cast eerie patterns on the walls, their glow flickering as though responding to the dark energy that crackled in the air. She carefully traced the inscriptions with her fingers, whispering ancient words that seemed to deepen the shadows around her. Her thoughts were interrupted by the storming entrance of the mysterious figure, their presence seething with disappointment and fury.

"What vexes you, my lord?" Lyra asked, her voice dripping with intrigue, each word carefully measured to mask her own ambitions. Her crimson gaze gleamed, ever eager to glean insight into the figure's plans—or failures.

The figure halted abruptly, their eyes narrowing as they spat the name like venom. "Zylron," they hissed, their voice slicing through the oppressive silence of the chamber.

Lyra raised an eyebrow, her interest piqued at the mention of the red dragon. "What of Zylron?" she asked, leaning forward, her curiosity barely concealed.

The figure's temper flared, their voice laced with cold fury. "He failed," they growled. "Failed to destroy Amara when the opportunity was laid bare before him. Kimras shielded her, and Keisha's magic was stronger than any of us anticipated."

Lyra's expression darkened, her mind already racing with the implications of those words. The thought of Keisha's growing power both unsettled and intrigued her. "So, Keisha's power grows... stronger than we anticipated," she murmured, her voice heavy with the weight of revelation. "We underestimated her once—never again."

The figure's anger simmered, their movements sharp and deliberate as they paced the room. "If Keisha and Ong continue to grow in strength, they'll become more than mere irritations—they'll become threats capable of unraveling all that we've worked toward."

A cold smile crept across Lyra's face, her crimson eyes alight with dark possibilities. "Then we must find a way to neutralize that threat," she said smoothly, her words like silk spun from shadow. "Keisha's power is tied to Kimras. We must separate them—divide their strength."

The figure stopped abruptly, their piercing gaze locking onto Lyra. "Indeed. We will strike while she is riding Kimras. Zylron's forces will create a distraction to demand Kimras's full focus. Meanwhile, Glaceria will target Purplefire Woods. We will divide the defenders, ensuring they are too scattered to protect their leaders effectively." Their voice dropped to an icy whisper. "There will be no failures this time."

Lyra hesitated for only a moment before carefully broaching a delicate subject. "You've forbidden us from harming Keisha directly before, concerned about provoking retribution from Kimras and her husband. If I may ask... has that concern changed?"

The figure turned sharply, their glare chilling. "You've been too fixated on Phoenix's failure," they snapped, their tone cutting. "A death in battle is different from outright harm designed to provoke vengeance. If Keisha falls amidst chaos, it is no different than any other casualty of war. Do you understand now?"

Lyra's lips curled into a wicked smile, satisfaction gleaming in her eyes. "Brilliant," she said softly. "Keisha's power may have grown, but it will be her undoing."

The figure nodded, their shadowy presence seeming to grow darker, more oppressive. "Then see to it that the plan is executed without error. Zylron and Glaceria know their targets. I will not tolerate another failure."

As their plotting deepened, the darkness in the tower pulsed like a living entity, feeding off the malice and treachery that filled the air. The flickering glow of the runes illuminated the room, casting ominous patterns across the walls as their plan took shape. This scheme would not only test Keisha's growing power but threaten to fracture the bonds of the noble dragons and their allies. And as the echoes of their laughter reverberated through the chamber, the shadow of impending conflict loomed ever larger over Vacari.

Chapter 25
Dragons' Vigil: Amidst Flames and Shadows

In the serene surroundings of Goldmoor, where sunlight danced upon the emerald leaves and a gentle breeze carried whispers of ancient tales, Ong and Keisha sat beneath the shade of a towering oak tree. Though the tranquility of their surroundings seemed a world away from the chaos they had recently faced, the tension between them lingered, unspoken but palpable.

Ong broke the silence, his voice cutting through the stillness with quiet intensity. "It was strange, wasn't it?" His brow furrowed deeply, his eyes focused on the distant horizon. "Zylron held back, only unleashing his full strength when he targeted Amara."

Keisha nodded slowly, her gaze distant, lost in the tangled aftermath of the battle. "It wasn't just strange—it was calculated," she replied, her voice steady but edged with cold understanding. "Zylron wasn't there to win. He was there to test something. To test Kimras."

Ong's expression darkened, his jaw tightening as the realization sank in. "Testing his loyalty," he murmured, the weight of his words hanging in the air. "To see how far Kimras would go to protect Amara."

Keisha's lips pressed into a thin line, her hands curling into fists as the implications struck deeper than she had anticipated. "It's not just a battle tactic—it's psychological," she said, her voice trembling slightly, betraying the emotions she usually kept so carefully in check. "Zylron wanted to exploit Kimras's bond with Amara, to see if it could be used against him."

The breeze that had once felt warm and welcoming now seemed colder, carrying a faint chill that mirrored the unease growing between them. Ong's eyes narrowed, his voice dropping to a low, serious tone. "Zylron didn't need to destroy Kimras in that fight. He just needed to plant doubt—to make Kimras second-guess his choices in the heat of battle."

Keisha's gaze snapped back to him, her eyes gleaming with fierce determination. "We can't let him get inside our heads," she said firmly, her voice filled with quiet strength. "If Zylron can make us question ourselves, he's already won."

Their eyes met, and in that moment, an unspoken understanding passed between them. This was not just about physical strength anymore. It was about resilience—holding their ground even when everything around them threatened to crumble.

Keisha reached out, placing a hand on Ong's arm. "We stand together," she said softly, her voice carrying the promise of unity. "No matter what they throw at us, we hold the line."

Ong covered her hand with his, nodding firmly. "Always," he replied, his voice resolute.

The peaceful surroundings seemed to blur, the weight of their conversation casting a shadow over the idyllic scene. Yet, even in the midst of doubt and fear, there was something unyielding in the bond they shared. Together, they knew they could face whatever trials awaited them.

Elsewhere in Goldmoor, beneath the dappled sunlight that filtered through the emerald canopy, Kimras stood beside Amara, his heart weighed down by unspoken fears. Though the world around them was calm, the memory of the battle burned within him, a gnawing ember that refused to die.

Kimras's golden eyes lingered on Amara, his gaze searching her as if trying to uncover hidden scars. The events of the battle replayed in his mind, each moment sharper than the last. "Are you sure you're alright, Amara?" he asked softly, his voice carrying an undercurrent of anxiety he could not quite mask.

Amara offered him a gentle smile, but a shadow flickered in her amethyst eyes. "I'm fine, Kimras. You protected me." Her words were meant to soothe, but she could see they did little to ease the worry etched into his features.

Kimras's claws sank into the earth as he shook his head, frustration, and fear colliding within him. "I came too close to losing you," he murmured, his voice strained. "Zylron was targeting you, and for a moment..." He faltered, his words catching in his throat. "For a moment, I didn't know if I could save you."

Amara's heart clenched as she watched the golden dragon—her steadfast friend, her protector—struggle with emotions he rarely allowed to surface. She stepped closer, her voice a soft anchor in the storm of his doubt. "You did save me, Kimras," she reminded him firmly. "You always have."

But Kimras's expression remained clouded, the storm within him refusing to abate. "What if next time, I'm forced to choose between protecting you and leading the others?" he asked, his voice dropping to a whisper as if saying the words aloud made them more real. "What if Zylron makes me choose?"

The weight of his question hung heavy in the air between them, the unspoken fears pressing down on both their hearts. Amara's smile faded as her own concerns stirred to the surface. She had seen the way Zylron fought—calculated and cruel. She knew his mind would twist every bond, exploit every strength until it became a weakness.

"Kimras," she began quietly, her voice steady despite the turmoil she felt. "You can't carry this alone. I know what you are thinking—that Zylron will use me against you. But we have to trust in each other. That's our strength, not our weakness."

Kimras's golden eyes met hers, but the flicker of doubt in his gaze remained. "I trust you, Amara," he said after a moment, his voice raw with vulnerability. "It's myself I'm starting to doubt."

The admission cut deeper than any wound. Amara felt her heart twist painfully as she looked at him, the dragon who had always been her rock, her unwavering pillar of strength. Now, she saw the cracks Zylron had driven into him, the seeds of uncertainty the red dragon had planted.

"You're stronger than you know, Kimras," Amara said softly, her voice brimming with quiet determination. "And I will stand by you. Whatever comes, we face it together."

Kimras's gaze lingered on her, the turmoil in his expression softening just slightly. In her steadfast eyes, he found a sliver of reassurance—a reminder that even in the face of doubt, he was not alone. They had faced countless battles side by side, and they would face this one, too, no matter the cost.

The sunlight filtering through the leaves above cast shifting patterns across the ground, a fleeting symbol of hope amidst the shadows of their fears. Together, they stood in silence, the bond between them a quiet yet unbreakable promise: no matter how dark the path became, they would walk it together.

As Ong and Keisha approached, the palpable tension between Kimras and Amara hung in the air like a fragile thread. Keisha's smile softened when she noticed the heaviness in their expressions, her eyes reflecting a deep empathy for what they were enduring. She understood, perhaps better than anyone, the weight of the unspoken fears swirling between them.

Ong, ever observant, leaned closer to Keisha as they walked. "Do you think it's only friendship?" he asked, his voice low but tinged with teasing, a subtle attempt to break the somber mood.

Keisha chuckled softly, though her heart ached for her friends. Her gaze lingered on the dragons, their bond evident even in silence. "For now, they call it friendship," she replied warmly, her voice barely above a whisper. "But that bond... it's something deeper. Something Zylron is trying to tear apart."

Ong's thoughtful nod mirrored her sentiment as they reached the dragons. The gravity of the moment settled over them like a shroud, yet there was a strength in their unity—a silent acknowledgment of the battle they all shared, even beyond the physical.

Kimras and Amara turned to greet them, their expressions a mix of weariness and gratitude. The golden dragon inclined his head slightly, his voice carrying warmth despite the lingering shadows. "Good to see you both," he said, his tone subdued but genuine. "Join us. We've been discussing the battle... and what comes next."

Ong's gaze sharpened, his warrior instincts flaring as he stepped forward. "We've been doing the same," he said, his voice firm. "There's a lot to prepare for. Zylron's attack wasn't just a show of force—it was calculated, something far more insidious."

Keisha stepped closer, her eyes meeting Amara's with a shared understanding. Her voice was quiet, but it carried a resolute conviction. "We think Zylron was testing your bond, Kimras. He wanted to see if he could make you hesitate—to see how far you would go to protect Amara."

Kimras's golden gaze darkened, his claws flexing instinctively as he absorbed their words. He lowered his head slightly, his voice a rumble of quiet frustration. "I felt it," he admitted. "He wasn't trying to defeat me in that moment—he was trying to make me question myself. To make me doubt."

Amara's amethyst eyes gleamed with a mixture of sorrow and resolve as she added, "And if he can plant that doubt in you, Kimras... he'll keep using it, over and over again. He'll find the crack and tear it open."

Ong, his voice steady and filled with urgency, spoke next. "We believe Zylron isn't just targeting noble dragons—he's going after the leaders. If he can take you down, Kimras, Vacari's defenses will crumble. He's playing a long game, and this was just the start."

Keisha's voice trembled slightly, but her determination was unshaken. "He's trying to break you, Kimras. And by doing that, he'll break us all."

A heavy silence settled over the group, the weight of their realization pressing down on each of them. Kimras, so often the embodiment of steadfast leadership, seemed shaken for a moment. His eyes flickered with doubt, and for the first time, the vulnerability he had been carrying was laid bare. He was not just a leader—he was a friend, a protector, and a linchpin holding their fragile alliance together.

But then, Kimras drew in a deep, steadying breath. The doubt in his eyes was replaced with a spark of defiance. His claws pressed into the earth, grounding him as his voice grew stronger, a fire rekindling within. "Then we cannot let him win," he declared, the words rippling with conviction. "We stay vigilant. We stay united. Zylron will not break me. He will not break us."

Amara's expression softened, a flicker of pride shining in her amethyst gaze. She stepped closer, her voice firm and filled with quiet strength. "Together, we are stronger than Zylron could ever imagine. He will never understand the bond we share, and that will be his downfall."

Keisha smiled, her heart swelling at their resolve. "We face him as one," she said, her voice carrying the weight of her unyielding spirit. "Always."

Ong nodded, his eyes scanning the horizon as if daring the shadows to rise again. "Whatever he has planned, we'll be ready."

The four stood together beneath the dappled sunlight, their bond unspoken yet undeniable. The shadows looming on the horizon grew darker, but the light of their unity burned brighter. Zylron may have sought to break them, but he had only strengthened their resolve.

And as they turned their gazes to the challenges ahead, there was no doubt in their hearts: whatever storm awaited them, they would face it together—and they would not falter.

Chapter 26

Symphony of Wings: The Sacred Partnership

The early evening sky over Goldmoor was painted in hues of orange and pink, casting a warm glow across the land. Keisha stood beside Ong, her Eladrin features illuminated by the soft light as they faced the two noble dragons—Kimras and Amara—who listened attentively. Keisha's voice was steady but laced with urgency as she posed a question that weighed heavily on her mind.

"Kimras, Amara," Keisha began, a mixture of curiosity and concern in her tone, "if Ong or I were on your backs, and Zylron or Glaceria attacked, what would you do?"

Kimras's golden eyes flickered with solemn resolve as he turned to meet Keisha's gaze. His expression was unwavering, reflecting his deep sense of duty since birth. "A dragon's first duty is to protect their rider, no matter the danger," he replied, his voice steady, carrying the weight of millennia of tradition. "Even if it means fighting alone, we would never endanger you."

Ong, his brow furrowed in thought, looked between Kimras and Amara. The weight of Kimras's words settled on him, stirring something deep within. After a moment of contemplation, he spoke, his voice quieter but filled with curiosity. "Kimras, Amara... what does this bond truly mean? How did this sacred bond between dragon and rider come to be?"

Amara, her amethyst scales shimmering as the sun dipped lower in the sky, inclined her head. Her voice was soft yet firm as she answered. "The bond between dragon and rider is ancient. It is more than a partnership—a covenant of trust and honor. When we choose a rider, we dedicate our lives to their safety and well-being. It's not just duty—it's a connection forged through shared battles and struggles, a bond that goes beyond words."

Kimras added, his voice filled with reverence, "This bond has been passed down through generations. Protecting our riders is our most sacred calling. It's not just about strength in battle—it's about trust, sacrifice, and honor."

Ong listened closely, his respect for the dragons deepening with every word. The bond between dragon and rider was not just a partnership—it was a profound connection rooted in trust and sacrifice. He glanced at Keisha, and his resolve strengthened. "I see it now," he said softly. "This bond makes us stronger. Together, we are united by purpose and destiny."

Moved by their words, Keisha felt a surge of curiosity. "Do you have a story from the past that shows the depth of this bond? Something that reveals its history and importance?"

Kimras and Amara exchanged knowing glances before Amara spoke, her voice flowing like a gentle breeze. "Centuries ago, in the realm of Aurelia, there lived a dragon named Thalor and his rider, Elara. Thalor was a noble silver dragon, and Elara was a fierce Eladrin warrior. Their bond was one of the strongest ever known. One day, an ancient evil returned to Aurelia, threatening to plunge the land into darkness."

Amara's eyes gleamed with intensity as she continued. "Elara and Thalor led the charge against this malevolent force. In the heat of battle, Elara was struck by a dark spell, her strength fading. Thalor, sensing her peril, fought with unmatched fury to protect her. He shielded her with his body, taking the brunt of the enemy's attacks."

Kimras picked up the story, his deep voice resonating with emotion. "In a desperate moment, Thalor made the ultimate sacrifice—he merged part of his life force with Elara's, giving her the strength to strike one final blow. Together, they defeated the ancient evil and saved Aurelia. Though weakened, Thalor survived, and their bond only grew stronger. Their story became a legend, a testament to the unbreakable bond between dragon and rider."

The tale captivated Keisha and Ong. The weight of its meaning hung in the air as they grasped the depth of the bond.

Amara glanced toward Kimras, her amethyst eyes shimmering with emotion. "That story reminds us of something deeper, doesn't it?"

Kimras nodded, his golden gaze warm but thoughtful. "It does. The bond is not just about battles. It is about sharing the weight of decisions, the triumphs, and even the failures."

Keisha tilted her head, curiosity flickering in her expression. "Failures?"

Kimras's voice softened. "There are times when even the strongest bonds are tested. A rider may falter. A dragon may hesitate. But it is how we come back from those moments, how we trust again, that strengthens the bond even more."

Keisha's voice was soft, filled with awe. "Thank you, Kimras, Amara. It's a powerful reminder of the strength and courage in this partnership."

Kimras smiled warmly at Keisha, his eyes filled with affection. "Do you remember our first battle at Goldmoor, Keisha? When Phoenix Shadowwalker's magic knocked you from my back?"

Keisha nodded, the memory was still vivid. "Yes, I remember."

Kimras's voice softened. "Even then, we were bonded. I dove after you, catching you mid-air, and pulling you back onto my back. I would've done anything to protect you."

Keisha took a deep breath, her voice trembling slightly as she asked, "Is that why you and Amara came to Afor when Vuarus was going to sacrifice me? Were you the ones who pulled me from the Abyss while Amara destroyed the altar?"

Kimras's gaze softened, and he nodded. "Yes, Keisha. Our bond compelled us to act. We could not let you be taken. The moment we sensed your danger, we knew we had to act. It was our honor to save you."

Tears welled up in Keisha's eyes as she recalled that harrowing moment. She stepped forward and embraced Kimras. "I understand the bond now," she whispered, her voice thick with emotion.

Ong joined them, wrapping an arm around Keisha. "We understand," he said, his voice filled with gratitude.

Keisha pulled back slightly, meeting Kimras's gaze with a resolute expression. "There's something I want you both to promise. Do not sacrifice your protection of one another for Ong or me. If the battle puts you in such a position, let us dismount. We can fight alongside you from the ground."

Kimras regarded Keisha with a mix of admiration and respect. "You ask this of us because you see the value in both of our lives. That is rare among riders. Many believe dragons exist solely to protect them, but you understand the true meaning of partnership."

Amara's voice joined, quiet yet firm. "It is not just our duty to protect—it is our choice. We choose this bond because it makes us greater together than apart."

Keisha's throat tightened at the weight of their words. She nodded, her voice trembling slightly. "And I choose to honor that bond by protecting you both in return."

Ong nodded. "We don't want you to risk yourselves for us. This battle is for the noble dragons as much as it is for us."

Kimras and Amara exchanged a solemn glance before Kimras spoke. "Your safety is our priority, but we understand. We will protect you—and ourselves."

Amara nodded. "We promise. If the situation becomes too dire, we'll ensure your safety and continue the fight."

With that promise, a sense of relief settled over Keisha and Ong. They stood united, ready to face the challenges ahead, knowing their bond with the dragons had deepened further—built on trust, understanding, and mutual respect.

Chapter 27
Darkening Horizon

The early evening sky over Flameford was painted in ominous hues of red and black, casting a foreboding glow across the land. Quellan strode into the shadowed tower, his footsteps echoing sharply against the cold, unyielding stone floor. The chamber was dimly lit, its flickering runes casting eerie, restless shadows that danced along the walls.

A mysterious figure cloaked in shadow glanced up from their work, their eyes gleaming with an intensity that pierced the dim light. Without lifting their gaze fully, they spoke in a voice laced with sharp command.

"Relay a message to Zylron and Glaceria: tell them to ready their clans. We launch a coordinated attack on both Goldmoor and Purplefire. But remind them—no destruction of the forests. Our focus remains on the amethyst and gold dragons."

Quellan nodded crisply, already preparing to turn, but the figure's voice cut through the air again, halting him.

"And Quellan," they added, their tone icy, "make sure Zylron understands—no more mistakes. He must not lose focus again."

A chill prickled down Quellan's spine at the reminder. Dealing with Zylron was always fraught with peril, but there was no room for hesitation. Bowing slightly, he slipped from the oppressive chamber, the cool night air outside a stark contrast to the stifling atmosphere within.

The weight of the impending battle pressed heavily on him as he made his way to Zylron's lair. The molten glow of the cavern radiated a suffocating heat, illuminating the red dragon's immense, imposing form. Zylron loomed over a pool of lava, his fiery gaze locked on Quellan with a fierceness that made the air itself seem heavier.

"Zylron," Quellan began, summoning every ounce of composure to steady his voice. "The figure commands us to prepare for a coordinated strike on Goldmoor and Purplefire. The focus is on eliminating the amethyst and gold dragons. The forests are to remain untouched."

Zylron's eyes narrowed, and a low, menacing growl rumbled from deep within his chest. Quellan instinctively stepped back, his pulse quickening in the face of the dragon's palpable rage.

"There's... one more thing," Quellan continued, his voice faltering ever so slightly. "No more mistakes."

A tense silence descended, so thick it seemed to smother even the heat of the lava. Zylron's massive tail flicked, and Quellan tensed as it swished dangerously close, its fiery tip scorching the cavern floor with a hiss. For one heart-stopping moment, Quellan braced himself, half-expecting the blow to land.

Instead, the tail stopped just short of striking him.

Quellan exhaled slowly, the wave of relief almost as overwhelming as the lingering tension. Zylron's dark gaze seemed to burn deeper, his claws digging into the stone floor as though restraining the impulse to lash out. After a long, excruciating pause, the red dragon gave a curt nod, his acceptance of the order as reluctant as it was ominous.

Before departing, Quellan hesitated, a flicker of uncertainty crossing his face. Then, summoning his courage, he cautiously ventured, "Zylron, I believe there is an advantage we haven't fully considered."

Zylron's fiery gaze lifted, his curiosity piqued. "Speak."

"If we eliminate Keisha," Quellan began carefully, weighing each word, "it would remove a significant threat. Her magic has become a persistent thorn in our side."

At the mention of her name, Zylron's lips curled into a sinister smile, his eyes gleaming with predatory delight. "Keisha…" he growled, savoring the sound of the name like a promise of vengeance. "Yes, that would simplify things."

From the shadows, Glaceria emerged, her icy eyes catching the molten glow of the cavern. Her voice was smooth, almost purring. "A fitting addition to our plans," she said, her tone both cold and calculating.

Quellan quickly interjected, his tone firm. "But our primary objective remains eliminating Kimras and Amara. Keisha is secondary."

Zylron's smile faltered, and his gaze darkened with thinly veiled irritation. After a tense pause, he grumbled reluctantly, "Of course."

Quellan exhaled, relieved to have delivered the message without further incident. As he turned to leave the cavern, the air seemed to ease, but only slightly. There was an ominous weight to this mission, an undeniable sense that this battle would be unlike any they had faced before—more decisive, more final.

Back at the dark tower, Quellan returned to find the mysterious figure still at work, their silhouette barely discernible in the dim light. The air around them was heavy with authority, their presence as imposing as ever. Quellan stepped forward and delivered his report.

"The orders have been delivered. Zylron and Glaceria are preparing their clans for the assault."

The figure nodded, their expression unreadable in the flickering light. Quellan hesitated, then added, "There was a suggestion... an additional target—Keisha. Zylron and Glaceria both agree it would strengthen our efforts."

A slow, sinister smile spread across the figure's face. "An excellent suggestion," they said softly. "It's time that Eladrin was removed."

A chill ran down Quellan's spine at the malice in their tone, but he nodded and withdrew silently. As he stepped outside, the darkness seemed to deepen around him, a foreboding omen of the storm about to descend on Goldmoor and Purplefire.

Inside Zylron's lair, the red dragon stood beside Glaceria, the glow of molten lava reflecting off their scales and casting ominous shadows across the cavern walls. Spread before them was a detailed map of Vacari, its edges singed from heat.

"I will lead the charge on Goldmoor," Zylron declared, his voice filled with fiery conviction. "Kimras will be there. I look forward to destroying him and watching Goldmoor burn."

Glaceria nodded, her icy tone a stark contrast to his fire. "Amara will be at Purplefire. I will ensure her end." Her glinting eyes swept over the map as she added, "We should merge our red and white dragons for this attack. Their combined strength will overwhelm any defense."

Zylron's gaze flicked to her, considering the proposal. Finally, he gave a curt nod. "Agreed. Together, they will not stand a chance."

As they finalized their strategy, the air in the cavern seemed to crackle with anticipation. Zylron oversaw the red dragons, ensuring their loyalty through sheer intimidation. Any murmurs of dissent were silenced by his searing glare, his authority unchallenged.

At the dark tower, the mysterious figure emerged from the shadows to survey the gathered forces. Cloaked in an aura of command, they approached Zylron and Glaceria, their tone razor-sharp.

"There will be no failure this time," the figure intoned. "Kimras and Amara must fall."

Both dragons nodded in unison, their eyes burning with resolve.

"And if the opportunity arises," the figure added, their voice dripping with malice, "eliminate the Eladrin."

Zylron's claws flexed, scraping deep gouges into the stone floor. "With pleasure," he rumbled.

The figure turned, their final command echoing through the still night. "Go."

With a deafening roar, the dragons took flight. Their powerful wings beat against the night sky, carrying them toward their targets. The flames of war had been stoked, and the time for battle had come.

As darkness swallowed the land, the stage was set. The fate of Vacari hung in the balance, poised between the onslaught of darkness and the defiant stand of noble dragons. A battle loomed that would shape the destiny of the realm.

Chapter 28
Eclipse of Destiny

Zylron led his contingent of dragons—reds and whites flying in perfect formation—toward Goldmoor. Each beat of his powerful wings echoed like a war drum, driving them closer to their target. Thoughts of revenge and conquest burned in his mind, the raw marks from his last defeat etched into his scales as a constant reminder. The memory of that humiliation gnawed at him like a festering wound, fueling his fury. Every breath he drew was a vow of vengeance. The tension among his forces was palpable, the air thick with anticipation. They were harbingers of destruction, their hearts set on razing Goldmoor to the ground.

Far above, vigilant patrols circling the skies of Goldmoor caught sight of the approaching threat. Alarms rang out across the city, their piercing cries a clarion call of danger. The warning reached Kimras swiftly. Standing watch atop Goldmoor's ancient walls, he scanned the horizon, his sharp golden eyes narrowing as he took in the sight of the advancing enemy. Goldmoor's weathered stone towers, proud and unyielding through centuries of storms and strife, gleamed faintly in the fragile dawn light. But even these storied walls would face a trial unlike any they had endured before.

Kimras's gaze hardened with unshakable determination. Around him, loyal companions—both dragons and warriors—stood ready. Their expressions were grim but resolute, their loyalty and courage a silent testament to their shared purpose. The weight of Goldmoor's fate bore down on Kimras's broad shoulders. The lives of the city's citizens, the legacy of his people—all rested on their defense. His heart, though steeled for battle, carried the burden of leadership. He could not afford to fail.

Turning to a group of mages and young gold dragons, Kimras issued his command. "Prepare the barrier," he said, his voice steady yet edged with urgency. Each heartbeat mattered now. The shimmering wall of magic would be their first line of defense, buying precious time against the oncoming storm.

In the heart of Goldmoor, Ong held Keisha tightly, his embrace fierce and protective, as though his arms alone could shield her from what lay ahead. "Be careful, my love," he whispered, his voice thick with unspoken fears. His heart ached at the thought of her flying into danger, beyond his reach.

Keisha lingered in his embrace, drawing strength from the warmth and love she felt. "You too, Ong," she murmured, her voice low and steady despite the storm raging inside her. The weight of their shared burden pressed against her chest. As they pulled apart reluctantly, their eyes locked in silent understanding. Ong was bound for Purplefire Woods, each of them charged with defending a piece of what they held dear. Their unspoken promise hung in the air—each would fight, not just for themselves, but for the other.

Keisha turned her attention to Kimras, who waited nearby, his massive golden form outlined in the pale light of dawn. As she approached him, her resolve crystallized. The familiar weight of her longbow rested across her shoulder, its presence grounding her. Beneath her skin, magic hummed, coiling just beneath the surface, ready to surge forth at a moment's notice. Her eyes lifted to the shimmering barrier rising over the city, its ethereal glow both a symbol of hope and a stark reminder of how close destruction loomed.

With practiced grace, Keisha mounted Kimras, her hands gripping the ridges of his scales as he took to the sky. Below, the citizens of Goldmoor watched, their faces a mix of awe and fear. Their prayers seemed to rise with the defenders, their hopes clinging to the wings of those who soared above. The barrier flickered, its light fragile yet defiant. Keisha could feel the weight of their trust, their desperation. Her heart steeled as they climbed higher. This was no longer just a battle for survival—it was a fight to preserve everything she loved.

The sight of Zylron's advancing forces—a formidable mix of red and white dragons cutting through the sky—was a chilling reminder of the battle to come. Each dragon moved with lethal precision, their elemental powers flickering ominously. Keisha's grip on her bow tightened as her mind raced through strategies, weaving plans to combine her magic with her arrows. The weight of the moment bore down on her, but she felt Kimras's reassuring presence beneath her. Sensing her tension, the golden dragon glanced back, his piercing eyes meeting hers with a silent promise: protection and partnership.

As they climbed higher, the first rays of dawn spilled over the horizon, bathing Goldmoor in a golden glow. The light cascaded over the ancient city, illuminating its towering walls and gleaming spires, turning it into a fortress of hope standing defiantly against the encroaching shadow. Below, the defenders—dragons and warriors alike—drew strength from the light, their resolve hardening. Yet Keisha knew that no dawn could halt the inevitable clash. The next few hours would decide the fate of them all.

Kimras and Keisha shared a final, wordless exchange, a moment of solidarity and understanding. The stage was set, the players in place, and the air around them felt thick with anticipation. Each heartbeat resonated like the ticking of a clock, counting down to the collision of forces. Goldmoor's fate hung precariously in the balance, poised between the light of hope and the shadow of destruction.

Zylron's contingent of red and white dragons soared toward the outskirts of Goldmoor, their massive wings slicing through the morning air. Below them, the Cerulean Expanse stretched endlessly, gleaming like a serene ocean, indifferent to the chaos above. Each beat of Zylron's wings carried him closer to his prey, his sharp eyes scanning the horizon until they landed on Kimras.

The sight of the noble gold dragon aloft in the distance stirred Zylron's rage. Perched confidently on Kimras's back, Keisha was ready—her bow in hand, magic crackling at her fingertips. Her presence was a taunt, a silent challenge.

A slow, cruel grin spread across Zylron's face as he called out, his voice dripping with disdain, carried on the wind like venom. "Ah, Kimras. Still clinging to that troublesome Eladrin and her feeble tricks," he sneered, his gaze shifting to Keisha. Malice gleamed in his eyes as he relished the thought of their defeat. "But don't worry, I'll rid you of both nuisances soon enough."

Kimras's response was a deep, resonant growl that rumbled like thunder in his chest. His golden eyes locked on Zylron, narrowing with disdain. Patience had never been Kimras's strongest virtue, but his composure was unshakable. Above him, Keisha let out a soft, defiant laugh, her voice cutting through the tension like the sharp edge of her arrows.

"Zylron, you never learn, do you?" she said, her tone light but brimming with confidence. "Your threats are as empty as ever. We have beaten your kind before, and we will do it again."

Kimras's lips curled into a subtle, knowing smirk as Zylron's expression twisted with anger. The tension between them hung heavy in the air, crackling like the charged sky before a lightning storm.

"Your arrogance blinds you, Zylron," Kimras rumbled, his voice deep and steady, resonating with quiet power. "Outnumbered, perhaps. Outmatched? Never. Vacari is our home, and we will defend it with our last breath."

The air grew heavier, thick with the charge of destiny. Above, the sky darkened as swirling clouds gathered, their churning forms mirroring the monumental clash about to unfold. The atmosphere trembled, laden with the weight of impending conflict. Kimras and Zylron circled each other, their ancient rivalry blazing in their hearts like an unquenchable fire. Neither would yield; only one could claim dominance over the skies of Vacari.

Their massive forms moved with precise, controlled power, cutting through the air as they locked their eyes in a deadly stare. The sounds of Goldmoor—the bustling city, its rich history—faded into irrelevance. Only the pulse of the looming battle remained, pressing down like an unspoken command. Every beat of their wings, every tense moment, carried the gravity of a war that would shape the future.

With a final, thunderous roar, Zylron gave the signal. His forces surged forward, and chaos erupted in an instant. Dragons collided mid-air, their deafening roars and the crackle of unleashed flames reverberating across the battlefield.

The first wave of red dragons dove with terrifying speed. Keisha, without hesitation, leapt gracefully from Kimras's back, landing lightly on the ground below. In one fluid motion, she drew her bow, its arrows already glowing with fierce, crackling energy. Each shot flew with unerring precision, streaking through the smoky air like comets. The enchanted arrows struck true, piercing through scales and flesh with lethal accuracy. One by one, Zylron's dragons fell, their bodies plummeting from the sky in fiery arcs.

Above, Kimras roared, unleashing a torrent of golden flames. His shimmering scales reflected the blazing light, casting an ethereal glow that radiated across the battlefield. The air around him shimmered with searing heat, forming a fiery barrier that repelled Zylron's forces.

Zylron retaliated with his dark inferno, his flames wild and violent, striking out with ferocious power. The two titans clashed in a deadly dance of fire and fury, their elemental attacks colliding with earth-shaking force. Sparks and embers lit the sky as each sought to overpower the other, their roars echoing like thunder across the heavens.

The sky transformed into a battleground of chaos and destruction. Firestorms raged, claws tore through flesh, and wings snapped with sick-ening cracks. Smoke billowed, obscuring the sun, while below, the citizens of Goldmoor watched in a mix of awe and terror. Their hopes and fears hung in fragile balance, tied to the defenders who battled fiercely above.

Despite the unrelenting chaos, Kimras and Keisha moved with perfect synchronization. Their bond, forged through countless battles, was a force to be reckoned with. Keisha's enchanted arrows and searing magic wove seamlessly with Kimras's overwhelming strength and fire. Together, they were a symphony of power and precision, countering every attack with unyielding resolve.

Zylron's forces pressed harder, but Kimras and Keisha stood firm, their determination unshakable. Each strike they delivered was not just a blow to the enemy—it was a defiant stand against despair. In the face of overwhelming odds, they fought not just for Goldmoor, but for everything they loved and vowed to protect.

As the battle raged, Kimras sensed the perfect moment to unleash his most devastating weapon. With a powerful beat of his wings, he surged upward, disappearing into the churning clouds. Hidden from view, he began channeling his most formidable magic—Cloudkill. His deep, ancient voice whispered the incantation, each word resonating with the power of ages. A sickly green fog began to form around him, coiling like a living thing. The deadly mist spread slowly, purposefully, snaking its way toward Zylron's forces below.

The poisonous cloud rolled silently over the battlefield, its lethal presence invisible to the enemy. Zylron's dragons flew straight into the trap, unaware of the creeping death enveloping them. Yellow-green tendrils of mist wound around their massive forms, their corrosive touch draining strength with every breath. Agonized cries shattered the air as the poison invaded their lungs, sapping their power and resolve. Zylron's forces faltered, their once-coordinated movements becoming sluggish and erratic. For the defenders of Goldmoor, it was the reprieve they had desperately needed.

On the ground, Keisha's sharp eyes scanned the battlefield, watching intently as the tide began to shift. She recognized the precise moment the Cloudkill spell had taken its toll. Raising her hand, she signaled to the amethyst and gold dragons to hold their positions, biding their time until the fog had fully ravaged the enemy. Kimras's calculated move had bought them precious moments—enough to regroup and prepare for the battle's final, decisive phase.

Amid the chaos, Zylron's enraged roar tore through the air like a thunderclap. "How dare you wield such power against me, Kimras!" he bellowed, his voice thick with venomous fury. The dark fog sapped his forces, his wings beating furiously as he struggled to keep control. His massive form swayed in the poisoned air, his desperation palpable.

Kimras emerged from the clouds, his golden scales shimmering even in the shadowed sky. His unflinching gaze met Zylron's wrath with calm defiance. "You always underestimate me, Zylron," he replied, his tone carrying a subtle edge of mockery. "Perhaps now you'll learn that our strength runs deeper than your arrogance allows you to imagine."

Kimras's eyes narrowed, his voice gaining a sharper edge. "And you dare to accuse me of wielding such power? If the tables were turned, you would have used it without hesitation—without a shred of restraint. Do not pretend to stand on higher ground."

The battlefield was engulfed in chaos. The sickly green fog of Cloudkill twisted through the air, mingling with smoke and flame as dragons clashed in a storm of teeth, claws, and fire. The atmosphere crackled with raw tension, the sky itself trembling under the weight of the battle. As the deadly struggle raged on, the fate of Vacari hung precariously in the balance.

With a frustrated snarl, Zylron barked orders to his remaining forces, commanding them to regroup. His voice, sharp and commanding, carried over the din of battle. His mind raced, desperation clawing at him as he searched for a way to reclaim the upper hand. Each faltering moment stoked the flames of his rage, but the tide was slipping from his grasp.

Amid the chaos, Kimras soared above while Keisha held her ground below, both unwavering in their resolve. The dark clouds of war swirled violently around them, but their determination remained unshaken. As Zylron's forces struggled to recover, they prepared for the next clash, ready to meet whatever storm the desperate dragon would unleash.

Zylron's fury intensified as his dragons were repeatedly repelled by the shimmering magic barrier protecting Goldmoor. His roars reverberated across the battlefield, an unrelenting chorus of frustration and rage. His glowing eyes burned with fierce determination as they scoured the battlefield, seeking any weakness in the defenses—a crack in the armor that would turn the tide in his favor. But with each failed attempt, victory seemed to slip further from his grasp.

Kimras, observing Zylron's mounting frustration, felt a flicker of satisfaction. Their defenses held strong, a testament to the unity and resolve of Goldmoor's defenders. His gaze shifted downward to Keisha, who stood with her bow at the ready, her posture radiating focus and strength. A glimmer of pride softened his expression as he addressed her.

"Your magic has proven invaluable once again, Keisha," Kimras said, his voice filled with admiration.

Keisha looked up at him, her heart swelling at his words. "We make a good team, Kimras," she replied, steady and warm. Her eyes returned to the battle, scanning for signs of the next assault. Their bond, forged through countless trials, felt unbreakable as they prepared to face the next wave of darkness. Side by side in purpose, their unity fortified them for what was to come.

As the noxious fog began to dissipate, the battlefield emerged in stark clarity. Dragons from both sides circled each other warily, their glowing eyes locked in tense assessment. The air was thick with unspoken anticipation, the calm before the storm of another inevitable clash. Each side bore the marks of the fight—their scales scorched, wings torn, but their resolve unshaken.

Kimras and Keisha remained vigilant, scanning the horizon with sharp eyes. Both knew the battle was far from over. Zylron, cunning and relentless, would not concede so easily. The defenders steeled themselves for the fight ahead, their hearts and minds bound by a shared determination to protect their home and loved ones from the encroaching darkness.

High above, younger dragons darted into the fray, their hearts pounding with the raw adrenaline of battle. Red and white dragons launched ferocious attacks, fiery breath scorching the air and sharp claws tearing through their opponents with savage precision. The sky crackled with flame and fury as the chaos of combat swirled around them, each dragon fighting desperately to gain the upper hand.

Amid this chaos, the young gold and amethyst dragons shone brightly, their bravery compensating for their lack of experience. The gold dragons, their scales gleaming like molten metal in the sunlight, conjured shimmering protective barriers, shielding their allies from incoming attacks. Balls of fire erupted from their maws, streaking through the sky to crash into enemy ranks. Meanwhile, the amethyst dragons unleashed devastating blasts of psychic energy, bending the very ground beneath them to their advantage. Their movements were raw and unpolished, yet their potential was undeniable, their courage blazing as fiercely as their attacks.

These young dragons fought with unwavering determination, each one eager to prove their worth in the crucible of battle. The weight of defending their home and their families pressed heavily on their wings, but their spirits never faltered. They dove headlong into the chaos, striking against the dark forces that threatened everything they held dear, their resolve shining brightly in the shadow of war.

From her vantage point on the ground, Keisha's sharp eyes tracked the gold and amethyst dragons as they moved in unison. Alongside their courageous riders, they swooped down upon the red and white dragons still weakened by Kimras's poisonous mist. A coordinated assault unfolded across the turbulent skies, each maneuver precise and deliberate.

The white dragons retaliated with freezing blasts of icy breath, their attacks sending waves of bone-chilling cold through the ranks of their gold and amethyst adversaries. Frost crept across their scales, a creeping cold that dulled their movements and threatened to sap their strength. The icy barrage slowed the once-graceful dives of the gold dragons, their wings weighed down by the relentless freeze.

In retaliation, the red dragons unleashed searing waves of fire, their flames roaring through the sky as they targeted the white dragons with furious intensity. Fire met ice in a violent clash, creating bursts of steam that obscured the battlefield. The air became a battleground of opposing elements, the harmony of nature twisted into a storm of destruction.

Amidst the chaos, the amethyst dragons drew upon their psychic powers. Shimmering barriers of energy sprang to life, forming shields that deflected the fiery onslaught. These ethereal defenses provided critical cover for their allies, allowing dragon riders to dart through the storm of combat with renewed confidence. The amethyst dragons, though young, fought with an unshakable resolve, their psychic energy protecting their comrades and turning the tide.

Their minds sharp and their wills unyielding, the amethyst dragons reinforced the cohesion of the defenders. Each shimmering barrier held firm, protecting vulnerable points in the fray and giving their allies the edge they needed. Though untested, their unity lent them strength. They fought not just for survival, but for one another—for the bond that connected them as warriors of Vacari.

Seizing the opportunity created by the amethyst dragons' shields, the gold dragons and their riders dove fearlessly into the heart of the enemy formation. Lances gleaming in the sunlight, they moved with deadly precision. Each strike was swift, purposeful, and devastating. Their lances pierced scales with unerring accuracy, tearing through enemy defenses. The gold dragons roared in unison, their power radiating across the battlefield as they pressed their advantage.

The cacophony of combat rose to a deafening crescendo. The clash of steel against scale, the roar of flames, and the cries of dragons filled the air, echoing across the Cerulean Expanse. Above, dragons twisted and turned in mid-air, their scales glinting as they fought with relentless fury. The gold dragons and their riders drove deeper into enemy ranks, their determination unbreakable. With every thrust of a lance, they struck down their foes, refusing to yield an inch of ground.

Amid this tempest, the young dragons fought with hearts ablaze, their courage shining like beacons against the darkness. They knew that the outcome of this battle would shape the future of Vacari. With every breath, every strike, they gave their all for their home, their loved ones, and the bond that united them in this desperate fight.

The battle raged on with neither side willing to give a quarter. The skies above Goldmoor churned with fire, ice, and psychic energy—a tempest that mirrored the ferocity of its combatants. Every clash of claws, every burst of flame, carried the weight of Vacari's fate, precariously poised between triumph and ruin.

Several red dragons faltered under the relentless onslaught. Caught off guard by the gold dragons' precision, they fell one by one. The gleaming lances of the riders found their marks, piercing thick scales and striking fatal blows. Crimson blood stained the azure sky as the mighty beasts plummeted earthward, their roars silenced by the unforgiving hand of fate.

Zylron, witnessing the fall of his brethren, let out a primal roar that reverberated through the heavens. His eyes blazed with uncontrollable rage as he locked onto Kimras with a glare filled with venomous hatred. ""Prepare yourself, Kimras," Zylron snarled, his voice a chilling growl that cut through the chaos. "Your reign ends here, and Vacari will fall beneath the might of the dark dragons."

Kimras met Zylron's challenge with unwavering resolve. His golden eyes narrowed, reflecting the fierce determination of a dragon who had weathered countless battles. Fear had no place in his gaze—only the calm, steady focus of a leader prepared to stand against the storm. On the ground, Keisha mirrored his resolve, her longbow ready and magic swirling at her fingertips. The weight of the impending clash settled over them like a shroud, but neither flinched.

Without a word, Kimras in the skies and Keisha on the ground braced for Zylron's inevitable assault. Their bond, forged through fire and blood in countless battles, was unshakable. Though separated by air and earth, they stood as one, ready to confront the darkness threatening to consume Vacari.

The sky ignited in a brilliant storm of elemental fury as Zylron's scorching flames met Kimras's searing fireball. Explosions of light and heat erupted across the battlefield, rattling the heavens and the earth below. Keisha's protective magic shimmered around Goldmoor, casting a radiant barrier that absorbed the brunt of Zylron's inferno, sparing the city from destruction. Above, the skies became a battleground of fire and fury, elemental forces colliding with unimaginable power.

Zylron fought with unrelenting ferocity, unleashing waves of malevolent energy that crackled with destructive force. Each attack tore through the air, shaking the earth and filling the sky with violent bursts of power. His strikes were not measured or tactical—they were pure, raw force, designed to obliterate everything in their path. His rage fueled his attacks, and the darkness around him seemed to grow with each devastating blow.

Kimras, undeterred by the onslaught, held his ground with steadfast composure. His golden scales shimmered brilliantly in the sunlight, radiating an aura of strength and defiance. Every strike he delivered was precise, each movement guided by centuries of battle-hardened experience. Kimras's attacks were deliberate, calculated strikes that sought to wear down Zylron's fury and test his resolve.

As the two titans clashed, their powers intertwined in a chaotic, violent dance. Fire and darkness collided with enough force to shake the heavens, sending shockwaves rippling across the battlefield. Cracks of energy streaked through the sky like lightning, illuminating the swirling tempest. Below, the people of Goldmoor watched in awe and terror, their eyes fixed on the sky. Every clash of dragons was a battle for Vacari's future, their hopes resting on the shoulders of their defenders.

On the ground, Keisha remained a steadfast ally, her heart pounding as she channeled her magic into the fray. Arcane energy crackled around her, alive and potent, as she bolstered Kimras's attacks. Her hands glowed with ethereal light, weaving protective barriers that shimmered around her dragon companion. Sparks flew with every clash of fire and fury, and the very air sizzled with the overwhelming power filling the battlefield.

Zylron lunged forward, razor-sharp claws extended, aiming to rip through Kimras's defenses. But Kimras moved with practiced agility, dodging and countering each strike. With a thunderous roar, Kimras unleashed a torrent of golden flames, engulfing Zylron in a blinding inferno. The fire scorched the sky, lighting up the battlefield in a blaze of fury.

Though battered, Zylron met the attack head-on, his dark flames colliding with Kimras's. The resulting explosion lit the heavens with a brilliant flash, sending shockwaves through the battlefield below.

Kimras roared, the sound echoing like a thunderclap across the battlefield. With a tremendous beat of his golden wings, he surged forward, his talons reaching for Zylron. In a swift, decisive maneuver, Kimras seized the dark dragon in his iron grip and carried him high into the stormy sky. For a fleeting moment, they hovered above the battlefield, the world holding its breath as light and shadow collided. Then, with a mighty heave, Kimras hurled Zylron toward the looming mountains.

Zylron hurtled through the air like a falling comet, his dark silhouette stark against the storm-laden sky. The collision with the mountainside was catastrophic, sending shockwaves through the earth and triggering cascades of snow and rock that thundered down in an unstoppable torrent. When the dust settled, Zylron lay amidst the wreckage, his once-mighty form battered and broken. Blood seeped from gashes carved into his dark scales, and his body trembled with pain.

But even in defeat, Zylron's resolve remained unbroken. Slowly, he rose from the rubble, his cracked scales gleaming faintly in the dim light. Blood dripped from his wounds, but his crimson eyes still burned with fury. He staggered to his feet, defiance radiating from his battered form.

"This isn't over, Kimras," Zylron growled, his voice low and venomous despite his injuries. "You have won nothing but time. Vacari will fall to me, and next time, there will be no mercy."

Kimras met Zylron's gaze without flinching. His golden eyes remained steady, unwavering even in exhaustion. Though his body bore the marks of the fierce battle, his presence stood as a towering symbol of defiance against the encroaching darkness. For a moment, the two dragons locked eyes—a silent clash of wills that promised more battles to come.

With a final snarl, Zylron turned to his remaining forces, his voice echoing across the battlefield. "Retreat!" he commanded, the word laced with bitterness and fury. "Live to fight another day."

The remaining dark dragons gathered swiftly around their wounded leader, their loyalty to Zylron unshaken despite their crushing defeat. Their eyes burned with an unrelenting desire for vengeance as they formed a protective formation around him. Together, their wings beat against the twilight sky, carrying them into the shadows of the looming mountains. Though battered and bruised, they were far from defeated—merely retreating to regroup, ready to rise again and pursue their relentless quest for domination.

As Zylron and his forces vanished into the distance, Keisha watched them go, a wave of relief tempered by exhaustion washing over her. The battle had been fierce, and though they had won, the cost weighed heavily on her heart. She took a deep breath, her chest rising and falling as she grappled with the enormity of what they had faced. Yet, amidst the weight of loss, a glimmer of hope began to grow. For now, they had thwarted the darkness, and with unity, brighter days seemed possible.

Kimras descended from the sky, landing beside Keisha with a rumble that echoed across the quiet battlefield. His golden scales, though dulled by soot and marked by battle scars, still caught the fading light of the setting sun, glinting with a quiet brilliance. Around them, the battlefield lay still—a sea of scars, fallen warriors, and the echoes of conflict. The air was heavy with silence, broken only by the whisper of the wind.

Lowering his great head, Kimras exhaled warmly, his breath brushing over Keisha. She stepped closer, placing a hand on his snout, the familiar strength beneath her touch grounding her amidst the chaos. "We did it, Kimras," she said softly, her voice a mixture of exhaustion and pride. Her words carried a quiet triumph, a recognition of their hard-fought victory.

Kimras rumbled in agreement, the sound deep and resonant, vibrating through the ground beneath them. His eyes, aglow with the light of the dying sun, reflected their shared relief and determination. "For now, we've won," he replied, his voice like distant thunder rolling across the horizon.

"But this is not the end. Zylron will return—and when he does, we must be ready."

Keisha nodded, her resolve solidifying beneath the weight of his words. "We will be," she affirmed, her gaze sweeping over the battlefield. The sight of fallen dragons—noble forms lying still amidst the wreckage—was a stark reminder of the price they had paid. Yet it also stoked the fire in her heart. This was their home, their people, and she would defend it with every breath she had.

As the sun dipped below the horizon, casting long shadows across the scarred land, Keisha and Kimras stood together. The battle had ended, but the war was far from over. They stood united, their purpose clear, their courage unyielding. Against the darkness that threatened to consume Vacari, they would fight on—dragon and warrior, bound by an unbreakable bond and an unwavering determination.

Kimras, battered but victorious, lifted his gaze to the horizon. His golden scales, even marred by the chaos of battle, gleamed faintly in the dim twilight, a testament to his strength and resilience. Though both dragon and Eladrin bore the weight of their wounds and the losses they had endured, their spirits remained steadfast. Together, they faced the coming challenges with the same unyielding resolve that had carried them through countless battles.

For now, Vacari was safe. And as the stars began to appear in the night sky, Kimras and Keisha stood as sentinels against the encroaching darkness, ready for whatever lay ahead.

Keisha watched with a swell of pride as Kimras approached, his golden scales glinting faintly in the fading light. They had faced insurmountable challenges together, yet here they stood—stronger and more united than ever. Amidst the aftermath of the fierce battle, she felt an unshakable certainty: their bond would endure, unbroken and unyielding, against whatever trials the future might bring.

As Kimras landed gracefully before her, Keisha moved quickly to his side. Her eyes were drawn immediately to the blood seeping from a jagged tear in his wing. Concern flickered across her face as she inspected the wound, her hands gentle as they traced the torn scales and reddened edges. Despite the pain, Kimras released a low, contented rumble at her touch, a soft smile curling at the corners of his mouth.

Together, they made their way back to Goldmoor, the city gates glowing warmly in the darkening sky. The gates stood as a beacon of safety and comfort, a promise of respite after the storm. As they approached, the mages standing guard lowered the shimmering magical barrier, granting them swift entry. Keisha dismounted with practiced ease, her movements fluid despite the weariness in her body.

Without hesitation, she called for the healers to tend to Kimras's injuries. Her voice was firm yet filled with warmth, a reflection of the deep care she held for her noble companion. As the healers rushed forward, their hands glowing with restorative magic, Keisha stood close by, watching with quiet relief as they began to mend his wing.

A smile tugged at her lips as she imagined Amara's inevitable fussing when she saw the battle-worn dragon. Turning to Kimras, she shot him a playful glance. "Get ready for some scolding, my noble dragon," she teased, her tone light but threaded with affection. "You know Amara won't let you off easily."

Kimras chuckled, his deep voice carrying the warmth of shared humor despite the fatigue etched into his features. His golden eyes sparkled with amusement as he replied, "I suppose I deserve it." He paused, his gaze softening as it lingered on her. "But seeing you safe and victorious was worth every wound."

A quiet peace settled over them as the moments stretched on, the chaos of battle giving way to a calm stillness. Their bond, forged and tempered through countless trials, felt stronger than ever in the wake of their victory. Together, they turned their gaze to the city they had fought so fiercely to protect. The glow of Goldmoor reflected the hope they carried, a testament to the resilience of its people and their defenders.

Though they knew the journey was far from over, neither wavered in their resolve. Shadows loomed on the horizon, and challenges awaited them still. But side by side, they would face whatever came, their courage unwavering and their bond unbreakable.

As the stars began to twinkle in the darkening sky, Keisha rested her hand on Kimras's snout, her touch light yet resolute. Together, they stood beneath the endless expanse of the heavens, united by trust, loyalty, and the shared promise to protect Vacari.

No matter what the future held, they knew one thing with certainty: as long as they stood together, they would be ready for anything.

Chapter 29
Shadows of Amethyst

Glaceria led her fleet of dragons toward Purplefire Woods, her icy gaze as cold and unyielding as the frost-covered landscape below. Crimson-scaled red dragons flew in formation beside her frost-white contingent, their fiery breath a striking contrast to the freezing power emanating from her forces. The air around them crackled with anticipation, a chilling promise of the devastation they intended to unleash on the unsuspecting defenders. Determination burned in the hearts of her fleet as they closed in, ready to strike and claim victory over Purplefire Woods.

Above the forest, vigilant patrols soared high, their sharp eyes catching the first glimpse of the approaching threat. A cry of warning echoed through the treetops, reaching Amara, who stood poised and ready. Her amethyst scales shimmered like radiant jewels under the dappled sunlight that filtered through the dense canopy. She coiled her body in readiness, every muscle taut with purpose. With a flick of her tail, she signaled her fellow dragons to prepare. Young amethyst dragons rallied to her side, their shimmering forms alive with energy. Joined by the nymphs, they began weaving a protective barrier around the woods. Their combined magic pulsed through the earth and air, creating a living force determined to shield their sacred home.

As Glaceria and her fleet descended, the temperature plummeted. Frost crept over leaves and branches, the chill of their presence penetrating deep into the forest. Ong stood steadfast beside Amara, his grip tightening around the dragonlance. His eyes, steady and resolute, reflected his unwavering determination. As he climbed onto Amara's back, the weight of the coming battle pressed heavily on his shoulders. Yet, his trust in Amara's leadership and the strength of their alliance held firm.

Amara's mind raced through strategies, her focus sharpened like the edge of a blade. The sight of Glaceria's fleet sent a shiver through her—not of fear, but of anticipation. She was ready. Drawing strength from the nymphs, dragons, and defenders gathered at her side, she felt the power of their unity. Together, they were a formidable force, prepared to meet the invaders head-on and protect the forest they called home.

The atmosphere in Purplefire Woods thrummed with energy, an unseen force rippling through the ancient trees and echoing in the hearts of the defenders. Amethyst dragons, nymphs, and warriors alike held their collective breath as Glaceria's fleet loomed closer, the tension mounting with every passing moment. Silence clung to the air, heavy and expectant, until the inevitable clash shattered the calm.

With a powerful beat of her wings, Amara launched into the sky, her majestic form slicing through the air with the grace of a born leader. Ong's heart raced with adrenaline as they ascended, the forest below shrinking as they climbed higher. Around them, the shimmering magical barrier protecting Purplefire Woods solidified—a radiant shield forged from the combined magic of the nymphs and young amethyst dragons. Its ethereal glow spread across the canopy, casting an otherworldly light that bathed the trees in a soft yet unyielding luminescence. Ong watched in awe, the sight filling him with renewed determination.

Arrogance marked Glaceria's approach. Her frost-white scales gleamed in the dim light as she led her fleet toward the barrier. Her icy blue eyes locked onto Amara, a sneer twisting her features. "Amara, you pathetic excuse for a dragon," she hissed, her voice laced with contempt. "You think you can stand against me? I'll make quick work of you and your pitiful clan."

Unfazed, Amara held her adversary's gaze, her amethyst scales shimmering with quiet confidence. A knowing smirk tugged at her lips as she replied, her voice steady. "Oh, Glaceria, always so full of bluster. You come here with your threats and cold winds, but Purplefire Woods is no ordinary place. Its strength runs deep—in every root, leaf, and stone."

Glaceria snarled, the sound cutting through the icy air. With a sharp command, she ordered her dragons to attack the forest, confidence radiating from her every move. A tempest of ice and fire erupted as her fleet unleashed their elemental fury upon the barrier. Frost crept toward the trees, flames roared, and the skies churned with their wrath. But as the assault raged, the trees stood unscathed, their ancient magic deflecting every blow.

Frustration flickered in Glaceria's icy eyes, her breath swirling like frost in the air. "What trickery is this?" she growled, her voice sharp with disbelief.

Amara chuckled softly, her eyes gleaming with amusement. "No trickery, Glaceria," she replied, her voice as calm as still waters. "Just the power of nature, and the strength of our bond with these woods. You may be powerful, but here, your might means nothing. You're no match for the magic that lives within this place."

The tension hung heavy, the stillness before the storm. The forest itself seemed to hold its breath, as if the very trees and creatures within knew that something monumental was about to unfold. With a thunderous roar, Glaceria's dragons surged into the sky, their wings slicing through the air as they circled above like a gathering storm. Amara and her dragons followed, their movements fluid and precise, a stark contrast to the brute force of Glaceria's fleet. Their gazes locked again, a silent challenge passing between the two dragonesses—each determined to emerge victorious.

Glaceria's voice cut through the air, cold and sharp as shards of ice. "Do not forget, Amara, that when you faced Zylron, it was only through Kimras's quick thinking that you survived," she sneered, her eyes narrowing with malicious satisfaction.

Amara's response was immediate, her tone unwavering and her confidence unshaken. "Yes, that's true," she acknowledged, her voice steady as she met Glaceria's glare. "Zylron is a powerful red dragon, I'll give him that." A smirk tugged at her lips, her voice hardening as she continued. "But you, Glaceria, are a white dragon—not nearly as formidable as he, and certainly no match for the might of the Amethyst dragons."

Amara's words hit their mark, and the tension between her and Glaceria deepened. Glaceria's icy gaze flickered with anger, but Amara held her ground, her amethyst scales glowing faintly as her power hummed beneath the surface, ready to be unleashed.

The atmosphere thickened with anticipation, the air crackling with energy as the two dragon forces converged over Purplefire Woods. Every wingbeat, every shift in the air felt charged, as if the sky itself braced for the storm of battle. Among the ranks of younger gold dragons, one stood out—a striking figure with scales gleaming like molten metal. It flew forward, approaching the young reds under Glaceria's command, its eyes blazing with determination.

The stage was set, and the battle between light and ice began.

With a fierce roar that echoed across the skies, the young gold dragon signaled the start of the clash, its defiance ringing clear. The red dragons responded with a deafening chorus of roars, their voices melding into the growl of an oncoming storm. They surged forward, wings beating furiously as the first strikes of battle ignited the skies.

Above, Amara and Glaceria circled each other, their eyes locked in a fierce, unbroken stare. The first blow had been struck, and both dragonesses knew only one would emerge victorious. The sky above Purplefire Woods became a chaotic war zone, alive with the roars of dragons, the beating of wings, and the crackling hum of unleashed magic.

Ong, perched securely on Amara's back, tightened his grip on the dragonlance. His heart raced with anticipation, each beat heavy with the gravity of what was at stake. He knew this battle would determine the fate of Purplefire Woods—and he was ready to fight with everything he had to protect it.

With a powerful beat of her wings, Amara surged forward. Her amethyst scales glittered like gemstones in the sunlight as she unleashed a blast of magical energy toward Glaceria. The shockwave rippled through the air, its force reverberating across the battlefield. Glaceria countered with a burst of icy breath, the frost-laden winds colliding with Amara's magic in a dazzling explosion of light and power. Sparks flew, and the clash sent tremors through the skies.

The battle raged on, filling the air above Purplefire Woods with a chaotic symphony of dragons clashing mid-air. Their roars echoed through the vast forest below, while the shimmering barrier pulsed with protective energy. Its ethereal glow cast a soft light over the chaos, shielding the sacred woods from the full fury of the elemental onslaught.

Amara and Glaceria fought with relentless determination, their elemental powers locked in a fierce, unyielding duel. Fire and ice swirled around them in a whirlwind of magical force, each dragoness giving everything to protect their allies and claim victory. The fate of Purplefire Woods hung precariously in the balance, the outcome riding on their strength and will.

Below, the young gold dragon fought valiantly, weaving through the sky in a blur of gold and flame as it clashed with the red dragons. Younger amethyst dragons joined the fray, their psychic magic rippling through the battlefield, sowing confusion, and disarray among Glaceria's forces. From the ground, the nymphs lent their power, their spells reinforcing the barrier and defending the forest against destruction.

Amidst the chaos, the young gold dragon swooped low, its wings beating steadily as it landed before the advancing red dragons. Its movements carried an air of confidence, and as it raised its head, its voice echoed across the battlefield with commanding authority.

"Listen to me, young ones," the gold dragon called, its voice cutting through the noise of battle like a clear bell. "We stand on the brink of conflict, but there is wisdom in dialogue and understanding. We are not true enemies. We share the skies and the earth of Vacari. Let us seek a resolution without needless bloodshed."

The gold dragon's noble plea was met with fiery defiance. The red dragons roared and snarled, their bloodlust drowning out any possibility of diplomacy. They were eager for battle, dismissing the notion of peace as a weakness. The air thickened with tension, heavy with the promise of war as the two groups faced each other, the space between them charged like a drawn bowstring.

Yet, among the red dragons, one hesitated. Its gaze flicked between the gold dragon and its kin, uncertainty flickering in its eyes. The moment was brief—so fleeting it might have been missed amidst the chaos—but it was there. A whisper of doubt. A crack in the unyielding facade of loyalty.

But reflection had no place on the battlefield. The white dragons surged forward, their icy breath frosting the air as they struck with ruthless precision. The gold dragons responded immediately, their fiery breath roaring to meet the freezing onslaught. The collision of elemental forces created a violent maelstrom, steam billowing into the sky as fire and ice battled for dominance. The battlefield became an arena of raw power, the furious clash threatening to engulf everything in its path.

Amidst the chaos, a sudden shift swept across the battlefield. Rain began to fall, cooling the scorched ground and extinguishing flames that had lingered in the sky. The deluge caught both sides off guard, momentarily halting their advances as the rain mingled with steam, cloaking the battlefield in a misty shroud. Visibility dwindled, the world around them blurring into a swirling haze of rain and vapor.

Ong's laughter rang out above the turmoil, a rare moment of levity amidst the storm. "Well, at least it's not ice and frost," he called to Amara, a grin spreading across his face as he glanced at the dark clouds above. "I'll take rain and fog over that any day."

Amara nodded, her sharp eyes scanning the battlefield below where young dragons fought amidst the rain and mist. "Agreed," she replied, a flicker of amusement lighting her voice despite the gravity of the situation. "Let's hope this rain gives us the advantage we need."

They exchanged a knowing glance, their shared resolve unspoken but clear. Even nature's unpredictability could not dampen their spirits. Amara's magic hummed beneath her scales, pulsing with power and readiness. Perched on her back, Ong tightened his grip on the dragonlance, his determination as unwavering as hers. Both stood poised, ready to rejoin the fray at a moment's notice.

The young gold dragon, its heartfelt attempt at peace rejected, returned to the battle with a heavy heart. The red dragons, consumed by their lust for battle, had cast aside the possibility of resolution. The gold's eyes burned with renewed determination, tempered by the bitter understanding that the fight for Purplefire Woods would not be won through reason but through fire and fury.

With a roar that pierced the haze, the gold dragon launched itself back into the chaos. Rain pelted its shimmering scales as it flew, its spirit undeterred. Below, the clash of dragons raged on, the sacred woods of Purplefire trembling under the weight of the battle that would decide its fate.

The rain poured in torrents, drenching the battlefield, and adding to the chaos. Steam from the clash of fire and ice rose in thick, swirling clouds, merging with the downpour to create a dense, fog-like shroud that obscured much of the fighting. Yet, even with visibility diminished, the dragons pressed on. Their roars pierced the storm, fierce and unrelenting, as the battle raged across the skies above Purplefire Woods.

Amara and Ong remained vigilant, their eyes locked on the unfolding skirmishes. They both understood the gravity of this battle—it would determine the fate of their sacred home. Ong's grip on the dragonlance tightened, his resolve hardening as he steeled himself for the trials ahead. Beside him, Amara braced her massive form, the magical energy coursing within her building to a crescendo. Together, they prepared to defend their home with every ounce of strength they possessed.

Despite the relentless downpour, the rising steam, and the ceaseless attacks from the red and white dragons, the defenders of Purplefire Woods held their ground with unyielding determination. The weight of their survival pressed heavily on them, yet they would not falter. This was their home, and they would fight for it until their last breath.

Amara's sharp gaze swept across the battlefield, her senses keen even in the storm's confusion. Her eyes caught sight of the young red dragon that had hesitated earlier. For a brief moment, their gazes met through the mist. In that silent exchange, Amara glimpsed more than aggression—there was a flicker of doubt, uncertainty, and perhaps regret. The moment passed quickly, but the seed was planted, a tiny crack in the red dragon's resolve. She tucked the observation away for later, knowing the battle left no time for hesitation.

Below, the young red and white dragons advanced on the gold dragons, their fiery breath cascading through the sky in waves of heat and flame. Yet to their shock, their attacks did little to break their opponents. The gold dragons, their scales gleaming with defiance even through the rain, stood firm. Their resilience was unmatched, weathering the relentless storm of fire without flinching.

The amethyst dragons retaliated with their unique, formidable powers. Explosive crystals and shimmering gems erupted from their mouths, streaking through the sky like shards of starlight. Each projectile detonated with thunderous force, disorienting the enemy ranks. The explosions threw the advancing red and white dragons into disarray, confusion rippling through their ranks as they struggled to regroup.

The white dragons, unwilling to concede ground, joined the fray with deadly precision. Their freezing breath sliced through the air, a stark contrast to the fiery assault. Sheets of frost cascaded downward, encasing some of the gold dragons in icy prisons. Movements slowed as the frozen shackles gripped tighter, threatening to immobilize them completely.

Caught between the scorching heat of the red dragons' flames and the bone-chilling frost of the white dragons' breath, the gold dragons faltered. Limbs stiffened under the icy assault, and the combined force of the attack pushed them perilously close to breaking. But even as they teetered on the brink, their fiery determination refused to waver. Drawing strength from one another, the gold dragons rallied. With roars of vengeance that echoed across the battlefield, they unleashed ferocious counterattacks. Their claws tore through the air with devastating precision, and their fiery breath blazed once more, scorching the battlefield in a display of sheer defiance.

The battle raged on, the skies above Purplefire Woods becoming a storm of fire, ice, and relentless willpower. Each clash sent tremors through the earth below, a testament to the stakes of this desperate struggle for survival.

The battlefield was a storm of elemental chaos—fire, ice, and explosive energy clashed in a swirling maelstrom as the dragons fought with every ounce of strength they possessed. Amidst the turmoil, dragon riders atop the gold dragons loosed enchanted arrows with deadly precision. Each projectile struck true, while bursts of magical energy from the riders' hands added to the relentless barrage. The red and white dragons, reeling from the combined assault, pulled back momentarily, seeking respite from the onslaught.

But the retreat offered no sanctuary. The amethyst dragons pressed their advantage, spitting explosive crystals with devastating accuracy. The shimmering projectiles filled the air with brilliant flashes of light, raining destruction upon the retreating forces.

High above the fray, Amara and Glaceria circled one another like predators. Their eyes locked in a silent exchange, each dragoness attuned to the ebb and flow of the battle. Despite the chaos below, their focus remained razor-sharp. Both knew the tide of battle could shift in an instant, and they braced for the critical moment when that shift would come.

Suddenly, a group of cunning red dragons broke away from the main conflict. With razor-sharp claws and snapping jaws, they swooped in behind the gold and amethyst dragons, launching a surprise attack. Their powerful tails lashed through the air, striking down unsuspecting riders, and sending some tumbling from the skies.

The defenders reacted quickly. Riderless gold and amethyst dragons darted to intercept the ambush, their courage shining amidst the chaos. With selfless bravery, they positioned themselves between the attackers and their allies, absorbing the brunt of the red dragons' ferocious assault. The air was filled with the thunderous clash of scales and the deafening roars of dragons colliding mid-air.

The young red and white dragons renewed their attack, combining fiery breath and icy blasts into a deadly barrage that threatened to overwhelm the defenders of Purplefire Woods. Flames roared through the skies, while frost coated the ground in a slick sheen. The defenders, however, were not so easily broken. Drawing strength from their bond with the forest and one another, they fought back with unyielding determination. Their spirits, like the woods they protected, stood strong against the storm.

Hovering high above the battlefield, Amara's eyes blazed with resolve. She focused intently on Glaceria, unleashing a torrent of magical energy that tore through the air, crackling with raw power. Glaceria reacted swiftly, exhaling a blast of icy breath that met Amara's attack head-on. Their powers collided in a dazzling explosion of light and force, sending shockwaves rippling through the sky.

Above the storm-tossed battlefield, the two dragonesses clashed with primal fury. Fire and ice ripped through the air in brilliant flashes, each strike more intense than the last. The sky itself seemed to shudder under the weight of their power.

Ong, his dragonlance gleaming in the dim stormlight, fought valiantly at Amara's side. His heart pounded in his chest as he struck at the red and white dragons, his aim unerring and his resolve unshakable. He knew the fate of Purplefire Woods hinged on this battle, and he was prepared to give everything to protect it.

All around, the dragons of Purplefire Woods roared in defiance, their cries echoing across the battlefield as a testament to their bravery. Despite the overwhelming odds, they stood firm, their bond and determination as unyielding as the ancient forest they fought to protect.

High above, Glaceria smirked, reveling in the turmoil she had unleashed. But her triumph was short-lived. Amara's voice cut through the storm, clear and commanding, brimming with righteous fury.

"Enough, Glaceria!" Amara's voice rang out, demanding attention amidst the chaos. Her tone carried the weight of a leader unwilling to yield. She turned to Ong, her expression sharp with urgency. "Be prepared, Ong," she warned, her voice steady but grave. "Glaceria will unleash her cold attack soon. We must be ready to face it together."

Ong nodded, tightening his grip on the dragonlance. His gaze locked onto Glaceria with steely resolve, ready for the battle that would decide the fate of Purplefire Woods.

Glaceria's icy gaze swept over the battlefield, narrowing as it landed on Ong perched atop Amara's back. A cruel smirk curled her lips as she taunted him, her voice dripping with malice. "Your elf wife is probably already dead, Ong," she sneered. "Along with that noble fool, Kimras."

Ong remained stoic, his expression betraying no hint of emotion as he ignored her provocation. Beside him, Amara let out a low chuckle, her amethyst scales shimmering as she waved a wing dismissively at Glaceria's words.

"Kimras is more than capable of handling himself against Zylron," Amara replied, her tone laced with amusement and confidence. She cast a sidelong glance at Glaceria, her eyes sparkling with defiance. "But is that all you have, Glaceria? Bluster and empty threats? You are giving me a headache with your whining."

Ong, stifling a grin, joined in. His laughter rang out above the battlefield, cutting through the storm of chaos. "A headache, Amara?" he teased, shaking his head. "Not exactly what I expected you to say, but I can't argue!"

Amara flashed him a quick smirk, her posture relaxed despite the battle raging around them. "Well, it's true," she quipped, her gaze never leaving Glaceria. "Some dragons are just full of hot air."

Her casual dismissal struck a nerve. Glaceria's icy breath flared, frost spreading across the ground beneath her as she took a threatening step forward. Her sharp claws dug into the earth, her lips curling into a furious snarl.

"You dare mock me?" Glaceria hissed, her voice cutting through the air like shards of ice. "I will tear your precious woods apart, Amara. You will regret this!"

Glaceria unleashed a torrent of icy breath, the frost cutting through the air with deadly precision as it surged toward Amara and Ong. Ong stood resolute, gripping the dragonlance tightly, his posture unwavering against the freezing onslaught. Amara moved swiftly, releasing her own breath weapon—a searing line of concussive force that tore through the air toward Glaceria. The opposing powers collided in an explosive spectacle, the clash crackling with raw energy and shaking the skies.

The two dragonesses circled with thunderous beats of their wings, their gazes locked in a deadly dance of calculation and defiance. Glaceria, her movements sharp and deliberate, conjured jagged shards of ice that shimmered with lethal intent. She launched them with precision, each shard a weapon of destruction. But Amara, unyielding, wove arcs of magical energy that intercepted the icy missiles, shattering them mid-air into glittering fragments.

Amara moved through the sky with fluid grace, her violet scales glinting in the chaotic light of the battlefield. As ice shards hurtled toward her, she danced effortlessly, her movements as seamless as flowing water. With calculated precision, she countered each attack with blasts of radiant magic, scattering the shattered remnants like broken glass across the chaos below. Dragons clashed amidst the falling shards, the battlefield consumed by a tempest of fire, ice, and relentless magic.

Ong's sharp eyes caught a flicker in Glaceria's relentless offense—an imperceptible pause, a crack in her icy composure. Recognizing the moment, Amara surged forward, her violet eyes blazing with determination. A pulse of raw power erupted from her, aiming to shatter Glaceria's focus and disrupt her momentum.

Glaceria snarled defiantly, her roar piercing the storm as her breath met Amara's magic in a dazzling explosion of opposing forces. The sky ignited with flashes of crackling energy, the collision sending shockwaves rippling through the heavens. Neither dragoness relented, their powers surging to the brink as they fought to gain the upper hand.

Below them, the battle raged with unrelenting ferocity. Dragons clashed in mid-air, their roars echoing across the storm-laden sky. Flames and frost collided, consuming the battlefield in a chaotic inferno. The defenders of Purplefire Woods fought on with unwavering resolve, their spirits unbroken even as the scent of burning trees and the hum of magic filled the air. The very fate of the forest teetered on the edge.

With predatory intent, Glaceria dove, her frost-encrusted claws poised to strike a decisive blow. She aimed to rip through Amara's defenses, but Amara reacted with lightning reflexes, twisting gracefully out of harm's way. In one swift maneuver, Amara channeled a concentrated stream of force, striking Glaceria with enough power to send her tumbling back. The resounding echo of their collision thundered across the battlefield.

The heavens blazed with the fury of their struggle, the storm-tossed skies illuminated by flashes of elemental power. Glaceria unleashed another wave of freezing breath, the air itself crystallizing in frost as it surged toward Amara. Amara retaliated with bursts of radiant energy, the dazzling beams slicing through the frost-like blades of light. Their clash was relentless—a symphony of fire, ice, and magic as two titanic forces waged a battle that pushed them to their limits.

Locked in their elemental duel, neither dragoness faltered, their powers shaking the very fabric of the sky. The struggle for dominance between

Amara and Glaceria became the heart of the battle, their clash embodying the stakes of the fight for Purplefire Woods.

As Glaceria closed in, her massive form cast a shadow over Amara and Ong. Amara's senses sharpened to a razor's edge, her focus absolute. With a swift mental command, she cast a psionic barrier around Ong, shielding him from Glaceria's impending strike. The monstrous dragoness's claws slashed through the air, inches from their target. The sheer force of her attack sent a powerful gust whipping around them, but Amara's barrier held firm, her will unyielding.

Glaceria, her frustration mounting, unleashed a torrent of icy breath, the frost surging toward Amara and Ong in a relentless wave. Ong stood his ground, his stance resolute, trusting Amara's strength. Amara countered swiftly, releasing a searing line of concussive force. The opposing powers collided in a dazzling explosion, the air crackling with raw energy as fire and ice battled for dominance.

The two dragonesses circled each other with powerful wingbeats, their eyes locked in fierce determination. Glaceria, calm and calculating, summoned jagged shards of ice, hurling them with deadly precision. Amara, undeterred, wove arcs of magical energy that shattered the projectiles mid-air. The remnants fell like glittering fragments, scattering across the battlefield below—a chaos of fire, ice, and relentless combat.

Amara danced through the skies with fluid grace, evading the icy assault with practiced precision. Each movement was deliberate, her counterattacks striking with bursts of radiant energy that fractured Glaceria's icy missiles into harmless shards. Below, dragons clashed in ferocious combat, their roars reverberating across the battlefield. Purplefire Woods trembled under the weight of the elemental forces unleashed, its fate hanging precariously in the balance.

Ong, ever watchful, noticed a flicker in Glaceria's relentless offense—an imperceptible pause, a crack in her composure. Seizing the opportunity, Amara surged forward, her violet eyes blazing with determination. A pulse of magical energy erupted from her, aiming to disrupt Glaceria's focus and momentum.

Glaceria snarled defiantly, meeting the attack head-on with another blast of icy breath. The opposing forces collided in a dazzling clash, lighting up the storm-darkened sky with flashes of fire and frost. Both dragonesses strained against the other's power, pushing themselves to their limits, neither willing to yield.

Below, the battlefield roared with chaos. Dragons of every kind locked in fierce combat, their cries echoing through the heavens. The defenders of Purplefire Woods fought with unyielding determination, their spirits unbroken even as the air grew thick with magic, fire, and frost.

Glaceria dove with predatory intent, her frost-covered claws outstretched to tear through Amara's defenses. Amara twisted in mid-air, narrowly evading the lethal strike. With a swift maneuver, she unleashed a concentrated stream of force, striking Glaceria with enough power to send her tumbling backward. The resounding clash thundered across the battlefield, a testament to the unrelenting intensity of their duel.

The skies above Purplefire Woods crackled with the brilliance of elemental power. Glaceria unleashed another wave of freezing breath, crystallizing the air in frost, while Amara retaliated with shimmering bursts of radiant energy. Their clash was unrelenting, a deadly dance of power and precision that pushed both dragonesses beyond their limits.

Caught in the frenzy of battle, Glaceria failed to perceive Amara's subtle ruse. Amara feigned surprise, her expression shifting to one of startled shock. The white dragoness hesitated, her attention momentarily diverted. It was the opening they needed.

Ong, sensing the critical moment, tightened his harness, securing his position with practiced precision. His hands moved swiftly as he prepared for the next strike, Amara's deception granting them precious seconds.

Glaceria unleashed another icy wave, her breath carving through the air like a frigid storm. Amara's mind raced, her resolve burning like a beacon amidst the biting cold. With a flicker of stealth, she vanished into the shadows above—not out of dishonor, but with the unwavering resolve to strike decisively and protect those depending on her. Ong gripped the dragonlance tighter, his knuckles whitening as he awaited her signal. This strike had to be flawless.

Glaceria, still scanning for Amara, remained oblivious to Ong's descent from above. His movements were swift and precise, the dragonlance poised for a devastating strike. In a burst of radiant energy, Amara reappeared, her shimmering form catching Glaceria's attention at the exact moment Ong struck.

With deadly accuracy, Ong drove the lance into Glaceria's exposed wing. The lance struck with a resounding thud, and Glaceria's agonized scream ripped through the battlefield. The force of the blow sent tremors through her body, forcing her to stagger mid-air. Amara and Ong pressed their advantage, unrelenting in their assault and giving Glaceria no room to recover.

Fury blazed in Glaceria's icy eyes as she whipped her gaze toward Amara. Her voice was a venomous hiss, the very air freezing around her words. "You dare to employ such trickery against me?" she snarled, her rage crystallizing in the air.

Amara met Glaceria's glare with an unwavering smile, her voice calm and cutting. "Trickery?" she echoed, her tone cool and confident. "If you had my powers, you would do the same. It is called strategy, Glaceria, and you should try it sometime."

Glaceria snarled in response, her icy breath flaring as she lunged toward Amara with raw ferocity. Yet, as the battle wore on, the weight of their combined assault proved undeniable. Each calculated strike of Amara's magic, every thrust of Ong's lance, chipped away at Glaceria's defenses. The once-unshakable pride that fueled her now faltered. Her breaths came in ragged gasps, her wings trembled under the strain of staying aloft, and cracks formed in her icy resolve.

For the first time, Glaceria hesitated. Her wings faltered, and in that fleeting instant, doubt flickered in her eyes. She realized that continuing this fight would only lead to greater losses.

With a begrudging growl, Glaceria pulled back, her pride battered but her spirit unbroken. Her icy eyes narrowed with frustration as she gave a sharp, commanding roar, signaling her forces to retreat. The dragons under her command responded swiftly, withdrawing toward the horizon and the distant safety of Flameford. Their mission was incomplete, but their spirits remained defiant.

Before departing, Glaceria shot one final, smoldering glance at Amara. Her eyes burned with a silent vow—a promise of vengeance. The message was clear: This is not over.

As Glaceria and her forces vanished into the distance, Amara and Ong shared a fleeting moment of triumph. They had defended Purplefire Woods, their bond and strategic prowess shining through the chaos. The battlefield, once roaring with the sounds of battle, now carried only the echoes of their hard-won victory. Above them, the storm clouds began to part, revealing slivers of sunlight breaking through—a symbol of hope for the days to come.

Ong, still perched on Amara's back, finally loosened his grip on the dragonlance as they soared above the battlefield. His eyes gleamed with admiration as he looked at his dragon companion. "We did it, Amara," he said, his voice a blend of relief and pride.

Amara nodded, her gaze sweeping over the battlefield below, where the remnants of their victory lay scattered. "Yes, we did," she replied, her tone steady but resolute. "But this is just the beginning. Glaceria will not stay gone for long. We need to be ready."

Their determination was mutual, a silent agreement passing between them. Amara and Ong turned their attention to their allies below, watching as dragons and defenders rallied amidst the aftermath. The victory had been hard-fought, and though exhaustion weighed on them, their spirits stood tall. Together, they resolved to help rebuild and prepare for whatever might come next.

Amara's eyes lingered on the horizon where Glaceria and her forces had vanished. Satisfaction mingled with unease as the memory of their clash played in her mind. Today's battle was won, but Glaceria's retreat felt more like a pause than an end. Turning her gaze forward, Amara steeled herself, knowing the fight was far from over.

Soaring above Purplefire Woods, the pair surveyed the quieting battlefield. The devastation left in the wake of the conflict was undeniable, yet the sight of their allies gathering to recover brought a tempered relief. Purplefire Woods still stood, resilient in the face of chaos, a testament to the strength of its defenders.

Amara's thoughts shifted to their friends. "We need to check on Kimras and Keisha," she said, her voice steady but tinged with urgency. Ong nodded in agreement, his expression mirroring her concern. Adjusting their course, they turned toward Goldmoor, the wind whipping past as they flew. The clash with Glaceria still lingered in their minds, a reminder of the battles yet to come.

As the outskirts of Goldmoor came into view, Amara and Ong exchanged a knowing glance. No words were needed; their resolve was etched in their expressions. Below, the resilient walls of Goldmoor stood as a beacon of hope—a reminder of what they fought to protect.

The sun dipped low on the horizon, casting a golden glow over the landscape as they approached the city. Amara's thoughts raced through their challenges and those still ahead. Their fight was far from over, but their bond—with each other, with Kimras and Keisha—renewed her strength. That connection was their greatest weapon, a force that gave them the courage to stand against even the darkest threats.

As Goldmoor's gates loomed ahead, Amara and Ong's hearts filled with determination. They were ready for the next chapter of their journey, a new dawn on the horizon. Their arrival brought hope that stirred the defenders within the city, reminding all that victory was still possible. This was not the end—it was a beginning.

Touching down at Goldmoor, Amara and Ong exchanged a final glance of shared purpose. Together, they would face the trials with courage, unity, and unwavering resolve. No matter the cost, they would protect their home and loved ones. And as the promise of a new dawn lit the sky, they stood ready to fight for Vacari's future—side by side, unbreakable,

Chapter 30

Shadows of Defeat: Return to Flameford

The sky above Flameford churned with dark, roiling clouds as Zylron and his dragons returned, their silhouettes stark against the stormy backdrop. Once a figure of unyielding might, Zylron now bore the unmistakable scars of battle. His wings, torn and tattered, moved with visible strain, each beat labored under the bitter weight of defeat. His gaze, once sharp and commanding, carried a glimmer of weariness, though his steps still exuded an air of authority.

As they descended onto the jagged outcroppings surrounding Flameford, an eerie silence greeted them. The air hung heavy, thick with unspoken judgment. It was as though the land itself held its breath, waiting to pass sentence on their failed mission.

Zylron landed with a resounding thud, his claws scraping against the stone and sending sparks scattering into the gloom. His followers touched down around him, their battered forms a mirror of his own. They had returned from their clash with Kimras and his allies bruised, battered, and burdened by the shattering realization of their foes' unyielding strength.

Yet amidst the defeat, a flicker of determination still burned in Zylron's eyes. He turned to his companions, his voice rumbling like distant thunder, laced with defiance. "Today's battle has scarred us, but our resolve remains unbroken. We will rise again, and next time, we will not falter."

His followers nodded in grim agreement, their spirits steadied by his unwavering resolve. But in the quiet corners of Zylron's mind, shadows of doubt began to stir. His pride bristled at the notion, yet for the first time, a cold uncertainty crept into his thoughts. He cast a wary glance at the storm-filled sky, wondering if this defeat was the first crack in his armor—the beginning of his undoing.

The echoes of failure reverberating in their hearts, Zylron and his dragons retreated into the depths of Flameford. The lair's oppressive darkness swallowed them, but it could not smother the flickering flames of hope—or the creeping tendrils of desperation—that simmered within.

Glaceria's group arrived shortly after, the air between them crackling with unspoken tension. Her wing hung limply at her side, blood seeping from the wound where Ong's dragonlance had pierced her scales. Her expression was dark and brooding as she surveyed the rocky expanse of

Flameford, searching for some remnant of hope amidst the wreckage of their failed mission.

She spotted Zylron among the gathering dragons, his hulking form unmistakable even in the dim light. Glaceria trudged toward him, her steps heavy with exhaustion and the sting of defeat. For a fleeting moment, she dared to hope that Zylron, despite everything, might have emerged victorious against Kimras. But as she drew nearer, the sight of his battered form and somber expression confirmed her fears.

Zylron met her gaze with a silent nod, his eyes mirroring her frustration. For an instant, Glaceria wondered if Zylron's confidence had been shaken. The thought unsettled her, but she quickly pushed it aside. Zylron's strength was a cornerstone of their cause—doubt could not be allowed to fester within him.

Zylron stepped forward, his commanding presence casting a shadow over the assembled dragons. His gaze swept over Glaceria, pausing on her injured wing. The torn flesh and dripping blood spoke of the ferocity of the battle she had faced.

"What happened?" Zylron demanded, his voice cold and sharp, cutting through the oppressive silence like a blade.

Glaceria's lips curled into a snarl, the bitter taste of failure thick on her tongue. "That cursed human, with his dragonlance, pierced my wing," she growled, her voice trembling with suppressed rage. "I failed to defeat them."

Zylron's expression darkened at Glaceria's admission, a grim acknowledgment of their collective failure. Together, they stood in brooding silence, their thoughts turning toward the inevitable reckoning with the mysterious figure who awaited their report. A shiver ran down Zylron's spine, unbidden and unwelcome, as if something cold and predatory lurked just beyond his awareness—watchful and dangerous. He shook it off with a growl, dismissing it as a trick of his weary mind. Yet the sensation lingered, gnawing at the edges of his resolve.

Quellan's heart raced as he made his way toward the chamber. Each step seemed heavier than the last, the weight of their defeat pressing down on him. He knew the mysterious figure's wrath would be as swift as it was unforgiving. The fate of their plans—and perhaps their very survival—hung precariously on the outcome of the report.

Upon entering the chamber, Quellan found the mysterious figure seated upon a throne of polished obsidian. Shadows flickered and danced across the cold stone walls, obscuring the figure's features, yet their presence was as imposing as ever. Beside them stood Lyra, her posture tense, her sharp eyes reflecting a mix of anticipation and apprehension. She, too, awaited word of the dragons' fate.

"Quellan," the mysterious figure intoned, their voice low and commanding. The sound resonated through the chamber, carrying an unyielding authority that sent a chill down Quellan's spine. "What news do you bring?"

Quellan hesitated, the weight of the moment pressing on him as he struggled to find the right words. "Zylron and Glaceria have returned," he began cautiously, his voice faltering for a moment. "Along with the young dragons."

The mysterious figure's expression hardened, their sharp gaze slicing through the darkness. "And the battle?" they asked, their tone edged with impatience. "Have they succeeded in their mission?"

Quellan's unease deepened. His gaze dropped for a fleeting moment before he admitted, "I have yet to speak with them. I came to inform you of their return."

A heavy sigh echoed through the chamber, the frustration in it almost tangible. The mysterious figure raised a hand, dismissing Quellan's lack of preparation with a weary wave. "Go," they ordered, their voice sharp and clipped. "Retrieve the report from Zylron and Glaceria, and bring their findings to me."

Quellan bowed quickly, his heart pounding as he turned to leave. The tension in the room lingered behind him, the unspoken weight of failure casting a shadow over the path ahead.

Quellan hurried through the grand halls of Flameford, his footsteps echoing against the cold stone as he approached Zylron. Anxiety gnawed at him with every step. Delivering news of defeat was a daunting task—doing so to Zylron, in his volatile state, was a near-impossible one. The battered dragon was infamous for his short temper, and Quellan could already feel the weight of his impending wrath.

As he entered the chamber, Quellan's uncertainty grew. Zylron's hulking form loomed over the space, his scales marred by deep cuts and bruises that glinted in the dim light. His wings, still torn from battle, hung low, adding to his imposing presence. Quellan hesitated, his throat dry as he attempted to speak.

"Z-Zylron," he stammered, his voice barely above a whisper. "Has Amara been defeated? And... what of Kimras?"

Zylron's head snapped toward him, his red eyes narrowing dangerously. A low growl rumbled from his chest, vibrating through the air. His lip curled back, revealing jagged teeth, as he fixed Quellan with a glare that could pierce stone. The sight of the nervous lackey daring to question him fanned the flames of his already frayed patience.

Without warning, Zylron's tail whipped through the air, striking the ground inches from Quellan and sending him sprawling across the cold stone floor. The impact left Quellan gasping for breath, pain radiating through his side as he struggled to regain his composure.

"Mind your place, Quellan," Zylron snarled, his voice a menacing growl that echoed through the chamber. He loomed closer, his shadow enveloping the dark elf, who remained frozen on the ground. "If the mysterious figure wants a report, let them come and ask me themselves. I am no servant for their petty whims."

Quellan scrambled to his feet, his body trembling under the weight of Zylron's wrath. The dragon's sharp gaze bore into him, unrelenting, leaving no room for argument. He swallowed hard, his voice a hoarse whisper as he managed to respond. "I... I will deliver your message."

Without waiting for dismissal, Quellan turned and retreated, his steps uneven as he stumbled out of the chamber. His heart raced, the memory of Zylron's rage etched into his mind as he disappeared down the corridor.

From the shadows, Glaceria's sharp laughter rang out, cutting through the tense silence. Her amusement was both mocking and defiant, her wounded pride masked by the icy mirth in her tone.

Zylron turned toward her, unbothered by the looming reckoning with the mysterious figure. He snorted, a plume of smoke curling from his nostrils. "I have no patience for that dark elf's games," he growled, his tone dripping with disdain. "If they want answers, let them come to us."

Glaceria smirked, her icy gaze gleaming as she folded her injured wing closer to her side. "I would like to see that. Maybe then, they will understand what it is like to face true power."

Zylron rumbled in agreement, his focus turning inward as he brooded over the defeat and the battles yet to come. For now, his frustration simmered, a storm waiting to erupt.

The mysterious figure's face contorted with anger as Quellan stammered out the report. Without hesitation, they stormed toward Zylron's lair, their movements sharp and filled with purpose. Their voice cut through the oppressive silence like a blade. "Zylron! I demand a report."

From within the cavern, Zylron's voice echoed, bitterness evident in his tone. "Kimras survived. We lost several red dragons in the battle. He injured me and—" his voice deepened, a flicker of restrained frustration seeping through, "—threw me against a mountain, effectively ending the fight."

The mysterious figure stepped closer, their sharp gaze piercing through the dim light. "And Amara?" they pressed, their tone icy and dangerous, a simmering fury just beneath the surface.

Before Zylron could respond, Glaceria interjected with a low growl, her frustration spilling over. "She and that meddling human tricked me," she snarled, venom dripping from every word. "Ong thrust a dragonlance into my wing. They had the advantage of the forest's magic—it shielded them at every turn."

The mysterious figure's pacing became erratic, each step heavier than the last as their frustration thickened the air. Their voice, when it came, was taut with barely contained rage. "Excuses," they spat, their tone razor-sharp. "You both failed to deliver results."

Zylron, already bristling, could not hold his tongue. His claws scraped against the stone as he spoke, his words clipped yet deliberate. "I warned you," he began, his voice a low, resonant snarl, "from the very start that Kimras was no ordinary dragon. His strength is unmatched, and Keisha's magic was a constant interference. It was not just his power—it was the way they fought together. Her spells disrupted our attacks and gave their forces an edge we could not easily counter."

"Keisha?" The mysterious figure's tone turned venomous, their disdain palpable. "You let her—a mere Eladrin—interfere? Pathetic." They sneered, their lips curling in disgust. "I expected better, Zylron. You should have accounted for every threat, including her."

Zylron's claws gouged into the stone beneath him, his muscles tensing as he resisted the urge to lash out. His red eyes narrowed, flickering with restrained anger. "You sent me to face Kimras and his allies without proper support," he said, his voice carefully measured. "And I fought until I could fight no more. But even a dragon cannot ignore the forces of magic, the strength of allies, or the inevitability of injury. You seem to forget—I still live. And I do not intend to fail again."

The mysterious figure halted mid-step, their expression unreadable as they stared at Zylron. The tension between them was a living thing, crackling and thick as it filled the space. For a moment, the air held its breath, the weight of their shared failure hanging heavy.

"See that you don't," the figure finally replied, their voice low and seething. Their gaze flicked to Glaceria, then back to Zylron. "We cannot afford any more failures."

They turned to leave but paused at the cavern's threshold, their shadow stretching ominously across the stone. Without turning back, their voice rang out, cold and commanding. "Recover your strength. We have no time to wallow in defeat. The black and obsidian dragons are en route. When they arrive, we will have the reinforcements we need to strike again—and this time, there will be no mercy."

With those words, they disappeared into the shadows, leaving Zylron and Glaceria to brood over their losses and prepare for the battles yet to come. The promise of reinforcements was a flicker of hope—but also a reminder of the greater darkness gathering on the horizon.

The mysterious figure stormed through the dark corridors of the spire, their footsteps sharp against the stone floor. Frustration churned within them, Zylron's failure gnawing at their patience. Yet, it was not his defeat alone that infuriated them—it was the mention of Keisha's interference and Glaceria's humiliation at the hands of Ong. How had their meticulously laid plans been so thoroughly disrupted by those they deemed lesser threats?

Their teeth clenched as their mind replayed the reports—Kimras, Amara, Keisha, Ong—each a thorn in their side. Their underestimation of the enemy had proven costly, and the weight of that realization fueled the cold fire of their rage.

They stopped before a massive, ironbound door deep within the spire. The air was heavy, the silence oppressive. With a slow breath, the mysterious figure pushed down their anger, forcing clarity to surface. If their dragons could not secure victory, then it was time to awaken something far darker—something that would bring devastation to their enemies.

Pushing open the door, they stepped into a secluded chamber lit only by the faint glow of ancient runes etched into the walls. The air within was cold, each breath visible as a pale mist. Slowly, deliberately, they began to chant, their voice resonating through the chamber, carrying ancient, forbidden words. As the incantation grew, the runes pulsed with an eerie light, the temperature plummeting further until frost began to creep across the stone floor.

The spell reached its crescendo, and the oppressive quiet was shattered by a low, guttural growl that seemed to emanate from the very shadows. The chamber trembled as the void itself seemed to split open, and from it emerged Voraxia, the shadow dragon—a creature wreathed in ethereal darkness. Her form was an abyssal silhouette, her eyes glowing with a cold, predatory light that seemed to pierce through the soul.

The air grew suffocating, heavy with her presence, and every flicker of her movement brought a pulse of unnatural, chilling energy. Voraxia's mere existence consumed the light, leaving the chamber bathed in a shroud of darkness that felt alive, crawling and encroaching upon every corner of the room.

The mysterious figure stood motionless, their breath caught in their throat as they beheld the ancient power they had summoned. Even in their position of control, there was no denying the sheer terror Voraxia evoked. Her voice, when it came, was a whisper that cut deeper than any roar.

"Who calls me from the void?" Voraxia's tone was both chilling and regal, her words laced with malice and ancient authority.

The mysterious figure lowered their head, a sign of deference mingled with calculated control. "It is I who bound you to this world. It is I who commands you now. We have enemies to destroy, and you will deliver my vengeance upon them."

Voraxia's lips curled into what could only be described as a predatory grin. "Vengeance," she murmured, her voice dripping with dark amusement. "A cause I can relish."

Outside the chamber, Zylron shifted uneasily in his lair. He did not know why, but a deep, primal dread coiled in his chest, colder than anything Glaceria could conjure. An ancient, terrible force had awakened, one that made even his fiery blood run cold. The air carried Voraxia's chilling essence, and despite his pride, Zylron could not suppress the shiver that ran through him.

Deep within Flameford, the shadows stirred. The battlefields of Vacari would never be the same.

Chapter 31
Echoes of Victory

Amara and Ong returned to Goldmoor under a sky still heavy with the echoes of conflict. The city bore the scars of battle—shattered walls, smoldering rubble—but among the devastation, glimmers of resilience emerged. Citizens moved with a determined purpose, their efforts to rebuild a quiet testament to their unwavering spirit.

Ong's heart raced as his eyes scanned the crowd, searching for Keisha. The tension of the battle, the lingering uncertainty—all of it faded the moment he saw her. Standing amidst the chaos, unharmed and resolute, she was a beacon of strength. Relief surged through him, a wave that swept away the remnants of fear. Without a second thought, he broke into a run, his footsteps growing faster with each beat of his heart.

"Keisha!" Ong's voice rose above the din, drawing her attention. In an instant, he was there, his arms wrapping tightly around her. The world around them seemed to fade, leaving only the solace of their embrace. Holding her, he felt the weight of the battle lift, replaced by the certainty that she was safe.

Keisha turned to him, her eyes wide with surprise before softening into a mixture of relief and joy. She melted into his embrace, letting the strength and warmth of his presence steady her. "Ong," she whispered, her voice trembling with emotion. "You're back."

He gently pulled away just enough to cup her face in his hands, his thumbs brushing her cheeks as his gaze searched hers. "Are you alright? Did anything happen while I was gone?" he asked, his voice laced with concern.

Keisha shook her head, a small, reassuring smile curving her lips despite the weight of the moment. "I'm fine," she replied, her fingers threading through his. "Zylron tried to threaten me again, but I wasn't afraid. I laughed in his face—reminded him how his schemes have failed every time."

A swell of pride filled Ong's chest, admiration shining in his eyes. Of course, she had faced Zylron without fear. Keisha's strength never ceased to amaze him. "You're incredible," he murmured, brushing a stray lock of hair from her face. The gesture, tender and deliberate, spoke volumes of his love and respect.

Keisha rested her head against Ong's chest, the steady rhythm of his heartbeat grounding her in a world still trembling from the aftershocks of battle. In his arms, the chaos faded, leaving only the unshakable bond they shared. "As long as we're together, we can face anything," she said softly, her words a promise etched in the quiet between them.

Ong tightened his hold, drawing her closer as her vow settled over him like armor. No matter what lay ahead, their love would be the light guiding them through the shadows. Together, they were unbreakable. In that moment, amidst the ruins of Goldmoor, Ong felt an unyielding resolve. With Keisha by his side, there was no storm he could not weather.

Above the city, Amara's elegant wings cut through the air, her sharp eyes scanning the landscape below. The remnants of battle were still visible—scorched rooftops, crumbled walls—but the sight of Goldmoor standing resilient brought a measure of relief. Her thoughts flickered to Ong and Keisha, hoping they had found solace in each other amidst the chaos. But her attention quickly shifted as a familiar glimmer of golden scales caught her eye.

With a graceful descent, Amara landed beside Kimras, her claws clicking softly against the stone. Her breath hitched at the sight of him—his golden scales, usually radiant, were marred by a deep gash that glistened ominously in the fading light. "Kimras," she exclaimed, her voice laced with concern. "What happened? Are you all right?"

Kimras shifted slightly, wincing as he adjusted his position. Despite the obvious pain, a playful glint sparkled in his eyes as he met Amara's worried gaze. "Just a scratch, Amara," he replied with a chuckle, his tone light, as if to downplay the severity of his wound. "Looks like I'm the one who needs to be more careful next time."

Amara shook her head, a teasing smile tugging at her lips even as her eyes softened with worry. "You, of all dragons, telling me to be careful?" she quipped, stepping closer. Her sharp gaze traced the edges of the wound, her movements careful as she inspected it. Relief coursed through her—it was not as severe as she had feared, though it was enough to leave its mark.

She let out a breath she had not realized she was holding, her voice softening. "I suppose this means I'll have to keep a closer eye on you from now on," she teased, her tone playful but underscored with affection. Their familiar banter, lighthearted as it was, eased the tension that had lingered since their return.

Kimras chuckled, the sound deep and resonant despite the ache he felt. He leaned into Amara's touch as she carefully tended to his wound, her presence a balm for more than just his physical injuries. "I guess I had it coming," he admitted, his smile tinged with ruefulness. "But I wouldn't have it any other way, as long as you're here to patch me up."

Amara worked with gentle precision, her focus unwavering as she cared for him. Each movement carried a quiet tenderness, a reflection of the bond they had forged through countless battles and shared trials. "You'd better not make a habit of this," she said, her voice light but carrying an edge of warning. "I have enough to worry about without you adding to the list."

Kimras smiled, his golden eyes gleaming with gratitude. Despite the chaos of the world around them, Amara's presence was an anchor—a reminder of trust, friendship, and shared purpose. In her care, he felt a rare sense of peace, a moment of respite amidst the storm. Whatever trials lay ahead, he knew he could face them, as long as Amara was by his side.

Amara's gaze drifted across the Cerulean Expanse, her sharp eyes drawn to a distant mountain where a thin plume of smoke still rose into the sky. Her brow furrowed as she studied the aftermath of what appeared to be a rather significant event, her mind racing with questions.

Turning toward Kimras, she raised a curious eyebrow, her expression expectant. "What happened over there?" she asked, her voice tinged with both curiosity and concern.

Kimras followed her gaze, his golden eyes sparkling with mischief. A slow grin spread across his face as he leaned back, his posture deceptively relaxed. "Ah, that," he chuckled, a glimmer of amusement dancing in his tone. "Let's just say it involved a rather... abrupt introduction to Zylron."

Amara's eyes widened, disbelief flickering across her face as she processed his words. "Zylron?" she repeated, incredulous. "What exactly did you do?"

Kimras shrugged nonchalantly, though the glint in his eyes betrayed his satisfaction. "I might have, shall we say, introduced him to the mountain—rather forcefully," he admitted, his tone light but carrying the weight of the battle they had endured.

For a moment, Amara stared at him in stunned silence before a laugh escaped her lips, the sound breaking through the somber atmosphere. "You threw him into a mountain?" she asked, her voice brimming with amusement. "Kimras, the poor mountain didn't stand a chance! Should I start drafting blueprints for any future geological renovations?"

Kimras chuckled, his golden scales glinting faintly as he shook his head. "I'll keep you informed," he replied, his grin widening. "Though I'm not sure Zylron would appreciate the diligence."

Their laughter intertwined, a rare moment of levity amidst the weight of their responsibilities. They watched the distant plume of smoke dissipate into the sky, the faint remnants of the clash fading with the passing breeze. For a brief moment, the two dragons stood side by side, finding comfort and camaraderie in the shared humor of the chaos they had endured.

Though the battles ahead remained uncertain, their bond shone steadfast—a reminder that even in the darkest times, there was strength to be found in friendship and laughter.

As Ong and Keisha approached Amara and Kimras, Ong's sharp eyes immediately caught sight of the injury etched across Kimras's golden scales. Concern flickered across his face, but before he could voice it, Keisha placed a subtle hand on his arm, silently urging him to hold his thoughts.

Understanding her unspoken request, Ong swallowed his worry and shifted his attention to the sprawling cityscape of Goldmoor before them. A quiet sigh of relief escaped him as his gaze swept over the bustling streets and intact walls. Despite the recent chaos, the city stood resilient, untouched by the ravages of war. Its people moved with purpose and determination, a testament to their unwavering spirit.

Their moment of reflection was interrupted by the arrival of King Alex. His regal bearing drew their attention as he approached, his gratitude evident in the warmth of his expression. Fixing his gaze on Kimras, the king offered a heartfelt smile. "Kimras, I cannot thank you enough for your swift action and decisive leadership during the crisis," he began, his voice resonant with sincerity. "Because of you, Goldmoor remains safe, and its people unharmed. You've given us hope in a time when we needed it most."

Kimras bowed his head humbly, a soft smile tugging at the corners of his mouth. "It was my honor, Your Majesty," he replied, his tone as respectful as it was genuine. After a brief pause, a glint of mischief sparkled in his golden eyes. "Besides," he added, a playful note in his voice, "I'd rather avoid the hassle of rebuilding the city—again."

Laughter rippled through the group at Kimras's jest, a much-needed moment of levity in the aftermath of the turmoil. Even King Alex chuckled, his shoulders relaxing as the weight of recent events momentarily lifted.

Amara cast a sidelong glance at Kimras, her lips curving into a wry smile. "You do have a knack for city preservation, Kimras," she teased lightly. "Perhaps you've missed your true calling as an architect."

Kimras chuckled softly, his golden eyes alight with amusement. "I think I'll leave that to someone with more patience," he quipped, earning another round of laughter from the group.

As they stood together, gazing out over the city they had fought so hard to protect, a sense of unity settled among them. The trials they had faced had only strengthened their bond, and though challenges undoubtedly lay ahead, they found solace in each other's presence. In that shared moment of lightness and gratitude, their resolve solidified. Whatever storms awaited, they would face them side by side, their friendship a shield against the darkness.

Kimras's gaze lingered on Amara, a knowing smile tugging at the corners of his lips. He shifted slightly, addressing the group with a tone that carried both mystery and quiet anticipation.

"I have a proposal," he began, his deep voice steady but laced with intrigue. "But it's not something I can simply explain. It is better experienced than spoken of. Meet me at the Hidden Isles when you're ready—I promise, everything will make sense then."

Amara arched a skeptical eyebrow, curiosity sparking in her amethyst eyes. Before she could voice the myriads of questions forming in her mind, Kimras raised a reassuring claw, his expression calm and resolute. "Trust me, Amara," he said softly, his golden eyes locking with hers. "You'll understand soon enough. All in good time."

Without another word, Kimras turned, his powerful wings spreading wide as he lifted off the ground. His golden form ascended gracefully, shimmering in the fading light as he flew toward the horizon. Within moments, he was gone, a distant silhouette heading toward the Hidden Isles.

The group exchanged puzzled glances, a mixture of curiosity and unease rippling through them. Amara's lips pressed into a thoughtful line as she considered his cryptic words. Her sharp eyes flicked to the others, silently gauging their readiness.

Finally, breaking the silence, Ong adjusted his grip on the dragonlance and nodded toward the direction Kimras had taken. "Whatever he's planning, it's worth finding out," he said, his tone resolute.

Keisha smirked, her fingers brushing lightly against Ong's arm. "Agreed," she said, her voice light but tinged with intrigue. "Kimras always has a way of keeping things interesting."

With mutual determination, they set off, their footsteps echoing against the cobblestone streets as they journeyed toward the Hidden Isles. The air was heavy with anticipation, each step carrying them closer to whatever revelation Kimras had promised. The path ahead felt charged with possibility—a blend of apprehension and excitement stirring within their hearts.

As they ventured into the unknown, the shadows of the city gave way to the open horizon, the distant glow of the Hidden Isles beckoning them forward. They knew, deep down, that whatever awaited them would shape not only their futures but also the fate of Vacari itself.

With minds brimming with questions and hearts full of determination, they pressed onward, their bond unshaken by uncertainty. The journey to the Hidden Isles had begun, and they were ready to uncover the secrets hidden within its depths.

Chapter 32

The Dance of Souls: Amara and Kimras' Courtship Ritual

Protected by an impenetrable magical barrier, the Hidden Isles remained untouched amidst the chaos of shadows. From afar, the shimmering veil of protection was barely discernible—just a subtle ripple in the fabric of reality that shielded the isles from harm. Within this sanctuary, nature flourished in its purest form, undisturbed by the darkness that plagued the world beyond.

As Amara and Kimras ventured toward the heart of the Hidden Isles, they were greeted by cascading waterfalls, their crystalline waters sparkling in the soft sunlight. Each drop seemed to shimmer with a life of its own, dancing and twirling as it fell from the heights above, filling the air with a harmonious symphony of sound.

The vibrant flora that adorned the isles seemed to beckon them closer, its hues more vivid and intoxicating than anything they had ever seen. Lush greenery blanketed the landscape, interwoven with bursts of color from exotic flowers, while towering trees reached for the sky like ancient sentinels. It was a paradise untouched by time, a haven of tranquility and beauty amidst the turmoil of the outside world.

At the very center of the Hidden Isles stood a golden castle, its gleaming spires reaching toward the heavens like beacons of hope piercing the darkness. It was a symbol of resilience and strength, a testament to the noble dragons and their allies who had fought tirelessly to protect their home from the encroaching shadows. Within its gilded walls lay the heart of the sanctuary—a place of refuge and solace for all who sought shelter from life's storms.

As Amara and Kimras approached the castle, a deep sense of calm washed over them, peace and serenity transcending the turmoil beyond. The very air around them hummed with a gentle energy, the magic of the Hidden Isles palpable in every breath, a reminder that they were stepping into a realm where ancient forces held sway.

Accompanying them were Keisha, Ong, King Alex, and a group of nymphs and citizens from Goldmoor. Together, they marveled at the beauty that surrounded them, their eyes wide with wonder as they took in the sights and sounds of the enchanted sanctuary. Everything here felt otherworldly, as though time itself slowed down in reverence to the magic that filled the air.

Little did they know that within the golden castle's walls, their lives would be forever changed, and their bonds tested in ways they could never imagine. But for now, they were content to explore the wonders of the Hidden Isles and revel in the magic that embraced them.

As Amara and the others ventured deeper into the heart of the Hidden Isles, they were greeted by a sight unlike anything they had ever seen. Nestled amidst a lush grove of ancient trees and towering cliffs lay a magnificent garden that seemed to have sprung forth from the very essence of magic itself.

Kimras had prepared this enchanting oasis—a sanctuary within a sanctuary—where waterfalls cascaded down tiers of rocks, their crystalline waters catching the light and reflecting the vibrant colors of the surrounding flora. Exotic flowers bloomed in every hue imaginable, their intoxicating fragrance filling the air with a heady perfume that stirred the senses and beckoned them to explore.

Amara's eyes widened in awe as she took in the beauty of the garden. Her scales shimmered in the dappled sunlight filtering through the canopy above, casting a soft, ethereal glow. She marveled at the intricate designs of the flowers, each petal arranged with care, and the shimmering pools that dotted the landscape, each a testament to Kimras's skill and devotion.

"When... when was all of this arranged?" she asked, her voice a soft echo amidst the tranquil surroundings, as if she dared not disturb the serenity of the place.

Kimras let out a rumbling chuckle, his wings unfurling slightly in a gesture of quiet pride. "It was a labor of love," he replied, his deep voice filled with warmth and affection. "I wanted to create a place where we could come together and find peace amidst the chaos of our world."

Amara nodded, gratitude swelling in her heart as she stepped forward to join Kimras by the edge of the largest pool. Its surface was so still and clear it reflected the azure sky above like a perfect mirror, an emblem of the tranquility they all sought. Around them, Keisha, Ong, King Alex, and the others followed, their eyes gleaming in the soft light as they marveled at the wonders of the garden.

Together, they gathered around the pool, their hearts lightened by the peaceful surroundings. This was a place of serenity and tranquility, a refuge from life's storms where they could find solace and camaraderie in each other's company.

As they settled in, Amara felt a deep sense of belonging wash over her, a profound connection to those around her. The unity and friendship they shared, forged in battle and strengthened by love, bound them together in ways words could scarcely describe. In that moment, surrounded by the beauty of the Hidden Isles and the love of those closest to her, she knew with certainty that she was exactly where she was meant to be.

As everyone settled into the tranquil beauty of the garden, Kimras took a deep breath, his golden eyes locking onto Amara's with a mix of determination and vulnerability. His heart pounded, the weight of what he was about to say heavy on his mind. Clearing his throat, his voice resonated with sincerity as he began to speak.

"Amara," he started, his words carrying through the serene stillness, "in the time that we have known each other, your friendship has meant more to me than words can express. You have been my confidante, my companion, and my unwavering ally through both joy and sorrow."

Amara blinked, her heart suddenly pounding in her chest. *What is he saying?* For a fleeting moment, she struggled to comprehend what she was hearing. Kimras had always been her closest ally, but love? That was something she had never allowed herself to consider. Yet, as his words sank in, something stirred deep within her, an undeniable truth breaking through the surface of her thoughts.

Kimras paused, gathering his thoughts, searching for the right words to express the depth of his feelings. His gaze never left hers. "But in recent years," he continued, his voice quieter now, more intimate, "I've come to realize that what I feel for you goes beyond mere friendship. It's a bond that transcends the boundaries of time and space, a connection that defies explanation."

Kimras's heart raced as he stepped closer to Amara, the weight of his confession hanging in the air between them, unspoken but unmistakable.

"Amara, I never thought I would find myself in this position, but I cannot deny the truth any longer. What I feel for you is more than friendship. It's a love that burns brighter than any flame—a love that fills me with hope and joy every time I see you."

Reaching out, his claw trembled slightly as he gently cupped Amara's cheek, his touch tender and reverent. "Amara," he whispered, his voice barely audible, filled with emotion, "will you do me the honor of becoming my mate? Will you stand by my side as we face the challenges of our world together, united in heart and soul?"

Kimras held his breath, his heart racing as he awaited Amara's response. His gaze remained fixed on hers, filled with anticipation and vulnerability. In that moment, it felt as though the entire world held its breath, waiting anxiously for her answer.

Amara's heart skipped a beat as Kimras's words washed over her, filling her with a powerful mix of astonishment and joy. She had never anticipated this moment, never imagined that Kimras—her closest ally, her trusted companion—would ask her to be his mate. The realization was overwhelming, and for a brief moment, she was speechless, her mind racing to comprehend the weight of what he had just confessed.

But then, like a warm flood, emotion surged through her, dispelling any doubts or hesitation. Her heart steadied, and a profound sense of certainty settled over her. Meeting Kimras's gaze, she saw the depth of his love reflected back at her, unwavering and pure.

"Yes," she said, her voice steady and sure, despite the swirling emotions inside her. "Yes, Kimras, I would be honored to be your mate."

A radiant smile spread across Kimras's face, his golden eyes bright with happiness and relief. Without a word, he pulled Amara into a tight embrace, holding her as though he had been waiting for this moment his entire life. Around them, their friends and allies erupted in cheers and applause, their joyous voices rising into the air, carrying with them a sense of unity and celebration.

In that moment, standing together in the heart of the Hidden Isles—surrounded by the beauty of nature and the love of those closest to them—Amara knew she had found her true home. Looking into Kimras's eyes, she felt the certainty of their bond, knowing that no matter what challenges lay ahead, they would face them together, bound by a love that would endure for eternity.

Amara's heart swelled with affection as she turned to Kimras, her gaze softening. From beneath one of her protective scales, she carefully retrieved a small, gleaming amethyst gemstone, its surface shimmering with an otherworldly glow. She had kept the stone close, its meaning and power as precious to her as the bond they now shared.

"Kimras," she began, her voice soft but resolute, "this is for you." She extended her claw, offering him the gemstone with a reverence that mirrored the depth of her feelings.

Kimras's eyes widened as he accepted the gemstone, turning it over in his claws with wonder. "What is it?" he asked, his voice filled with curiosity, his gaze never leaving the stone.

"It's an amethyst," Amara replied, a fond smile playing on her lips. "One of my favorites." She paused, meeting his gaze with unwavering sincerity. "But it's more than just a gemstone. It's imbued with a protective aura that will enhance your resilience and shield you during battles."

Kimras blinked in astonishment as the significance of her gift sank in. He could feel the faint pulse of magic from the stone, its protective power resonating through his scales. "And that's not all," Amara continued, her tone gentle yet determined. "It also has calming properties to help you stay focused, even amidst chaos."

Reaching out, she placed her claw gently over his, her touch warm and affectionate. "This is my gift to you, Kimras. A token of my love and gratitude, and a symbol of our bond."

Kimras was speechless, his heart overflowing with love and gratitude. He gazed into her eyes, his own shimmering with unspoken emotion as he realized the depth of her feelings. The weight of the gemstone in his claws felt like more than just a physical gift—it was a reflection of the trust and love they shared.

"Thank you, Amara," he whispered, his voice thick with emotion. "I will treasure this always and carry it as a reminder of the love we share."

With reverence, Kimras tucked the amethyst close to his heart, holding it carefully beneath his scales as a symbol of their bond. In that moment, standing in the heart of the Hidden Isles, surrounded by the beauty of nature and the love of their friends, they knew their journey together was just beginning.

Just then, Keisha approached with a warm smile, holding a stunning necklace crafted from intricately worked gold, inset with precious gemstones that sparkled in the soft light. Each stone seemed to catch and reflect the magic in the air around them, casting a delicate glow.

"This is for you, Kimras," Keisha said warmly. "A gift from the Eladrin jeweler who crafted a necklace for Silvara. When you first began creating this sanctuary, you confided in me about your feelings for her. Knowing how special this place is to both of you, I asked the finest jeweler to craft something that would symbolize the love and unity you two share."

Kimras accepted the necklace with awe, his claws tracing the delicate patterns etched into the gold. Each curve and gemstone seemed to carry meaning, representing the depth of the bond he and Amara shared. "Thank you, Keisha," he said, his voice filled with deep gratitude. "It's magnificent."

Turning to Amara, determination flickered in his eyes. "Amara," he began, his voice steady despite the emotions swirling inside him, "this necklace isn't just a gift for me. It symbolizes my love for you and my promise to keep you safe."

With trembling claws, Kimras gently fastened the necklace around Amara's neck, his touch tender and reverent. As the golden chain settled against her scales, Amara felt a surge of warmth and emotion flood her, the weight of the necklace reminding her of the love they shared.

She looked into his eyes, her own shimmering with unspoken feelings. "Kimras," she whispered softly, "thank you. I will cherish this always, as a symbol of our love."

In that moment, surrounded by their friends and the tranquil beauty of the Hidden Isles, the necklace became more than just a piece of jewelry—it was a testament to the unbreakable bond they had forged, a bond that would guide them through whatever challenges lay ahead.

Ong's eyebrows shot up in surprise as he turned to Keisha, his expression filled with curiosity. "I thought you said they were just friends," he whispered, his voice barely audible above the soft murmur of conversation around them.

Keisha smiled, her eyes twinkling with amusement as she leaned closer to Ong. "No, I said *Kimras* stated they were just friends," she replied, her tone playful yet knowing. "But we had to accept what he said at the time. Things do change—*as you're fully aware.*"

Ong chuckled softly, a mischievous grin tugging at the corners of his lips. Wrapping his arm around Keisha's waist, he pulled her close, warmth radiating between them. Watching Kimras and Amara, he couldn't help but reflect on how much their bond mirrored his own connection with

Keisha. They had all come so far—each friendship deepened by the battles they had fought and the victories they had shared.

With their gifts exchanged and their commitment to each other reaffirmed, Amara and Kimras stood side by side, their hearts intertwined. The connection between them was palpable, an unspoken bond forged in both love and loyalty.

As they spread their wings and launched into the sky, a sense of exhilaration coursed through their veins, their scales shimmering in the golden light of the setting sun. They soared together, their movements in perfect harmony, a testament to their shared strength and unity.

Ong and Keisha watched from below, their hands clasped as they shared in the joy of their friends' union. In that moment, surrounded by the beauty of the Hidden Isles, they knew that no matter what challenges lay ahead, they would all face them together—bound by unbreakable ties of friendship, love, and loyalty.

Their friends and allies watched from below, their voices hushed in awe as they witnessed the majestic sight of the dragons taking to the skies. Keisha and Ong stood together, hands clasped tight, sharing in the joy of their friends' union. Around them, smiles and quiet murmurs of admiration filled the air as the beauty of the moment swept over everyone.

Amara and Kimras soared high above the Hidden Isles, their wings beating in perfect harmony as they danced amidst the clouds. With each graceful arc and elegant swoop, they declared their love to the world, their bond shining bright against the canvas of the evening sky.

Then, from the distant horizon, two shimmering forms emerged—Talleoss and his mate, Silvara, the majestic silver dragons, joined them in flight. Their scales gleamed in the golden light, casting silvery reflections as they flew in elegant synchrony alongside Kimras and Amara. Together, the four dragons created a stunning display of unity and grace.

The celebration didn't stop there. One by one, other dragons from the Hidden Isles began to ascend, their powerful wings lifting them into the sky. They joined the dance, their formations intricate and beautiful, a tribute to Kimras and Amara's union. The sky became a tapestry of colors and scales—bronze, emerald, sapphire, and ruby—all coming together in a breathtaking aerial celebration of love and loyalty.

Below, the crowd watched in awe, their hearts swelling as the dragons celebrated the mating of Kimras and Amara in a grand, airborne display. The sky above them was alive with movement, each dragon's presence adding to the magnificence of the moment.

Amara and Kimras, at the center of it all, flew as if the world itself had been transformed for them alone. Their love and unity seemed to set the heavens ablaze, the celebration of their bond echoing in every beat of their wings.

As the evening faded and the stars began to twinkle in the darkening sky, Kimras gently guided Amara toward a secluded alcove nestled within the depths of the Hidden Isles. It was a place known only to him—a secret sanctuary, untouched by the world, where they could retreat and revel in each other's company.

As they stepped into the alcove, Amara's eyes widened in wonder at the sight that greeted her. In the center of the space hung a magnificent tapestry, its colors vibrant and alive with magic. The intricate weaving depicted a scene of natural beauty—a mythical landscape that seemed to pulse with energy and life, as if the very threads themselves were enchanted.

Kimras smiled as he watched Amara's reaction, his heart swelling with pride and affection. He had created this sanctuary with her in mind, a place where they could share in each other's presence away from the chaos. "This is our private lair," he said, his voice soft with emotion. "A place where we can come together and escape the world outside."

Amara nodded, her gaze lingering on the tapestry as a deep sense of peace washed over her. "It's beautiful," she whispered, awe filling her voice as her eyes traced the vibrant, shifting colors.

Then, something incredible happened. As they drew closer to the tapestry, its colors began to ripple and shift, transforming before their eyes. The landscape within the tapestry came alive, the scene evolving into an immersive world. Amara gasped, her senses overwhelmed by the magic enveloping them, drawing her into the heart of the mythical realm.

Together, they lost themselves in the magic of the tapestry, transported to another realm where time seemed to stand still. They laughed, talked, and shared moments of quiet intimacy late into the night, their hearts brimming with love and gratitude for one another. It was a world just for them—timeless and boundless, a reflection of the depth of their bond.

As dawn's first light filtered through the trees, casting a soft glow across the alcove, Amara and Kimras emerged from their sanctuary, their connection stronger than ever before. They knew their journey together was only the beginning, and that no matter what challenges lay ahead, they would face them united, in heart and soul.

With a final glance back at the tapestry—now a symbol of their eternal bond—Amara and Kimras turned and spread their wings. As they soared into the sky, the cool morning air beneath them, their hearts were filled with hope and excitement for the future. And as they journeyed back to Goldmoor and Purplefire, they knew that their love would endure for eternity, a beacon of light shining against the world's darkness.

Chapter 33
Sentinels' Watch

In the tranquil depths of Purplefire Woods, Ong and Keisha treaded carefully along winding paths, their steps muffled by moss and leaves. The crisp, earthy scent of the forest mingled with the faint hum of distant birdsong, a comforting reminder of nature's resilience. Yet beneath the serenity, a quiet tension clung to the pair—echoes of the recent clash between Amara and Glaceria still fresh in their minds.

Their mission was clear: to ensure Purplefire remained unscathed after the battle and offer support to their allies in the aftermath. As they walked, a shared determination settled between them. Though victorious, the battle had taken its toll, and the weight of responsibility lingered in the air. Keisha glanced up at the towering trees, their vibrant canopy a testament to endurance. She could not help but reflect on how far they had come from those early days of uncertainty and doubt.

As they approached the woodland's heart, the glow of Aeliana's magic shimmered softly against the towering trees. The nymphs moved with tranquil grace, their serene expressions starkly contrasting the chaos Keisha had braced herself to find. She stepped forward quickly, her voice catching slightly as she called out.

"Aeliana, please tell me Purplefire is unharmed. Did the battle cause any lasting damage?"

Aeliana's eyes sparkled with calm reassurance as she replied, "You needn't worry, Keisha. Although the barrier sustained minor damage during the clash, we were able to mend it swiftly. Thanks to Amara's quick thinking and the nymphs' restorative magic, Purplefire is as it should be."

Keisha's shoulders sagged in relief, the heavy weight lifting from her heart. Her thoughts briefly wandered to the countless battles they had faced, each threatening to disrupt the delicate balance they had worked so hard to preserve. "Thank the stars," she murmured, gratitude thick in her voice. "I was worried sick."

Ong gently squeezed her hand, sensing the depth of Keisha's relief. "You've carried this worry alone long enough," he murmured, his voice low but steady. "We'll face whatever comes next—together." Keisha met his gaze, her heart swelling with gratitude for the unspoken strength he always seemed to offer.

With a final nod to Aeliana, they turned toward Goldmoor, where new trials and reflections awaited. Yet for now, the bond they shared—and the enduring beauty of Purplefire Woods—offered a fragile but precious reprieve.

As Ong and Keisha arrived in the bustling streets of Goldmoor, the vibrant energy of the town enveloped them. Merchants called out their wares, children's laughter echoed from narrow alleyways, and the rhythmic hammering of a blacksmith's forge rang in the distance. The mingling scents of fresh bread, leather, and horsehair filled the air, creating a symphony of life. Yet amidst the lively commotion, Ong and Keisha sought the familiar solace of the stables, where their faithful companions awaited.

Ong approached Thunder's stall with a fond smile, his heart swelling with affection as he reached out to pat the sturdy black stallion's flank. "Hey there, Thunder," he said warmly, his voice carrying an unspoken camaraderie. "Missed me, boy?"

Thunder responded with a soft whinny, nudging Ong's hand with his muzzle as if to say, Of course I did. Ong chuckled, scratching behind the horse's ears. Their bond, forged through countless trials, felt unshakable—a steady constant in an ever-changing world.

Nearby, Keisha approached Celestia's stall, her anticipation blooming into joy as the elegant mare lifted her head, ears twitching at the sight of her. Celestia greeted her with a soft nicker, her bright eyes alight with recognition.

"Hey, girl," Keisha murmured, running a hand along Celestia's sleek coat. "You missed me, huh?" Her voice carried a warmth reserved for her closest companions. Celestia nudged her shoulder gently, as if to affirm that she had. In these quiet, tender moments, tending to their horses, Ong and Keisha found an anchor amid the storms they had weathered.

Ong's teasing voice broke through her thoughts, drawing her gaze. "Remember when we found Celestia in Purplefire?" he asked, grinning. "You didn't even want a horse back then."

Keisha laughed, her melodic voice cutting through the sounds of the stable. "I know, I know," she replied, shaking her head in mock exasperation. "But Celestia had other plans. She decided to follow me, and, well, who was I to argue?"

Ong joined her laughter, his rich tones blending effortlessly with hers. In a rare display of affection, he wrapped his arms around her in a tight embrace, the strength of his love clear in the gesture. For a moment, the world outside the stables faded, leaving only the warmth of shared memories and the quiet rhythm of their companionship.

Together, they turned back to their horses, falling into an easy rhythm as they brushed coats and adjusted tack. Thunder's strong, steady presence and Celestia's grace seemed to reflect the bond between their riders—a connection rooted in trust, strengthened by every trial they had faced. Their horses were more than companions; they were symbols of endurance and loyalty, anchors in a world that often felt like it could shift beneath their feet at any moment.

As Ong and Keisha discussed the possibility of returning home to E'vanaho once Amara and Kimras returned, they were interrupted by the approach of King Alex. His expression was warm and sincere, a reflection of his gratitude.

"Ong, Keisha," he greeted, his voice carrying a heartfelt tone. "Thank you for all you've done for Goldmoor. Your bravery and loyalty have not gone unnoticed."

They turned to him, their attention drawn by the weight of his words. "Of course, Your Majesty," Ong replied with quiet respect. "It has been an honor to serve."

King Alex raised a hand before they could continue, a gentle smile softening his features. "There is something my wife would like to show you," he said, gesturing toward the palace garden. "Queen Jeanne wants you to see how much Casper has grown."

Ong and Keisha exchanged a curious glance, their interest piqued by the mention of Casper. "We would be honored," Keisha replied warmly, a fond memory of the cougar stirring in her mind.

Following King Alex into the palace garden, they were greeted by a serene, sunlit haven. The vibrant blooms and the gentle hum of the breeze created an atmosphere of tranquility. Amid the beauty of the garden, Queen Jeanne appeared, walking gracefully alongside a magnificent cougar. Casper, now fully grown, moved with the confident strength of a protector, his sleek coat glistening in the golden light.

Ong and Keisha could not help but laugh, delight sparkling in their eyes. "Casper has certainly grown!" Ong exclaimed, his voice tinged with awe.

Queen Jeanne nodded, pride lighting her face as she rested a hand on Casper's broad shoulders. "Yes, indeed," she said with affection. "He has proven himself to be more than a companion. Not long ago, during one of my walks, he saved me from the clutches of the dark Druchii, Quellan."

Keisha's expression softened, admiration shining in her eyes. Her heart swelled with gratitude for the noble creature. "He's bonded with you deeply," she said, her voice filled with warmth.

The queen's smile deepened as she looked down at Casper, who nuzzled her hand with affection. "He truly has," she said, her voice tinged with emotion. "And I cannot thank you enough, Keisha, for bringing him into my life."

As they watched Queen Jeanne share a quiet moment with Casper, a sense of peace settled over Ong and Keisha. The weight of recent battles and uncertainties began to ease, replaced by the gentle comfort of seeing lives touched by their efforts and connections flourishing in their wake.

But duty, as always, soon called. With a final bow of gratitude to Queen Jeanne and a lingering look at Casper, Ong and Keisha departed the palace garden, their steps turning back toward the bustling streets of Goldmoor. The city awaited them, its people looking to them for strength and guidance.

Walking side by side, Ong glanced at Keisha, a soft smile tugging at his lips. Words felt unnecessary as his heart swelled with gratitude—for every battle they had fought, for every moment of calm she had brought to his life.

As their hands brushed lightly against each other's, a quiet understanding passed between them. Whatever challenges lay ahead, they would face them as they always had—together, united by their unwavering commitment to protect their home and the people they held dear.

Chapter 34
Destined Paths: Reflections and Unanswered Questions

As the sun dipped low on the horizon, casting a golden glow over the landscape, Amara and Kimras soared through the skies toward their respective destinations. The gentle breeze carried the mingling scents of pine and earth, and their scales glimmered like jewels in the fading light. Below, the sprawling edges of Purplefire Woods came into view, its ancient trees stretching toward the sky like sentinels.

Amara glanced at Kimras, her amethyst eyes catching the light with a determined gleam. "I'll join you later in Goldmoor," she said, her voice resolute yet calm. "I need to check on the amethyst dragons first."

Kimras nodded, his golden wings beating with steady rhythm as he veered toward Goldmoor. "I'll see you there," he called back, his deep voice trailing in the breeze as he disappeared into the distant horizon.

Amara descended through the canopy of Purplefire Woods, the forest greeting her with its vibrant energy. Shafts of golden sunlight filtered through the towering branches, casting intricate patterns on the forest floor. The hum of life surrounded her—chirping birds, rustling leaves, and the faint whisper of magic that lingered in the air.

Touching down gracefully, Amara wasted no time in seeking out the young amethyst dragons. They bounded forward eagerly, their shimmering violet scales catching the dappled light. Chirps of greeting and playful nudges warmed her heart, though she kept her tone firm as she addressed them.

"Rest well, my friends," she said gently, her voice carrying the authority of a leader. "You've done well today, but there are more patrols ahead. Use this time to regain your strength."

The young dragons nodded, their bright eyes reflecting a blend of weariness and determination. With her reassurance, they curled up among the protective roots of the ancient trees, their breaths settling into a calm rhythm as they drifted to sleep. Amara watched over them for a moment, pride and protectiveness mingling within her.

Satisfied that her charges were safe, she turned her gaze toward the horizon, where the faint glow of Goldmoor beckoned. Her heart swelled with purpose as she set off again, her steps steady and her resolve unwavering.

Meanwhile, Kimras descended into Goldmoor, where the city bustled with the lively hum of recovery. Its golden spires gleamed in the last rays of sunlight, a beacon of resilience in the waning day. As he landed, the ground beneath him hummed with the strength of a city that refused to falter.

Kimras wasted no time, making his way to the garden where the young gold dragons rested after the recent battle. He inspected each one carefully, his keen eyes searching for signs of injury or distress. Relief washed over him as he found most of them unharmed, their scales glistening brightly in the soft evening light.

As the dragons settled into the garden, the sweet scent of flowers mingled with the soothing sound of cascading waterfalls, creating a haven of peace. Kimras paused to take it all in—the resilience of Goldmoor, the strength of its people, and the steadfastness of the young dragons who had fought so valiantly.

Perching atop a sturdy tree, Kimras surveyed the city below. The protective barrier shimmered faintly in the distance, a testament to the strength of its magic and the will of its defenders. Pride swelled within him as he reflected on their efforts. Though the battle against Zylron had passed, the fight against darkness was far from over. But for now, Goldmoor stood strong, a city unyielding in the face of adversity.

As Kimras gazed over the city, the familiar figures of Ong and Keisha appeared in the distance, their steady strides a welcome sight. A warm smile spread across his face as they approached, his heart swelling with gratitude for their unwavering support and friendship.

"The battle is over," Ong said, his voice carrying a blend of relief and exhaustion. Kimras exhaled softly, his golden gaze lingering on the horizon, a shadow of unease flickering in his eyes. Sensing his friend's unrest, Ong tilted his head in concern. "What's on your mind, Kimras?" he asked gently.

Before Kimras could respond, the sound of rustling leaves announced another arrival. Amara emerged from the forest edge, her amethyst scales catching the fading sunlight in a dazzling display. With a graceful leap, she perched herself on a low-hanging branch, her presence commanding immediate attention.

"Amara," Kimras greeted warmly, a hint of relief threading through his voice. The two dragons shared a brief, knowing glance, their bond as leaders unspoken but palpable.

Amara nodded in return, her gaze steady as it met Kimras's. "I couldn't help but overhear," she said, her voice calm yet laced with resolve. "And I agree with you, Kimras. The battle may be over, but the threat still looms large over Vacari. This was just one victory. I fear there will be many more battles before this war is truly over."

"Indeed," Ong added, his tone grave. "But for now, at least, the fight with Zylron and Glaceria is behind us. That is something we can take solace in."

Kimras's shoulders sagged slightly under the weight of their words, his wings shifting as if bearing an invisible burden. "I fear our struggles are far from over," he admitted, his voice low, uncertainty lingering in its cadence.

Even in the face of his doubt, Amara's gaze did not waver. "We may not know what lies ahead," she said, her tone firm but reassuring, "but as long as we stand together, we can face whatever challenges come our way."

Her words hung in the air, a quiet but powerful reminder of the bond they shared. For a moment, the group stood in reflective silence, the soft hum of Goldmoor's life filling the space around them. The light of the setting sun bathed the garden in warm hues, a fleeting moment of peace in a world still shrouded by uncertainty.

As the three pondered the uncertain future, Keisha, who had quietly joined them in the garden, interjected with a thoughtful observation.

"You're right," Keisha remarked, concern lacing her voice. "We still don't know who's pulling the strings behind the dark dragons. It would take someone incredibly powerful to orchestrate such a coordinated attack. Dark dragons are notorious for their solitary nature. The fact that they're working together now is deeply troubling."

Her words hung heavy in the air, a sobering reminder of the threat still looming on the horizon. Ong, Kimras, and Amara exchanged knowing glances, each grappling with the implications of Keisha's observation.

"It's a mystery we'll need to unravel," Ong said, his voice firm with resolve. "But for now, let's focus on strengthening our defenses and preparing for whatever comes next. Together, we stand a better chance of facing this threat head-on."

The group nodded in agreement, their determination unwavering in the face of uncertainty. As the sun dipped below the horizon, casting a warm glow over the garden, they knew the road ahead would be fraught with challenges. But with their bond as allies and friends, they were ready to face whatever darkness awaited them.

Amara's voice cut through the quiet contemplation like a blade, her concerns echoing the unease that had settled over them all. "While our battle against Zylron and Glaceria ended in our favor," she began, her tone heavy with apprehension, "I fear for the safety of the other noble dragons. If Zylron and Glaceria were willing to launch such a brazen attack, who is to say they will not strike again? And we won't know who their next target will be."

Kimras, his expression grave, nodded in agreement. "Indeed," he said somberly. "That's why I'm glad I sent the message to the other noble dragons. They will be on alert now, watching for signs of danger. We can't afford to be caught off guard."

His words carried the weight of responsibility, a testament to the careful planning that had already begun. The others nodded, the gravity of their situation settling more deeply upon them.

"The threat is ever-present," Kimras continued, his gaze fixed on the horizon where darkness was slowly encroaching. "And the shadows hold countless dangers. We must remain vigilant and ready to defend our kin at a moment's notice."

Amara placed a steadying claw on Kimras's shoulder, her amethyst eyes reflecting a mix of gratitude and resolve. "And we will," she said softly. "Together, we'll protect our kin and our world, no matter the cost."

The group stood united in the dimming light, their bond of trust and determination their greatest strength against the coming storm. As the last rays of sunlight faded, casting the garden into twilight, they knew their fight was far from over. But they also knew that as long as they stood together, they would endure.

Amara noticed Kimras tense, his golden scales seeming to darken in the dimming light. Concern flashed in her eyes as she stepped closer. "Kimras, what's wrong?" she asked, her voice soft but probing.

For a moment, Kimras did not respond. His eyes were distant, as though searching the edges of an unseen void. When he finally spoke, his voice was low, almost reverent. "It's... a coldness," he said at last. "Something ancient and dangerous, lurking just beyond the shadows. I felt it earlier, during the battle—a darkness far more sinister than Zylron or Glaceria. It was watching, waiting. And I fear it still is."

Amara's expression hardened, her concern deepening into resolve. "Do you think it could be related to the shadow dragons?" she asked.

Kimras's gaze remained fixed on the horizon, his wings shifting uneasily. "Perhaps," he admitted. "But this feels... different. As an ancient dragon, I am attuned to these forces, and this presence feels older—more malevolent—than anything I have encountered before. Whatever it is, its power eclipses even the strongest of the shadow dragons. We must prepare. I don't know when it will strike, but I feel it moving, calculating, even now."

His words sent a chill through the group, the weight of their situation pressing down like a shroud. In the growing darkness, their resolve to protect Vacari only burned brighter, their determination forged in the crucible of fear.

Kimras straightened, his golden eyes blazing with newfound purpose. "I will send word to Radiantus, the Platinum Dragon," he declared, his voice steady with resolve. "His wisdom and power are unmatched. Perhaps he can help us understand why the dark dragons are uniting—and offer guidance on how we can rally the noble dragons to stand against this ancient threat."

Ong and Keisha exchanged a glance, their agreement unspoken but immediate. "We will return to E'vahona and inform the Eladrin of what we've learned," Ong affirmed, his voice steady with determination. "They must be made aware of the looming danger. If this darkness reaches the Elven cities, we must be ready."

With a shared nod, Ong and Keisha turned to leave, their mission clear and urgent. Retrieving their horses from the nearby stable, they prepared to embark on the journey home, their hearts heavy with the weight of the news they carried.

Kimras and Amara remained behind, their watch over Goldmoor and Purplefire unyielding. As the sun slipped below the horizon, shadows stretched long across the land, and an eerie stillness settled over the garden. Both dragons sensed it—a presence just beyond the veil, like a predator circling its prey. They knew their duty to protect their home, and their world had only just begun.

Standing side by side, their scales glimmering faintly in the twilight, they resolved to face whatever challenges awaited. The road ahead was uncertain, fraught with peril, but they drew strength from their bond and their shared determination. Together, they would stand against the encroaching darkness, ready to face the ancient evil stirring in the shadows—and whatever else fate might throw their way.

Epilogue

In the suffocating darkness of the caverns, Zylron shivered, his scales bristling as if the very air had turned against him. The silence was heavy, broken only by the occasional drip of water echoing through the vast, unseen expanse. Something cold—something ancient—had awakened. Though he could not name it, he felt its presence, an icy whisper brushing against the edges of his mind.

Beside him, Glaceria stirred, her dark, sleek form blending seamlessly with the gloom. Neither spoke at first, the weight of their failure hanging thick between them. The memory of their last encounter with the mysterious figure gnawed at Zylron's thoughts, a threat that loomed ever larger in the cavern's oppressive shadows.

"Glaceria," Zylron murmured at last, his voice low and taut. "Do you feel it too? That cold... something's changed."

Glaceria's luminous eyes flickered in the dim light, narrowing as they turned to him. "I thought it was my imagination," she whispered, her voice carrying an uncharacteristic edge of uncertainty. "But now... now I'm not sure. Since our last encounter, I have sensed it. Something old. Angry. Like it's been waiting... watching."

A growl rumbled low in Zylron's throat, his unease growing like a shadow crawling across his soul. "It's not waiting anymore," he said grimly. "It's awake. And it's furious."

A heavy silence fell between them, thicker and more oppressive than before. The darkness felt alive, pressing against their scales with an unrelenting chill. Glaceria shifted her wings, unease radiating from her every movement.

"The mysterious one won't tolerate failure again," she muttered, her words barely more than a breath. "And now... this presence. If they sense it too, we're already living on borrowed time."

Zylron's gaze drifted toward the unseen exit of the cavern, his red eyes narrowing in determination. "We need to prepare," he said, his voice cutting through the quiet like a blade. "Whatever this is, it's coming. And we can't afford another mistake."

Glaceria nodded, though her expression remained tense. Her voice was brittle, carrying the weight of the question neither dared answer. "The real question is—who, or what, has awakened? And how do we stop it?"

The silence that followed was absolute, as if even the cavern itself held its breath. The unseen force stirred in the world beyond, cold, and malevolent, its intent unknown but undeniably dark. Zylron and Glaceria shared a glance, a rare moment of mutual dread. This presence was not just a threat—it was a harbinger of something far worse.

And in the shadows, far beyond their reach, the mysterious figure who once commanded their loyalty watched. Their wrath simmered, boiling just beneath the surface, waiting for the perfect moment to strike. The cold presence was no ally of theirs, but they knew how to wield fear—and fear was a weapon they intended to use.

Dragons of Vacari

Teaser
Shadows of Betrayal

The wind shifted as they crossed the border into Vacari, carrying the sharp scent of pine and the faint hum of life stirring in the land. He reined in his horse, pausing as the scene unfolded before him. Years had passed since he last set foot here, yet the land now felt strangely unfamiliar. The rolling hills and dense forests were the same, but something had changed—something unspoken, lingering just beneath the surface.

Behind him, his companions followed in silence, their presence a steady shadow as they ventured deeper into the territory. He could sense their unease, though none dared voice it aloud. The silence between them stretched, punctuated only by the steady rhythm of hooves on the soft earth.

As they pressed forward, a flicker of movement drew his eyes skyward. The sun, bold and steady moments ago, dimmed as shadows passed across its light. His gaze narrowed, catching sight of vast silhouettes gliding effortlessly above the horizon. His breath hitched.

Dragons. Their wings cut through the sky with a grace that seemed almost unreal, their forms majestic yet imposing.

"Dragons," one of his companions murmured, their voice low and edged with unease.

He watched the creatures in silence, their wings slicing through the sky with an elegance that seemed otherworldly. The sun caught on their shimmering scales, noble and brilliant, as they flew in deliberate formation. Noble dragons. Rare. Elusive. For years, they had existed only in whispers and half-forgotten tales. Yet here they were, soaring freely above the land he once knew.

"Don't worry," he said finally, his voice calm though his mind churned with questions. "That's a noble dragon. They don't pose a threat."

But even as he spoke, he couldn't shake the unease twisting in his chest. The noble dragons weren't supposed to be here. Their kind had withdrawn from this world long ago, choosing isolation over interference. Their sudden return couldn't be a coincidence. Something had drawn them back.

He forced himself to look away, gripping the reins tightly as they continued forward. But his thoughts remained fixed on the creatures above and the questions their presence raised.

Why were they here?

Why now?

As the silhouettes vanished into the horizon, unease settled over him like a shroud. Whatever had brought the noble dragons back to Vacari, he feared it was only the beginning.

Acknowledgements

Jean McEvoy

To my wonderful mother—your red pen and unwavering belief in me will never be forgotten. Thank you for always standing by me.

Caroline Otto

To my best friend from high school, Caroline, thank you for taking the time to read the rough drafts. Thank you for also being there for me during high school and believing in me now. Her friendship has meant a lot to me. She is more of like a sister.

Steven Thomas

To my dear friend, Steven, who took the time to read early drafts of the chapters. Your friendship and feedback mean the world to me.

Special Acknowledgements to the Fur Babies (whose names are used in the book

Pumpkin

I rescued my little black panther over five years ago, and her playful spirit became the inspiration for Pumpkin in this book.

Casper

To Casper, Caroline Otto's spoiled fur baby, who brings joy to every moment.

Milton Keynes UK
Ingram Content Group UK Ltd.
UKHW041241061224
452010UK00020B/290